Solve the World Part Two

by Dante Stack

Published by Stockade Amusement at Smashwords

Other Works by Dante Stack

Fun with the Apocrypha
Solve the World: Part One
Solve the World: Part Three (coming February 2019)

Table of Contents

The World According to Jennifer Dash

Jenn has already begun her hunt to solve the world. This is why the chapters of this book begin at 19.
She has learned some things already.

- Truth must be discovered. Being taught is not enough. It needs to be experienced to be believed.
- There may be a villain. If such a thing exists, his name is Pied Piper.
- If Leviathan is real, then the supernatural is quite natural.
- It feels bad to have your head shaved against your will.
- Theme parks have secrets.
- Take every opportunity.
- Act fast. The world does. You need to too.

This book is not the beginning.
This book is not the end.

To the Pacific

<u>Main Cast</u>
Jenn Dash known as Jennifer Free
Captain Alfred Bacon
1st Mate Emmanuela Godard
Elizabeth Schumacher known as Lizard
Alexandra Keitel referred to as Lex
Doctor Anthony Merkyl referred to only as Merkyl
Father Benjamin Thomas
Timothy Isaac referred to as Sir Isaac
Miles Faa
Jorje Robles

Chapter 19: Aboard the Orion

"Welcome aboard the *Orion*, young love," said the ship's Skipper, Captain Alfred Bacon. "I am to be your dutiful and always punctual, energetic, perhaps a wee-frivolous, Captain Alf, at your service! It is very fine indeed to have on board another young lady."

"Pleased to meet you, Captain... Alf." Jenn reached out to shake the jolly older man's hand, but rather than shake, the Cap'n bowed at his midpoint, an impressive feat. Jenn found it curious how a man of the Captain's girth and age could manage such a bendy posture.

"Everyone, minus one Sir Isaac and one Lizard has gone ashore to fetch themselves some urban grub. You and I then may slop something together in the cabin while going over the lay of the land and ensuring that this'll indeed be a jolly good fit for you as well as for the rest of us. Come one, come all, right?!" The white-bearded, bald-headed Captain caressed his facial extension in sudden contemplation. "That's not quite right is it?"

Jenn snickered, admiring the voracious energy of this man. She was hoping to find a good leader to get behind once Lillith set her heart aflutter with the vision of the expedition.

"Oh, for goodness' sake, it's not come one, come all, it's all for one, one for all! That's the ticket! Alexandre Dumas, how could I commit this vicious injustice on you? I beg your sincerest apologies." Captain Alf pulled out a crucifix hanging underneath his buttoned-up shirt, kissed it lovingly, and set his eyes upon the clouds, as if earnestly praying to the ghost of *The Three Musketeers*. Returning his gaze upon Jenn, the Captain motioned for Jenn to move about the ship. "After you, young love."

"My name's Jennifer... Jennifer Free. But I go by just Jenn."

"Yes, yes, take it all in, young love, every nook and cranny, your salvation and damnation all wrapped in one! That bow that now induces such awe will soon enough be your point of humiliation. The mysterious cabin below will inevitably metamorph into a hauntingly unbearable isle of claustrophobia."

"Aisle of claustrophobia, you say?"

"Quite right! Shall we venture inward?"

"After you, Captain!" Jenn was enjoying this overly ceremonial dance.

Alf began the descent before suddenly stopping in his tracks. "Oh, my dear young love, one thing I must say, and one thing you must hear with all your concentration and cunning of will, you hear?"

"Aye, Captain." Jenn couldn't help but snicker at herself.

"Uh, yes, so, Elizabeth Schumacher, more affectionately known to the crew of the *Orion* as Lizard...."

"Yes?"

"You see... I mean, of course, you will see immediately...."

"Yes, Captain." Clearly the verbose leader needed some help, "What will I see immediately?"

"Are you able to recall the man by the name of John Merrick."

"No."

"Dammit woman, you are to refer to me as Skipper, Captain, or if you can't recall such high honors, a mere Sir will do. You hear?"

This sudden unravelling of the Captain's jovial demeanour was disconcerting, but Jenn decided to lap it up to his uncomfortableness regarding this John Merrick character. She'd continue to play the game deftly... for now. "I'm sorry, that is... I mean to say, 'No, Captain'."

"Good, good. That's... that's much better young love. Very good. Very good indeed. You are doing fine. Nothing to worry about."

"Yes, Captain."

"I only mean to say, as a means of respect and such, that you... I mean, I mean to suggest that you act appropriately when you meet Lizard. Is that understood?"

An honest answer would be absolutely not understood. Jenn had no concept of what the Captain meant. What was appropriate? The nearest guess Jenn had was that Lizard, aka Elizabeth Schumacher, was indeed a bona fide reptile.

Maybe it was the ship's mascot. "Understood, Sir."

"Very good, very good." Relieved, the Captain pivoted, took another step, and, just as abruptly as before, stopped. "Oh yes, you must not take Sir Isaac's composure as an insult. He acts that way to everyone." He spun around again, only to hesitant and turn right back around. "He won't tell you, so I might as well. His name is Timothy Isaac. He's a very, very focused and studious mathematician. Trigonometrist, or something of that painful ilk. But like I said, he'll never tell you any of that. He'll never tell you anything. He's just... here. If it were up to me I'd have him walk the plank for insurrection, but in these dark times a Captain doesn't have the will of the people in the palm of his hand as he once did... as he should." And with that... they descended into the cabin.

The schooner, built mostly by the hand of an eccentric retired Navy officer, and commissioned seaworthy by him in 1961, was refurbished immaculately in 2009. If Lizard hadn't drawn all Jenn's eyes on her, then the exquisite woodwork of the cabin would have. Amidst the rather spacious central hall was a long, half circle plush bench seat. In the coming weeks the bench would remind Jenn of Da Vinci's *Last Supper*, as all ten-plus crew-members could at once—and rather comfortably—sit round the bench and eat off the rectangular dinner table.

But for now all attention fell on the demon lounging in the center of the cabin. Jenn's first reaction of utter revulsion was unconcealable. A vicious compulsion to vomit welled and gagged in Jenn's throat as she beheld the atrocity spooning mashed potatoes into a hole at the far right of its head.

"I'm Elizabeth, but I go by Lizard," the beast said cordially to Jenn. "You are very pretty. What's your name?"

Jenn raged against every internal screaming instinct to run away and managed to speak with a hushed monotone, "I'm Jenn. Everyone calls me Jenn."

"I have elephantiasis. Don't be scared. Don't be cruel. This is who I am." The arm that Lizard used to pantomime ended not in fingers but a flat flap, as if God gave this woman a pancake for a hand, as if someone melted down a hand into a flat glob of bones and tissue.

8

"You were born this way?" Jenn said at a level of astonished whisper.

"No. Not quite like this. As I've matured, many things have changed." Lizard clearly struggled when speaking, but Jenn thought she caught a chuckle in her tone. "Have you met the others yet?"

"Just you and me so far, my lady," Captain Alf butted in. "When on duty, you'll find Miss Lizard manning the helm, steering our old gal! Due to the nature of Lizard's, uh, her formation, it's dangerous, well, uh, difficult to say the least, for her to do the types of jobs that come as necessity to the rest of us. So it works out that she can turn our wheel most deftly."

"A word to the wise," Lizard said to Jenn, ignoring the Captain, "Don't bother to learn people's names. Just learn their wants, and that'll be satisfactory. We're all just a bunch of stereotypes."

"Oh really?" Jenn said. She was thankful Lizard was bringing a conversational topic to the table. She didn't know what to ask her, her only thought being if Lizard's skin was made out of clay—and whether her nose, ears and various bumps could pop right off, or be rubbed out like day-old, semi-hardened Play-doh. But this mention of stereotypes put Jenn somewhat at ease. She knew stereotypes. All her recent adventures could be diagrammed as a series of brush-ins with obscure stereotypes: the fat mob boss, the old eccentric artist, the fraud boyfriend, the jealous roommate, the man behind the curtain. Or rather, as it came in the form of Lillith Babbit, woman behind the curtain. "So what's your 'want'?"

Lizard cleared her throat before answering in full: "I'm Sublime. Then there's math, forgiveness, creatures, miracles, legacy, power, and immortality. Now you. And next week I understand we'll pick up another. 10 + 1, right boss?"

"Yes, yes my lady. Ten plus one, that's always been the goal," said the Captain.

Jenn turned her attention to the old man, "Which one are you? ... Sir?"

"Oh hogwash, you don't need to know any of that, my love. Come-come, why don't you meet Sir Isaac? Or at least, try to."

Jenn followed the Captain left down a narrow hallway.

"We've got four rooms for sleeping. The gentlemen in one. Myself and First, that is, the First Mate in another, the ladies' cabin of which you'll be a part down here at the end, and Sir Isaac, for reasons that can never be understood, gets his own room."

He knocked on the door in the middle of the hallway on the left side. "Alright, we've done our due diligence. Why don't you go in and have a peek-see?"

"Me? You're not coming in?"

"Now, now, you're the greenie. Greenies gotta learn the ropes for themselves. Go ahead, go in. He won't bite."

Jenn was a little afraid that he might indeed bite. After Lizard, Jenn wondered if the *Orion* was meant to be a freak show. That was a disconcerting thought: Come one, come all to marvel at the 10 + 1 freaks of the high seas! Coming to NBC this Fall!

Pushing the thought aside, Jenn nudged herself into the room. It was dark with no windows. Just a little desk lamp and a man hunched over, scribbling notes on a page, fully unaware of Jenn's intrusion. "Uh, hello?"

No answer.

"Hello, hi! I'm Jennifer. Jennifer Free. But you can just call me Jenn."

Nothing.

"What's your name?"

In a barely audible voice, a reply: "I'm coming quite close to a breakthrough. I'd appreciate it very much if you'd let me be. I'm sure I'll make your acquaintance more formally at a later time. Good day."

"Oh boy," Jenn said to herself as she exited the room. She had only been aboard the *Orion* for two minutes, and so far she'd met what seemed to be a bi-polar captain, a severely deformed person called Lizard, and a man who refused to take two seconds to meet a new crew-member. A precarious start, to say the least.

Captain Alf and Jenn joined Lizard on the bench while Jenn received the basic protocol of the voyage. As a member of the *Orion*, Jenn was under the direct authority of the Captain. If disputes grew to a level of either mutiny or physical endangerment, then Lillith Babbit was available to intercede. She was the end of the line. Beyond that there was an arsenal of maritime rules, regulations, and knots to learn. It was explained to Jenn that she, having no tangible way to go about her goal of solving the world, was to find her answer experientially, and therefore, would not be allowed to work on special projects during the day, as most other crew-members were entitled to. She was to be ship-hand all the livelong day. She would learn the ropes fast, and her greenness would recede ever more towards a ruddy hue of expert seamanship. When Jenn inquired as to what the other special projects were, Lizard gave a swift response.

"The *Orion* is a Destiny Ship. Do you know what that means? It means we've been tasked by the auspices of Miss Lillith Babbit to make a great discovery. In doing so we'll bring more fame to her name. We then, as one unit, are striving to bring her glory. And it just so happens that each of us has a different means by which we seek to attain this glory."

"I don't get it," Jenn admitted.

"It means," Captain Alf piped in, "that it doesn't matter what it is that we discover, only THAT we discover."

"Oh."

Lizard continued, "Lillith believes that thinking is best done in a focused environment. The ship is the focus. It confines the mind to a certain framework. It's her belief that in locking us into a constant state of adventure, she's nursing the very best of us."

Jenn was given three days to rest up. Lillith had set Jenn up with a security guard at a hotel outside the main stretch of Vegas. Jenn mostly slept the time away. She felt like she could have used another week or so of R&R, but she had a direct flight to San Francisco where she was to meet up with this ragtag bunch of genius explorers. The hustle and subsequent uneasy meet-and-greet had left Jenn fatigued, easily equipped to sleep for a few more days straight. Politely then, Jenn asked if she could go to bed and meet up with the rest of the crew in the morning. The Captain thought this a swell idea and showed her to her top bunk, above "Lex's bed",

11

whoever she was.

"Oh, one more thing," Captain said, pulling Jenn aside from her bed. "The rest of us, well, you see, we've just been through a hell of an experience. It's just that, well, to put it mildly, things got heated for a while. Yes. Things were quite hot. Actually, no. We neared the North Pole, so obviously we were bone-chillingly cold. All the time. But internally speaking—yes, that is what I mean—internally, there was a lot of hot stuff. Hot stuff, yes, like... hot strife, even. Hot strife, ha! I like that. It's a good turn of phrase, if I don't say so myself! How about a fresh brewed pot of hot strife coffee, eh?!"

"What?"

The Captain made a sheepish *you get it, right?* look.

"What... what happened? Up north, you said?" Jenn tried to yank the Captain back on topic.

"Ah yes, well, obviously, as you could imagine, as anyone could imagine, things got rough. Everyone cold and hungry, and it became bone-chillingly, bone-breakingly, bone-obliteratingly clear that things weren't going as according to plan."

"Okay...."

"Yes. Well, then. Okay indeed. Good night, young love."

"Wait, what? I don't get it."

"You say that a lot, young lady! Either you're quite dimwitted or you don't know what that phrase means."

Ignoring the insult, Jenn pushed on. "What was the point? All this about your last adventure, the North Pole...."

"I didn't say that we went to the North Pole. I never said that. I said we NEARED the Pole. Just close by. That's all I meant by that—as a means of direction."

"Okay, sure, but was there something in that story that you need me to know?"

"Ah, right. A very perceptive little lady you are! I bet you'll get on smashingly well with Miles Faa when you meet him."

"Who?"

"Oh, who am I kidding? A girl like yourself, all boxed up with the likes of us and him along for the ride? You never even had a chance. He'll bundle you to himself before we set off south wind!"

12

"What now?"

"Never that mind, you young lover! What I mean to say in all this who-dee-who... well, Lemony Snicket, what do I mean to say? Ah, just that we're glad you're here, if nothing else, just for the sake of new blood. You know, spin the center of power a bit on its axis."

"No, I don't know."

"Spin the axis on its... oh, yes, I guess you really don't know." The Skipper paused examining his thoughts. "Well, then, another time then. Goodnight!"

"Goodnight."

Jenn found her bunk and slept before she allowed a moment's reflection.

The nights since her fortunate encounter with Lillith Babbit ended the same. Each night, each pre-dawn dream brought forth the same ruddy image. It started with the room, that same room Jenn had dreamed of seemingly every night of her life. Gray walls. But now, since Las Vegas, since Magical Kingdom, a transparency. One wall shimmered, bled through. It was like a wall of transparency paper suited for an old slide projector. And on the other side, two figures: Thomas Flusher O'Malley and his inherited sister of the streets, Tiff. Flusher stayed quiet. He just stood there, on the other side of that wall. His head bent low. Sometimes, as Jenn peered at the boy in the way that one looks at someone without seeing—the way of dreaming—he changed. Cartoonish. He became some twisted creature. A man with a twisted face. Rounder. And his eyes... they were slit. Grotesque. And the grotesque Flusher snarled, like the Cheshire cat, only more hideous. But Jenn's attention never remained on the Flusher abstraction. No, it was Tiff who demanded Jenn's subconscious stare. Focused—all of Jenn's soul focused in, not merely on Tiff as a whole, but more finely, more exactly and expectantly, on her lips. Those lips were priming to speak, to release something. A deep truth. Or... a deep question?

Tonight, unlike the evenings prior, Jenn awoke before her dream reached its pinnacle of devastation.

A grisly sight welcomed Jenn. The distorted mug of Elizabeth Schumacher, the Lizard.

13

"I need to ask you something."

"Wha?"

"Where's the highest place?"

"Elizabeth—"

"Call me Lizard."

"Okay. Lizard, I'm asleep. Can't we talk in the morning?"

"Just answer the question. Where's the highest place?"

"I don't know, Mount Everest."

"No. Think better. Where's the highest place?"

"I'm... I'm pretty sure that Mount Everest is the tallest place on Earth."

"No, stupid. Think higher."

"Liz, is there something you want to tell me?"

"Don't call me that."

"Oh, I'm really tired. I haven't had much sleep recently, and you kinda woke me up."

"What's higher than the mountains?"

There was no getting out of this. Whoever Elizabeth Schumacher was, she was not someone who would be bowled over by sympathy. She clearly had no care for Jenn's comfort. She needed something, she needed it now, and she needed it out of Jenn.

"Pay attention. Listen. Answer. What's higher than the mountains?"

Jenn's mind went to Leviathan. What if she wasn't just big? What if she was massive? What if her measurements eclipsed the mountains? What if Godzilla was just an egg next to her? Jenn tried up-sizing her Leviathan. She thought briefly of the Ziz, the bird so large it's wingspan blotted out the sun. Jenn imagined being in a rowboat all alone on a breezy, overcast day. She envisioned a wall suddenly jutting out into the heavens beside her rowboat. Up and up, water falling off her hide as big as tidal waves. This colossus, too big for this earth.

"You've got it, don't you?" Lizard said.

"Excuse me?"

"Your eyes went up and to the right. You were picturing it.... Tell me."

"It's nothing."

Lizard drew her mug closer to Jenn's fair skin. It wasn't just

14

that Lizard's face looked like a Picasso on steroids. Her face space was a miasma of red sores, flakes, and permanent measles. It was a grotesquery, no way to make it pleasant, a face lacking any redemptive qualities. Lizard's shell of a body was proof alone that the world was unjust. Nature had proven not to be a benign mistress to mankind. "Tell me, Jennifer Free. Tell me now."

"I saw Leviathan."

"Leviathan."

"Yes, that's what I saw."

Lizard turned and began to hobble away.

"Wait. What's the right answer? What did you want me to say?" There was more desperation in Jenn's voice than she herself expected.

"It doesn't matter."

"Then why'd you ask?"

"You can't help me."

For some time, Jenn lay in her bed, trying to sort out the meaning of this late-night encounter. *What's the highest place?* Did Lizard mean the stars? The sun? The ends of the cosmos? What could possibly be the right answer? Thinking on this, Jenn once more brought up the vision of her in a rowboat witnessing the leviathan albatross arise from the deep like a planet ascending into the universe proper. Leviathan wasn't a bad answer. If only Lizard could see her as Jenn saw her, then she'd understand. Maybe then she'd agree.

Before the mix and mingle that the morrow brought, before the myriad introductions that were to follow under the coastal blue sky, Jenn finished her sleep. And it always ended the same.

Tiff's lips, white as stone, beside the ghoulish outline of Flusher, purse and finally uttering:

"Why are we dead, Jennifer?"

~~~

This begins the next stage of Jenn's adventures. She's met three of her crew-mates on the *Orion*. Next week she'll meet six more. Take heart, and get to know these characters.

Jenn's stuck with them now, come hell *and* high water. Choose your favorite. Root for them. But I'll tell you this, dear reader—one of them's a traitor.

Chapter 20: Eight Conversations

Conversation 1: 1st Mate

Jenn: Hi, Miss Godard... uh, Emmanuela?... Hello. Ma'am?

1st: If you insist on calling on that name, you'll live a lonely life on this boat.

Jenn: Excuse me?

1st: I am the ship's First Mate, not some Ma'am. You will call me First. Understood?

Jenn: Yes, ma'a—First.

1st: You're green, but if you listen well, work hard, and stay on deck, you'll become something less than an embarrassment to yourself soon enough.

Jenn: Wow, okay, so I guess as First Mate your role is to play the hard ass?

1st: This vessel is a myopic fusion of ignorants and ignoramuses. The ignorants are fine. I can teach them how not to be ignorants. But the ignoramuses on this boat, those ones, you can't teach them, can't help them help themselves. You can't even talk to some of them. I know what I sound like. I don't need you to act all pretty and naive. We barely survived our last outing, and those mother-ignoramuses dug our grave. Babbit's "wild expedition" has the luck of the gods to thank for any of us even being alive today.

Jenn: What happened? I keep hearing about "your last adventure," but no one's told me what ya'll went through.

1st: Are you ready to tell us why Lillith Babbit decided to thrust a 17-year-old bald girl onto the deck of my ship?

Jenn: Your ship?

1st: You'll see soon enough who runs this place.

Jenn: Ok... I'm sorry if I'm an inconvenience to you. But I'm here now. That's not going away. So you can label me an ignoramus, ignorant, whatever. You can make me walk the plank if you really want, but you're going to have to deal with me, one way or the other. If you're really the person that makes everything run smoothly around here, then you might as well reckon yourself to the fact that I'm here, I'm alive, and I'm ready to learn and to work. Okay?

1st: Now that's the first intelligent thing I've heard you say!

Jenn: That's... good, right?

1st: I assumed Babbit was sending me another idiot genius who'd just cripple us even further. But if you're ready to work—to man up, then I am pleased to have you aboard, Jennifer Free.

Jenn: Just call me Jenn.

1st: I'll call you whatever I want to call you.

Jenn: Right. Of course, label me an ignorant or an ignoramus.

1st: Look around before you judge me. Have you seen these people?

Jenn: What, the crew?

1st: Ha! We don't have a crew! We have the world's most eclectic bunch of aspiring minds, who all seem to think that this boat runs itself, and that their transcendental dreams somehow fuel the ship.

Jenn: You said there are ignorants and ignoramuses: two groups, right?

1st: Merkyl and Gimli, the only two worth their weight around here.

Jenn: And the Captain.

1st: Ha! Ha-ha-ha! Best joke I've heard all week.

Jenn: Why's that funny?

1st: If you knew the Captain like I know the Captain, you'd laugh too.

Jenn: Okay... what about Lex and Miles? They seem young and athletic.

1st: Lex is too scatterbrained. She'll be working, true enough, but then suddenly, like a haunting miracle floating on a day breeze, her face goes blank. No one's home. She's gone somewhere else. I damn near have to hit her to bring her back.

Jenn: And Miles?

1st: Who, Faa? He's too busy over-analyzing himself. The man is a god of psychology, and yet he finds himself more fascinating than anything else in nature. A narcissist, through and through. I despise his type.

Jenn: So... how do I not be an ignoramus?

1st: Here. For starters, grab onto this.

Conversation 2: Merkyl

Jenn: Hi, uh, Merkyl?

Merkyl: Yes. Hello, Jennifer. How are you liking the Orion?

Jenn: I don't really know yet. To be honest the last few days have been so... so... out of the ordinary. I'm having a hard time making much sense of the world.

Merkyl: Is that why you shaved your head?

Jenn: Oh... uh....

Merkyl: I like it. It means business.

Jenn: Ha, well, the First Mate said you were all about getting down to business!

Merkyl: Yeah, me and Godard get along pretty well. Boats don't sail themselves, you know.

Jenn: Yeah, that's what she said.

Merkyl: She tell you much else?

Jenn: Not really. I don't think she likes me very much.

Merkyl: She's an interesting one, that Godard. She really should be the Skipper on board.

Jenn: I think she pretty much feels the same way.

Merkyl: Well, if the situation were any other, I'm sure she'd have staged a coup and mutinied already 'til she got her way.

Jenn: It's that serious then?

Merkyl: Every situation is serious to Godard.

Jenn: Oh... so what's so special about the current situation that keeps her from, from mutiny... from mutinying, mutinizing?

Merkyl: You mean besides the fact that she's married to the Captain?

Jenn: What? I had no idea! Nobody told me!

Merkyl: Yup, you'd never know unless someone told ya. Neither of them like each other much. They don't share a bed. They don't wear rings. I've never even heard Godard say his name. It's always "Captain" for her. Always.

Jenn: But they must love each other to sign up to sail around the world together like this.

Merkyl: Your guess is as good as mine.

Jenn: So what do you do to stay on the First Mate's good side? It seems everybody else is in the doghouse.

Merkyl: Have you looked around? Have you seen who's on this boat?

Jenn: I just... what makes you different?

Merkyl: It has nothing to do with me. I'm the normal one. It's them that are different. Take Lex, for example.

Jenn: She seems normal enough.

Merkyl: Alexandra Keitel is crazy. Sure, she's a sweet girl and all, but the crazy just keeps bubbling up.

Jenn: Oh. I think I may know what you mean. I had a roommate who would freak out at me. She'd be normal, and then all of a sudden attack me. Crazy stuff.

Merkyl: Well now, it's not like Lex is mental in the classical sense. She's not bipolar or nothing.

Jenn: Oh.

Merkyl: It's just the things she believes in. Honestly, and this is the God's honest truth, and I feel I have to say that because it's so preposterous... Lex Keitel believes her mother is/was—I'm not sure if she's dead—a selkie.

Jenn: A what-ie?

Merkyl: A selkie.

Jenn: I've never heard that word before.

Merkyl: A selkie is a person who's a sea person... usually they're associated with seals.

Jenn: Just like someone who is obsessed with swimming?

Merkyl: Nope, that'd be a swimmer. A selkie is a human on land, but turns into a seal when they're in the ocean.

Jenn: A mermaid!

Merkyl: No, full seal. No Starbucks fin business. Full-on metamorphosis into a seal.

Jenn: Wow. That's a new one for me.

Merkyl: And she's the least of our worries!

Jenn: How so?

Merkyl: Well, you got Father Thomas, who's literally trying to live up to his name.

Jenn: Thomas?

Merkyl: The Apostle Thomas, the follower of Jesus who

refused to believe that Jesus resurrected. He's the Bible's great doubter. Meanwhile our Thomas is so plagued with self-doubt that he got himself signed up on the *Orion* here just to search the world for God. He wants a miracle, a true, anti-science, no-way-to-explain-it-but-divinity miracle. He spends more time staring at the clouds and sky than he does anything else. Then you get Sir Isaac and Lizard—both of whom are more or less door weights. I mean, I know it's not Lizard's fault, the elephantiasis, but I don't see Babbit's thought process in assigning a woman of her condition to a boat bound to battle the seven seas.

Jenn: And what about Isaac? Does he not like people?

Merkyl: Oh, I'm sure he likes people fine. He's just never met anybody. No social skills. He spends every waking minute of his life thinking about numbers.

Jenn: He's an accountant?

Merkyl: Worse. A theoretical mathematician.

Jenn: Oh, so like, he's trying to solve some ultimate equation or something?

Merkyl: Hell if I know.

Jenn: And is the Captain as the First Mate says?

Merkyl: Just call her Godard. No one calls her First.

Jenn: But she said—

Merkyl: Yes and no. She tells everyone that, but no one listens to her. The Captain's not as bad as she likes to say he is. He's just not quite as hard-nosed as we need him to be.

Jenn: I don't understand.

Merkyl: He's a peacetime leader, good for the soul when times are good. But when times get bad, he's not the guy you want in your foxhole, if you know what I mean.... Besides him, there's just Miles Faa and Robles, who we'll pick up tomorrow. You heard about Robles?

Jenn: No.

Merkyl: He was with us before the whole Alaska debacle. Gimli brought news that Robles' woman—well, one of them—was about to have a baby. So he went off to go see the birth and meet his son. We're picking him back up tomorrow. The lucky mongrel, got out of dodge just when things went downhill for the *Orion*.

21

Jenn: What happened in Alaska? Everyone's whispering about it.

Merkyl: Nothing good, I'll tell you that much. So yeah, Miles Faa... Faa's young enough, strong enough, athletic enough to be a great crew-member, but he's always looking for a mind he can control. Usually, that just leaves him thinking about himself. That's the only diamond just beyond his reach, methinks.

Jenn: And who's Gimli?

Merkyl: Ah, Gimli! Gimli's the best of us!

Conversation 3: Lex

Lex: Convinced you're trapped on a boat full of lunatics yet?

Jenn: Oh, hey, you snuck up on me. Sorry, what did you ask?

Lex: Having second thoughts about the *Orion*? Babbit made it sound so great, right?

Jenn: Haha, yeah, something like that. I just... I'm not sure how to fit in. Everyone seems pretty isolated, you know? It doesn't feel like a team, or a crew.... I don't know... I don't know what I expected. I guess I thought there would be something here that I could be a part of—something to plug into.

Lex: You have to keep in mind we just went through a horrible ordeal. We're lucky to be as stable as we are. Everyone's just on edge. We haven't yet figured out our next mission, so, I think, until that's cleared up, everyone's a little bite-y, afraid of ending up in another Alaska situation. Once we're on our way somewhere, you'll see, we'll get to gellin' again.

Jenn: How's it work? Like, we'll just up and choose a mission?

Lex: Pretty much. I joined before the campaign to the underwater volcanoes off the coast of Hawai'i.

Jenn: Wow. How was that?

Lex: Actually, that was a pretty successful campaign... but then Captain Alf had to have his way.

Jenn: So, everyone will have a pow-wow or something to

decide what's next.

Lex: Ah, well, the semi-annual great debate.

Jenn: What's it like?

Lex: It's pretty much the only time all of us act like a crew—the only time we're all together. It's amazing how 10 of us—well, 11 if you count Gimli—can perpetually find so many separate places to be on a small boat.

Jenn: So, uh, can I ask you another question?

Lex: Someone telling stories about me?

Jenn: Just... I was talking to Merkyl.

Lex: Yeah, Merkyl has a way of getting into everybody's business.

Jenn: What's his thing, anyway? Everyone here seems to have a thing, but he didn't tell me what he's all about.

Lex: He's an evolutionary biologist. He's been trying to find a cure for death.

Jenn: But everyone dies.

Lex: The funny thing is in all this—we're a bunch of broken people. You don't turn into an obsessed idea-aholic without having a series of breaking points in your life. Pretty much everybody here has gone through something horrific that's made them that way. Cap, Godard, obviously Liz, even Faa. We've all been through the ringer of emotion and suffering. So when I heard Merkyl had this destiny to cure death and discover immortality, I presumed he'd lost an only child, or witnessed a loved one die in his arms or something. But no! He's an only child, Gimli brings him mail all the time from both parents. I mean, the man's in his late 50s and both of his parents are alive. He's never married, never even been in a deep relationship, as far as I know. So, where does he get this zealous need to cure death? I'm lost on that one.

Jenn: So you've been through some rough stuff, huh?

Lex: Well, my mom left when I was seven, so Dad took us kids and immigrated to Toronto.

Jenn: Your Mom just left you... abandoned?

Lex: Pretty much. She'd put it another way, but...

Jenn: Merkyl said—

Lex: Jennifer, or, it's Jenn, right?

Jenn: Yeah, Jenn is good.

Lex: Jenn, I don't really want to get into all that right now... with you. I'm just not the type of gal who opens up to people I don't know yet. I'm sure you're a nice girl and all, but trust has to be earned.

Jenn: Sure-sure. Of course, I totally get that.

Conversation 4: Miles Faa

Jenn: You're Miles Faa, right? I don't think we've been formally introduced.

Faa: Yeah, uh, hi.

Jenn: So, everyone says you're the nerd and somehow also the jock of the group. You're a high school drama unicorn!

Faa: Sorry, I, uh, I need to clean the lavatory right now. It's my day for it, and it's kinda a one-man job. You should talk to Merkyl or Godard. They'll give you something to do.

Jenn: Oh, right. Thanks....

Conversation 5: Father Thomas

Thomas: We didn't get a chance to meet before. I'm Father Thomas.

Jenn: Hi, Father Thomas. I'm Jennifer Free. So, you're Catholic, you're a Priest? I've been learning a lot about Saints and Catholicism lately.

Thomas: I'm glad to hear that, but I'm afraid to tell you, I'm Anglican.

Jenn: Anglican... is that like, like, an Angel church?

Thomas: No, not angels, angles.

Jenn: Huh?

Thomas: You know, angles. We're really into geometry!

Jenn: You're pulling my tail.

Thomas: I am... Anglican is just another type of Christianity.

Jenn: Oh, okay. So are you the boat's pastor?

Thomas: You don't yet quite understand what you've joined, do you?

Jenn: I thought I did, but, excuse me for saying this, but, ya'll are so weird!

Thomas: Ha. That's the truest sentiment I've heard all

24

week. What were your expectations when Mrs. Babbit offered you a position on the *Orion*?

Jenn: I don't know. Adventure. Interesting sights... hmm... I guess now that I think about it, I thought, for some reason, that I'd be able to understand what's true out here. I just came out of a gross situation, and I've been so confused. I thought that the open water, the physicality of this voyage—I thought that would make everything clearer, you know?

Thomas: Makes sense to me. But sadly, in my experience, nature is just as obscure as the metro.

Jenn: So why are you here?

Thomas: Oh, I've been here for ages now. I predate this entire crew. I was here when the *Orion* was helmed by Captain LaMarcus LaSalle, way back in the day.

Jenn: How long has the *Orion* been... like, in office, in commission?

Thomas: I don't rightly know. She's been at sea in one iteration or another for centuries. Suffice it to say, Alfred's a good Captain. You've come at a good time.

Jenn: Really? Because I kinda got the idea that I've come at a really bad time.

Thomas: Nonsense.

Jenn: It's just, people seem pretty closed off. Tight lipped. And no one, I guess, except you, seems to think highly of the Captain.

Thomas: Alaska didn't do us any favors. That's really all there is to it. If you'd come before, right after the volcanic outing, then you'd have found us a much jollier gang. Especially with Robles around. He's a firecracker, a real energy giver.

Jenn: So why'd do you say I've come at the right time?

Thomas: I think because, even though none of us enjoyed going through it, what happened in Alaska was good for us. Especially for the Captain and First Mate. Maybe no one realizes it yet, but once the shock wears off, and the bitter edge of the experience is blunted with faded memories, all of us have come out better people.

Jenn: Why?

Thomas: Sometimes, at least in my experience, the only

way to recover after a horrible experience is to go through another grueling one. The new covers up the old. Now, when Alf and Godard think on hard times, the most recent memories, aka Alaska, come first to mind. The older stuff doesn't bubble up. The faces of their two little ones won't come to surface.

Jenn: Two little ones?

Thomas: About, what, maybe four years ago now, Godard gave birth to twins. A little boy and little girl. They were so happy. They made plans to leave the *Orion*, to start a new life on land with their growing family. We were off the shores of Tonga, at the time. Then, before they had a chance to get away, the little one died. The little boy. It was awful. We all felt the pain, of course we did, living in such proximity, but to this day I still can't imagine what Godard and Alf must have felt, must still feel. We had a funeral at sea for the little boy and I tried to do a service that honored God, but... but it was a tough time. Then, slowly, things seemed like they were getting back on track. Alf still said they planned to leave, but they didn't want to leave the only place where they ever knew their son.

Jenn: How horrible.

Thomas: And then, a few months later, the little girl left us too.

Jenn: How?

Thomas: Both of them, they just left in the night. For the second one, we tried to do a funeral just like the first. I wanted to do a service that honored God, but... but it was a tough time.

Jenn: I had no idea.

Thomas: This is a hard world.

Jenn: So, are you, I mean, do you... do people give, that is, do you take confession?

Thomas: Is there something you need to get off your chest, Jennifer?

Jenn: I... I was just wondering. You know, in case, in case there comes a time!

Conversation 6: Liz

26

Jenn: How's the steering, going?

Liz (Lizard): Leviathan could work.

Jenn: Excuse me?

Liz: Leviathan could work.

Jenn: Why does everyone on this boat talk in riddles?

Liz: I shouldn't have scolded you last night. Your answer wasn't bad. It might not even be wrong.

Jenn: Okay, well, glad I could help.

Conversation 7: Captain Alf and Sir Isaac

Alf: How's your first day going, young love? Meet everyone? Got the lay of the land down much yet? Godard assign you daily tasks?

Jenn: Um... yeah, it's a... it's a process, right?

Alf: What now, brown cow?

Jenn: Huh?

Alf: What now, brown cow? You know the one, young love! What now? Brown cow!

Jenn: Like, it's a first step... ya'll are a lot to handle.

Alf: But you at least connected with everyone? I think that's important. Sure, I introduced you, but that's not real conversation. I want to make sure you have genuine conversations, genuine connections. That's the only way we'll become one mind, one organism. So...?

Jenn: Yes, sir, Captain?

Alf: Did you make meaningful connections?

Jenn: With most everyone.

Alf: Most? Not all?

Jenn: Well, there's Sir Isaac....

Alf: Didn't even look you in the eyes, did he?

Jenn: He seems pretty busy.

Alf: I'll wring his neck—come on, follow me. Let's work this out.

Alf: Isaac. Isaac. Isaac! Wake up, man!

Isaac: I wasn't asleep.

Alf: You had your bloody eyes closed, Isaac.

Isaac: I was thinking.

Alf: It's two in the afternoon! It's bad enough you don't do anything on here, but for Pete's sake man, this isn't the time to nap!

Isaac: I wasn't napping.

Alf: You have your eyes closed, your head back, you're leaned back—when you're actually hard at work, I know the look. You'd be bent over like a hunchback at that desk of yours! Whatever this is, whatever you're doing "not napping", it sure as Bloody Mary acts like sleeping.

Isaac: What are you here for?

Alf: No, it's not like that. In the real world, Isaac, in the real world we talk to one another like men. We look each other in the eyes. We shake hands. We explain ourselves. And we work to meet each other halfway. I'm tired of bending so far backwards I'm pretzel-walking forward just so that you can reach out just 1%—not even 1%, Isaac! You understand numbers and percentages, 0.002%—that's all I'm asking you to give me on a day-to-day basis. 0.002%. And tickle me bruised, you're still not able to give me that much of yourself. Not even 0.002%. You know what this is, young love, you see what this is? I'll tell you what this is! 0.00000004%. That's what Isaac is giving us, right here, right now! Tarnation! 0.00000004%. Can you believe that, Jennifer Free? Helloooooo! Have you even noticed she's bald!

Jenn: Hey now!

Alf: Sorry love, I was just pointing out the obvious. Trying to make this lug-weight have a reason enough to look up.

Isaac: What do you want, Alfred?

Alf: I want you to acknowledge the existence of our newest crew-member!

Isaac: I met her yesterday.

Alf: That's not what she expressed to me.

Jenn: Captain, it's okay. I'm sure we'll be pals in no time. You can't force these things.

Alf: Maybe you can't, but I'm the Captain. I'm the Papa! TALK. Now, Sir Isaac. TALK.

Isaac: Hello.

Jenn: Hi.

Alf: Ask a question of the young lady.

Isaac: Why are you here?

Alf: Say her name!

Isaac: Miss....

Jenn: Free. But you can just call me Jenn.

Isaac: Miss Jenn.

Alf: Now ask your question.

Isaac: Why are you here, Miss Jenn?

Jenn: I'm... I'm searching for the Leviathan.

Alf: Good, good! Well, look at that! Real conversation! Even I, the all-knowing Captain, learned something new. That's what real conversation does for you, young love! Marvelous!

Conversation 4 Returned: Miles Faa

Faa: Hey, I need to talk to you.

Jenn: Are you sure? Because it seemed earlier that you'd do anything to avoid talking to me.

Faa: Yeah, about that... you're not exactly someone entirely new to me, Jennifer Calling.

Jenn: It's Jennifer Fr—How do you know that name?

Faa: I bet you've heard my name before too. Before the *Orion*.

Jenn: I don't... think... so.

Faa: How about the name Mohammad Najjar?

Jenn: He attacked my giraffe.

Faa: I was his therapist.

Jenn: You're a psychologist?

Faa: An occupational hypnotherapist.

Jenn: Oh. Do you know why he attacked me?

Faa: Yeah, that's kinda what I wanted to talk to you about.

Jenn: Oh.

Faa: I guess, I was kinda afraid to talk to you.... I don't know why that happened. But I'm sorry.

Jenn: What are you sorry for?

Faa: My technique, one of my techniques: it's pretty controversial. It involves making the situation much worse before it gets better.

Jenn: How's that?

Faa: Mohammad Najjar came to me because he was

deathly afraid of snakes. His brother and daughter both died from snake bites.

Jenn: Should you be telling me this? Doesn't this break some client-doctor creed or something?

Faa: I owe you an explanation. And who out here's going to prosecute me? The form of therapy I used on Mr. Najjar is called "Convergent Hate-Fear Assimilation". When I found how deeply embedded Mr. Najjar's fear and hatred of snakes went, I was convinced there was no way to simply erase it. Because the center of his suffering was based not on just one event, but two separate traumatizing incidents differentiated and distinguished by years and years, there was no way I could find to get him let it go. So I sunk him deeper into his trauma. I caused him to fear all animals. Every creature. Ideally, once that's established, once he hates and fears the entire animal kingdom, then I can break down his whole system of fear and hatred. I break 'em so I can rebuild 'em. The problem is... that time period when he's broken... that's a vulnerable and dangerous time. I had him in isolation. Living on a ranch at my retreat... a solid two-hour drive east of Los Angeles.

Jenn: So his attack was all because of a fear of snakes? That's it?

Faa: No... there's something else too....

Jenn: Yes.

Faa: Najjar believed... he said he saw... the snake that bit his sister... he said... his words, his belief, was that the snake came out of the desert looking for him, but bit his sister instead, then... after it bit her, meta-morphed into a man and ran away, back into the desert.

Jenn: Okay... what are you telling me? To be on the lookout for Transformers?

Faa: No, I'm telling you that someone, and I don't know who, but someone, SOMEONE, let Najjar out. Someone let out a very unstable man before he was fixed. And I believe that someone sent him to Magical Kingdom that day. I think that THAT someone knew exactly what they were doing.

Jenn: You're saying he was sent to take out my giraffe?

Faa: I'm saying he was sicced on you like a dog. Be careful

who you trust, Jennifer Calling.

Conversation 8: Lex on Robles

Lex: How's your first day gone?

Jenn: Okay, I guess.

Lex: I'm sorry if I came off brusque. I just don't like it when other people gossip about me.

Jenn: I get that.

Lex: Well, I hope despite everyone's aloofness, I hope you feel welcome.

Jenn: I'm not sure if welcomed is quite the right feeling.

Lex: It'll be better tomorrow. Robles will overhaul the mood. You'll see.

Jenn: So who is he? What's he like?

Lex: He's a pagan extremist. He pretty much lives to experience the craziest stuff he can.

Jenn: Oh... and that's... good?

Lex: He's always the life of the party!

Jenn: Gotcha. Oh—and who's this Gimli? When's he coming?

Lex: Gimli is our postman... well, our post-gull.

Jenn: Huh?

Lex: He's Merkyl's trained gull. He flies all over the place, picks up our mail from various locales, and brings it back to us.

Jenn: But if the boat's always sailing, how does the bird find us?

Lex: Pretty cool, right? We may be a motley crew, but there's some magic amongst us.

Jenn smirked, pondering what adventures lay ahead of the Orion.

~~~

Jenn's met 8 out of the 9 fellow travellers on the *Orion*. On day three of Jennifer Dash's voyage on the high sea, Jorje Robles makes his triumphant return to the ship. Robles' appearance also dictates Jenn's first encounter with the "Theatre of

31

Remembrance"—and the opening of a new style of
storytelling.

Chapter 21: Theatre of Remembrance

Jenn's second night on the *Orion* was not a peaceful one for our young protagonist. The day's conversations tossed in her head while she turned in her bed.

What must it have been like to lose two children at sea? And from what? From nothing. Just gone. Gone in the night. Gone in their sleep.

Lex, who seemed so normal compared to the others—did she really believe her mom turned into a seal? Jenn had never heard of such a thing, not even in fairy tales.

What about Liz? It was bad enough that Jenn couldn't resist flinching every time she gazed at the presence of elephantiasis, but that the woman didn't make any sense when she talked—that makes befriending her tricky.

And then there's Faa.

Running through the story in her head, Jenn concluded Faa had to be lying. But why? Maybe he knew exactly why Najjar attacked her mechanical giraffe, but wanted to play the fool so that she'd trust him? Maybe he orchestrated the hit. Maybe he hypnotized Najjar specifically to attack her. The smoking gun of Faa's story was in omitting the lawyer, Mark Janner, from his story. Jenn faintly remembered Janner mentioning that Najjar was someone's client, though honestly the name Faa never stuck with her. Nevertheless, Faa was now connected to Najjar who was clearly connected to Janner who was connected to Lillith Babbit, the billionaire who gave Jenn her ticket onto this clown-boat. So, someone up that line had to be responsible. If Faa's story had any truth in it at all, that Najjar was hypnotized and secretly let out of Faa's desert retreat, then somebody in that line had to be the cause of the attack. Everyone couldn't be innocent. Jenn lay in bed contemplating whether she should trust her new shipmate, or choose to continue trusting the people who got her here.

"Why are we dead, Jennifer?"

The next day Jenn tried hard to get to work, to be productive.

She wanted to be on Merkyl and the First Mate's good side. This attempt, however, fell to shambles. She was taught over and over how to tie a bowline knot, but whenever she tried to do it in real time, all her bowlines came out as sad pretzels. Even the simplistic clove hitch eluded Jenn's motor abilities.

By mid-day, the *Orion* was again ashore, picking up the pagan extremist known as Jorje Robles. The event went not at all as expected. Jenn supposed that this "energy kicker" (as Father Thomas had described him) would come hooting and hollering, making a general ruckus. Jenn was ready for a party... she didn't get it.

Jorje Robles climbed aboard the *Orion* in silence. Worse, the crew didn't bother to acknowledge him. And worse yet, everyone on the deck, seemingly in unison, kept their eyes at their feet. Only Jennifer's eyes beamed at the gristled, bearded, Hispanic pagan. For a moment, just one instant, Robles caught Jenn's gaze. He threw her a smile and a wink before submerging below deck.

It wasn't until nightfall, after at least another 50 failed pretzel knots, that the atmosphere on board the *Orion* changed.

The sky was clear. Thousands of stars beamed down. The ocean was calm. If Jenn had been more observant, she would have spied Merkyl yanking ropes around high up on the mainsail mast.

"Everyone out! The Theatre of Remembrance has begun!" Captain Alf boomed. A spotlight shone up at the sails. Merkyl, twenty-five feet up, yanked a lever and down swooped the mainsail. Below, Godard, the First Mate, grabbed an edge and pulled it port side. Godard tied down the edge of the fabric, and it took a moment for Jenn's eyes to absorb the scene. They had made the mainsail into a stage backdrop, a convex arena.

In that semi-circular space, Jorje Robles, the pagan extremist, stood tall. The spotlight swirled about before landing on his face. Jenn peered around and noticed nearly the whole crew sitting on the deck behind her, glaring up with gleeful anticipation at their own prodigal son. The anchor was set, Jenn took a seat, Robles cleared his throat.

It began:

Theatre of Remembrance
Come take this chance.
Hear what will be heard.
Quiver not at fates foretold.

Once upon a lifetime,
Whence Zeus sat in his prime,
An angel called out to me,
An angel whose name is Gimli!
And he said, my son, my son,
you no longer are the only one.

I cried, I shouted, I demanded!
"Pray tell, don't leave me stranded."
That Gimli, with weary wings,
Recalled that a woman near sings.
She sings the old song
Of a son soon to birth headlong.
I bolted, I ran, I swam.
To my birth home in the far land.

Some call it Mexico,
I say that's a low blow.
I say my woman gave birth in Bethlehem
Of this, dear friends, do not condemn.
For one sees what one wishes,
And for a son one endures many bitches.

While at first I came upon the land,
I saw my woman sinking in the sand.
She breathed and she cried and she hissed,
Telling me that from my own mother I am missed.
"Who cares what she feels," I recanted.
"'Tis your allegiance" she chanted.
"If we dismiss our families,
Then we damn our future cruciallys. "

"For in this day we must above all bear

Our past family with all care.
Then if in haste we quickly diminish
The gods of fortune to us will finish
That never forward shall our baby rise,
But only regress and regress until he dies.
This is the law of the goddess tradition.
And so now this must be your mission.
Go to your mother, hear what she shall say.
And in this way we will seize the day.
For then our son will be born without fortunes turn,
And malevolent Lucifer he shall spurn."
"Lucifer, Lucifer, what talk of devils?
Our son shall reign in all the world's annals!"

So out I left the very day,
To find my dearest mother of May.

It took awhile, scrapping through forest.
To find my old mother, always the earnest.
But found her I did, true as can be.
In our old abode, sewing so formulaic-ally.
I called out, "Mama, mama, que esta mal"?
She cried out, oh how she cried, "The curse won't fall!"

Such news met me with no satisfaction,
For I never heard that there lay some deep infraction.
On my head and the brow of my only begotten,
As sure as I tell you now, I thought all was forgotten.
Yay, "No, no, no," my mother didst proclaim,
"From your father's deeds lay this claim.
There's but one way to end the curse.
You must seek and kill your father first.
Before that babe is born today,
Your dreadful father must you slay!"

"Why, oh why!" to my mother I did protest,
"What is this curse that puts me this insidious test?"
She stole some breath, and filled her lungs,
my mother did, before she hung the fable of tongues,

36

Of how my father never drank his fill
Until one day it drove him to kill.
And who indeed should he kill dormant in Bethlehem?
But the town's own mayor by the name of Saludamem.
Pierced him in the heart he did,
With bottle broken at the lid.

"This was many years ago," she said.
"Long before you grew in my belly's bed.
Yet who should be this Saludamem's wife,
But the descendant of the Mayan life!
A witch of much fame and repute,
Who still could cast spell without dispute."

And curse my murderous father she did,
Under dark sky of Mayan pyramid.
The wicked witch spelled misery in the sky,
And punished us hombres to never feel high.
Never should we believe our fortunes so grand,
We were cursed to perceive all life as bland.

The bottle, the beer, tequila, the gin,
Such spirits gave rise to unforgivable sin.
My likeness, my padre, he who blasphemed,
Bore the virus of toxic Mayan scheme,
That left both him and me full of void.
This void in me, this emptiness, like an android,
Is the cause of my wandering heart.
From this depression I can never part.
My destiny is set.
My future's met.
There's no Valhalla awaiting me.
Nothing more for me to see.
I am the bastard saint of schizoid,
Listen, hear, refrain from being annoyed.
For as if I had meditated under Freud,
I knew what mission now must be employed.

'Tis true, due to my Father I am left devoid,
But I shall bless my son and not leave him destroyed.
By the most vicious of diseases, the vilest of crimes,
Which is seeing darkness where there is light.

Friends, my confession is that I am blind.
Yes, blind in the ways of ecstasy and sublime.
The eyes of my soul are covered with grime.
This is my cruel heart curse.
The bottom of Pa's purse.

Theatre of Remembrance
Come take this chance.
Hear what will be heard.
Quiver not at fates foretold.

You know what must be done.
The thing I couldn't shun.
Yes, that thing, the great Oedipus
Long worshiper of the god Bacchus,
Blind now, sees the future true.
His father must be slew.

So I traveled, friend
I flew as if a godsend,
to my father's first home.
The tavern, his catacomb.

Our eyes met.
Destiny's set.
He asked how I was.
I said, "My babe gives no pause.
Know what I must do,
To end this curse true."

My father, the tyrant,
bellowed a hideous grunt,
And laughed an immortal's laugh.

He said, "I tell you this on your behalf,
If you slay your father today,
You will surely fall prey."

Incredulous, I shouted back,
"I'm already prey of your hijack!
You've ruined me, and my son too,
unless you die this day anew."

"Idiot!" he stammered.
"I'm not talking of Mayan chants deferred!"
"A worm lives inside me."
I truly didn't understand his plea.
All I thought was my soon to be baby.

I shoved my knife into his chest.
Churned it in and out of his breast.
To death, to die, to fates eternal.
I sent my Pa to quick funeral.
Blood he spat from out his lips,
And died red, mouth to fingertips.

I sighed, but before I turned away,
Out came a worm as big as Yahweh.
A sickening twisty invertebrate,
The size of well-round piglet,
Flew through the air towards me.
I later discovered from where it got its glee.
It grew fat on alcohol, the squirmy beast.
Day by day my father refused to be policed.
And drank and drank and drank his fill,
Which nursed this worm like Winston Churchill.

An alcoholic has many enemies,
Whomever fed him this worm,
Believed he served him a disease,
When in fact the worm did affirm,
To father that the bottom of the bottle,
Has an unseen protector's will to battle,

39

Or avenge any wanderer for fodder.

This worm did fly
Entirely to my surprise.
He had no teeth, but rather,
Vicious suckers that gather
And glue onto one's skin.
Much to my chagrin.

But I did grab that poison.
And like a Viking Norseman,
Smashed him back down my father's throat.
You may say I was cutthroat.
Having no pity on the creature,
Too bellicose to wiggle out of its leacher.

Nay, I say, and walked away from that place.
To see my son born with beautiful face.

I found him, head pushing free from his Mother.
"What a beut!" I bluther.
The boy, he smiles to this day.
His life he will not betray.
For I gave him a gift.
That he may never know the rift.
The rift I feel so steeply.
The pain of which knifes me deeply.

As for me, experiences I cannot store.
Neither lore, nor score, nor whore,
Can make me whole again.
I cannot make my amend.
Besides to say that even seeing my son for the first time,
Didn't inspire me to feel anything of the sublime.

I am cursed to feel the Mayan trap.
Destiny has already written my map.
I shall never be happy, senor,
For my soul shall be lifted, nevermore.

Theatre of Remembrance
Come take this chance.
Hear what will be heard.
Quiver not at fates foretold.

The Theatre of Remembrance had ended.

Everyone came up, and one by one, hugged and kissed the indomitable, Senor Jorje Robles.

Jenn found Miles Faa and asked, "Was that all true? Did he really kill his Father? Was there really a worm living inside of his Dad that fed off of alcohol? Is there really a Mayan curse?"

Miles looked at her smugly, "You were a Patriot, you saw the tunnels, you should know more than the rest of us what the Mayans are up to." Miles snuck away from Jenn and warmly greeted Robles.

Behind Miles, Lex waited in line to greet the rhymer. Jenn repeated her inquiry, "Was that all true? Did he really kill his Father? Was there really a worm living inside of his Dad that fed off of alcohol?"—Jenn left off the part about the Mayans... she couldn't deal with that right now.

"Sure, it's all true," Lex answered. "At least, thematically. Maybe Robles didn't really kill his Father, and there probably wasn't any real curse, but there's truth there. With the birth of his own son, he was able to get past, to destroy the sins of his Father, to break the chain. You get it? That's how the Theatre works."

"Oh," Jenn said.

A shadow suddenly bathed Jenn in darkness. She crested her eyes towards the eagle's nest of the ship, wherein Gimli the gull perched himself above the rest of the crew of the *Orion*. At his side, a fanny pack, overflowing with newspapers and mail.

~~~

The Theatre of Remembrance will one day return to us. But

41

not yet.

For now, Jenn's left to unravel one confusing mystery after another. If the *Orion* wasn't already crazy enough, the emergence of Jorje Robles just made life on the high seas more than a little zany. From this moment, however, it's time for the *Orion* to set its path. It's time for the obsessive crew of the *Orion* to choose their next adventure. Will Jennifer finally set course to find Leviathan? The next chapter awaits your eyes, and with it, a promise of direction.

Chapter 22: The Great Debate

The following takes place on the fifth morning of Jenn's stay on the Orion. The discussion includes ten of the eleven members of the crew (minus only Gimli). Because such meetings always begin in the most boring of manners, I bring this transcript to you, picking up the meeting in mid-conversation.

Cap: What would your goals be in that venture?

Liz: There's a neuro-toxin I know of, a quick trip to the coast, and we could accost it.

Lex: You want to experiment on blue whales, Lizard?

Liz: Not precisely—if the chemical works as I suspect, it'll retard the growth of the animal without causing any detrimental side effects. We find the pod off the Japanese coast, inject a youngling with the neuro-agent, separate her from the rest—which should be no problem. If we hover around the pod for weeks, the group will accept our nearness as no peculiarity at all. Ideally, the pod will slowly start to reject our chosen one. They'll ostracize her, sensing something foreign about the whale. We swoop in, feed her, accept her, cherish her. Expunged from her family, the mammal will choose the *Orion* as mother. We'll migrate away from the pod, and—again, ideally—the youngster follows. If not, we'll of course have a tracking beacon on her, so finding her shouldn't be a problem.

Jenn: I had a tracking beacon injected into me once.

Robles: You want a midget blue whale as a pet?

Liz: Blue whales are the biggest life form on Earth, and yet, we know very little about them. We don't even know what their normal life span is... we think 80 years. We think! But there are arctic whales that we know are at least 200 years old. I think blue whales are similar.

First: Why not go hunt an Arctic whale then?

Cap: I'm all for that!

Liz: Because I, like the rest of us, have no desire to go back north at this moment in my life.

Lex: What's the point? So we get a baby blue whale. Where does that get us?

Liz: Two possibilities, both very real, both very impacting. One, once we know the neuro-agent works, we repeat the process with another infant, mate our two specimens together, migrate them somewhere away from other Blues, and let nature take its course.

Cap: I don't get it.

Liz: I think the agent should affect the whale's chemical make-up, meaning, she'll pass on her size to her newborns.

First: Thus introducing a sub-species to the ocean.

Liz: Yes, precisely. It'd be a rare glimpse for humanity to witness what a completely foreign, new species does to the environment. Being a differing size, they'll have new predators—but yet, they'll not require the same energy intake, food consumption. They'd have to come up with their own new survival tactics. Evolution will take them in an entirely unforeseeable direction.

Merkyl: A direction you'd like to us to witness.

Liz: And secondly, research on blue whales, or arctic whales or any large whale for that matter, is inherently overwhelming due to the creature's size. With a stunted blue, research becomes much more conductible.

First: And what sort of research are you thinking of?

Liz: Ideally, longevity.

Robles: You crazy mother—as hideous as you are and you're still searching for the fountain of youth, like all the bearded white men that preceded you! You crazy doll!

Cap: Alright, alright, old chap, hold your water buckets! We're all still in the phase of tossing ideas to-and-fro. Let's keep our judgments steady until it's time to see what sticks and what falls over board.

Lex: What've you got, Robles? Something diabolical, no doubt.

Robles: I have indeed, the thing we all must lock arms and agree to! We must.

Merkyl: ...and that would be....

Robles: Come back to me. Let the others go first.

Merkyl: No, you were asked, so you go.

Robles: I do as I please. My idea is the best, so I shall go last.

Merkyl: This isn't second grade show and tell. You've been asked to go, so you go!

Robles: Skipper didn't ask, just our local Crypto.

Lex: Hey!

Merkyl: You need a good spanking, son!

Robles: Ooooh, mother may I!

Cap: By Jove! these are fun times, fun times! I'm glad we're all feeling so passionate already! That's just the right type of enthusiasm we've been looking for. But I say, this is your Captain speaking, make no mistake! Let's let youth speak up. Young love, do you care to make a suggestion?

Jenn: So, I don't... I don't fully understand what we're trying to accomplish.

Lex: It can be anything, really.

Merkyl: No!

First: Not anything. We need to choose an adventure. One that we can all support.

Liz: Something that brings fame upon the name Babbit.

Thomas: One that unifies us under a common cause.

Cap: Precisely, so what say you, young love? Got any grand expeditions hiding up your sleeve?

Jenn: Not really... would it be okay if I think about it a little bit?

First: We need to decide today. We've put off this meeting long enough.

Cap: That's not exactly how I'd put it, but unfortunately, yes, the current of time swiftly breaks against us.

Lex: Jenn, you can vote for someone else's idea. You don't have to come up with a solution all on your own.

Cap: We'd like everyone to bring something to the table, Alexandra. And yes, that even means you, Sir Isaac.

Isaac: Oh, I'm quite ready to present our future destitudinal plans.

Cap: Alright then, let's hear it.

Robles: Okay here's thing: I know my plan isn't... how do you say... amenable to the rest of the crew. I want to travel from the tip of North America to the bottom tip of South

America. Or versa vice! Now, I know, I know, this is not a good mission for the crew, but you dropped me off before... maybe you'll drop me off again on the way to your next adventure. So... yeah, I'm for whoever is going furthest North or South. There. Are you happy? Are you really happy now, all of you? I'm outta here!

Jenn: Where's he going?

Father: Mr. Robles has arguments in his head before he actually speaks up. It's sometimes hard for him to discern the real conversation from the one in his head. I'm sure we shot him down a hundred times before he opened his mouth.

Faa: He'll be back in a moment. The anger runs its course through him pretty quickly. He'll be jovial as ever in a moment or two.

Lex: It's really quite a sight to behold, how quick his turn-arounds are!

Cap: Isaac, I am eager to hear your idea.

Liz: Yes, so am I.

First: Go ahead, Isaac, tell us.

Thomas: Yes, I for one, would very much like to hear.

Isaac: The black stone—the Ka'aba of Mecca.

Jenn: The what?

Isaac: Various calculations report that the cube, that place, is one of the seven strong points on Earth.

First: Seven strong points?

Isaac: Gravity is not dispersed evenly on Earth. Roughly speaking, the Earth is most bulbous at the equator, and therefore there's a higher gravity field there. The Earth than flattens at the poles. But, there are seven notable anomalies, places where the gravitational field is not what it should be.

Lex: And Mecca is one of those places?

Isaac: It's the third strongest in the world.

First: Where are the first two?

Isaac: The strongest is in the middle of the Atlantic—which may give scientific cause to some of the Bermuda Triangle beliefs. The second is in Northern Scotland.

Lex: Scotland? Really?

Isaac: But Mecca interests me most. Its obvious religious significance can't be overlooked.

Robles: What do you mean by that?

Lex: See? All better already!

Robles: I heard everything.

Isaac: If a place is historically venerated, the way the Ka'aba is, there usually is some mathematical reason for such zealotry to evolve.

Cap: You think the most revered site in all of Islam is because of a scientific anomaly?

First: What do you actually want to do there?

Isaac: I want to trap gravitons.

Jenn: What's a graviton?

Merkyl: It's just theoretical; gravity may be stored in sub-atomic particles we call gravitons. But nobody has isolated them. It's impossible.

First: How would it be possible, Sir Isaac?

Isaac: If there's more of them there, then they should be easier to catch.

Liz: Sounds simple enough.

Cap: Okay, before we raise our hands for Isaac's religious quest, let's all have our ideas spotted. So far we've got me: going back North, further North to find Hudson's real route.

All: Ugh!

Cap: Lizard wants to give coffee to an infant blue whale, and Sir Isaac wants to sneak into Saudi Arabia. Who's next? Father Thomas?

Thomas: Yes, well, I have no actual expectations that any of you will like this idea, but I've heard rumblings of underground church meetings in North Korea. Apparently, since the border between North and South is pretty well attended by guards, there are these partially man-built running caves that go from the Communist side to the religiously-tolerant South. From what I've heard, members of the church from both North and South meet in these caves for secret services.

Jenn: Like the Underground Railroad!

Thomas: Yes, I think it's very similar—a connective tissue between the free and the oppressed.

First: And why should we visit them?

Thomas: I thought maybe we could aid them? Maybe help

expand their underground network.

Faa: Don't you think that any "help" we give them would leave them more vulnerable to being discovered by the DPRK?

Thomas: The what?

Faa: The Democratic People's Republic of Korea. Whatever we do, wherever we go, we have to report back to Babbit. I'd hate for our mission to help a hiding people be invalidated by our duty to report back to an unknown quantity.

Cap: That's true. Whatever our mission, I'll certainly have to report it back to Lillith. She's funding this expedition. We can't very well leave her in the dark.

Jenn: We could... we could tell her that we're doing something else.

First: You'd lie to your boss—for that? For nothing?

Cap: No, no. I'm sorry Father Thomas, the logistics of your proposal just don't compute.

Thomas: I wasn't expecting anyone to raise my flag. Thank you, Jennifer, for your kind words.

Jenn: You're wel—

First: Don't congratulate her for musing insubordination.

Thomas: Oh, I just—

First: Jennifer, can I have a word with you aside?

Robles: Ooooohhh... young blood is in trouble with da Momma!

First: I want you to know that what you said in there is entirely out-of-line. If I see glimpses of that sort of attitude again, I'll see to it that your stay on the *Orion* is brief, one way or the other.

Jenn: I'm sorry, I guess I don't really understand what the big deal is?

First: Don't you be flippant with me, slut.

Jenn: Excuse me! Don't speak to me like that.

First: See, that's an example of acceptable anger. Both my response and words. It's okay to be angry, Jenn. Really. Most any emotion is acceptable on my watch.

Jenn: You just called me—

First: What I have no tolerance, no patience, no good will

48

towards, is any semblance of insurrection. It'd be intolerant and atrocious enough for you to say those words to the Captain or myself. That'd be bad enough. But you invoked it against our philanthropist. You're here because Lillith Babbit, one of the greatest women of our age, had pity on your slutty soul. Don't disgrace her... especially in front of the rest of the crew. If I catch you acting out again, AND SO FLIPPANTLY, you're gone.

Jenn: You're trying to intimidate me.

First: I'm telling you that on this boat, when you look at me, you should see that I'm Lillith Babbit embodied. And I will not tolerate sluts.

Jenn: Stop calling me that!

First: How can I trust you after what you said?

Jenn: I was just trying to be helpful!

First: Helpful. Helpful? By lying to your master and commander?

Jenn: I'm sorry. It was a silly thought... next time I have a silly thought, I'll keep it to myself.

First: I don't know how you're going to gain my trust back. Now whenever you say anything, how am I to believe that you're not beyond lying to make your personal situation better? Only sluts lie, Jennifer. That's why I call you one.

Cap: Welcome back, Lex just finished explaining her selkie search.

Lex: I—

Cap: I think we're all in agreement that ultimately it, like Father Thomas' idea, is an untenable plan. Moving on: First Mate, you got something for us?

First: During the Second World War, a fleet of German U-Boats made it as far as the Gulf Coast. I'd like to dredge the coast in search of sunken U-boats. That s all.

Cap: Okay... any questions?

Faa: Seems pretty self-explanatory.

Cap: Okay, Merk, what say the bastion bulwark of the *Orion*?

Merkyl: I want to go to the Galapagos.

Cap: Ah! We've been through this. The world is still, what, half-undiscovered. Why do you want to go to one of the very most previously discovered places?

Merkyl: I'd like to take some blood samples. Maybe work on some genetic synthetic variations.

Cap: We don't have the lab equipment needed for your deep experiments, Merkyl buddy. Come on, everyone, we haven't exactly hit the jackpot of ideas yet, have we? Give me something we can work with! If not, then for sure, back North to further search for the pass has got to be the continued mission for us.

Faa: There's a room in Minneapolis. It's internationally recognized as the quietest room in the world. No non-deaf person has been able to handle the room for longer than 45 minutes. They say when you're sitting there, in utter darkness, in that room, everything gets confusing. You start to hear your body at work. Not just the sound of your heart and your lungs, but the sounds of your stomach at work, the rhythm of your kidneys, the very synapses in your brain turning on and off.

Lex: You want to go to Minnesota.

Faa: No, Miss Keitel, I want to go to Cajamarca, Peru, where the real quietest room has just been built. Early reports say this one drives people insane in less than 15 minutes. I've never been mad. But my whole profession, my whole way of life, is about examining the mad, sympathizing with the insane. This is a chance to have that temporary experience. Doesn't it pull at your imagination to know there's a room that can't be fathomed by mankind? We could be the one's to endure it. And document it. And surpass it. I vote that the *Orion* experiences this room, and with our collective intelligence, rediscover the world in a way no other team of investigators could.

Lex: Wow... that sounds... intense.

Liz: How do you know that this room is truly greater than the Minneapolis one?

Faa: Because a coalition of major world power governments helped build it. Currently, it's used as an international truth serum. This room is the future of torture.

Liz: You want us to torture ourselves?

Faa: Opportunities created in which we can bend our minds

inward are rare in this life. I want us to seize this opportunity while the room is still get-able.

Merkyl: This opportunity is going away?

Faa: It was made through various government agencies. Once the room proves its worth, one tribe will try to strip the others of its access. This'll begin a proxy fight for the room. Those never end well. For now, it's a sleeping giant. I want us to steal the giant's gold before he wakes.

Lex: I'm not sold.

Faa: Captain, while you're in the room, you'll experience what's called tendrilism, the experience of losing your disconnection from the world. Meaning, you'll become unable to disassociate yourself from your surroundings. That may sound frightening, and to most, it is, but if you're calm and think on it, you'll see that's nirvana in its truest form— becoming one with the space around you. And once there, once there! Once you feel that height of euphoria, I sincerely believe you'll find access to your Resource State.

Cap: Resource State, am I supposed to know what that means?

Faa: Your purest state of being, a place of mind that allows you to tap into your most novel realms. Most of our lives are played out like a bad recording. Our brain feeds from the same cognitive frameworks day after day. However, from the womb until about 8 months of age, our brains are just gooey goodness, a mush-like substance... and that's really exciting. Only with time does everything freeze up and harden. Hardening is good, or maybe a better way to put it is, necessary, because it allows us to draw conclusions and make decisions. But the mush phase, that's when our potential is completely unlimited. When you have access to your Resource State, your brain again functions as if in infancy. That's bad if it completely resets, but the goal, and what readily happens to adults who experience the Resource State, is that when you come out, your mind reconfigures and has a new lens by which to investigate your experience in the Resource State.

Liz: It's a profundity center, a place that gives you truly novel thoughts.

51

Faa: Sure, that's a great description.

Lex: Sign me up. My vote's with Faa.

Cap: Whoa, whoa, whoa! Let's not take our horses to the feed trough before we're ready to dismount! Let's hear all the ideas first, before we start throwing our weight around one way or another.

Merkyl: I think—

Cap: Oh, and by the way, I'll say this on the out-front just to be clear. You know I support each and every one of you... well, except maybe Sir—

Liz: No one's voting for Alaska again.

Cap: Not Alaska! Canada. If you'll just look at the map here....

First: Miss Free, I believe you are last.

Jenn: Umm... yeah. I just would like to find the mythical Leviathan.

Lex: Any idea where to look?

Merkyl: What would you do if you found her? Do you know what she looks like? How would you actually know if you found her?

Thomas: Which legend are you basing your theory on?

Jenn: Theory?

Cap: Is that everyone then?

Lex: My vote's for Faa's plan.

Faa: Thank you, Alexandra.

First: Why with him?

Lex: I can just imagine myself being stretched in that room. My life is still a mystery to me. Maybe I've got answers locked away somewhere inside... like a hidden lost memory.

Faa: Often what can happen in a Resource State is a pulling of background data. It's like watching a video of your memories; you can press play, you can even zoom in on details that took place in the background that your conscious mind never noticed, but your brain diagrammed and filed nonetheless.

First: Lex, dear, this is just Faa doing his usual thing. He's manipulating you, dear.

Lex: No he's not. It's a really intriguing idea. It beats looking for hidden Nazi treasure.

First: Fine, I vote for Isaac's idea.

Cap: Honey, no! You can't!

First: I most certainly can. And I have.

Cap: But what about Canada... you promised!

First: None of that matters now. We were stuck in the ice for weeks, Alfred. You think anyone is going to volunteer for that hell again? If you veto our wills and take us North, there'll be a mutiny. We'd eat your liver before we let you take us back to that freezing graveyard.

Cap: I can't believe my ears.

Merkyl: I also vote for Isaac's proposition. I'd very much like to carbon date the black stone in the Ka'aba.

Cap: Oh, big surprise there—do you have a will of your own, Tony, or do you just wait for the First Mate's approval to take a crap?

Thomas: Alf, this isn't how you should be acting.

Cap: Oh, isn't it? Isn't it! Where's your allegiance, Father? Who's fish are you frying?

Thomas: I don't like the idea of messing with a Muslim holy site. And Faa's quiet room sounds like a soulful place with minimized distractions, where prayers can be thought in peace. I'd like to pray in this quiet room, Miles. I'm with you.

Cap: Great, so it's the manipulator versus the dead weight. Those are our options. What about you, Lizard? You got any sense in that abominable mug of yours?

Liz: Classy, Captain. I vote for finding the blue whales.

Cap: You vote for yourself. Cool.

Merkyl: That's 3 votes for Isaac's Mecca voyage, 3 votes for the silent room, and 1 vote for blue whales. Jenn, Jorje, it's you 2 and the Captain.

Jenn: I'll vote with Lizard.

Merkyl: Okay, 3 for Mecca, 3 for Peru, 2 for blue whales.

Robles: I'm with Sir Isaac. Maybe I'll find God.

Merkyl: 3 for Peru, 4 for Mecca, 2 for blues... and I suppose you're voting for yourself then, Captain?

Cap: If it's mud wrestling between the psycho and the psychic, I'll choose the psychic. South America.

Merkyl: The Captain's double vote makes it 5 to 4 for Peru.

Cap: At least we'll stay on this ocean. Maybe a little

equatorial sun will change your minds about ol' Hudson and his un-found pass.

Liz: I change my vote to Mecca.

Cap: What! No. The voting's over. The deal's done.

First: She can change her vote if she wants to!

Cap: No, she can't. If we let people swap around then we'll float here 'til Summer. We all spoke our votes into being, as you all know, my vote as Captain counts for two, and now we move on with life. I'll set coordinates for Peru, and we'll set our sails South in the morning. End of show. End of debate!

First: No. Lizard rightly saw that her vote didn't count. This was a two-horse race, so she chose the party she liked best. Isn't that right, Lizard?

Liz: That's how it is.

Cap: Fine, fine. But even if I grant you that, it's 5 to 5. We're stuck.

Merkyl: Not if Jenn changes her vote too.

Robles: What's it gonna be, little girl?

Lex: Mecca or Peru?

~~~

I don't need to explain to you the impact Jenn's decision will have for the ten human souls of the *Orion*. Her decision locks in a particular destiny, and we're about to find out just how far that adventure will lead her.

Mecca or Peru.

Next week the crew sets sail for their destination, but before Jenn can fully commit to the future, she'll wrestle anew with the ghosts of the past. She'll also receive word from Atticus via Gimli the gull, the very words you read in Chapter 17.

Chapter 23: On Open Seas

Eyes closed. The gray room. Of the gray house. Of the gray continent. Of the gray dream.

Jennifer Dash hadn't had a restful night's sleep since joining the *Orion*. Weeks of tumultuous, undulating gray walls were wreaking havoc on her disposition.

Most nights, viewing her surroundings from a forced 3rd-person perspective, staring down at herself from somewhere above, Jenn hid from her own dream-state. She'd managed, on nearly a nightly basis, to crawl underneath her bed. There, underneath the great weight of the levitating mattress, she'd cover her ears, trying not to speculate on how she could still somehow watch herself from up above, even though she hid away under the bed.

The reason for hiding, of course, was what lay just beyond the menacing walls which shook, wilted, and seemed to breathe with every passing moment. The cat-themed man. A furry body, with shrill, high ears, a tail, whiskers, and the unmistakable mug of Thomas Flusher O'Malley.

He beckoned her. Flusher beckoned the sleeping Jenn to come through the gray walls, to push through, to where the dead sleep. This beckoning, more than just audio, played out in the room like a rippling sound wave. It was a cat call, yes, but in the perversity's meowing, a hidden voice whispered, "Come Jenn. Come to us. See how it really is." For this reason, night after night, unwanted visit after unwanted visit to that dream house, Jenn plugged her ears and hid herself.

Dreams don't work the way waking life does. One's efforts to avoid conflict, to suppress fear, only elicit further confrontation. There's no denying the dream witch her curse.

Deep in her mind, Jenn surmised on this night, during this particular dream, that maybe the only way to end the torment, the hell of repetition, was to wade into its depths. Flusher the cat couldn't hurt her here, right? He couldn't reap his vengeance for real... could he? Not in this life. And so it was only prudent, it was only reasonable, to answer his howling siren song—to face the music and push through the gray.

Tonight.

Right here.

Right now.

Jenn reached through the undulating grayness. There was nothing to feel, pushing her hand into the wall like it was liquid mercury. No, no feeling. But there was taste. In the way that only makes sense in dreams, Jenn tasted the wall, tasted the gray... tasted it all, in her hand, and in her arm. And the taste was of blood. Metallic, gray blood. The taste oozed its way up her arm, as if eating her from the inside out.

Inside the wall. Inside the wall! This. This was inside the wall. If Jenn had ever seen the *Lord of the Rings*, she'd be reminded of the way Frodo's world looked when he put on the One Ring of Power... a blurred realm of misshapen forms. But she hadn't seen those films, and so Jenn's shock exploded.

Of course, all of this was Jenn's own doing. This dream didn't come from outside. This was Jenn on fire in her own mind. This was her own working out. So while there was fear, there was a certain anticipation. She wondered where the Flusher cat went, and as soon as she asked it, she arrived at an answer. Flusher was leading her. He was just ahead of her, a blurry vision of the near future. And as she came to this conclusion, she spotted his silhouette. The interior of the inside-wall world was not one of focus, but, as Jenn zeroed her attention on following the white rabbit, aka the cartoon cat man, she watched her feet step down a spiral wooden staircase. There weren't more than one or two steps in full view at a time. But each step brought another.

Down and down Jennifer Dash twirled. Down and down she followed the hideous poltergeist. Down and down until—an end. No more steps. Jenn looked up from the ground. Below her toes lay not another spiraling wooden step, but a white marble floor, to take in an entire wide room of white marble. In the corner Flusher pointed. He pointed towards the middle of the room. He pointed to nothing.

No. Not nothing, Jenn's mind concluded. *There is not nothing there. There's my fear. There's my roommate. There's my Tiff.*

56

Tiff, Jenn's slain roommate from Magical Kingdom, a long-standing member of the underground homeless circuit known as the Patriots, sat, arms outstretched, her eyes pinned on Jenn.

"Hello, Jenn."

Jenn wouldn't speak. She couldn't speak. She had nothing to say.

"Nothing to say," Tiff smiled wickedly. Tiff's right arm was hooked up to a bag of blood. Her left, just as Jenn's once did, lay sliced open, spilling into a pool of burgundy. Jenn stared at the pool. The blood was so dark. Far closer to black than red.

"Aren't you going to say thank you?"

Jenn didn't respond. Instead she took her eyes off the pool of blood, off the slashed wrist of Tiff, onto the baggie of blood. It too was something less than red. Not black, but yellow... yellowish-green.

"Not exactly a fair trade, was it?" Tiff said. "You got my blood, now I get yours... but I gave you the best of me. My pure heart's blood, that's what you got."

As Jenn tried to comprehend Tiff's words, she looked at Tiff's head, trying to see if the head-wound she endured was visible. Maybe the injury had healed. Maybe Tiff was okay.

"The funny thing is, now you carry me with you everywhere you go. It'll be my blood in your eyeballs that first beholds great Leviathan. It'll be my blood in your heart that finally solves the world... in a way, you're more me than you. You've been drained and filled up with all of me. Kinda romantic in a way, isn't it?"

The walls caved in on Jenn, her heart racing. Cat Flusher appears in front of her face, nary an inch away from Jenn's lips.

He says, "Jennifer Free Dash, will you marry me?"

The cat man moves in to kiss Jenn.

Eyes open. Out of bed.

It's the middle of the night on the *Orion*. Jenn, fear and loathing coursing through her veins, decides it's best to get some fresh air, to check on Lizard who steers the schooner whilst the others sleep. Jenn hopes seeing another real person will snap her back to reality.

Every night had gone by like this. Jenn awaking from the same grotesque dream, then making her way in long johns out to talk to the Lizard at the helm. Every night beside the deformed, Jenn beheld the deep black of the Pacific's unending night horizon.

She'd chosen South America, and had, mostly, felt good about that decision. Jenn didn't like that the *Orion*'s fate rested on her decision. How was a seventeen-year-old supposed to make a decision like that? She'd never been on a boat before, let alone traveled to South America or Africa. Was Mecca even in Africa? Jenn wasn't altogether sure. At any rate, the crew of the *Orion* accepted Jenn's decision with relative ease. There were some snickerings of how of course Miles Faa, the resident mental magician, got his way, but overall no dissenter outwardly appeared to treat Jenn any worse for her conclusion.

That was weeks ago, and now, just days out from shouting "Land Ho!" and making inland for the eponymous quiet room, Jenn felt at ease on the ship. Except, of course, for the dreams, and the exhaustion derived from the nightmarish nocturnal tradition.

On this night, as Jenn arose and walked through the galley to the deck, she found a chorus of activity aboard the ship. And yet each little unit was entirely ignorant of the others, fully convinced they acted alone under the cover of dark night.

First, Jenn passed the bathroom. The door was closed, but light streamed from under the door. The ship's bathroom was a tiny little thing, and being the only bastion of internal relief, a line often formed for its usage. Jenn had assumed she'd have a free pass to its services at this late hour, and so she cringed at her misfortune finding said lavatory occupied. Jenn supposed she could wait until after her rendezvous with Lizard to pee, but as she passed the door, the strange sounds coming from the small room caused for pause.

The grunts were unmistakably those of Jorje Robles, the ship's eccentric, extremist pagan.

Self-flagellation. Robles was whipping himself. Why? He was no self-loathing monk. Surely he didn't view himself as a reprobate that required penance through suffering. So why do this? Why torment thyself in the middle of the night?

Under his moans, his aches, Jenn heard the Mexican mutter, "Thy will be done. Thy will s hard. Thy will be done. Thy will is perfect. Thy will. Thy will."

This odd event would have rumbled through Jenn's mind until she came up with some internal rationalization for Robles' strange behavior, had she not then been overwhelmed by another sight.

On the kitchen table, on full display for any passerby, as Jenn so happened to be on this evening, Merkyl and the First Mate of the *Orion* hunched themselves over the body of small monkey. There was no denying the sight. There it was, as plain as day, a midnight autopsy. Both "doctors" wore masks over their faces as they cut at this poor simian's brains. The two were in such ecstasies of concentration that neither noticed Jennifer as she tiptoed right on by, ascending the stairs up to the deck.

The ocean air in her hair and on her face did Jenn some good. The ocean was real, the waves confident and consistent. These realities had concreted themselves as forces of good for Jenn. Sure, everyday for the first six days on board brought with it vomitous bouts of seasickness, but that was a small price to pay for a fine reality. A pulsing, thick reality, not like the dreams beyond the gray walls, manic dreams, ever undulating and brim-full of guilt married with deception. The ocean blew away such illusions and made visions of monkey autopsies lose their luster. Thankfully.

Jenn made her way to the helm. Lizard, faithful woman she was, peered ahead as she kept her hands on the wheel.

"Good evening, Miss Free."

"Good evening, Lizard. Any Blake-ian visions tonight?"

"None yet."

Lizard had so obsessively spoke of William Blake, that Jenn had begun to address Lizard with a new vocabulary menagerie. A thought of inspiration was a "Blake-ian vision". A new plan or idea was a "compass path", while new experiences that one couldn't understand were to be labeled

"Songs of Innocence". That left experiences in which one could gain insight as "Songs of Experience". To this end Lizard currently spoke.

"I had a song of experience today."

"Oh, how's that?"

"I passed Sir Isaac's room while he talked with Alf. The Captain wasn't angry."

"Really? And you understand this?"

"He asked Isaac why he wanted to go to Mecca."

"Isaac's answered that question a hundred times already."

"He gave a different one this time."

"Really? Isaac has a secret agenda?"

"I don't think so. But he said that the stars point him there."

"Like... how? Is that a metaphor?"

"No. Sir Isaac's an astrologist."

"What? No! Isaac's a man of mathematics."

"These two are not divorced in the way you imagine they are."

"So you know what he was talking about? You know what the stars are saying?"

"No. But Alfred seemed to understand."

"So what's your conclusion? What insight did you gain? I'm left with more questions than answers. Still sounds like a Song of Innocence to me."

"I believe Isaac and Captain Alfred are not so against each other as they appear."

"They're faking mutual contempt?"

"I think so, yes."

Had Jenn had more faith and trust in Liz, she would have opined about the monkey autopsy she just witnessed, but as things were, Jenn still was yet to feel particularly chummy around the elephantiasis victim. Years ago, Jenn had caught a documentary on TV about a one Mr. Joseph Merrick, the man well known for the circus title "The Elephant Man". He died a sad life, but Jenn recalled that the man had a sweet disposition, and one short poem Merrick often quoted stuck with her. The poem read:

'Tis True my form is something odd -

60

But blaming me is blaming God,
Could I create myself anew,
I would not fail in pleasing you.

Elizabeth Schumacher was not like Mr. Merrick. She talked with consistent fervor of a future, a future or a vision, a vision or a destiny, a destiny or... God knows what. Jenn could never quite grasp Lizard's M.O. And because of this, Lizard remained, day-in, day-out, an obscure figure to Jennifer Dash who felt that at any given moment, Lizard would sell Jenn off to the highest bidder, if it offered Lizard a glimpse at the divine. Therefore, it was best not to speak of midnight monkey postmortems.

The next day was difficult—not because work on the bow of the ship required any unusual feat from Jennifer. It was merely the addition of yet another day without sufficient sleep.

In those days, there were many continual tasks and trivial aspects of life aboard the *Orion* that surely would be well worth mentioning, which would create a kaleidoscope through which to better view Jenn—to embiggen your view of her seafaring world. But those days riding atop the waves of the sea are behind us now. For sanity's sake, and for the sake of our ever-dissolving memories, we must forsake the mundane details of the life aquatic, and stick to the narrative.

One event that day is worth mentioning, however: The return of Gimli the Gull. The fowl bore in its beak the contents of many pieces of mail, and—very perceptively, Jenn thought—yesterday's newspaper from Cajamarca, Peru. Jenn giggled at how Gimli fawned over Merkyl's petting and soft words to the bird. It was the sweetest Jenn had seen the rough-necked Merkyl, this act of gentle regard to the mail-bird nearly erasing the sullen image of Merkyl the monkey brain excavator.

"What do we got?" Lex called out.

Merkyl tenderly grabbed the mail bag from Gimli's mouth.

"Let's see... Godard, looks like something from your father. Sir Isaac's got some sort of certificate from the University of Columbia. One for me. One for Miles. And, one for Jennifer...

Dash? Jenny, I guess this one's for you? You from Jennings, Louisiana? Or did Gimli grab the wrong mail?"

"No, no. That's mine. It's... it's just a pet name."

"Ah, a pet name from Atticus Further, then."

Jenn ran and grabbed the letter, smothering it to her chest.

Atticus remembers me! Atticus still thinks of me! Atticus misses me! Humphaliandra from Atticus!

HUMPHALIANDRA FROM ATTICUS! YIPPEEE!

Jenn was a new woman. Who cared for sleep when words from Atticus Further were so close! This letter, she could touch it, caress it.

A bashful thought then overwhelmed Jenn. Did she really like Atticus so much? She nearly called out, "My love!" to herself in the ecstasy of the moment. But she didn't love Atticus... did she?

No. That'd be silly. That'd be like the time Antonio D'anconia said he loved Jenn—love didn't work that way. Love's a slow bleed, a slow transfusion of virtue into the bloodstream. Not stupid Tiff's blood. Not poisoned blood. This Jennifer, the one called Jennifer Free, wasn't worthy of a letter from the noble Atticus, the perfect, gentleman boy, the darling saint of the pelican state. He was so far better than Jenn. He was perfect and pure. Jenn? She was used, worn down, jaded. Could she even claim to look at Leviathan with an honest heart? Once upon a time she wanted to find the mythical beast for reasons of honest curiosity. But now, Jenn was unable to do anything honestly. Everything had the burden of stain. Jenn was stained, stained with the blood of her roommate. Stained with a dutch prostitute's bald head. Stained with the recent memories of mayhem, already worn to nubs by obsessive observance and reflection.

Meanwhile, half the crew was breezing through the local Peruvian newspaper. Jenn would come to find out later that everyone onboard the *Orion*, save Miles Faa and herself, spoke Spanish fluently. That's what Jenn got for climbing aboard a ship of idiot savants.

Not the headline, but a sidebar column of the newspaper reported the reappearance of the fabled figure Pishtaco. The report spoke of three people, one of them a child, who claimed to have spotted a fat 'white demon' feeding on some sort of carcass. Naturally, being collectively of good cheer and having no real concept of the dangers that lie ahead, no member of the *Orion* put much stock in the article.

Gray room. Again. Curses.

There's the cat-man. Here's the blood taste in the arm. Now the spiral wooden staircase, one step at a time. The marble room. Tiff, blood in one arm, blood out the other.

But wait. Look again. There's a change. The pool—the pool is gone. Gone is the cylindrical pond of wrist gore. In its place burns a green flame. Blood falls, drip drop, into a vacuous green flame, same as the one Dolores Burden had danced around. St. Vitus' fire. The flame of Pied Piper. The vengeance of that cruel angel, that childnapper.

Jenn awoke suddenly. Father Thomas was shaking her.

"I'm sorry Jennifer. You were moaning in your sleep... I was praying... and... I thought I... I understood it to be best to wake you."

"Father, get Miles Faa for me."

"Why? I'm sure he's sleeping."

"Father, if you sin in a dream, do you sin in real life?"

"Why, I... I don't know. Sin is a complicated subject."

"Would you wake Miles for me?"

"Of course."

Father Thomas obeyed. Miles Faa came. Something about being woken in the middle of that recurring horror leveled a surge of decisiveness in Jennifer Dash. Her blood swelled with instant clarity. She couldn't go on like this, couldn't live day to day with night-to-night horrors. She was ending this. Tonight.

"Miles, will you hypnotize me?"

"Why would I do that?"

"I can't sleep."

"There are lots of cures for that. Hypnotism is a bit drastic."

Father Thomas spoke up, "May I speak to you alone, Miss Free? I'd like to talk to you about this. Hypnotism... it's not at all safe."

Miles answered, "Safety's not the issue, Jenn. It's more a matter of—"

"I'm stuck."

To this, Father Thomas replied, "I beg your pardon?"

"I can't escape the past. It just keeps replaying and replaying, every time I close my eyes."

"But why not try something else? I'll pray with you through the night, if you like."

"I'd be happy to help Jenn," Miles said.

"I just... would you excuse us for a moment, Miles?"

"Why, Tom?"

"No. He doesn't need to leave," said Jenn.

"Yes, but... there are some matters I really think you should take into account."

"You woke me, Father Thomas. Do you want to know what I was dreaming?"

No answer from either man.

"There's this man, dressed funny... old timey funny... medieval even. And he's playing a flute, dancing—tiptoeing—around a green flame. It's a beautiful flame, reaching all the way to the stars. But there's this bar of wood lying horizontally above the green fire, and I'm strapped to it. I'm just high enough not to burn completely, but I can smell the ends of my hair—I have my old hair in the dream—burning black." Jenn indeed intended to lie about the contents of her dream, but why this particular lie, why this particular vision came to mind, was well beyond her. But now was not the time to question such things.

I know that this is the moment that Miles became sure. He knew who Jenn was without exception now. He knew her role, and his finally made sense. Nevertheless, he listened to Jennifer Dash stoically, fearful that any facial response would give his position away.

Jenn continued, "I know for certain that if I do nothing, if I just leave things be, then I'll end up dead. Burned alive by the green. But something in the silly flute player's song gives me the answer. It tells me that if I just promise to follow him, the medieval dancer, then I'll be all right. The flame won't overcome me. All I have to do is believe in him, this one guy."

Jenn turned her attention now specifically to Father Thomas. "I asked about sin because I know in my heart that

64

it's wrong to pledge allegiance to this man. Somehow, I know he's evil. It's a sin to follow him."

Jenn turned her gaze then to Miles, "And so I keep my mouth shut... every night. And every night I'm lower, closer to being devoured by the flame. One of these nights I'm going to break down. I'm going to follow the flute player. I'm scared of what that'll mean. I'm scared of what happens after...."

The methodical crashing of the ocean against the boat was the only sound heard by the three souls that moment. Jenn liked it that way. She was selling her story whole-heartedly, and the two men were eating it up. She'd set the table well enough, now to feast. Now to get what she really wanted.

"Miles, can you replace my dream with something else?"

"Under hypnosis?"

"Yes."

"Theoretically, yes, I don't see why not."

The priest stammered, "I can't abide by this. Do what you wish. Good night."

"Wait," Jenn said firmly. "Miles, you'll put me under. Father Thomas, I want you to replace my dream. Replace it with something good. Something whole."

"I... I don't understand."

Miles said blankly, "She doesn't trust me, doesn't trust what I'll fill her with."

Slowly, Father Thomas smiled, "Smart girl.... What shall I say, Jennifer?"

"Just tell a story. A good story."

"I... I don't know any good ones."

"Tell her a Bible story," Miles offered.

"No," Jenn said resolutely. "The last Bible story got me into this whole big mess. Just, tell me a story from your heart."

Father Thomas saw in his mind a field of wheat, an image that appeared to him whenever he found a peaceful answer to his internal questions. He smiled again, "I think I've got something."

"Will you do it, Miles?"

Half smirking, half grimacing, Miles responded, "So you trust me enough to let me take control of your mental computer, just not enough to add my own software."

"Something like that."

"Well, it's two in the morning, why the hell not?!"

So it began.

Miles took control.

Father Thomas told the story he held closest to his heart.

~~~

Soon, the *Orion* will be forced to make yet another decision: make contact with a lone boat that violently doesn't want to be reached, or continue on, ignoring the ominous warnings signs.

Thankfully, for Jennifer, despite whatever troubles she finds herself in, she'll now be able to take refuge in the dreamworld. By the combined efforts of Miles Faa's hypnotic trance and Father Thomas' heartfelt story, Jenn can sleep merrily.

Chapter 24: Stranger Danger

Father Thomas found Miles Faa alone. "I'd like to know what you would have done," he asked.

"Tom, you're going to have to be more specific. But I'll tell you this: if given the knowledge I now know, I most certainly would have stopped watching *Lost* after season three. If I'd stopped there, I could have loved her 'til the day I died." Faa's reference went unnoticed by Father Thomas, who hadn't watched anything on a screen since the movie *Westworld* terrified him on his ninth birthday.

"Jennifer Free. Before she asked me to fill the space, to tell her the story, what were you planning on feeding her?"

"Why do you assume I had something in mind?"

"Because you always know what happens next."

"Ol' Tom, you speak as if I'm the boat's conniving villain."

"I know what you are."

"Father, must I quote the letter of James to you?"

"Which part?"

"He that wavereth is like a wave of the sea driven with the wind and tossed. For let not that man think that he shall receive any thing of the Lord. A double minded man is unstable in all his ways."

"Why do you antagonize me?"

"Because you're so easy to knock down. Grow some balls, Father. Have some conviction. If I'm the enemy, believe it. If I'm evil, let me know I'm damned."

"There's always time for change."

"Is there?"

"I... I will not get sucked into your games. What did you intend to pour into the young lady's head? Tell me. What was your plan?"

"Why should I tell you, of all people?"

"You must tell me!"

Miles laughed magnanimously. "Yes. Yes, *I must*. Okay then, if the good priest orders... I was going to tell her about Elagabalus and the baetylus."

"Elagabalus... he was... he was a Roman emperor, yes?"

"Very good, Tommy! Well done. Someone got a fancy education, didn't he?"

"He was... pagan, no?"

"Oh, worse than all that, Tom. Elagabalus was as decadent and morally perverse as they come."

"Why use him? What story does he keep?"

"His ma' got him the job. He was the chief priest down in Syria before he became emperor. And when enthroned, he brought his god with him."

"Yes, I remember now, his name, Elagabalus—"

"Is actually the name of the god he worshiped, yes."

"Are you following hell's orders, Miles Faa? Why do this? Why fill her mind with such tripe?"

"Elagabalus worshiped his god in the form of a certain black stone, a certain meteorite.... He placed it in Jupiter's hall, and then, when the boy king was slain, when Rome returned to her former gods, the stone traveled east."

"Why is this important, Miles?"

Miles responded, "*You must tell me Miles, child of Lucifer. You must tell me your dark secrets.* Is that it, Father? Have I got the tone right? Are you ready to plunge a stake into my undead heart?"

"Be serious."

"Fine. Since you're as dumb as a chinchilla. The black stone of Elagabalus', what we call a baetylus, traveled east where it was venerated by Arabs for hundreds of years. Until, that is, it was exalted by the prophet Mohammad, and enshrined as the Ka'aba."

"But why... Sir Isaac wanted to go to Mecca. If you're convincing Jenn to go there, why not just vote it into place?"

Miles slapped the Father on the back amused, "She's got to go to Mecca, Tom! We all know that deep down, don't we? I'll help push her there, but she's not ready yet."

"Not ready for what?"

"Do you really think you'll live long enough to see what she'll find?"

"Why do you hate me?"

"You act like I'm the one writing the script. I don't hate you at all. You see through a glass darkly, but your fear, fear from God knows what, keeps you from doing what's most prudent."

"Which is?"

"Spitting on the glass, rubbing it clean with your shirt! There's a whole world to see out there. I dislike you, Father Thomas, because your petty fear holds you forever back."

"There are things... there are rules I must uphold."

"Don't use your religion to excuse your inexhaustible trepidation. Are we done, here, Tom? Are you satisfied? Or shall I hurl more insults at you?"

It sang through Jennifer's mind like a small play, like a band of performers dressing up for the show on a small town-hall stage, with only a dozen or so in the audience. The new dream, the vision that replaced Tiff and Flusher. Here. Now.

The play began like this:

Once there was a kingdom in the clouds. Many, many countries lived within the valleys below, but all looked up to the kingdom in the clouds. It was believed that the kingdom was ruled by one of the gods of creation.

The great mountain Pelagus, at its zenith, reached up to the high door entrance, which led unto the kingdom in the clouds. From time to time intrepid men teased death by embracing the trek. No one ever came back alive. Many bodies were found at the base of the summit, as if pushed down from the kingdom's walls.

A rumor circulated among one tribe, and over generations became embedded as an eternal truth. The tribe believed that when one ventured to climb Pelagus and reach the god who dwells above, that adventuresome spirit must offer the god a gift. If that god does not approve of the gift, he destroys the climber. But if the gift is accepted, the believer lives forever amidst the kingdom in the clouds. It was further believed that the god who ruled there loved only precious stones.

There came a time when life became so unceasingly difficult that every soul lifted their eyes to the clouds, imagining a way to gain entrance into the celestial kingdom. Rich men spent their fortunes mining for gems, forever unsure of how many jewels precisely would gain them entrance beyond the gates of splendor. The poor devised schemes to steal what they could not earn.

One boy burned with indignation. He sneered up at the heavens, hating the gods for damning him to his wretched state. He could never afford to purchase one gem, even if he worked night and day all the years of his life. The boy knew the fate of those who tried to steal their way into eternity. They all failed, and worse yet, suffered torture at the hands of the unforgiving courts.

The boy took all his anger, all his strife, all his pain, and he suited himself up with it. He pinned it to himself like armor. Then he took to mount Pelagus.

His plan was simple. He'd reach the walls of the kingdom, and once in sight of the god of the realm, he'd punish that god with verbal justice. He'd curse this god for being so cruel, for fixing the universe against the poor, against the needy. The boy was brave, for he knew there was no chance the god would hear truth in his vitriol. He knew his sentence would be final. But at least he'd go out on his terms, not as a beggar like all the rest.

Night and day he climbed. It was arduous, but he was relentless. It was tough, but he was tougher. It was perilous, but he feared not the reaper.

When at last the boy reached the summit, a knight opened for him the gates to the kingdom. An arsenal of giant guardians marched him to a great room. There, they told him, the boy would have his counsel with god.

The boy had memorized his lines a thousand times, and now he mumbled them to himself once more as he awaited the king.

As the king approached, the boy fell to his knees. This king, this thing, this god radiated more brightly than the sun. The boy collapsed to his hands, both in fear and self-protection. He couldn't bear to gaze at the king. The king spoke nothing.

At once the boy knew everything he had planned was wrong. This god, he was more beautiful than all the gems and rubies in all the worlds combined. Whatever he asked for from the tribes, it would pale in the sight of this god. The boy knew he was miserable, knew he was wretched—not because of his

70

lot in life, but because he dared to judge and critique that which he never knew.

Before the king spoke a word, the boy bellowed, "HAVE MERCY ON ME, OH TRIUMPHANT LORD! I AM BUT A BOY! SPARE ME THIS DAY AND I WILL SPEND THE REST OF MY DAYS SERVING YOU AND BRINGING A GIFT WORTHY OF YOUR BEAUTY! PLEASE, HAVE MERCY, OH MERCIFUL GOD!"

The king said, "Go in peace."

The boy left.

He descended the mountain.

Initially, he dared not tell his story. But over time, he began to tell others that he alone saw God and lived. The boy was always quick to add to his strange story that, indeed, this god is worth all the gems of the world.

The boy made it his lifelong duty, that no matter what, he'd find enough gems to honor his god, and be received past the walls of mercy.

Over much time, the boy became a man. He became first a miner, then a manager, a landowner, and eventually, a tyrant. The face of god blazed on his face forever, and with unrelenting zeal he pillaged the earth for its treasures. He whipped those who failed to impress him. At times, he even whipped them unto death, for how could they know the importance of this quest? If only they saw the god he saw, they too would work harder. And this hard work, it wasn't merely selfish ambition, but honest loyalty and extreme love. For more than anything in the world, more than wealth, women, or conquest, the man yearned to see the face of god once more.

And at the end of his days, when he was an old, old man, the boy looked at the riches he'd collected: diamonds, rubies, pearls of every color, emeralds, and hardened ambers. Yet, when his eyes cast down on his great wealth, he wept greatly, for it was not enough. And the old boy knew it.

He climbed Pelagus one last time, bringing none of his treasure. Rather, he gave it to the poor of his birthplace. His back ached, his muscles screamed, his feet bruised black and brown, but he made it.

71

The guardians marched him to the hall of the king. The boy's heart leapt out of its frame. He'd awaited this moment since that first day up on this very hill.

When the king appeared, the boy, once more, fell to hands and feet, crying out, "OH GOD OF GODS, I HAVE NO GIFT FIT FOR YOU. DESTROY ME NOW, IF IT PLEASES YOU. I AM AT PEACE AT LAST IN YOUR PRESENCE."

This king welcomed the old boy into the kingdom in the clouds, where he still lives to this day. It was never rubies or pearls the king desired.

Jenn awoke, as always these days, with a smile on her face. She also awoke to the face of Alexandra Keitel.

"Come on, get up. Whole crew meeting."

Besides the Theatre of Remembrance and a few meals where all happened to attend, Jenn wasn't familiar with "whole crew" meetings aboard the *Orion*.

She rose to the deck to see the barely-dawning sky with a dense mugginess to the air that made breathing feel like an exercise in over-eating. Too early for the likes of Jennifer Dash.

Everyone else sat alert, Jenn apparently being the last to come to. The ship sailed, by this point, just a few clicks north of Peru, and only two or three days away from making landfall and heading inland to find the world's quietest room.

First Mate Godard started the meeting. "One hour ago, Lizard noticed something on radar. We quickly concluded that it was a ship of some sort, roughly the same size as ours. We tried communicating with the vessel, but received nothing back. We suspected their electronics were debilitated or that they were ignoring us."

"Okay..." said the captain.

"We thought it prudent to connect with them. We set a course to follow the signal. We quickly gained on them... then."

"About 20 minutes ago, Godard and I heard a sound," chimed Lizard.

"It came with a swift hum. Not too loud... but clearly something foreign."

"I knew it right away."

"We found on the bow, this." Godard held up an arrow. A real-to-goodness, arrow, seemingly sent on a voyage from a bow. Godard pulled out a scrap from her back pocket. "Attached to the arrow was this note. Its message reads in Portuguese, Spanish, and a third language I'm not familiar with... probably a local, tribal tongue."

Godard held up the scrap for all to see. Jenn couldn't make any sense of the three languages, but that didn't matter. What caught Jenn's attention, what refused to relinquish Jenn's mind, was the form the hand-written note took. It wasn't just scribbled out. It wasn't just metered one language, then another, then another. It was written in a circular fashion—the letter starting at one point and spiraling quickly out to the edges of the paper.

Looking at Jenn, Godard said, "It reads, 'Beware Pishtaco and his monster. Stay away from us. We are plague.'"

"You mean, 'We are plagued'." Captain Alf suggested.

"No. It's written very purposefully. We are plague."

"We stalk them. Keep our distance, but watch them. We should take precaution, but not be hindered," Merkyl said with authority.

"I agree," said Godard.

The Captain jumped into gear: "They are shooting arrows, people. Arrows. These are not pirates. They aren't military. Our plan's to go inland soon. We read the paper about Pishtaco. Maybe there is something to it. This ship of fools might just be the intel we need before going shore-side. Lizard, keep us on their heels. Merkyl, Robles, can you two fashion a bow and arrow out of whatever you can lay your hands on?"

"Yes, sir," each replied.

"Good. We'll talk to them on their level. Who speaks Portuguese?"

Lex and Godard raised their hands. Lizard nodded.

"Great. Lex, go with the boys and help translate the note. Let's exchange an English translation for their local brand. Got it?"

"What are we going to say?" asked Lex.

Captain Alf looked to the stars, hidden by the thick, dewy oncoming morn. Jenn hadn't yet witnessed composure like this in the skipper: a look of serendipitous introspection. "Write: We've defeated Pishtaco. We've come to aid you."

"They won't believe us," Lex said.

"It won't matter. Alf wants to create dissension among them. They've already chosen to alienate themselves from us. The Captain wants to fuel doubt in that decision. A coy move," Faa responded.

Jenn butted in to address Lex, "What does Pishtaco mean?"

Lex was busy moving below deck, but Robles offered an answer, "Pishtaco is an old myth that just won't die. A white stranger comes and kills locals, usually because he wants their fat. It's been a recurring fear for the local tribes ever since the Spaniards first showed up."

"So... how could a boat be plagued by it?"

Godard butted in, "We don't quite know the answer to that, buttercup, now, do we?"

The *Orion* was abuzz. Everyone had a job a to do, and everyone faithfully, without hesitation, fulfilled their task. Jenn found, somewhere in these intervening minutes, a freedom and peace she hadn't yet felt aboard the schooner. She was now, truly, a cog, an important gear, in the operation of this adventure ship. What a thing to be a part of! What an adventure indeed!

It didn't take long for the boys to come devise a bow. Giddily they boasted to the Captain that they used the lining of Sir Isaac's door to craft the bow.

"Henceforth," Merkyl insisted, "Isaac's door will never properly shut. It will forever remain ajar." The men, acting like boys waiting for a gold star from teacher, did not receive the cajoling they were expecting.

Captain Alfred Bacon frowned at his rambunctious schoolboys. "After this incident finds itself a conclusion, it shall be your duty, the both you, to repair Sir Isaac's door at once!" Overhearing the conversation, Jenn couldn't help but recall Lizard's Song of Experience in which she suggested to Jenn that the Captain and Isaac's show of animosity was only surface deep. Maybe she was onto something. It occurred to Jenn that the relationships on the *Orion* were more complicated than she gave them credit for.

By 9 in the morning, through the thinning fog, the boat Merkyl had wanted to stalk, the arrow-slinging carrier, was in view. Its appearance was that of a Pirate ship. Long and bulwarky, dark wood and dark sails emitted an ominous vibe from its mast to its stern. Most oddly, however, was not the structure of the design itself, but the numerous lines and shapes etched into its wood. Like a paper hijacked by burgeoning 5th-grade mathematicians, the boat had geometric doodles all over. These markings immediately conjured images of witches and demon-hunters—stories of people who mark their bodies with strange symbols to ward off evil spirits.

Jenn was standing beside Father Thomas as he first sighted what lay ahead. "Dear God," he whispered.

Atop the foreign boat, above its main sail, the ship's flag was simple: a white-outlined right triangle against a black backdrop. Jenn perused the boat with her glance, searching for a name. She didn't find one... that is, until Emmanuela Godard noted it.

"It's Pi. The name is the number." She pointed to a series of numbers carved into the dark wood of the stern.

Fffffeewwwww!

Robles shot off the *Orion*'s returning arrow.

The crew stood in silence waiting for a response. It dawned at once on everyone how very odd it was that not a single soul was visible on deck of the Pi.

Binoculars in hand, Captain Alf spied the *Orion*'s message arrow, successfully supplanted near the helm of the ship. For moments, the arrow stood completely solitary, thoroughly isolated and alone, aboard the geometric ghost ship.

"There!" the Captain shouted. A robed figure emerged just long enough to steal the message from the arrow and return below into shadows.

"What did he look like?" Lizard asked from the wheel.

"Just a dark robe," Alf called back.

"Monks?" Merkyl suggested, turning towards Father Thomas.

75

"So, what next?" Lex asked.

"We wait," said Godard.

"We wait, and draw nearer," replied the Captain.

Ten minutes later and the intricacy of the woodwork, of the exotic etchings, were on full display. The two ships neared each other rapidly.

"Lots of Fibonacci Sequences," Lex said.

"What are those?" Jenn responded.

"A pattern that keeps showing up in nature... something like a perfect spiral."

Jenn had no clue if there was any real significance to such a sequence. "Does it mean anything?"

"Does anything mean anything anymore?" Lex brushed off.

Fifteen minutes later and the ships were a mere twenty meters apart. Godard had cautioned Lizard to slow their tracking of the mysterious ship. It was always possible that the strangers were in fact plagued with some sort of disease. There was no need as of yet to get too close and risk subsequent infection. More to that reasoning, this could all be some sort of elaborate pirate plot to use the *Orion*'s fervent curiosity as bait.

"There's a certain sea snake," Godard told Lizard, "that acts dead at the bottom of the sea. Its performance is so convincing that it even allows fish to take little bites out of it. It endures such pains to lay the ultimate trap."

"If this is a trap, it's worth it."

"Why do you say that?"

"Whoever devised it is someone worth meeting."

"HEAD'S UP!" the Captain roared.

Pffffplunk!

Another arrow. Merkyl was the first to it. He unraveled the note, this time, three pages worth.

"It's in Spanish... only."

"Give it here," Godard butted in and snatched up the pages. She translated out loud. "Do not come closer. Save yourselves. Set us alight. Please. You must do this. If you fail, your company will be the hell we now experience. Please. Perhaps this is why you've come. Finish us. Set us alight. Let us burn and sink to the depths. Save us from our madness before it takes us further. We want you. We are the plague now. We want you."

"There's more." Godard flipped to the second page. "We want you. It's wrong. We want you. We want you, for hell is with us. We want the whole world now. This is the plague. Don't you see why you must do this? You must send us to the depths, far from any man. If you fail, we die of madness. Or still worse, we find land, and the world's sorrows will have no end...."

"Lizard! Turn us around, put two kilometers between us and them," the Captain blared. "Do it now!"

"Wait, there's still more," Godard said, and she turned the second page around. "Do not welcome Pishtaco's monster. She brought the plague into us. Now we want to eat you. We want your flesh. Your beautiful flesh."

As the *Orion* turned around, a robed figure emerged from the shadows and dove into the sea. Splashing around like a poisoned rat, an unspeakable, guttural scream arose out of the drowning, robed thing.

"Lord Jesus," Father Thomas prayed, "Be with us this day. Lead us not into temptation, and save us from the evil one."

That thing, that hideous shadow creature, screaming mercilessly, was paddling toward the *Orion*... and as it did so, white excrement puddled out into the surrounding sea.

"It's... it's his skin!" Miles Faa said in awe. If this blasphemous sight caused even Faa to stumble, what under heaven was happening?

Jenn watched, catatonic, the wretched sight. She did, however, catch Jorje Robles in her periphery, as he ducked swiftly below deck. Something about the way he moved signaled warning upon warning in Jenn's heart.

Jorje Robles knew something... something that scared him.

"Look!" Lex cried.

Two dozen robed figures appeared instantly on the deck of the Pi.

Had the sun shone that day, their features would have been brought to light. Had the sun shone, Jenn would be reassured that these beings were indeed just mortal men... not a brood of witches and warlocks.

77

One of the robed creatures raised a bow and arrow. Instinctively, Jenn ducked, fearing the alien colony was about to wage medieval war on her.

She rose just as suddenly, as the horrible screams ceased.

Jenn saw just the top of the monster's head as it sank into the Pacific, an arrow nestled stiffly through its head. They had shot their own. Maybe it was mercy. The creature appeared to be melting in the sea. Maybe it was mercy.

Or maybe it broke the rules by jumping overboard.

Or maybe they were stopping it from swimming to the *Orion*.

Maybe the note was telling the truth. Maybe the ship had turned into a house of flesh-craving ghouls.

Maybe.

Then, the robed ghoul-crew of Pi removed their robes from their heads, revealing their true nature.

The *Orion* jerked. Lizard had cut the engine and was promptly re-routing the boat back towards the strangers. She was experiencing a song of innocence. She wailed with surprise and glee, "They look like me! They're my people!!"

'Tis True my form is something odd -
But blaming me is blaming God,
Could I create myself anew,
I would not fail in pleasing you.

~~~

This day has brought surprises to the crew of the *Orion*, and they shall not leave this encounter untouched. Each member of Jenn's boat has their own worries and assumptions concerning these new strangers.

Captain Alf sees a welcomed opportunity to divert course. Who knows, maybe this new adventure will lead the hearts of his crew back north, back to where he feels they all belong.

Godard senses a connection of the fabled Pishtaco to real lost history. She'd rather investigate the past than be stuck engaging with her self-destructive conscience in the quiet room promised to come.

78

Lex wonders if this monster and Pishtaco fit into her ever-widening worldview of cryptozoological realities.

Lizard thinks she's found a homestead of like-minded diseased people.

Miles Faa is afraid. This encounter was unexpected.

Father Thomas knows demons when he sees 'em.

Sir Isaac is despondent that his door's been disassembled.

Merkyl knows more than he'll let on.

And Jorje Robles is about to make a life-altering decision.

Chapter 25: Ship of Fools

If the effects of elephantiasis on Lizard once repulsed Jenn, she had no idea how far the depths of ugly plunged. These robed creatures, these dissolving hordes, didn't resemble humans at all. Before one could make sense of their faces, the smattering of color blurred through. Each face contained streaks of red and purple, fused with deep browns and blacks. Their skin had a closer resemblance to some form of tie-dyed sand paper. One would be challenged to figure out what ethnicity and skin tone these creatures once were—one would be at a loss to fit these bodies into God's creation.

The word "perverse" barricaded itself inside Jenn's mind. She suppressed an urgent gag reflex and veered her eyes away from the horror she saw on the right triangle boat. This was perverse. This was wrong. Morally. Somehow.

"We need to leave," Godard blurted out very uncharacteristically. The whole crew caught the glimpse of fear in the First Mate's voice, and none dissented. At least for a moment.

Jenn returned her horrified gaze to the strange ship of monsters. Beyond their discoloration, they were missing parts. One figure not only was missing its right ear, but the whole right third of its head looked indented... or missing. Another had no nose. Still another looked entirely like an alien being, as Jenn saw no evidence of shoulders—a deranged stick figure brought into light, begotten into three dimensions.

And it didn't end there. Where there were correct body parts, there was also excess. Boils and skin flabs. Rotting points swamped eyes, mouths, skulls. All Jenn wanted to do was get away from this. She'd sigh and meticulously work on forgetting these creatures in the coming days. No one should live with this.

No one should see this, Jenn thought. Maybe Miles could take it away. Maybe the *Orion* could embark on a mass dosage of hypnosis to remove this stain on their collective memories. Jenn closed her eyes, but the figures remained.

80

The worst had no lips. No nose. Over its eyes were bulbous skin growths, purple and red. The result was a relic of Edvard Munch's "The Scream", a rudimentary creature made of a circular hole for a mouth, a rectangular abyss where should be nostrils, and an ungodly excess where one should be able to see the world.

"NO!" Captain Alf yelled, a long, stupefied response to Godard's demand to leave. "Whatever their plague, we need to know it. They could be patients zero, or the last remnants of a world gone mad. We need to know."

"Why?" Miles blurted out. "There's plenty of horrible things in this world. We need not tunnel through them all. Leave the pitiable ones be."

"Lizard, I want you to get us as close as possible to their boat, side by side. But be vigilant, we don't want to be touching them."

The engine roared as Lizard spun the *Orion* around, back towards the impurities.

At the feel of the turning of course, Robles peaked out from below deck. "What are we doing?"

"We're getting close enough to them to communicate. Lex, grab one of the walkie-talkies and turn it to channel two. When we're near enough, spy out their Skipper, and toss the walkie-talkie to him. Can you do that?"

"Aye-aye, Captain."

Jenn watched Jorje Robles struggle to breathe. He was anxious. The daredevil extremist was on edge. He gulped for air, as if preparing to dive underwater. Then he dove back to his cabin below. What was going on with him?

Happy to contrive an excuse to go away from the wretched sight at hand, Jenn moseyed below deck, announcing to no one in particular, "I'll check on Robles."

Below, Robles had locked himself in the bathroom. He was flagellating himself again. "Thy will is hard." Whip. Sting. "Thy will is just." Whip. Sting. Breath. "I will not fail you."

"Jorje?"

"Uh... Just a minute."

"It's Jenn."

"Just give me a moment, will you? I'm... I'm pooping!"

"Can I come in with you? You can keep the door closed."

Pause. Then, the door unlocked.

Jenn swung the door open. Robles' beady eyes glared back at her, his shirt off, his weeping back on full display—centuries of wounds healed with patchwork indecision.

"Close the door."

Jenn followed orders, but the twosome couldn't fit in the stall-room without some bending and twisting. Jenn tried her best to keep away from Robles' bloodied back. It looked sticky.

"Why are you doing this?"

"Don't you know? I'm a pagan."

"I... I don't really know what that means."

"I take orders. And I follow them."

"Whose orders? Why? Why do this? You're ordered to beat yourself?"

A tear rolled down Robles' cheek.

"*Slow!*" Godard was faintly heard yelling up above.

"*Easy, easy, Lizard!*" The Cap chimed in, "*There we have it, there we have it! Lex, do you have the walkie-talkie? You have your man?*"

"*I think so,*" Lex yelled back to Alf.

"When you get to heaven's gate, put in a good word for me, okay?" Robles muttered.

"What? No, I'll meet you there."

"I picked the wrong horse, Jenn. But maybe they'll have mercy on me up there."

"Up where?"

"In the afterlife."

"*Go! Toss it!*" roared the Captain.

"*Good throw!*" Miles applauded.

Jenn pleaded, "Why are you talking this way? Something on that ship, isn't it?"

"I've seen it before."

"What is it?" Jenn whispered.

"More Mayan wizardry."

"This? How do you know? Everything can't be Mayan, Jorje."

"Mayan, Celtic, Egyptian, Sumerian—we're talking about

82

the same thing, Jennifer."

"What's that?"

"Emissaries of the old knowledge."

THUMP!

"What's that?" Jenn exclaimed, alarmed.

Quickly, Jorje, just inches from Jenn's face, kissed her, flung the bathroom door open, and ran up deck, swiping his shirt on while he did so.

Jenn stood hunched over and unclear as to what just occurred. Jorje's kiss wasn't romantic. It was intimate, but fast, and... like a goodbye. Jenn wished she had known Robles better before this moment to better gauge the situation.

"Awww, god! Merkyl, Miles, come look at him!"

"He's dead. Don't touch 'em!" Merkyl yelled.

At this, Jenn hurried up through the hatch, climbing past the foresail and the foreboom towards the quarterdeck. There, a body lay, it's arm a foot away from its body, detached rather bloodlessly. One of them. One of the monsters.

What felt like the entire crew surrounded the new corpse.

"What happened?" Jenn asked in astonishment.

"He... He must have climbed their eagle's nest and dove."

"Dove?" Jenn repeated incredulously.

It happened like this: as the *Orion* neared the strangers, all eyes were on Lex and the figure to whom she prepared to toss the walkie-talkie. The crew's attention diverted, one of the robed ones climbed up their highest mast. With twenty vertical feet of clearance, the monster had plenty of air to land upon the deck of the *Orion*. But his weak body didn't withstand the deck floor, and he died instantly, his innards plopping like jelly inside his chest cavity.

"We've got some heavy duty disinfectants locked in the hull. I'll get them and clean up this mess. Nobody touch anything. We don't know how this disease is transmitted," Merkyl barked.

"Do we know it's a disease?" Lizard called out.

"Godard, will you join me?"

"See if they'll tell us what the hell is going on, Lex!" Lex fumbled at her walkie-talkie.

BANG. BANG!

Gunshot, from below deck!

Jenn followed the crew below deck, everyone reacting like ants, following the nearest and most recent loud sound.

Another body lay by in kitchen. A bullet in its head, a bullet in its chest.

"You shouldn't have stripped my door," Isaac said stubbornly.

"You've had a gun this whole time?" Father Thomas asked.

"I thought only the skipper and Merkyl had guns," said Lex.

"I had to do it," Isaac said.

Merkyl rushed in from his search for the disinfectant. "EVERYONE ON DECK. NOW! There could be more hiding!"

One of those things had managed to sneak below deck without anyone spotting it. If not for Isaac's gun and his newly-unhinged door, the monster would have moved on, gotten at least one of the crew. Lizard took the helm and bee-lined as fast as possible away from the monster ship.

Over the walkie-talkie, a voice spoke in Spanish. Lex heard, and responded. The translation of that conversation follows:

"We're sorry. We're so sorry."

"This is Alexandra Keitel of the *Orion*. We are an American adventure schooner. Please tell us who you are."

"We're sorry. We're hungry."

"Hungry!? Then why not ask for food!? We would have given you food!"

"We know it's wrong. It's wrong of us to want. It's wrong of us to ask."

"Please tell us who you are."

The voice began to cry. "We want to eat. We want you. We want you all."

"You're cannibals?"

No answer.

End transmission.

The crew searched the *Orion* but found no appearance of another creature. There was, however, a skiff beside the *Orion*. Whilst everyone turned their intention to the jumper, the real mission was taking place on the skiff. The diver, the one arrowed in the head, had sacrificed his life as a decoy. The monster in the skiff paddled out to the *Orion*, flanking the crew, thinking first to go below deck, maybe to corner the crew one-by-one. It was a godsend that Sir Isaac carried a gun with him... a gun that supposedly no one knew about. A gun not listed on the ship's manifest.

The *Orion* purred away from the demon ship, but the demon ship now followed.

"Captain, what do we do?"

"Keep going," First Mate Godard answered, "They'll tire. We'll out ride them."

The Captain's face was blank.

Before the chase got a foot, the world changed, the end game card played.

Jorje Robles jumped and climbed aboard the monster's skiff. He steered his small vessel back towards the stranger danger.

"Robles, what on God's earth are you doing, man?" The Captain blurted out.

Jorje waved a pistol in the air and responded, "Isaac's gun!"

"We can't let him get there," Godard stated to the Captain.

"What can we do?" said Captain Alf.

"We could shoot holes in the skiff," Merkyl answered.

"What good would that do?"

Godard looked hard into her husband's eyes. "If he gets on that boat, we can't let him back on ours."

"She's right," Merkyl affirmed.

"Of course we can... we'll just quarantine him for awhile."

"You'd risk the entire crew, the entire expedition?"

In protest, the Captain yelled out, "Robles, don't do this! If you do... they'll be no saving you this time!"

Lex too, "You don't have to go!"

Father Thomas, "You are loved, Jorje, come back!"

Miles Faa watched silently.

Tears rolled down Jenn's face. *He knew as soon as we made contact with that evil vessel. He's not planning on coming back. That's why he asked for a good word in Heaven. He's worried about his soul.*

Jenn couldn't help but add onto the shouts urging Robles to change course, "This won't save you! This won't get you into heaven!"

Father Thomas turned a queer look Jenn's way.

Merkyl re-appeared with a rifle. He aimed at the skiff, but wavered. "I don't want to hit him," a moment of uncharacteristic trepidation from the rogue journeyman.

"Do it now, or forget it," Godard added.

Hesitation.

Jorje Robles made it to the boat. A team of robed ones helped boost him aboard. As they reached down, Jenn paid attention to their pussing, oozing, lactating sores and missing parts. Robles had now touched them.

It was true, then.

He wasn't coming back.

All the boat's robed ones encircled Robles. Maybe a dozen or more. They were enveloping him.

A scream. From Robles.

The *Orion* hummed with worry as they watched their friend and shipmate overwhelmed by flesh. He dropped out of sight, hidden beneath the cavalcade of the robed indwelling.

"They're eating him. They're eating him!" Lex cried out.

"For God's sake, shoot 'em!" Godard yelled at Merkyl. Before he had a chance to respond, she swiped the gun from his hands and lowered her aim.

BANG-BANG-BANG-BANG BANG-BANG-BANG!

7 bodies fell to pieces. The remaining five robes scampering off to the furthest corners of the boat.

"Great shot!" Captain Alf yelled exultantly at his wife.

"I... I didn't do it," Godard confessed.

No. Robles stood with Isaac's gun in his grip. He'd snuck away with it. He planned to murder the monsters.

Why?

He called back to the *Orion*, "I'm out! Can you..."

He stopped mid-sentence. Robles had spotted something on the deck. The walkie-talkie.

"Hello. Come in, *Orion*?"

Lex nearly jumped out of her skin. She'd still been holding the two-way in her left hand.

"Robles. This is Lex."

"I know. I can see you."

The two stared at each other from opposing ships.

"What are you doing, Jorje?"

"I'm going to talk to the Captain before... before the end. But I'm out of bullets. Can you take out any others on deck? I don't wanna be... surprised."

Lex turned her attention to Godard, "You catch that?"

"There's one."

BANG. Godard plugged a bullet into a monster hiding behind the mast. He too fell to pieces. Dead instantly from Godard's rifle.

"That's the spirit," Robles responded. "I'm going to go under, see what I can see. Stay on the line."

"Robles, are you hurt?"

"Give me that!" The Captain swiped the radio out of Lex's hands.

"Jorje, this is your Captain speaking... are you hurt?"

"Does it matter?"

"Do you have any wounds?"

"I'll make it long enough. Whatever this is, we need to find out the cause. Give me radio silence while I'm below deck."

"Okay. We'll be here."

The intervening minutes brought silence save for three bangs from Godard's rifle, two of which hit their mark.

The hushed crowd waited in utter arrest for Robles' voice to return. No room for anxiety or worry of any kind. To survive, you live in the now... only, the now had nothing for them to do. So, as one unit, the *Orion* stayed motionless.

And then the voice. "Lex."

"Yes, Jorje, we're here."

"Here's what they know."

Godard peaked her head close enough to the walkie-talkie for her voice to be picked up, "Robles, start with who they are."

"Yeah, well, I got their skipper here. He tells me they're a part of a bigger group, a group dedicated to solving the riddles of existence. They are an ancient group.... Generation after generation has passed down their knowledge, and they lived throughout the world in different times. But... okay.... Apparently, they follow the Greek Pythagoras They're

87

Pythagoreans."

Jenn never took any higher-level math courses. The name Pythagoras sounded familiar, but no Eurekas struck her at the sounding of his name.

"A2 + B2 = C2" Lizard whispered.

"Okay, what else?" Godard insisted Robles go on.

"Ah, okay... I'm going to try to make this quick... I'm losing a lot of blood."

"Are you okay?" Lex worried.

"I probably don't have much time. I need to... I need to tell you, and then prepare."

"Prepare for what?" Lex asked dumbly.

"Pishtaco—the Pythagoreans thought they knew what it was. A man came to them, came to their camp a few years ago, raving about his accomplishments in genetic splicing. He had some vision of home genetics and geometry, that the two have never been married, and that with the Pythagoreans' help, this man could start the world over again. He could re-write life's script."

"Did he give them the plague?" the Captain yelled.

"Not exactly. The skipper here says once the rumors started circulating around locally, and they appeared to be true, the crew set sail for an island they believe... they believe Pishtaco creates at?"

"Creates?" Lex asked.

"The belief was that this man—"

"What's the name of the man, Robles?" Miles butted in.

"The man... he moved to an island and started his work with a few followers... wait... 'believers' the Skipper says."

Godard, "And the plague?"

"He said the man gave the Pythagoreans the coordinates of the island when he first tried to partner with them. When this ship, 'The Known triangle', got within eyesight of the island, there was a pulse. An electromagnetic pulse."

"An EMP?"

"Yeah."

"That explains the arrows," Merkyl added.

"They thought the EMP was some sort of solar flare. They say they physically felt it when it hit. So they anchored several kilometers off the coast of the island for the night... But during the night it came."

"What came?" said Lex.

"They say it was... they say it was a griffin."

"Ludicrous," Merkyl mumbled.

"It landed on the ship. They knew it had to be from the island... a creation of Pishtaco. But one of the crew wanted to catch it. He, excuse me, she—"

"There's women on that boat?" Captain Alf asked rhetorically.

"She threw a net on it—tried to wrangle it in and the griffin's talons managed to scratch her."

"That was it, wasn't it?" Lex added.

"He says the griffin wrestled free and flew back to the island. But fear struck the crew. No one knew how to handle the existence of this monster flyer. The Captain decided to go back to land, report their findings, and regroup with a later expedition.... After four days, the lady who was scratched started to show odd signs. She wanted to eat fish raw. She got really touchy with all the crew. Handsy. She started crying. Wanted to touch everyone. Lots of hugs. Then she got a bad fever. By that point everyone saw what was happening. Her nose turned black. She tried walking to the bathroom, bumped her black nose, and it cracked off completely. So... they killed her."

Silence from the *Orion*.

A frog caught in Robles' throat. Their wretched fate was now tied to his. "But it was too late. One by one they all started showing the signs. The disease makes them mad. I've pinned the Skipper down, but with a free leg he keeps rubbing his foot on my leg. The plague wants to live. It wants to live out.

"Listen. There's plenty of lighter fluid in this cabin. I'll find other flammable materials. But you need to do it. I don't want suicide on my soul."

Lex sobbing, "No. No. No!"

"Shhhhh. Honey, it's okay. Alexandra, pass the walkie-talkie to Godard, right now, sweetie. Would you do that for me?"

"No! I won't do that. We won't let you do this!"

"It's okay... it's okay, Lex. I just need you to pass that walkie to Godard. Do this one thing for me."

Lex relinquished the radio to Godard's firm grasp.

"Robles. I'm here."

Lex ran off to her bed, head in her hands.

"Good. You understand what's at stake here, yes?"

"We can't let that ship make contact with anyone else."

"One more thing. There's a book here. The Skipper says it's a bound copy of an ancient stone carving. It's small, pocket-sized, but fat. I'll drop it into the skiff. Once we're gone, get the book. Be careful not to let it touch skin... they've touched the book, so it might be carrying... it."

"We won't do that."

"As you wish... just passing on direct orders from this side."

"You do not take orders from them."

Robles was frustrated with Godard's ever-exacting nature.

"Emmanuela, I'm dying here. Don't quarrel with me."

Silence on the other side of the line.

"Pass the radio to Alf."

Godard did so wordlessly.

"Alfred?"

"Yes, Jorje, this is your Captain," Alfred said as solemnly as possible.

"In my bags there is a small stone idol. His name is Metztli. She is a god of the moon. He looks like a rabbit in the moon."

"It's a he or she?"

"Maybe both. Maybe neither. He doesn't tell us much about herself. Get him and he'll aid you. She'll be a charm on all the house of *Orion*."

"Alright! Jorje, you mad pagan, we'll faithfully do what you ask."

"Thank you, my friend. Please pass the radio to Jennifer... Jenn."

"Yes?" Jenn said.

"Remember what I told you."

"I will."

"That's the biggest responsibility I've ever asked of anyone. You will remember, right?"

"I will."

"Promise me, Jennifer Free."

"I promise."

"Good. Hand the walkie-talkie back to Lex. I'll be ready in a few moments."

Jorje popped up and down a few times amidst the deck of 'The *Known Triangle*' soaking the wood with lighter fluid. At one point another monster came up from the shadows. Jorje shoved him down, and the imbecile looked to be shattered. It was obvious, however, even without binoculars, that Jorje was oozing blood, a mouth-sized gash on the right side of his neck. His right check dangled by the strings of a few pieces of skin. The cannibal crew of the *Known Triangle* had at least gotten two good sinks into Robles.

Then, without hesitation, and without any apparent remorse, the *Orion* watched Jorje Robles mount the main sail of the *Known Triangle*. He scooted up to the eagle's nest, the old boat's highest lookout point. From there he yelled, "I'm ready. May the gods bless each and every one of you."

Nothing from the *Orion*.

"Blast it, woman, don't draw out this small moment. Do it!"

Godard held a long pole, with a swaddled, inflamed cloth at its edge: a DIY javelin engulfed in flames.

"DO IT, YOU BASTARDS!"

Godard threw the pole.

The fire ate at the deck of the *Known Triangle* immediately. Black clouds of smoke at once hid Robles' image.

From the dark fumes, a voice rang out:

"I love you all! Though I am not able to love, I love you still! Tell my boy, he's free! The curse is broken!"

And then a shrill cry—fear and agony from the man.

It didn't take long for the ship to go under. No one spoke.

Despite her earlier resentment, Godard dutifully retrieved the old book from the skiff. Using latex gloves (Jenn suspected the same gloves previously used to vivisect that monkey), she dropped the book into a plastic baggy. No one had any curiosity about its contents. Not today. Not on this day of death.

They anchored right there that night. It didn't seem right to move on so soon. Everyone felt that way.

Jenn went to bed as fast as possible. Sleep was now Jennifer Dash's one safe haven. Come hell or high water, the peaceful dreamworld of Father Thomas beckoned her anew for comfort and repose.

Before she faded to that nightly realm, Alexandra Keitel asked Jenn, "What was it? The thing Robles asked of you?"

"He wants me to put in a good word for him at the gates of heaven."

Lex asked, "Will you?"

~~~

Jorje Robles is dead. The day after his passing, after that dreadful encounter with the plagued Pythagoreans of the *Known Triangle*, the crew of the *Orion* will memorialize him in a Theatre of Remembrance. They'll enlarge their collective memories of the man, spreading his tales as big as the sea, small chapters of his life turned into exotic odysseys which no human save Robles has endured.

But the consequences of Robles' death will be far more immediate than mere grief. We don't now have time to retell the tales of Jorje Robles' life as the crew did, but we'll follow the dramatic events that follow his passing in detail.

And dramatic they are.

Chapter 26: Rogue

From *50 People I Pity*
Entry #46
Akhenaten

*Learn this, and learn it well. Cause change in one arena of life
and you'll be remembered as an innovator. Better still, if you
gain some steam towards this change, but never actually
make it to the top of that mountain, fret not, for you will still be
remembered as a dreamer. There is no danger in wanting to
change one thing. People are multi-faceted, so they can bend
on one thing, no matter what that may be. Case in point—the
man in charge of the first great civilization: the pharaoh. In
Egypt's long, elephantine history, a young ruler by the name of
Amenhotep IV came into his own. We could bark at him right
out of the gate for using his one thing on the menial labor of
changing his name from the aforementioned Amenhotep IV to
the newly minted Akhenaten, fresh enough to not require a
number after its pronouncement. But, I'll give old Akh'y a
freebie on that one. Where Akhenaten uses all his valuable
points is on the deferment of Egypt's religion away from the
Ras and Horuses towards a new solar-disc God. One god to
rule them all. A preeminent god. Aten. And the whole of Egypt
scratched their heads and mumbled, "Ah, that's what's going
on with his new name Akhen-aten. I get it." Akhenaten had his
one thing—great. Good for him. One could even say that he
shrewdly converted Egypt. He didn't appear to murder
dissenters of the new faith, he made synergistic attempts to
associate Aten as a new name of Ra. Aten was not merely the
new god on the block, he was, in essence (a quite literal
essence), the amalgamation of all Egyptian gods. You see,
this new monotheism did not require the betrayal of Egypt's
many hosts of heaven. Nay, it was merely the result of the
people's fervent religiosity. All things were summed up in one.
All the gods found their true identities, their final god-ness in
Aten himself. You see? Right there. If Akhenaten stopped with*

that, he'd be the greatest innovator of not just his age, but all ages. He'd be the great innovator of Egypt. And if by some chance, a later generation, a son or daughter, a King Tut or a Queen Nefertiti, undid all of Akhenaten's labor in service of the solar-disc Aten, fear not, for we would still elevate him to this day as the greatest of all idealistic dreamers. But the devastating truth is that Akhenaten couldn't stop there. He moved the capital to... wait for it, Akhetaten. That's right, Akhenaten lived in Akhetaten worshiping Aten. And that's not all. Akhenaten loved his wife just a little too much. Nefertiti, whom we remember along with the likes of Cleopatra as being one of Western history's famous beauties, was the monotheist's wife, lover, and apparently, co-ruler. In his later years, Akhenaten began to serve two divine rulers: his god Aten, and Nefertiti. Unfortunately, Akhenaten's feminism came just a few millennia too early for the rest of the developing world. Perhaps if the good Pharaoh was ultimately so charismatic, so pragmatic, as well as so wise, he could survive the triple-change he havocked upon Egypt. But alas, he embalmed himself in failure when he changed his image. Akhenaten gave orders to have his image be revealed on stone reliefs as having a forever long chin, an alien-ish lengthened skull, twisty legs, and finally, the cherry on top, a sagging stomach. Who could survive this Dali-like surrealism? How could the people take such a caricature seriously? If you change one thing, you're an innovator. Change two and you're a wizard. Make it three, and you may still get lucky and be counted as a hopeless romantic. But woe to him who goes beyond that. Akhenaten tried for four, and so upon his death, all his work was undone. Egypt returned to their old gods and ultimately doomed itself because its once-innovative King couldn't stop at one... or two... or three. Remember Hadrian? He did one thing for Rome: he grew a beard. Thus, after him, every successive Caesar had to have a beard. That's innovation. Constantine went monotheistic, but tried to stretch his luck to two by moving the capitol. Is it any wonder that Alaric sacked Rome less than a century later? Constantine was moderately successful because he stopped at two. Because Akhenaten's appetite for change knew no ending, he stands alongside Nero, Elagabalus, Pied Piper, and Rasputin as a ruler who could have at one time been thought of as an innovator or dreamer poet, but instead lives in historic purgatory. And purgatory, my friends, for power hungry tyrants, is a fate for worse than hell.

Remember Remember: One change per dictator. Anything more, and you risk legacy ruin.

Jennifer read this entry in the little book that Joseph Further gave her before falling asleep. The day had been exhausting, beginning with an improvised Theatre of Remembrance.

Unlike Jenn's first experience of this performance art on the high seas, this one was handed to-and-fro from storyteller to storyteller aboard the *Orion*, a funeral service wherein the grieved remembered tales gone by that never quite were. Jenn surmised that no one knew how to end the Theatre when its conclusion concluded so very much. So the tales just kept coming, with sailors going back and forth three, four times. Jenn figured that Lex came up on the "stage" five separate times.

The Theatre descended into some form of modern absurdity when a new custom was instantly embraced as tradition; each speaker, when they came to rise onto the stage, took an article of clothing from Robles' things and inorganically dropped it into the sea as they told their tall tale of the mad Mexican. It didn't take long to empty out all of the dead man's belongings into the sea, save Metztli, the prized moon idol of the pagan. Indeed, when Captain Alf found the small idol amongst Robles' belongings, he propped the small god on a mast giving it a clear, crisp view of the Theatre's Remembrancing.

It watched the memorial unmoved.

Jenn felt bound to listen to the hyperbolic ceremony in limbo forever, until, during one of Lizard's addresses, a 25-foot wall of water socked the port side of the *Orion*.

Jenn tumbled to her knees, skidding on a silk stream of water across the deck. The crew collective decided the violence came from nothing more than a rogue wave. Jenn surmised that perhaps the wave was a godsend, as it ended

95

the theatre before it languished into real rough waters.

But there would be no reprieve from drama after the rogue wave. A vicious debate erupted, far more heated than the debate weeks before in which it fell upon Jenn to decide the *Orion*'s destiny. This one centered on the notion of whether or not the crew should seek out the island of Pishtaco.

"This is that moment, THAT MOMENT! Here's the white rabbit, taking a pocket watch out of his waistcoat pocket. WE DON'T FOLLOW HIM!" Miles was in an uproar. "Lex, surely you see the truth for what it is! You can't be for this!"

Miles eyes were red and boiling over with fiery tears.

"You're right, Faa," Lex answered calmly. "It's a doorway. Robles is gone, just like that." Lex snapped her fingers. "We could all be gone just as soon. Let's follow the rabbit."

"YOU'RE INSANE!"

Lex would later confide to Jenn that she'd never seen Miles lose his cool. Not even a little. But here, he was manic.

There was no vote. Captain Alfred Bacon decided to move forward with the search... to chase the white rabbit. Dissenting voices were few. Miles and Thomas. Lex, Lizard, Merkyl, Godard were vocal proponents. Isaac and Jenn never spoke a word.

Around suppertime and a rare appearance by Sir Isaac, another rogue wave hit, this one worse. Rivers of salt water burst below deck, as if hit by lightning.

A sudden jolt, the floor below you disappearing.

You lose all sense of direction, all sense of safety.

What do you do in that moment, when the world's colliding in on itself?

It just so happened that at the moment it hit, Sir Isaac was vocalizing a complaint—no one had bothered to reprimand Robles for stealing his gun but just watched him paddle away. He charged Captain Alf of dereliction of duty.

"The Captain should ensure that personal property is not stolen, least of all by fellow crew members," he politely argued. No one acknowledged his complaint; no one vocalized validity to the mathematician's protestations. He railed that the boat was sinking into anarchy. It was then that the wave hit.

There were minor foundational damages to the *Orion*, but nothing a few hours of fixer-up-manship in the morning couldn't solve. Sir Isaac, having been the only one standing when the wave hit, was the lone sailor injured. He had a gash in his right thigh that caused Jenn to grimace, as well as a laceration on the top of his head. Godard functioned as the night nurse and saw to the man's wounds.

Before bed, Lex shared more thoughts about Miles Faa with Jenn.

"I think it must be an act."

"What is?"

"Faa's anger."

"Why?" Jenn responded.

"Quiet!" Lex whispered. "There's no reason for Miles to shout and make a pissy-fit to try to get his way."

"Emotions are high, Lex. Everyone's on edge. I know I can't get those monsters out of my head. Did you see the one that... that didn't have shoulders?"

"It's not that. I've known Miles long enough now, and he's too smart for all this. If he really wanted to avoid this island place, he'd make sure we all thought the same way. He has that kind of power of people."

"But we don't all think that way."

"I know. That's the point. Miles can make us think anything he wants."

"I don't think he's quite like that," Jenn reasoned.

"He is, Jenn. He manipulates everyone and everything. He's the guy you only want on your team because you're more scared of the other side getting him."

"What are you saying, Lex?"

"I don't know. Faa's up to something."

"Can't it just be that he's worried? Maybe even scared?"

"The day Miles Faa is truly scared is the day I die."

The unnerving conversation sent Jenn into her book—though Jenn never understood why Train Conductor Further chose to give her this small book of tirades, the consistency of the essays somehow soothed Jennifer Dash. On this particular night, however, reading about the folly of Pharaoh Akhenaten did not bring the relief Jenn was hoping for. There

97

was something in that list that unnerved her, namely, the Pied Piper.

Why was the Piper listed among real, authentic historical figures? Nero, Ela—Elag-Elag-a-bu-lus, Elagabulus! And Rasputin. In truth, Jenn had never heard of Elagabalus, but the names Nero and Rasputin were known quantities. Nero was that wicked emperor, famous for playing the fiddle while Rome burned. What did those names have in common?

Maybe they all played instruments. Nero the violin, Pied Piper a flute... but what did Rasputin, that un-killable Russian play? That theory sank; nothing in the essay purported Akhenaten as any kind of musician. Then what? What connected Pied Piper, not even a proven figure in history, with a pharaoh, an emperor, and a Russian monarchy destroyer?

This quandary rattled through Jenn's mind as she sank into sleep.

In the dream world, that ever returning solace wherein a boy climbs a mountain to heaven, something was happening... the boy was ascending the mountain to God, as he did every night. But on this replay, he was not climbing but falling. Not off the mountain. Up. He was falling up towards the heights.

Quick.

Suck in the air.

Jenn opened her eyes.

She'd been thrust onto the ceiling.

A miasma of chaos. The world was inside out, the world was upside down.

Faintly, Jenn heard shouts. Shouts and screams. Shouts of voices she knew. Screams from a primate.

Then, like a clock spinning into gear, her mind focused. Jennifer Dash was drenched, her body shivering in a layer of salt water.

The *Orion* was upside down.

Another rogue wave. This one must have been the big brother of the others. What size must this wave have been to knock the *Orion* over with such force?

The capsized boat would right itself and its wounds would heal. Besides some scratches, bruises, and in the case of Lizard, a severed cyst, no monumental damage was endured by any aboard the *Orion*.

Everything was okay. For now.

The once vivisected monkey, Godard and Merkyl's midnight surgery patient, had split its head open. Jenn heard it moan for five minutes or so, coming from the storage closet. She spied Merkyl surreptitiously sneaking into the closet, followed by an end to the primitive moans.

No one went back to sleep that night.

Lex and Godard took turns manning the radios, trying to get to the bottom of the rogue waves. A rogue wave was a thing of nature, but not a common one. In fact, Merkyl quickly pointed out that the waves that crashed against the *Orion* were small in comparison to the infamous rogue waves of history. But three hits within one 24-hour day, each bigger than the last, that was the disturbing feature that didn't match the data. Rogue waves did not come in triplets. Adding to the ominous scene, ten minutes after the wave smashed into the *Orion*, the sea was as serene as could be.

On September 9th, 1980, the MV *Derbyshire*, a British oil carrier, measuring 1,000ft in length, was annihilated by a rogue wave at least 92 ft. high, but none of the crew lived to tell researchers how nephilim-esque the wave truly was.

That was one wave.

If anything that big were to strike the *Orion*, the ship would go down faster than the *Known Triangle* went down in flames.

The thought on everyone's mind now: would there be more?

Radio contacts echoed one singular, disturbing story. No one had seen any large waves. It seemed like the whole of the pacific was calm. Up and down the coast—they called everyone. No other ship's radar showed anything. A cargo ship less than 100km from the *Orion* reported nothing unusual.

Whatever the *Orion* was experiencing, it was experiencing it alone.

An unexplained phenomenon.

Jenn recalled a movie she'd caught on TV one day years ago. It was based on a true story; something about a high school boat, where a bunch of boys were taught their remedial studies whilst sailing the seas. The climax of that film occurred

99

when that ship (the skipper was played by Jeff Bridges, Jenn recalled) sailed into a white squall.

"Is it a white squall?" Jenn asked everyone, and no one. At 4 am on the deck of the *Orion*, a clear sky full of white stars blinked down at her.

"No," Miles Faa responded, "It's happening because we're not going where we're supposed TO GO!" He screamed.

Lex and Jenn shared a look.

"A white squall is more like a traditional storm," the Captain chimed. It was clear, despite the chaos, he was rather enjoying this sea battle.

"More likely a microburst," Sir Isaac mumbled.

Jenn was not alone in giving double take towards Isaac. He was on deck! He never came on deck.

"What exactly is a microburst?" Lex asked.

"A pocket of energy is trapped above," Isaac pointed toward the sky. "That energy is released as a burst of air—a burst of wind. Straight down."

Merkyl picked up the pieces, "Think of it like a tornado, but instead of the air current swirling around, it's streamlined in one direction. It shoots down, hits the surface of the ocean, and sprawls out horizontally in every direction. That could easily account for the waves, but there would be 70-100mph winds in front of the wave. Maybe even stronger. We'd know the wave was coming."

"Did anyone feel high winds before the hit?" Someone asked.

No answer.

There had been no winds, no warning. The waves came as specters.

Just before dawn, only a few minutes before the fourth wave came, Jenn asked Father Thomas if he had a theory.

"I think it's the man-eaters of Tsavo, revisited."

"Are those... cannibals? Like the... the boat? You know, Robles' boat... *Pi*... the *Known Triangle*?"

"I'm not sure if it has something to do with that or not."

"So you think its man made?"

"Certainly not. No, the man-eaters were two lions in Africa.

The Brits were trying to build a bridge, using lots of local help, but these two lions, they just started killing. Some say they slaughtered over 100 people. They killed for fun, or sport... or something. They didn't eat them. They weren't eating the people for food. You understand?"

"No."

"Nature doesn't work that way. Lions don't go ballistic just because. That's not evolution. Killing for fun is not in a lion's DNA. They were sent, Jennifer."

"Sent by whom?"

"Maybe the devil. Maybe God."

"Why would God do such a thing?"

"He may not be who we think he is. D d Robles ever tell you why he was a polytheist?"

"No."

"He believed that following one god was an old pharaoh's play for power—that monotheism was an attempt to centralize power. Freud thought that was how monotheism came to Moses and subsequently the Jewish people. And from the Jewish people, the Christians and Muslims inherited One God to rule them all."

"Robles thought that Judaism was a hoax?"

"He told me that the gods, the pantheon and all the others, they all want to claim the top spot. So when we monotheists play, all the gods listen, because they all think we're praying to them."

"You think he was crazy?"

"No. I think maybe there are many spirits, even many humans, who want all the prayers of the saints to be theirs for the taking. And God will not let them pretend forever. He humbles the many with his wonders."

"The rogue waves are judgment?"

"How should I know? I'm just an old priest who can't hardly pray at all anymore. Is it ever hard for you to pray, Jennifer?"

It was then that Father Thomas' stare meandered past Jenn. His eyes grew wide. His mouth dropped. He saw destiny.

Lizard cried out, "It's coming!"

"Below, get below! All hands below!" The Captain cried out.

Jenn saw it before she fled away from the sky.

A wall of water—Merkyl would later say it had to have been seventy to eighty feet tall—like a monolith hovered toward the *Orion*.

Going below deck frightened Jenn. She feared she'd be trapped between floor boards when the water swamped in. She didn't want to drown stuck in the bowels of the boat. She'd rather drown in open water than stuck in such a tight space.

Worse still, it was cramped below deck.

Bodies hyperventilating.

Awaiting fate.

A giant wave was coming.

Any moment now.

Jenn looked at the faces huddled around her. These geniuses, beacons of reason and wit—small powerless eyes peered out from their faces! They waited, and became children once more, innocent little boys and girls at the mercy of a relentless parent whose name is nature.

We are all children now, Jenn thought.

Jenn experienced the crash in slow motion, watching, with objective feeling, the world turn upside down. It just kept on going, spinning right back up again. There wasn't even time to fall on one's head. It came, shook the world, and passed.

Miraculously, somehow, this wave, though bigger than all that came before, left the *Orion* almost entirely unscathed.

Jenn raced aboard deck, exhilarated to see the sky, secured in the hope that she wouldn't drown below deck. She wasn't the first to hop on deck. Merkyl was already there, his back facing her. He was holding something—dropping something into the ocean. A body. Had someone died? The monkey. Merkyl was putting the dead corpse of the monkey to rest in the heart of the sea.

The rest of the crew came to deck, searching for the vital artery, the snapped board, the internal bleeding that would signal slow demise. Somewhere there was going to be a leak. But unbelievably, nothing of that ilk would be found. The *Orion* had survived this hit. The uppercut was not to be a knockout.

Smiles.

A certain euphoria rose from the crew. A general sense migrated from one laugh to the next, as each person sucked in sweet gasps of life. They'd survived, and surely the worst was over. Uniformly, the *Orion* believed it had survived the worst, the biggest hit the sea had to offer. Its fourth punch had surely been its worst, and it was over now.

All done.

No.

There.

On the horizon.

Another.

Bigger.

Taller.

The end.

The last was a precursor.

Now came judgment.

Now came chaos.

On deck, Father Thomas noticed something that gave him pause. Metztli. The idol. Robles' idol. It stood on the mast, plain as day. It even looked dry. How could it have stayed in the exact same place since yesterday? Captain Alf had placed it there during the Theatre of Remembrance ceremony, minutes before the first rogue hit. Now there had been four. Each bigger than the last. And yet, the idol remained.

Father Thomas grabbed the idol, held it in its hands, and awaited the oncoming monster wave.

Jenn, like minutes before, waited below along with the rest.

Was this to be the second suicide in just days?

Father Thomas held the idol into the face of the behemoth, ninety-foot wave.

An offering to the god of the sea.

Before it struck, Miles Faa agonizingly said to himself, huddled next to the others, "I should have known better. I should have foreseen this."

Then, the last rogue.

103

~~~

The *Orion* will not survive.

To the Island

<u>Main Cast</u>
Jenn
Lex
Merkyl
Miles Faa

Chapter 27: Two if by Sea

After the sinking of the *Orion*, after the crew split into two groups, after the reunion, and after the second great debate, Father Thomas found himself recalling his experience to a group of Anglican missionaries. He'd been back only a few weeks when propositioned to speak at a weekend conference regarding spiritual burnout. He led a seminary on healthy vs. unhealthy doubt, offered up morning prayers, and on the last day of the conference, was a part of a panel on "finding God in the world".

Towards the end of the hour-long panel, an attendee asked the question, "What has God used in the world to pull you back to him?" The panel had the usual responses, "The smile of an orphan, acts of charity by strangers, the example of faithful servants who have completed lives of integrity for God." Then it was Father Thomas' turn.

He held the microphone with two hands and began. "As I mentioned earlier, for many years I was a faithless corpse. I was supposed to be the priest for this exciting expedition. I was supposed to be the moral high ground for a boat of dreamers. It was my job to be a spiritual counselor and comforter. But I did none of that. I was... a zombie.

"But God pulled me back two times. Well, really, one time... but I needed a foretaste so that the real experience would stick.

"The first time, our expedition, was stuck way up north near the Arctic Circle. We had been barricaded in by ice and storm for weeks. We couldn't stay warm. All the computers and electronics onboard had betrayed us. We were alone, freezing, stuck, and slowly starving. But then, on the day of our redemption, there was a break in the ice. That alone would be reason to sing praises.

"Out of a hole, out of one, ice-less circle, we witnessed these tremendous spears javelining out of the water. Narwhals! A pod of narwhals were coming to surface, coming to breathe in sweet air, right beside us, right in our break in the ice! They were magical, truly wondrous. Seeing those creatures up close exceeds any nature documentary. Trust me, we don't need unicorns as long as narwhals are around. I'd like to start a petition to call them uni-whales—maybe then they'll get the love they deserve!

"I didn't know it then, but that was God sending us a gift. Things got better for us from that day on. One small break of ice led to another led to another... until we were free, we could breathe again."

"The narwhals prepared us for what came next. A few months later, we were sailing off the coast of Peru. Over the course of one day, we were hammered by five rogue waves. The last one, there's... there's no way to describe it. I was on deck when it came. It was like the hand of God swooping me up. A cliff of water that blocked out the sun, knifed down and through our ship, and lifted me clear off the boat. For a moment, I felt I was flying, weightless. I've since imagined that it must be a similar feeling to be caught up in a tornado.

"I decided—by this time I'd been so nervous, anxious, and depressed—I decided I wasn't going to fight this thing. I was going to let this titanic wave be the end of me. I wasn't thinking about heaven or hell or even God. I was just thinking about it all ending. I wanted to pull the release valve. I wanted all the gunk in my head to be flushed out, and if dying in the palm of this god-forsaken wave was how I achieved that flush-out, then so be it!

"I thought, since I'm going to die down here—oh, and let me just say—when you're controlled by a wave such as that, you're thrown in all directions. I had no conception of up. Even if I wanted to live, how could I find up? I was somewhere underwater. I had no idea how deep or what direction I was pointed. I opened my eyes. I wanted to die with my eyes open.

"And there it was.

"This creature, so enormous, so gentle, so... mystical, floating beside me. It was the biggest thing I've ever seen. Who cares about rogue waves? This thing felt like it must have been bigger than any wave in the world.

"It was a jellyfish. Some sort of jellyfish. Pink with darker, purple stripes. It was the most gorgeous thing I'd ever seen.

How could I lose faith in God, when he has made such splendor on the Earth as that?

"The jellyfish moved horizontally, from my vantage point. I wanted to follow it, so I swam in its direction, and as I did, I noticed the light getting brighter. The jellyfish was directing me up. God used the jellyfish to get my head back above water. My perception of horizontal movement was actually upward movement. I made it to the surface. I still can't believe it. I was doomed—should have been.

"So, how do I say this? God has used his ocean creatures to re-inspire me. To give me hope. And to re-ignite my faith in a God who's watching me."

Father Thomas stopped talking. The room was quiet.

After the panel, a younger man approached the Father.

"Can I ask you?"

"Yes?"

"When that wave hit, did it kill anyone on the crew?"

"No. I was the only one on deck. We all saw the wave minutes before it hit. There was plenty of time to get below... I... I..." Father Thomas sized up his inquisitor. "You've read the book of Jonah?"

"Sure."

"You know that God causes a storm, and the storm won't subside until Jonah jumps overboard."

"Of course."

"Our God is truly the jealous type."

Thomas turned to walk away.

"Wait, what do you mean? God was angry with you? You were Jonah?"

Thomas turned back, speaking softly. "There was an idol aboard the ship, an idol containing an evil spirit. Its master had just died, and that spirit blamed us. It was angry. I held onto the idol as the final wave hit to make sure the idol would be driven to the depths of the sea. I wanted it to be undone by the very force it called upon."

"No. That's not how God works. Demons don't have power over nature."

Thomas smiled coyly. "Where'd you read that?"

Four things happened when the fifth wave hit the *Orion*.

One: Miraculously, no one died.

Two: Father Thomas was battered and tossed more than a mile away from the *Orion*. He would tread water and bob for an hour before choosing a direction to swim. After twenty or so minutes moving in that direction, the bedraggled priest spotted his group. The *Orion* was united, if only ever so briefly.

Three: In a heroic effort to save the lives of her fellow crew, Lizard took to the wheel moments before the freak of nature struck. She did her best to ride the wave up and over the behemoth. Just before cresting the zenith, however, the *Orion* reached its angle of repose, slipping back down the thundering wall. The force of the current somersaulted the ship numerous times.

Four: During the blow, Jenn's wig slipped off. Lacking wig-oriented cosmetic supplies aboard the ship, Jenn had used an industrial strength tape to keep her false hair situated pristinely atop her head. When it ripped off, it took a bushel of newly minted real hair with it, as well as a top layer of scalp. The result, which everyone would notice but none acknowledge, was that young, beautiful Jennifer looked like she had mange. This disaster, as well as the self-evident truth that she no longer had access to wigs, led Jenn to vow to live life as she was... if she was bald, so be it. She'd sport her baldness boldly.

One should note here that although this became Jenn's personal mantra, she was keen to grow out her hair and indeed, when available, Jennifer Dash was faithful implementing an arsenal of cosmetic make-ups and supplies whenever possible to present the most brilliant and refined Jenn as achievable.

By the time Father Thomas' head poked up above the water on the horizon, the waning crew of the *Orion* had successfully abandoned ship. The vessel itself was somehow still bobbing bottom-side up, but its demise was inevitable, its death as certain as the sunset.

As for the crew of the *Orion*, they had divvied themselves up between two smaller boats: the *Orion*'s skiff (a small metal boat with a motor), and an orange emergency raft.

This world is one wherein things tend to happen all at once. Revelations come at the most bewildering times, and in clumps. Upon revelation that his ship was sinking into the depths of the pacific, Captain Alfred Bacon of the *Orion* searched furiously for a reason to survive, for a reason to endure, for a reason....

He gripped a small book in his claws. The lone artifact from the *Known Triangle*. He opened it. As he did so, a small scrap floated loose. On it, direct coordinates. More intriguing still, the coordinates were nary a day away.

Pishtaco's island!

They were so close. So damn close!

And then a rapturous thought captivated the Captain. They could still make it... at least, some of them. The mission didn't have to end. Not for everyone. The spirit of the *Orion* could endure. Alfred had lost his two children onboard this ship. He couldn't bear for it to just descend, like the souls of his offspring, into the deep abyss. It had to live on. He wouldn't accept this dismal end, this finale without reason, without hope.

No, hope was indeed to spring eternal. And here it was, presenting itself.

The emergency raft would wait for rescue. Lizard managed an SOS that reached several authorities before abandoning ship. Yes, the raft would wait. But the skiff... the motorized skiff. It didn't have to stay. It could journey on, following the shadow of Pishtaco.

As much food and drink was snagged as possible before all eight (Father Thomas was not yet found) huddled onto the two dingies. Jenn, being of the more acrobatic ilk and in the midst of the years before one's body betrays oneself, took to the orange life raft, leaving the more structurally sound and thus easier to waddle into vessel for the likes of Lizard, the Captain, Isaac and Merkyl. So, quite naturally then, the boats were segregated by age: the old in the sturdy boat, Miles, Lex, Jenn, and Godard in the inflatable.

Jenn didn't grab anything save her backpack (which included her book and her letter from Atticus). No wig. She was now, more than ever before, a traveling vagabond, with nothing but the shirt on her back. A shirt, one should note, that was torn at the hip rather badly.

Good worker bees like Godard and Merkyl grabbed (what appeared to be) plenty of water, food, and first-aid kits. Somehow Sir Isaac managed to carry a whole arsenal of seemingly pointless mechanical protestations. Wiggly-woos and wonky-doos. Jenn couldn't make head-from-tails of the mechanical gyrations.

It was about this time when everyone was getting settled in their new temporary home, when they spied Father Thomas out on the horizon.

Once aboard, it was clear the man was exhausted. His muscles all drooped like jelly. But somehow he still had his wits about him, at least enough to ask, "So... what happens now?"

"We wait to be picked up." Merkyl said.

"It's over," Godard echoed, to herself if no one else.

"That might not need be the case," the Captain optimistically offered. "I happen to have on me the coordinates to the island."

Silence.

"It's not far. If we were on the *Orion* still, it'd be but a day's voyage... maybe less... it's really close."

"We're sunk."

"Not all of us! We're half sunk, half hopeless, half dead, whatever you want to call it. But there's victory in our clutches, yet!"

"What chance?" Lex said.

"This skiff has a motor. Half of you could still make it to the island. The rest of us, we'd wait for rescue, gather up resources, find a new boat, and come get you in a few days."

"You'd abandon us?" Lex said.

"Not abandon... you'd... the people who choose to go, well they'd be... they'd be covert ops. They'd spy out the mission before the rest of us arrive in force."

"In force?" Miles repeated.

"If necessary." Merkyl said.

This was not the time for a vote. No one was thinking profound thoughts. Everyone was waterlogged.

"If you want to go on, raise your hand."

The Captain raised his own first. Godard's and Merkyl's followed. Then Lex's. Neither Isaac or Thomas looked apprehensive about their decisions. They kept hands down. Lizard raised hers, then added, "I believe we should go... but I would be a liability."

"We're not voting aye or nay, just on whether you personally want to go. So if you think you shouldn't, then abstain."

Lizard lowered her hand.

Should I wait for rescue, or go onward, searching for an island of plague demons? Jenn wondered. A decision needed to be made now.

"I... I want to go. Badly. But, I shouldn't," said the Captain, "I need to stay with the ship. Whether that be the *Orion* 1.0 or 2.0."

Then came the shuffle. Sir Isaac, Father Thomas, Lizard and the Captain himself clumsily relocated onto the raft. Godard and Lex made their way to the motorized transport.

So it was to be Godard, Lex and Merkyl headed to the island of Pishtaco.

"It would be best if it were 4. Four going, five left behind. If there's any hiccup with the emergency services, if there's no one coming for awhile... six makes it hard. Five on the other hand, though just one less..." the Captain let his voice trail off. He knew he couldn't strong arm anyone to go on a mission like this, especially on a potentially fatal mission with no clear objective, no real reason. In Alfred Bacon's mind it boiled down to what it was always meant to be: adventure.

For Jenn, the decision to go came rather easily when she looked around. On her raft was Lizard, a woman with an inexhaustible appetite for strange discussions, the Captain, who was fine on his own, but when in a confined space with Isaac was simply disastrous. Those two were bound to touch each other over the course of the next few hours, and one, if not both, were going to fly off the rail... and there would be no escape. Add to that, Sir Isaac had killed someone with a gun no one knew he had. He clearly was a man of secrets not to be entirely trusted. That left Father Thomas and Miles Faa. Both had helped Jenn overcome her re-occurring nightmare, but in the last twenty-four hours, each had seemed deranged. She had watched Thomas make the decision to stay on deck for the last wave. Did he have a death wish, like Robles? And Miles, who supposedly could control everyone with his power of will, why was he so angry? Was the silent room really that important to him? And why? It belied a notion that Miles Faa had some surreptitious, perhaps dark motives for yearning to venture to the silent room.

These were to be the five people she'd be stuck with.

Or: Lex, the only person on board who actually knew how to small talk, a value Jenn was starting to highly value, Merkyl, and Godard. Though they assuredly were strange in their own ways, they were easily the most competent sailors of the *Orion*.

Jenn bounded up, and latched herself to the motorized skiff.

Miles Faa followed. No hesitation.

"Okay! Miles and Jenn, you're a pair, it seems! Okay, then I believe we're set!"

"We're not a pair!" Jenn protested. "We're not a pair," she repeated at Miles.

"I know. I just happened to have changed my mind right when you did."

"Well, I change my mind again. I'm not going." Jenn feigned departure, stood up, but a small wave brushed her back down.

Godard and Merkyl were whispering... whispering in another language.

"I'm off," Godard announced and bounded to the inflatable. She chose reunion with her husband. Interesting.

The table set, the game was on.

Captain Alf copied the coordinates so that each side had their own copy, handed it to Merkyl, and the two parties said their "adieu". That was that.

Jennifer Dash, known as Jenn Free.

Miles Faa the mind reader.

Alexandra Keitel, the cryptozoologist and perhaps daughter of a selkie.

The gruff heavy-laden Merkyl.

These were the members of the *Orion*: Special Ops

113

Division. And now they motored away.

It was hard to hear anything over the sound of the motor, so the foursome stayed quiet while they roared on the surface of the sea. The orange emergency raft shrank against the endless oceanic horizon until it disappeared entirely.

Jenn lost track of time. She dozed off, not quite dreaming, not quite awake, falling into that void where lucid thoughts meet unexpected images.

High noon—evening—night.

They rationed their water and food, enough for about a week of decent meals. Double that if they wanted to really bear down.

Three hours after sunset, they were refueling. They had enough gas for maybe four refuelings, enough to get them where they needed to go... not enough to get them back. Once they got to the island they would be stuck there.

Given the opportunity to actually use their ears while they sat and refueled, Jenn asked Miles, "Why'd you change your mind?"

Miles smiled and shrugged, "I looked at who was going where. What if help took awhile? Could you imagine being stuck on that dinky raft while Isaac and Alf went at it? Madness."

"So, it was me then. You changed your mind when I changed boats."

Lex turned her attention from pouring fuel to gazing at the awkward couple. She had always wanted Miles to like her. Not necessarily romantically, but she wanted to be considered interesting enough to catch the gaze of someone as intrinsically intriguing as Miles Faa. To be liked by him was to know you were important, above average. It would be the ultimate form of validation.

"What do you want me to say, Jenn?" Miles said.

"I just... I don't really know anything about you."

"Well, now we have the time to get to know each other, don't we?"

"Where were you born?" Jenn inquired.

"Where do you think?"

"Umm... New York?"

114

"Nope. Try again."

"Beijing," Lex tried.

"Nope."

"Canada." Jenn offered.

"Close. I was raised near Toronto."

"I give up."

"Istanbul."

Jenn was struggling hard to remember which country Istanbul belonged to... "You're Istanbulish then?"

"Turkish... and no."

Engine ready. Off again.

By now, Jenn thought, gazing up at the many sparkles in the night sky, *the raft's been rescued. Captain Alf and the other four are headed to land. They probably have a warm meal in their bellies. Maybe Father Thomas is being attended to by some nurse or doctor. He didn't seem well at the end. How did he survive that wave? What if another comes?*

Somehow, Jenn knew, just as everyone else did in their heart of hearts, that the rogues were over. There would be no more. The waves existed to destroy the *Orion*. That happened. *Orion* destroyed. No more. So there would be no more waves. Every member of the Orion believed this superstition, that nature was somehow bound to honor this purely speculative pact. And because of this, there was peace.

Rest.

Morning—day—high noon—evening...

It was boring, but not bad. The ocean was calm, the speeding of the motor consistent. Aside from a few scattered conversations, everyone was quiet, calm, and meditative.

Life was okay. Everything was working out fine.

Just as full dark came on, the boat rattled. The engine still worked, but all three of the compasses on board began to somersault and veer off in separate directions.

"The EMP!" Merkyl shouted, "We're close!"

"We better be!" Miles yelled.

They tried their best to stay the course, go on straight-as-an-arrow. No one thought on what would happen if they missed the island, or if there was no island. They'd die out here.

And in that dark night, four from the *Orion* found what they thought would be redemption.

This was not the type of island gorgeous movie stars stumble upon in movies. There were no coconut trees. No high mountain peaks overlooking a luscious rain forest.

No.

This was a plateau. The whole island looked like a mountain cleaved off evenly at its base. Cliffs rose forty feet, and then a barren flat land.

Somewhere between midnight and sunrise, they reached the base of the cliffs. And began to climb.

~~~

Jenn, Miles, Lex, and Merkyl will discover what Pishtaco's island has in store for them. The island is not an Eden waiting to be discovered. It's not paradise lost and now found by half the crew of the *Orion*. It is a dark place, ruled by a force stronger than they can yet fathom.

We'll continue to follow Jenn while the rest of the *Orion* goes on a separate journey. We'll reunite with them eventually. But our attention must stay with Jenn. These are trying times, and she'll need us with her, praying with her in the darkness, in the heart of the god-forsaken island.

Chapter 28: The Island

A certain story is predetermined to soon rumble through our adventure. Not a story, exactly, but more of a theme. Or an idea. Ideas give rise to nations and infect the healthy. Ideas are the undercurrent to life itself. Ideas are the future, and the past is full of the consequences of ideas gone by.

Jennifer Dash, like every youngling on Earth, every child who has yet to resign herself to the fatalism of a world beyond one's control, beyond one's grasp, had thought minimally about the concept of identity. Though she'd re-branded herself multiple times—Jennifer Dash, Jennifer Calling, Jenn Free—she'd not taken the time to evaluate what these namesake changes entailed. She'd never bothered to embrace their representations, never realized that she held a certain conviction: that different venues of life require self-change.

One personality is better than another in particular situations. Jennifer had accepted a chameleon's life in a de facto manner. When she left Louisiana in search of an answer to life, she did not set out to reinvent herself, yet here she was, middle of the night, middle of the Pacific surmounting a vertical island cliff with what looked like a splotchy buzz cut with three suspicious crew-mates

She was Jennifer Dash, the once imprisoned double agent of Magical Kingdom, the Patriots, and Lillith Babbit, now scaling these island walls as Jennifer Free, a mercenary shipwrecked off the adventure schooner *Orion*.

The walls of the island broke off under one's feet into a sordid black dust. Merkyl explained that it was a form of molten ash. The island was a volcano, and according to Merkyl, a recently active one.

A silence cascaded over the foursome. If the island was a volcano, an active one, then this was no island paradise. There'd be no knocking coconuts together with toucan birds any time soon.

117

A certain story is soon to be told... not a story, exactly, but more of a theme. Or an idea. The idea involves the simplest of concepts. So very simple. Number the people. Remove their names. The land will no longer bear the names of old. The Carters, the Robertsons, the Smiths, the Youngs, the Stoddards, the Miyazakis, the Disneys, the Stacks, the Corleys, the Burundis, the Slovaks, the Bulgars, the Indians, the Celts, the Russ, the Armenians, the Carthaginians, the Romans, the Assyrians, the Phoenicians, the followers of Baal and Balaam. The Earth will spew them out. Vomit them up like rotten meat. The names of old will vanish into dust and cloud. Every countenance will fail, every creed fall by the wayside. No more selfish tears, for the self will cease to be. This is the idea. This is the belief.

This is the story of Pishtaco, and the very beginnings of his master stroke.

Enter and beware.

The night sky was trying to bless Jenn's group with moonlight, but persnickety clouds kept veiling the near full moon. As the clouds passed, before other floating giants covered the glare of the lesser light, Jenn glimpsed the dark and bare wasteland. The cliffs had no features whatsoever. They hung there, ever vigilant, dark monoliths. And yet, below the dark side, trudging on the dark ash, Jennifer Dash, Miles Faa, Alexandra Keitel and Merkyl made progress. They slowly ascended and conquered these dark hills.

Unfortunately, the clouds tapered over the large moon as they mounted the summit, betraying any opportunity to preview what lay before them. On the plateau, what they could make out was not reassuring. "There's nothing here," said Lex.

"How could anything live here?" Miles said.

Jenn peeped up, "Is this the right island?"

"I don't see how it could be," Lex responded.

"We don't see anything. We don't know anything," Merkyl grumbled, and marched ahead of the other three.

The island's strength made itself known in the form of its vastness. The plateau extended out far past one's imagination. Jenn kept narrowing her eyes, trying her best to

118

fight the darkness and catch a glimpse of the island's end. No luck. The flat, formless mass betrayed any dimensions.

Although the plateau was as flat as a pancake, with not even any large stones to trip over, Miles, Lex, and Jenn took every step on the alien island gingerly. Merkyl, by contrast, marched with relentless zeal, as if a war general, making claim to a new territory.

Then came the fall.

While our story involves many characters, Miles and Lex perhaps chief among them at present, this is, and will always be, a story about Jenn. And so it is that the fall started with her.

It was sudden, and so unexpected that it might as well have been an earthquake or an alien's tractor beam. Jenn took a step with her right foot.

The ground just wasn't there. Jenn would later remember it similarly to taking an extra step up a flight of stairs, only to stumble and realize that that last step doesn't exist. Jenn's foot fell through the step... fell through the air.

In a desperate panic, as she fell, Jenn flailed out for help. She reached out and pulled on the right shoulder of Miles Faa like a drowning person. Miles, in return, lost his balance, fell backwards towards Jenn (or rather, towards where Jenn once strode), and in his own astonishment, grabbed Lex's hand, who also then fell back toward the thrust of Miles' pleading discombobulation.

Jenn fell. Her stomach dropped. The shock was too much for her. Survival tactics didn't pipe in. She fell far enough that she could have broken her back. She didn't pivot. She didn't try to arrange her body in any sort of way to break her fall more gracefully. Jennifer Dash does not have the instincts of a cat. Jenn Dashes do not fall on their feet.

Jenn, Miles, and Lex fell fifteen feet. They landed on tightly coiled netting. The fabric leeched itself onto the body. Jenn and the others found themselves suspended in a hole, a deep hole, imprisoned in a netting not unlike a spider's web.

Jenn lay entangled on her back, staring up at the sky far above her trench. Her left arm lay pinned somehow, somewhere under Lex's stomach, while her right was twisted

119

back behind her head. Miles, when he fell back, twisted in such a fashion as to arrive in the netting headlong, his head by (beneath?) Jenn's legs, his legs left sprawling vertically up towards the horizon. Lex was probably the most comfortable of the bunch, having landed face-down on her stomach. She was the first to realize what had happened.

"MERKYL! MERKYL HELP! WE FELL! WE FELL!" Lex cried.

Miles hopelessly tried to rearrange himself. No avail. It was like being trapped in time. The webbing so embroidered itself to them, so latched itself to their flesh, that any sort of rearrangement was a futile dream.

Jenn had, of course, taken her backpack with her when vacating the *Orion*. In it, besides *50 People Whom I Pity* and two tightly-bound ensembles of clothes, were several granola bars, three cans of fruit, a dozen or more packages of beef jerky, and a chocolate bar. Miles and Lex also carried with them supplies of food and drink, but what good were they, if all three of them remained entombed in island webbing?

Jenn, being the only one of the three with a view toward the pit's entrance, made out the silhouette of Merkyl.

"Hey," Jenn called up to Merkyl, "We fell." She couldn't see Merkyl's face to judge his expression.

"Can you move at all?" Merkyl said.

"I can't," Lex said.

"Me neither," Jenn said after trying to wiggle her right arm free.

"Negative, alpha rider," Miles said.

"Anyone hurt? Anything broken?"

"I can't tell," Lex said.

"I think we're so tightly packed in, that whatever's broken, if anything, it's molded in place. I don't think there's any immediate cause for concern," Miles concluded.

"Okay," Merkyl said. "I'll find something."

Jenn watched the monkey surgeon's form vanish. "He left us," she whispered.

"What?" Lex said.

"He left us."

"No. No! Merkyl! MERKYL! DON'T LEAVE US! Merkyl, you

bastard, come back here!" Lex yelled.

"Calm down, Lex," Miles said. "I don't think there's much he can do here. It's better for him to see if he can find something further along."

"Further along? What do you expect he's going to find? We fell into a trap, Miles, a trap devised on a remote, godless island! The only thing to find is the monster that made the trap. I don't think we want Pishtaco to find us."

"He might be able to find a branch or limb or something to help get us out of here. Jenn, you can see up from where you're at?"

"Yeah."

"How far down would you estimate we are?"

The darkness made it difficult to gauge distances. Merkyl's outline seemed tiny when it overshadowed the hole. Jenn's initial thought was they must be twenty-five, thirty feet down, but then she tried to track the darkness up. She inched up the sides of the walls with her eyes. She used Miles legs as a measuring rod. Assuming Miles' leg was two feet long from knee-to-toe, Jenn measured seven or eight knee-to-toes to the mouth of the cave. "I think maybe fifteen feet."

"Quiet!" Lex whispered harshly. "Do you hear that?"

At first, Jenn heard nothing. There was a breeze audible from the mouth of the hole. Jenn actually thought the sound of the wind blowing over their pit in the earth was rather pleasant. But then she heard it.

Scratching.

From where?

"What is it?" Jenn asked.

Miles responded. "Maybe an insect? Insects."

"No. That's no insect. It's bigger."

"Ahhh!" Miles tried to suppress a yelp of surprise.

The two ladies tried to hold back screams themselves, but alas, squeaks came out.

"What is it?!" Lex asked Miles, "You saw something?"

"Just. Just a shadow."

"What sort of shadow?" A memory flashed in Jenn's mind. Once upon a time she was dying. Poisoned. She was getting a blood transfusion kn Mrs. Moose's mansion. Mrs. Moose

121

had left. Left the room. But there was something there. A shadow. Some kind of presence. Jenn had turned, twisted to look at the absence. The lightless one. That's how Jennifer Dash got covered in her own blood, trying to spot that shadow. And now, somehow, the shadow had returned? Was it death, come for Jennifer once more? Who else could find her in this desolation? What had she seen on that day? What had she really seen?

"It... I think it... it must have been some sort of rat. Or mole."

"How big?" Lex asked.

"Big."

"So it was a Rodent of Unspeakable Size?"

"Yeah! I think it was."

Jenn had never seen *The Princess Bride*, so the reference went over her head, but she appreciated the levity, nonetheless. "Is there any chance that this... that we're not trapped in a man-made contraption?"

"You think we're not in a Swiss Family Robinson pirate trap?" Lex said, and thankfully, Jenn got that reference.

"Is there any chance that the shadows... the rodents... that they made the netting?"

Lex responded immediately, "There's nothing in nature that can make something this complex. No. It's not possible."

Silence fell on the troop. Alexandra Keitel's assessment didn't feel reassuring. If Pishtaco was some sort of mad scientist, if he was able to fashion together grotesque, plague-bearing griffins, then maybe he could make web-slinging rodents. It wasn't out of the realm of possibility... right?

Lex was beginning to lose her cool. "Where's Merkyl? He should be back by now!"

"If he hasn't found anything of use, there's no need for him to come back," said Miles.

"Sure there is. We need to know he's okay. We need to know there's someone up there looking out for us. We need to have a watchman. What if Pishtaco comes with a band of cannibals?"

"How long until sunrise?" Jenn asked.

"Why?"

"Well, I'll be able to see out once the sun comes. Maybe

122

there'll be something useful to spy out."

"I wouldn't hold my breath for sunlight." Miles said.

"Why not?"

"What happens when morning comes? Most probably, whoever made this trap comes to see what he caught."

"Can't you do something, Miles?" Lex asked.

"Like what?"

"I don't know. Use your super powers."

"Super powers?"

"You know, your mind reading, omniscience powers."

"Being perceptive and knowing some tricks does not particularly assist me in climbing out of a net."

"Don't you have a knife or something?"

"Merkyl does. Merkyl's got a machete... I do have a book of matches in my pocket."

"Can you reach them?"

"Can you?"

Frustrated silence.

"Okay... okay. How about this? What's your favorite memory?" Miles asked.

"How's that helpful?" Lex snarked.

"It's just something to talk about, something to take our minds off the current predicament. How about it, Jenn? Got a favorite memory?"

Atticus Further. He was at once the most comforting person Jenn had ever met and the most unpredictable. How could that be? How could someone who is good, who is kind and warm, also be unpredictable? That seemed like a contradiction.

"Okay... yeah. One time I needed make-up. Really bad. I went to the store and got some. But on my way out I ran into this person I really liked. We sat down, and I didn't want... this person, to know that I had this make-up. So I stuffed the make-up in my back pocket. But it had a sharp edge, which was cutting into my butt. I tried to re-arrange my sitting, but no matter how I fidgeted, it still was sticking me."

"This is your best memory?" Lex asked incredulously.

"Well, it's the first one that came to me."

"You've led a miserable life, Jenn," Lex said only half

123

sarcastically.

"Just listen," Miles said. "Go on."

"Anyway, this... person was telling me his thoughts on this book, and for some reason, I was completely enraptured. We had this tremendous conversation."

"Ah, the famous transcendent conversation," Lex said.

"What?"

"Oh, I remember asking my Dad once how he knew he wanted to marry my mom, how he knew she was the right one. He said that one day they had this conversation that kept getting better and better. It kept going up and up. He described it as a transcendent conversation, the connection point wherein both parties are adding perfectly to a masterstroke, like painting a portrait together, but in conversation."

"Oh."

"Sorry to interrupt. Go on, finish the story."

"Okay... well, there's not much to tell. I just remember feeling this unreal sensation. I was in a good deal of physical pain. And all I had to do to get rid of the physical pain was to stand up, to leave. But the conversation was so comforting, so absorbing, that the pain didn't even matter. I've never experienced anything like that before or since."

"That's really beautiful, Jenn."

"Thanks."

"Your turn," Miles said to Lex.

"My turn. Let's see... I'm young, three or four. Five, max. It's summer. We're on the beach. Me, Ma and Da, all together. I'm searching for shells. There aren't many, just a few here and there. But that's not a problem. It makes finding them all the more special. I find little ones, pieces. Lots of fragments. Da is holding a paper bag. I put all the fragments in the bag. I'm holding both Ma and Da's hands. They're doing that thing, you know, that happy parents do with their kids, where they're swinging me up and down... it's wonderful. A strong wind comes, a cold wind. We decide we need to go. The beach isn't as nice when the wind comes. But I want to look into the paper bag my Da's holding. I want to choose one sea shell to remember this day. I'm hoping that maybe I had put one

124

perfect shell in the bag, even though I know I didn't find anything perfect. I reach in, feel around with my little fingers. I can't find anything whole, just shards. Maybe some really tiny ones, but nothing perfect. I'm a little sad, but not much. It's been a good day. I tell Da just to dump out the bag. It's okay I didn't find the perfect shell. Then Ma says something. I don't remember what. Da gives the bag to her. She reaches in with her hand. She's smiling at me. Da's smirking. He knows what's going to happen. I stare up at her, waiting for the magic.

"Ma pulls out a giant, enormous shell, the size of my hand! It's a gorgeous, conical, pearly white shell of perfection. I let out a yip of glee. Ma hands it to me and I rub it in my hands, not yet knowing that magic isn't real. I believe Ma made this shell. I truly believe she somehow made all the shards and pieces come together. She swirled them up somehow in that bag. She swirled them with the tips of her magic fingers and made this perfect gift for me... that's my best memory."

"Wow," Jenn said.

"You used the word perfect a lot, Lex," Miles said.

"Yeah."

"That's good. That's a good ebeneezer to hold onto."

"What's that?" Jenn asked.

"An ebeneezer is a memory that keeps you you."

"I don't understand."

"When you face events or trials or things like this that threaten to change you—change your personality or your identity somehow, you hold onto these ebeneezers that remind you who you are," Miles said, "or at least who you want to be."

"Okay, Faa, you're up," said Lex.

Miles Faa told his favorite memory. Well, he told a story, a very intricate, long story that put both women at ease, calmed them as they lay stuck in the hole, stuck in unknown webbing. He told them what they needed to hear to not worry about their troubles. And in the telling of this very tall tale, Miles Faa calmed down too.

The story went on and on, so long in fact, that the sun rose with very little notice from the threesome. Until that is, the noises returned.

Louder and louder now.

Lex could see clearest of the three. Enough light cascaded down the hole to reveal that they lay entangled in a mesh coffin four feet above the floor. The ground below appeared black and papery-ashy, not unlike everything else surrounding them.

"Look, look," Lex whispered vehemently. "There's a tunnel!"

At the base of the hole, at what appeared to be the far left side from Lex's viewpoint, a small tunnel—no more than six, seven inches in diameter—appeared to shimmer.

"It's coming through that shaft. The rodent!" Lex said too loudly.

They held their breath, awaiting whatever travesty revealed itself from the little hole at the bottom of the big hole.

A backpack. A backpack plopped through the hole! Then, a whoosh of air and a sweet sigh of relief. Merkyl had returned.

Once through, Merkyl rummaged through his backpack, snagged a pocketknife, and cut the threesome free from the meshing.

The affair took an hour or longer. Getting free of the netting was tedious work. Once free, the four members of the sunken *Orion* sat at the bottom of the ditch, this earthy abyss, exhausted from the long night's events.

They learned quickly that escaping up was useless. There was no escape up. You simply couldn't climb the hole. The island was made of strange stuff. Anytime they applied any pressure to the walls, any time anyone tried to climb out, the earth gave way like quicksand, like the island was made of sinking sand that somehow, unless messed with, held its frame.

As for Merkyl, he'd searched the island far and wide. He said he'd just about traversed its four corners. There was nothing on the island. It appeared to be utterly uninhabited. There were no buildings. No trees. No plants. No food of any kind. And no Pishtaco. When he'd circled around, he hit a trap-door drop similar to the one the three fell into... the only difference being there was no net in this hole, and there was a small opening in the base of his pit. It was too narrow for him, so he needed to scrap his way through it. As he battled inch

126

by inch through the minuscule tunnel, he began to hear a voice. A little further and he knew it to be Miles.

"I figure, when someone comes for us, as long as we hear them coming, we can crawl into the tunnel. At the very least that'll buy us a little time."

"That's reassuring," Lex said.

"The good news is, there's no way this tunnel is organic OR man-made."

"What is it?"

"By the patterns, I'd bet it was made by some kind of mole."

"How is that good news?" Jenn asked.

"It means we have a food source waiting to be caught."

Jenn peered out at the sun now cresting just above the hole, wondering what the next few days could possibly entail.

~~~

As one may suspect, the island Jenn's trapped on is not as uninhabited as it appears. For the weak of mind and spirit, it will prove to be just as inhospitable as imaginable.

The world came into being through imagination. But imagination too can be corrupted. For Jenn to solve the world, she'll need to peer down the depths of imagination's endless tunnels. Pishtaco's island may just hold the keys to unlocking the very mystery of life itself.

Chapter 29: Way Down in the Hole

Charles Dickens coined the word "boredom" in his novel *Bleak House*. But the reality of boredom far predates the word's existence. A Roman official in the second century had a memorial dedicated to him for having "saved a town from tedium". How he managed that feat remains a mystery to us moderns.

Before the fall down a deep hole, Jenn had only experienced something akin to boredom once since her journey to solve the world began. When she first got off the train in Los Angeles, she had no idea what lay in store for her. She wandered the streets, but two things kept her from really absorbing in an all-encompassing sense of true boredom. This first was fear. Stepping off that train, Jenn was stumbling into her first great adventure, her maiden voyage into mystery. That alone brought with it an energy that pushed out against the closing walls of tedium. The second was that despite Jenn's lostness, Los Angeles represented a cavalcade of sensual newnesses. Sights to see, smells to inhale, a consortium of objects to touch.

Here, way down, the hole worked as a poor man's sensory deprivation chamber. Within a few days, Jenn's eyes dimmed from having nothing to take in. Dark walls, dark land, dark destiny; everything dark.

After two weeks, the rations were just about empty. Nothing to eat, nothing to drink.

Conversations ranged miasmically. A lone voice, often Lex's or Merkyl's (though truth be told, on more than one occasion, Jenn found herself disgusted at the subject matter of a particular monologue she overheard, only to realize with stunned shamed that the voice was her own), would trumpet on about some morose, dark, or delirious topic. In most cases, Miles Faa would turn the dialogue towards something more manageable, something more palatable for the emotions to endure.

One would expect that the dread of the situation, the reality that the most likely outcome to this particular standpoint was starvation would inspire enough fear to ward off boredom... but one would be wrong.

Boredom flowed like rivers through Jenn's being. Worse still, the boredom interlaced itself with a brand of melancholia which had now infected the whole tribe down in the hole.

Only Faa looked to the heavens. He was at once the group's ringleader, cheerleader, and eternal optimist.

"Gimli will come. He'll bring us news," Miles said. "And we'll send news back with him. The others will come. Once they understand, they'll come."

"No one's coming for us. We're on our own," Merkyl would answer.

"We've got the mole men with us... somewhere," Jenn offered. The reunion with Merkyl did not lead to an end of the scratches and squeaks. They persisted from all around. At times, when she used all her strength to incline her ear towards the mystery, Jenn swore to herself that the noises came from underneath. Her mind filled up with machinations of a whole network of tunnels underneath them.

Sometimes the noises were so loud, so seemingly close, that the group braced for an appearance of the scratching apparitions.

"What do you think they talk about?" Miles asked.

"Who?" Lex said.

"The mole men. What are they up to today?"

"You think they can talk?"

"Of course! How else could they accomplish all this?"

"All this?" Jenn mimed with a degree of disgust.

"Don't think about them that way!" Merkyl grumbled.

"Why not?"

"Because if we keep adding this complex mythology to them, if you actually believe they talk to one another, then you might move that much slower when it's time to catch them. That split second hesitation will be the difference between starvation and a full tummy."

Merkyl, while not possessing anything close to the optimism Miles had, found strength in the notion that he was going to catch and eat one of these mole men.

Time slid.

Miles had declared himself the tribe's reader extraordinaire, and he took his duty quite seriously. He had read every page of Jenn's copy of *50 People Whom I Pity*, often with scrupulous personal reflections and disagreements. He found the author to be unduly condescending and flat-out wrong on most occasions.

After reading the write-up on Cleopatra, Miles slapped the page, ripping it straight out of the book. Jenn, much to her own surprise, didn't find Miles' display of noble indignation alarming. She didn't yell at him for destroying a piece of the only thing that connected her to Atticus Further. No. Jennifer Dash smirked. She knew Miles knew that she played Cleopatra at Magical Kingdom. He was defending her honor. Faa was making a point: the Cleopatras of the world are not to be pitied, by no means! They are to be held in high reverence. And if Miles has to forcibly remove Cleopatra from bad company, then he's willing to go that distance.

Jennifer's heart couldn't help but flutter.

She picked the torn page off the ground, reading the author's warning at its bottom once more:

REMEMBER REMEMBER: Guile and wisdom alone won't spare you from destruction. Never tie your fate to the selfish aspirations of lesser souls. Be angry.

A day or two later, while a calm sat upon the remnants of the hole, Jenn penned a short letter atop the torn out Cleopatra page:

Atticus,

You helped me once before. Help me again. Save us. We're starving on an island in the Pacific. West of Peru. Atticus, we fell in a hole searching Pishtaco's island. We're going to die. Please find me. Save me. I love

-Jenn

She couldn't quite say, "I love you". A sort of pride had bubbled up and made her stop. She'd never told a boy she loved him before. She wasn't about to start now. Beautiful words should come from beautiful moments, not from a pit of despair.

Before the moment washed away into the next doldrum of boredom, before Jenn smashed the note into her ashen pockets, close at hand so that she could offer it up to Gimli at a moment's notice, she scribbled this postscript:

PS: Lillith Babbit—

Once again Jenn stopped mid-sentence. She wanted to say something like 'Lillith Babbit will help you find us,' or, 'Lillith Babbit can figure out where we are', or even, 'Lillith Babbit knows what to do', but Jenn wasn't sure of any of that anymore.

Jennifer Dash had a penchant for qualifying people in categories of either 'good' or 'bad'. For obvious reasons, and perhaps necessary ones as well, Jenn had fastened Lillith securely in as an empress of the good. But look where Lillith had brought her: to this hole in the Earth. More than six feet under.

Time slid by.

In boring, desperate places, interesting things happened in bundles. One day, after multiple days of nothingness, four interesting things happened.

Interesting Thing #1: the end of the rations. Merkyl had stopped eating anything but crumbs for a week already, so the measly food crumbs and water droplets had stretched a bit longer than expected. But today it all came to an end. Examining the dearth, Lex started crying.

"Stop it!" Merkyl yelled. "You can't afford to cry!"

For some reason, that was it. The notion that one shouldn't cry in order to reserve water just battered the walls down. Miles, eternal optimist extraordinaire, dissolved into hysterics. Lex grabbed Miles, pulled him into her dirty shirt, and the two cried together.

Jenn was angry. "Why are you here, Merkyl?!" And as she spat vitriol at him, Jenn's eyes watered. She broke down. Way down in the hole, Miles reached out to Jenn, and pulled her in. The three friends cried together in a huddled mass, thankful in their desperation for one another.

Merkyl, the isolated one, crawled into the small passageway connecting his hole with the group's. The others

131

were unaware, but I'll tell you this secret now. Alone, in that small cave, Merkyl cried too. But he didn't like to share his pain.

As the three cooled down from their ceremonial cry fest, Interesting Thing #2 began.

Squeaks. Lots of them.

"It's so loud!" Lex said.

"Merkyl, you hear this?!" Miles called.

The older man crawled back into the main hole.

"They're coming!" Merkyl grabbed his machete and held it in ready position. "They're right underneath us."

"How many?"

"At least three. Probably more. Maybe lots." Merkyl said with too much confidence.

Then silence.

"What's going on, why'd they stop?" Lex asked.

"They're prepping for an attack." Merkyl's gaze informed the troop of a coming battle.

Lex grabbed Merkyl's pocketknife, flicking it to the ready position.

Miles and Jenn stared at each other, as if asking, "What are you going to use?"

Miles grabbed at his feet, unlacing his shoes. He slipped them off and handed one to Jenn.

"Here. It's steel toed."

Jenn took the shoe and raised it above her head, ready to slam it on whatever hideous thing came up from the dirt-ash beneath them. Miles snagged his matchbook from his pocket. Two matches left. They'd used most of the book a week back when Lex had the "genius idea" to make a smoke signal. It didn't work.

Jenn shot Miles a bewildered yet amused look as Miles held his match at the ready.

"Maybe they're afraid of fire."

Jenn shrugged.

They held their breath waiting for the eminent attack.

Drip. Drop.

132

Drop. Drip.

Rain.

"Merkyl howled, "They knew it was coming!"

The poor group huddled in their hole, figuring ways to trap as much rain as possible.

It continued to pour down for 35 minutes, and then puttered to a drizzle off and on for the next two hours or so. The hole filled several inches full with water. Every bottle and container filled to the brim. Jenn, Lex, Miles and Merkyl weren't going to die of thirst. At least not yet.

Interesting Thing #3 occurred around sunset. Jenn had a bowel movement. This indeed was news, and welcomed news at that, for Jenn hadn't had such an experience in well over a week.

The troop figured pretty early on that they needed a designated defecation area. It didn't take much imagination to figure out that Merkyl's pit was the perfect candidate for a makeshift outhouse, being the only place isolated from the group. Add to that, it gave a level of privacy to the act, which allowed the group to maintain some degree of dignity between one another, despite their inhospitable circumstances.

It was a wet, soggy situation, and after so many days of unsuccessful attempts, it wasn't exactly a pleasant endeavor. It also hurt. Nevertheless, it was an event, a change, something by which to mark and remember the day.

As it turned out, sometime after sunset, while under a moon-y glow, it wasn't the poop that made this particular day so memorable.

Interesting Thing #4 would cement the day as one Jenn would never forget.

Nights in the hole were difficult because of there being just enough heat to make things uncomfortable. It was never an overwhelming heat, no one sweat themselves into submission, it was just a couple ticks too high.

Lex took to the crawl space for rest. She was dainty enough that the tunnel didn't crowd her in as it did the other three. That left Merkyl, Miles and Jenn. The diameter of the hole

133

wasn't long for anyone to sleep fully outstretched from edge to edge, so a system was put into place. Miles, the tallest, slept on the outside ring of the circle, Jenn, next tallest, rested her head by Miles' knees and slept on a second-semi-circular track, while Merkyl, the shortest, slept in a fetal position at the center most point of the circle. The trick allowed everyone to sleep without having to touch each other, which was the one sure-fire way of sweating in the night and causing universal crankiness amongst all hole-going dwellers.

Sometime after everyone took to their muddy places for rest, a little earlier than usual, the day's excitement seeping extra ounces of energy from the quartet, a fifth being came amongst them.

No one saw it for who knows how long. Ironically, Miles, not Merkyl, was the first to see it. It stood on its four legs inches from Merkyl's feet. Miles awoke. Stared at it. Nudged Jenn.

Jenn opened her eyes to see the new sight. Its body looked to be that of a hedgehog, spiky and round, maybe a foot long from nose to tail. But its face divorced the creature from any hedgehog Jenn had ever seen before. The face wasn't pointy but broad and large... far too large for its body. Almost human. Looking at it, its features made its appearance look somewhere between cute and hideous.

It caught Jenn's stare, gawked back motionlessly for a moment, and then rolled right onto its back revealing a small, 'what-would-you-call-it... fanny pack', Jenn guessed. Halfway in the fanny pack pouch was an unopened Baby Ruth candy bar, hanging out like a joey in its mother's pouch. A folded note lay taped to the candy bar. On the outside, the note read, "TAKE ME".

The hedge-creature remained motionless on its back, apparently waiting for Jenn to take the note.

"Merkyl," Jenn whispered, "Merkyl, don't move."

Merkyl opened his eyes, and without moving, caught Miles line of sight. The two gestured to one another and slowly, Merkyl felt for his machete.

"I think it wants me to take it," Jenn said.

"Take what?" asked Miles.

Merkyl slipped his feet away from the beast and slowly,

silently, steadied into a position to hack the intruder.

"He's got a Baby Ruth on his belly!" Jenn cried in surprise.

It seemed as though the creature's eyes were growing, becoming big doughy discs like some sort of sympathetic Disney animation.

From the crawl space: "Guys, are you whispering about me?" Lex called out as she shimmied into the main hole.

Like a bullet, Merkyl's machete hammered down—

—too late. Jenn had watched as the creature tossed the Baby Ruth out of his fanny pack, turned into a ball, and nearly teleported into the ground below. He must have clawed at the ground, but it happened so fast it seemed to Jenn like the thing evaporated.

Merkyl's machete beat the ground. The little creature even managed to cover his newly minted hole as he descended into God knows what underneath them.

"Jeez, Merk, you nearly hacked off Jenn's leg!" Jenn hadn't even noticed that Merkyl's machete came no more than an inch from her shin.

"Where'd it go?" Merkyl shouted.

"Guys! What's going on?" Lex cried.

"A visitor came!" Miles answered.

"The vermin!" Merkyl sneered and began searching for a tunnel under his machete.

As Lex scooted into the hole, she saw what was left behind, "What's that?"

In a matter of minutes the Baby Ruth was divided up. No rationing. Lex ate a third, Jenn ate a third, and Miles ate a third. Merkyl claimed to have peanut allergies. Said the allergy was bad enough that even food touching peanuts could make him deathly ill. No one argued. In the hearts of Lex and Jenn, both secretly felt convinced that Merkyl was lying, just becoming a martyr for the cause. What can you do if a person refuses to eat? You can't force feed him; try to call his bluff. If you're wrong, you've just murdered a man, not to mention wasting some of the precious candy bar.

"I'll eat well enough when I skin that critter."

The note.

It was folded in half. Lex opened it and read it out loud.

"Welcome to Hole #043. You will be hearing from the Numbered Man soon. Enjoy your stay."

"I'm gonna kill that critter with this machete," Merkyl said in response to the note. "I'll lick his blood off my blade."

Who was the Numbered Man?

Jenn surmised that he was the boss of this place. She'd run into bosses everywhere she'd been so far. The Patriot, the security of Magical Kingdom, Mark Janner, Mrs. Moose, Lillith Babbit, Captain Alf, and now the Numbered Man. *An ominous name*, Jenn thought to herself. *No chance he's a good boss. Good thing I'm not alone.*

Although the note was exciting, and the rain and Baby Ruth both quite tasty, similar to the day after Christmas, the quartet didn't know what to do with themselves after all the hoopla settled down. Great, there was another man on the island. Can we talk to him? No. Can we search for him? No. Maybe the game pieces had been set, but there was no play. Not yet. At least, that was how Miles, Jenn, and Lex saw the script.

Merkyl on the other hand, knew exactly what he needed to do: stay vigilant. Merkyl was not to sleep. Not to talk. Not to do anything but stay always at attention, machete in hand, ready to whack a mole whenever the right moment arose. He was caught sleeping at the job once, he would not be found lacking again.

The next morning the three sane members of the apparent Hole #43 found in themselves an extra zest for life. Yesterday had new adventures in it, maybe today would as well. Maybe they'd hear from the Numbered Man. Anything was welcome at this point. Any action considered a blessing.

But the day came and went. They played jukebox-on-demand a dozen or more times. Jenn always lost. The rules of the game were simple: You had to sing a song, as much or as little of the song as desired. Whenever you stop singing, the next person in line immediately has to start singing a new song. No repeats allowed. The game is challenging in that it's hard to think up a new song when you're listening to one. All this is made infinitely harder when you're begging and praying in your mind that another little hedgehog-monkey-thing comes and brings you some new scrumptious treat. Jenn kept finding herself fantasizing that the little rodent-man-dwarf would somehow unfold a giant pizza from his handy pouch on his next visit.

No luck.

The day came and went.

No rodent. No message. No Numbered man.

Everyone but Merkyl slept. The next day, his eyes were so blood shot it looked as if the man had gone blind. When questioned, he'd just grumble some answer and say that he can't leave his work—a work which entailed him incessantly staring at the ground below.

From time to time they'd hear the scritchings and scratchings again. But nothing ever came of it.

Time slid right on by.

Jenn lost the days.

Then came Merkyl's big moment.

Sometime in the night, in his fetal position spot in the hole, he had dug two small holes for his arms, hoping that the tunneling demons would unexpectedly run into his hands, where he had his pocketknife ready to rip into something.

He nearly pulled it off.

With his hands buried below the ground, the rodent emerged once more, not however, from underneath, from the side. It waddled in to catch Merkyl's glare. He immediately scurried his arms as quickly as possible out of the holes he'd placed them in. If only he'd stayed vigilant and kept watch with his machete, he would have had the drop on the thing, no problem, but here, now, things didn't go as planned.

"Aaaahhh!" Merkyl yelled.

Everyone woke up, the creature buried itself, but this time, Merkyl leaped in time to catch the hole it left. Apparently, Merkyl had grabbed its tail, to which it swung around and bit his pointer finger. It bit him, and retreated when Merkyl retracted his arm in panic. He held up his hand in the moonlight to stare at the evidence.

The creature had bit him.

"You're infected," Miles said emotionlessly. "What have you done?"

Lex once again shimmied into the hole. "What happened? It

came back? Did it leave any food?"

Everyone was motionless. Lex caught the sight, the line of blood oozing down Merkyl's hand.

"I'm fine... it... it was the griffin that carried the disease, not... not this thing."

"You're right, we don't know what diseases this one has."

"It's just a type of rodent, mole, right? Not some genetic freak like the grif—" Lex trailed off.

"I saw its face. It didn't look normal to me." Jenn confessed.

"What do we do with you, Merkyl?" Lex said.

"What do you DO with me?! WHAT DO YOU DO WITH ME! I'm the only one trying to keep us alive down here!"

"No. Last time that thing came, it brought food. You scared it off, didn't you? You tried to kill it." Lex said.

"We can't live on candy bars! How many ribs can you count right now? We're already starving! That thing was going to buy us another week, maybe two!" Merkyl defended himself.

"We were never going to eat it, Merkyl," Miles said.

"What?" Jenn said.

"We can't roast it... if we were to eat it, we'd have to eat it raw... which, unless we're at the very precipice of death, we're not going to do because the likelihood of it carrying bacteria and a whole host of things that could poison us unto death nears 100%." Miles turned his attention away from responding to Jenn back towards Merkyl, "I was letting you play hunter because I thought it was important to you to have a mission, to feel you were remaining in control. But I was wrong."

Merkyl grinned something sadistic. "You want me dead, don't you?"

"No. But you can't stay with us. You very well might be infected with that... that thing. Or, you'll just get sick and die. Either way, it's too dangerous for you to be around the rest of us."

"But there's nowhere to..." It dawned then on Merkyl what Miles was saying.

It would take Jenn a moment longer. Until she watched Merkyl trudge away, it didn't really sink in.

Merkyl was banished to the poop hole.

No one spoke.

138

He went to his waste space silently, without protest.

No one slept that night.

Quarantine is a tricky operation living down in a hole.

Miles had taken to an unfortunate form of leaking. A day earlier, before that "thing" bit Merkyl's finger, Faa had utilized the "outhouse" to do his uncomfortable duty. Now that area was off-limits. That left only the tunnel to the quarantined one as a viable option. Miles would scoot into the crawl space, rummage onto his back, and lay there while moderate cramping and leakage ran its course.

Lex took to singing. Her throat was too sore, tired, and malnourished to produce much of a tone at this point, so the singing, though sounding quite adequate in Lex's mind, came out as undulating warbles and screeches.

As for Jenn, she spent most of the day standing, looking up at the sky far above, dreaming of a renewed life, a start-over button.

Most of all, she thought about Atticus Further.

Between Faa's leaking bouts, he'd whisper to himself, long, long diatribes about unknown things. The myriad memories and ideas still trapped in Miles' head were using his broken body to claw out anyway they could.

No one heard any word, whisper, or shout from the quarantined corridor.

It was maybe an hour before sunset, right around what would have been time for rationed dinner, when it came. Jenn, still standing, knew at once who it was.

Like a dove, he descended upon them.

The majestic Gimli, savior of Hole #43, welcomed postman of the adventure schooner *Orion*, champion of the seven seas, hardened pilot of all the winds of the Earth, the great trumpeter, the eternal newsman, the bringer of truth, the harbinger of certainty; at last, at last the noble and eloquent, gentle bird had found the miserable ones of Pishtaco's pit. How long had Jenn yearned for this moment, eagerly sought out the fowl's silhouette in the sky? Hope springs eternal; life gives way to life anew. Hope springs eternal.

This meant so many things! Perhaps even word from Atticus!

Gimli had proven his worth once already by bearing that message from the Pelican State boy. And Jenn had sent word back to Louisiana with Gimli weeks, maybe months prior. This could be it! The real deal! And beyond breathless words from Further, they could send an SOS to the *Orion*, to the once departed members. This meant rescue, this meant safe return! This meant reunion.

Tears of happiness trickled down Jenn's eyes. She pulled out the dirty scrap of Cleopatra's story on which she'd scribbled her words to Atticus and raised it high in her hand, up for Gimli to snatch with his message-bearing talons.

"Gimli, Gimli! Here! We're here!" Jenn screamed with glee.

The gull descended. He was so large. Enormous, really. His form seemingly filled the entirety of the hole.

"Gimli, you made it! Here! Here!"

Those talons, so large, more like a lion than a bird... Jenn had never noticed how stunningly grand Gimli was.

"JENN! JENN, NO! GET DOWN! THAT'S NOT GIMLI!"

Jenn didn't recoil in time. Miles found the machete and raised it towards the flying freak!

"AAHHHHHH!!!" screamed Miles.

Talons clasped onto Jenn's outstretched hand... and sunk into her flesh.

~~~

Is Jenn infected with the leprosy-plague? Is she doomed? The griffin's talons have pierced her skin, just like the doomed woman of the *Known Triangle*.

Adventure always seems so carefree from the outset, but its perils know no humanity, no mercy.

Chapter 30: Good Things

Pain.

Shock like I've never known.

I've heard it said that emotional turmoil is as blisteringly painful as physical torture. But have those who've expressed such thoughts ever lost their limbs?

I haven't.

I'm at a loss to describe Jenn's experience.

Here are the facts.

It was not Gimli that descended upon Hole #043. It was the griffin. It clung onto Jenn's hands. Miles, quick thinker that he is, grabbed Merkyl's machete, screamed at the top of his lungs, and hacked off Jenn's left hand at the wrist. Perhaps stunned by the commotion, the griffin flew off, taking Jenn's hand with her.

More than that, I cannot express. Instead, I offer Jenn's own words as insight. She wrote this letter on a page from the journal she later collected as a peace offering from the Numbered Man.

Dear Atticus,

I'm not who I once was. I'm different now. Forever altered.

But I want to be who I once was. I want that back. I'd do anything to go back. Back to Louisiana, back to your couch.

We were starving in the hole. I thought I saw Gimli. I reached out my hand. I wanted to give you something, so I reached out. I reached out my hand, and now it's gone.

I never said goodbye. I never consented to this. Isn't that a stupid thing to want? I even want to see my hand, just to say goodbye to it. I know that's weird. I know it's dumb. I'd like to build a little coffin to put it in. I want to bury it in the ground, underneath the sun.

I want to see the sun again.

It was there, my hand, and then it was gone.

I know in my mind that if Miles hadn't done what he did, I'd be done. I'd be one of those boat people, ready to swan dive onto the deck of the Orion just to go splat. I know this in my mind, but in my heart, I can't forgive Miles. He's supposed to be so smart, so seductive with words, but he can't undo this.

He gave my hand to the monster. How can I forgive him for that?

After we ate, after we heard from the Numbered Man, he tried to apologize. I guess. It wasn't enough. I can't even look at him.

Okay, enough sobering gilbery-gook. I'm okay. I really am. I'm just different. New me. Now, with twenty-five percent less digits!

I can recollect the moments after if I focus. It's funny, the memory of it, it's like there's this red and yellow splash of fog over the videotape. The first thing I remember is falling. And then thinking that I was blind. Then, I saw lack. My hand was gone and there was my blood spurting straight out of me.

As Jenn wrote that sentence, she nearly erased it, but thought better of it. She had wanted to write, "My hand was gone and there was Tiff's blood spurting out of me."

Miles tore his shirt, made a tourniquet. I think I was shouting. I know Lex was. I remember her shouting for Merkyl, over and over again. I think Miles yelled at her to shut up. Merkyl was nowhere to be found. He still is. He evaporated into the walls. We think he must have found one of the tunnels on his own. He's around, somewhere. He just won't forgive us, won't show his face. I may not be able to forgive Miles, but I still have manners. I haven't lost my Southern-ness yet. But if I do, I sure could use a hand!

I blacked out soon after, so I didn't get to see the spectacle. I didn't witness the train of hedgehog-y critters. Before, when they first came, I just saw the one, with its cute little fanny pack. Merkyl was right all along. There was never just one. There are dozens.

Lex told me that we should have been able to hear them, but none of us were really taking in any senses except for what was happening to me. Anyway, the ground dropped out underneath us. I was unconscious. Everyone dropped like ten feet deeper down the hole. Then, while Miles and Lex were trying to figure things out, the critters carried me off. You see,

142

our hole was positioned just a few feet above one of the main tunnel arteries of the Numbered Man's networked highway. It kinda reminds me of Patriot's underground. The tunnels are much bigger than our hole in the earth. They're tall enough to stand up in. No crouching necessary.

The little hedge guys grabbed me on their backs, so says Miles, and carried me to the chamber. I'm in a chamber kinda like that one now. There's no light. I mean, there's no fire or electricity. And we're like a hundred feet under ground! How am I writing this, you ask? How am I putting pen to paper? Well, in these chambers, and all along all the tunnels, the rocks glow! All sorts of colors! The first one they took me to, all the rocks glowed green.

Don't believe me?!! It gets better! Lots better!

The first thing I remember is sitting in her lap like an infant. Her arms and legs swaddled me and cocooned me to rest. Sure, with my eyes I was betrayed, destroyed and terrified, but the soothing felt so good. My arm was soooooooo coooool. It had been on fire, spurting out lava and agony. Now it was bathing in a cool bath. She was so strong and gentle. It was, if you can imagine, like nestling into the bosom of a giant, real, Buddha. She had those dimensions!

I'm sure I'm not making any sense. Let me back up a moment, maybe it's better if I explain what Lex told me they saw.

She said she was rummaging up through the dust and ash of the fall, trying to reorient herself and prepping for the worst. That's when she saw at least a dozen of the hedgehogs carrying me off.

And she noticed the green rocks glowing, kinda lighting a path. Lex and Miles were able to follow us, just ten feet or so behind. They were too in awe of the lights and these things carrying me to attack them or come up with a plan or anything. They were just following. Follow the green rock road.

Lex said, in her own words, I remember them clearly, said, "I couldn't input what my eyes saw."

In the chamber, there were piles of food. All kinds of fruits and vegetables, fully cooked rotisserie chickens, whole slabs of ribs. Anything that makes your mouth water, it was there.

But more to the point, in the corner of that chamber room was a beaked, froggy woman. She had a round human tummy and torso, but green, frog-like skin, and frog legs with flappers for feet. But her face, that's what I remember best, it was feathered, at least partially, and beaked. The only thing we have in our normal world that mirrors it are some of the old photos of Egyptian gods. Which one? I can't remember their names. This woman is probably an amalgamation of all of them. Just like that. The bird-frog-woman-goddess. Her beak was pointed, and out of it came this slime. She was holding me, and the slime from her mouth was sealing my wound, healing me.

Are you believing any of this?!!

Uh-oh. One of the hedgeys are here. I gotta go. I'll write more later.

Jenn put down her newly minted diary. She wasn't the only one with a journal. At one of the 'meal chambers', as the group came to call them, three journals, beautiful brown leather bound books, lay beside the mounds of sumptuous food. Both Miles and Jenn took them. When Jenn decided to open and write in hers, it was a horrible experience. Life with one hand was going to be challenging—stretching in almost every mundane detail. So this 'letter' Jenn had managed to pen on this day was quite an accomplishment (or was it night? All three had long lost any ability to discern what time a day it was).

The roly-poly hedgehog mutation walked into their chamber, seemingly smiled gently, according to Jenn's intuition, and rolled onto his belly.

"It's a tape recorder," Lex said, stating the obvious after staring at the blunt object dangling out of the hedgey's fanny pack.

"Grab it," Miles said.

"You do it," Lex responded.

Miles didn't hesitate. He grabbed the recorder and pressed play.

"Hello. How are we today? In a few moments, #361, 362, and 109 will come to bring you bathing suits. Just so you

144

know, 361 comes for the one you call Lex, 362 for the one-armed girl you call Jenn, and 109 for the man, Miles Faa, I believe. I'd like to invite all three of you, my guests, to try out one of our three premiere spas on the island. I'll warn you, however, that the spa has a habit of getting a bit too warm. When you arrive, you'll notice strings hanging near the edges of the spa. Those strings are attached to buckets of ice. If you get too warm, feel free to pull on the strings. Pulling on them will tip the buckets over. Just be sure to stay out of the way of the falling ice. More than one of us has been bruised from the descending frozenness. It's fair and true to remark that this premiere spa is perhaps the least eloquent of our offerings. Indeed it's the oldest one on the island I've furnished... I promise you the newer spas are far more spectacular. Like everything on the island, the evolution is apparent, older things far surpassed by newer incarnations. But, alas my guests, I don't want to overwhelm you. That is why I choose to show you the smallest of our glories first. We must desensitize your imaginations to wonder. You'd explode, spontaneously combust if I let you see my kingdom in its fullest fruition. Imagine yet still how great your explosion would be if we harnessed the power of a time machine. You'd blow up to a million, bajillion pieces. And that's a promise. Don't worry, I care well for my guests. I wouldn't do that to you. That's why I'm being so scrupulous, so magnanimously patient with you three. Were I any less wise, less cunning in my benevolence, I would have rescued you from your pit of despair on that first day. But I'm smarter than that. You see, I've learned that you must always start with what the mind expects. If you give the people something they can't fathom right away, then guess what? It's just like that! They lit-er-al-ly CAN-NOT fa-thom it! It's wholly remarkable. I've watched it happen. They say that when the Europeans first sailed to the new world, the Indians of the coast couldn't see the boats. It's as if the Europeans floated on invisibility cloaks.

"Come, come to our exemplary spa. I'll be speaking to you there. Some things of greater relevance I believe you are now able to hear. The warming glow of the spa too will help dampen your inhibitions and calm your nerves.

"Do you have any concerns that we can attend to?"

The recorder continued to run silently to a closed-mouth room.

"You can tell 242 whatever it is that needs attending. He'll carry your messages for you."

More silence.

"Go ahead. Just open your mouth and tell him. He can understand you."

Jenn thought about opening her mouth and asking for a sling for her arm. Though her limb had pretty much healed from the bird-frog-woman's saliva, she still couldn't manage to walk with her arm at her side. She carried it with her good hand, held it close to her breast. Perhaps it was part of the grieving process, but Jenn Dash couldn't let go of her arm.

But before Jenn could figure out how to ask for such a thing, the tape kicked in again.

"Very well. I, whom you may call the Numbered Man, will be hearing from you soon at the spa."

The tape clicked to a stop. The hedgey, number 242 according to the Numbered Man, reached out his claws toward Miles. The gesture was strange, but easy enough to translate. The hedgehogy wanted Miles to hand back the recorder. Miles did so, and the creature grabbed a hold of it with relative ease and dexterity. He plopped it into his fanny pack, reversed directions, and waddled on out of the chamber, into the vast network of glowing rock aisled tunnels.

"What do we do?" Lex asked out loud.

"Shhhh!" Miles sneered.

"What?" Lex whispered.

"He knows our names. He may be listening to our conversations."

"How?" Jenn asked.

"Who knows? We were never supposed to come here! I have no idea what's going on. Maybe he's rigged this place with microphones."

"You keep saying that... you said that back on the boat. You were so mad that we decided to head this direction. When we split up, you never wanted to come aboard." Jenn was searching for more reasons, more evidence to cast Miles Faa as an enemy, a demon in disguise.

"Jenn's right. Why are you here? You were adamantly against coming here. What do you mean, 'we were never supposed to come here'?" Lex was jumping onto Jenn's train. The Numbered Man wasn't here, wasn't showing his face. There needed to be an enemy... and the only option was the mind reader standing right in front of them.

"We're not doing this. Ladies, we're not having this conversation right now."

"Ladies? Don't you go patronizing us now, Miles. Answer the question."

"This isn't productive."

"I don't care what's productive! We've been starved, terrified, betrayed by Merkyl—"

"We don't know Merkyl betrayed us."

"Microphones in the walls, Miles. Are you deliberately being so dull? There's not even electricity down here... there's just iridescent rocks! He knows our names because Merkyl told him."

"We don't know that."

"Answer the question, Miles."

Jenn rubbed her stump. The end was so smooth... what magic was in that saliva?

"Jenn lost her hand, Miles. You need to tell us what you know."

"I don't know anything."

"Lies!" Lex stuttered and stumbled. "I don't get it. I've seen you do things. You're one of the cleverest people on this planet. You can make anyone like you, make anyone think what you want them to think. Why are you letting Jenn and I hate you? Why don't you calm us down! You know something, and the fact that you're so miserably trying to cover that up is pathetic! You're better than that! And I'm terrified!!!"

Jenn's mind trailed back to her first conversation with Miles. The one about Mohammad Najjar.

Jenn: So his attack was all because of a fear of snakes? That's it?

Faa: No... there's something else too....

Jenn: Yes.

Faa: Najjar believed... he said he saw... the snake that bit his sister... he said... his words, his belief, was that the snake came out of the desert looking for him, but bit his sister instead, then... after it bit her, meta-morphed into a man and ran away, back into the desert.

Jenn: Okay... what are you telling me? To be on the look-out for Transformers?

Three hedgeys entered and waddled right up to their prospective human. Jenn remembered the Numbered Man's prophecy. #361 for Lex, 362 for Jenn, 109 for Miles. Each rolled onto their bellies revealing smashed up clothes.

Lex pulled hers out first. A bikini. A teenie-weenie polka dot bikini.

"You've got to be kidding."

Jenn pulled hers out. Same situation. A tiny little thing.

"That freak. What a misogynist," Lex lamented. "I'm not wearing this."

The two women looked to Miles Faa to fully embrace the sexism when his polka dot board shorts revealed themselves. Miles Faa smirked. His bathing suit, if one could call it that, was just as skimpy as the women's. The piece of cloth looked to be the love child of a speedo and a thong. Miles was unsure of what the point would be to wearing something that revealing... might as well go in a birthday suit.

The hedgeys squeaked the same type of squeak the group heard long before they knew these humanoid, fanny-pack sporting mutant hedgehogs existed. The three shimmied on out of the chamber into the big, tall, shimmering rock-lit tunnel. Once there, the three split, going three different directions.

"Changing rooms," Miles said.

"Excuse me?" Lex said.

"They're giving us private changing rooms," and Miles, speedo-cloth in hand, followed his hedgey.

"Uh-uh, no way. I'm not giving that freak the pleasure." Lex crossed her arms and clearly made haste to stand pat in defiance.

What would Jenn do? She didn't know. Abstractly, she watched herself follow her hedgey. The thing motioned her

148

towards a small, dimly-lit hole, not unlike the one they fell into, except this one had no outlet up into the heavens.

She did as she was told.

Jenn squeezed into the bikini. She felt silly for doing so, certainly immodest, but what did it matter? Since losing her hand, everything was foggy, and she didn't feel like herself. Her normal self may have balked at the idea of showboating her body in front of her friends (was Miles a friend?) and maybe this weird island-Lord. But now, left-hand-less Jenn just didn't care so much. Be a sex doll for an underground creep. Sure. Once on, Jenn sheepishly made her way into the large tunnel, the underground highway.

It was hard not to think about her hand. The instinct was to subtly cover her body when revealing herself to Lex and Miles, but with no hand, she felt all the more bare.

There's nothing left to hide anymore.

Lex came out into the tunnel, spied Miles, and examined Jenn head to toe, "You guys look ridiculous." She couldn't suppress a laugh.

Miles Faa was quite the specimen. Jenn couldn't help but notice his toned physique. Chiseled was the word that came to mind.

The three followed the hedgeys through the tunnel wandering this way and that, zigging here, zagging there, until at last they reached the summit of the spa. Jenn tried her best to memorize their path, but it was useless. After seven or so left turns and another half-dozen right turns, not to mention one star-intersection wherein they seemed to make a near 180 turn, Jenn gave up hope of holding onto any semblance of a memory. There were very few physical markers from turn to turn, besides the color of the rocks changing. Every color was on display somewhere; purples, yellows, reds, even bright browns and grays. Jenn hoped that in some life she could take one of these rocks away with her to show Atticus.

Oh Atticus, where are you now? Jenn's temperament swung so freely from pole to pole way down here where the sun doesn't reach.

The spa was fifteen feet below them. The tunnel traversed up to a cliff edge, and a great pool lay far below. A ladder awaited them at their feet, but it clearly was deep enough to dive in.

Dive. That's exactly what Miles Faa did.

The spa was especially colorful. The rocks below the water were a special hue of orange, a variant of which Jenn had never seen before.

Both Lex and Jenn couldn't help but fear that Miles was going to melt or evaporate or spontaneously combust in the pool. Nothing was taken for granted on this island, and if saliva could heal an amputated stump, who's to say what a spa would do? But, to the two girls' relief, Miles returned to the surface and called up,

"Come on in! It's warm, but quite nice! Like bathing in a sauna."

"No," Lex stated matter-of-factly.

Once again, Jenn found herself responding before thinking through an answer. She carefully tipped-toed down the steel ladder. She plucked her toes in, found it to her satisfaction, and waded in.

The feeling was almost instant. A sense of peace.

Miles and Jenn found themselves smiling vigorously as they tread the temperate water. Jenn had very little experience swimming before, but the water was naturally ultra buoyant. She could almost float without even trying. Almost.

The peace spa.

What a blessing.

What a good thing.

In fact, everything since the griffin had been pleasant. The Numbered Man had taken care of her. Miles didn't do that. Lex couldn't. Merkyl was MIA. Jenn was starving, the Numbered Man fed her. Jenn was going to bleed to death, but the Numbered Man made sure she didn't. And she was clean, no infection... and it was all painless. There's no pain on Earth like losing a limb, but, in the days since the incident, the Numbered Man had made sure she felt as little as possible. He even gave her pen and paper to write down her thoughts. So what if he wanted to ogle her in a bikini? Maybe he wasn't the villain everyone made him out to be. Jenn thought these thoughts as the spa soothed her whole being. Miles pulled one of the hanging strings. Sure enough, just as the Numbered Man had said, a bucket of ice tipped over, and a sweet coolness plunged into the pool beside Faa.

Lex sat at the mouth of the entrance, her legs hanging over the side.

Then the speakers came on.

"I'm happy to know that at least a majority of you are enjoying the fruits of my labor and imagination. It's a shame though; I would have so enjoyed watching this Lex swim in my spa.

"You've come to my island, come to my home as guests. I want you to know that. You are my very special guests. In time I'll yet show you things that will make your mind race and your heart flutter. If you don't yet, you WILL come to love my creation. This island is special, and you're special for witnessing it in its nascent form. You see, I have big plans. I so want to share them with you. I love you. Each of you. I really do. The rest know that. You may not yet be convinced. You will be.

"I must confess now, that I've played my cards close, and I may have tried to manipulate the situation in my favor. You see, I know I'm doing great work, wondrous work. I know that. But I also know humans; we're a simple lot. We like what we know. We're slow to accept change. And so, at a place like this, my fortress, my defense, my alma mater, all this change and newness might seem a bit much. PEOPLE ARE SO STUPID! How they can't see what we're here to do, EMPHASIS ON DO, is just utterly beyond me. If I'm dimwitted in anything, it's that. I can't conceive of how the masses have missed the point of life.

"Ah, look at me, I'm distracting myself. You see, the spa has a certain chemical in it, don't worry, it's not like a drug that leads to addiction, nothing like that. It just has calming agents in it. I wanted to give myself as much chance for success as possible. You understand, if a man has a chance to rig the game, even just a little, you can't blame him for doing so. Don't you agree? Of course you do! Whether you realize it or not, you all do! That's why you're here.

"Each of you has rigged your own destiny, that's what you

151

were trying to tell the women, isn't that right Miles? That's what you were stuttering to tell them. You had great plans in store for you and Miss Jennifer Dash—oh, I'm sorry, I mean, Jennifer Free. Didn't you, Miles Faa? You can confide in me. I'm trustworthy.

"The spa, it's on my side, you see. It's here to help my cause, as all of my creation is. You'll see. Too bad your Alexandra Keitel is unwilling to go for a dip. Unfortunately the truth is, my guests, that I need something from you. I'm going to give you three options... and, I know, I KNOW, because I understand what its like. You're not going to like your options, but you have to remember that you are my guests. MY guests.

"Just remember, I've given you so many good things, and so many good things await you yet.

"All I ask of you is that you make this one hard decision."

~~~

Jenn's lost a hand, but if she wants it, she's about to inherit a future. A future unlike anything us regular folk have ever known.

The Numbered Man holds all the cards, and the decision he's forcing upon Jenn and Miles and Lex is not pleasant.

A wrong choice will kill them all.

Chapter 31: Three Paths

"All I ask of you is that you make this one hard decision."

Lex's knees buckled. She was regretting not diving into the relax-a-spa. She peered down at the other two. Despite the Numbered Man's strange and frightening words, they seemed peaceful down there. Serene even.

"I am a man, just a regular man. SoooOOOooo, I, of course, like options. Don't we all—all of us regular mans. We like our options. We like strolling down that aisle examining closely all 432 varieties of detergent. We feel wise for having chosen one out of 432. We are not racked with self-doubt or a debilitating sense that we've surely chosen the wrongest detergent of them all, that we've had the veil pulled over our eyes, that, IN FACT, the right detergent was that one we didn't even give a second thought to. We scoffed at it. It didn't say linen fresh on the label, so we thought nothing of it. We were so very, VERY, very, confident that all the best detergents say "linen fresh" on the label. The fact that detergent choice number 104 said nothing about linen freshness, but only exclaimed in large print, DETERGENT: WORK GOOD was the final nail in its sad, sad coffin, wasn't it?

"Speaking of coffins, thanks for the hand, so-called Jenn Free. It's really been handy to have it around. Number 819 brought it to me. Should I build a coffin for it? Bury it in the sand? Or will you be wanting it back? I can get it back to you, you know. Your hand can be stitched up ever so delicately. It won't even hurt. I promise. And you know my promises are trustworthy... because I AM trustworthy." The Numbered Man abruptly pivoted to a tone of overwhelming anger. "Trustworthy! You'd pay a million dollars to be as trustworthy as I am! You can't even dream of my trustworthiness! YOU CAN'T EVEN DREAM!"

Wading in the underground spa (or was it just a natural lake?), Jenn stared up at the speakers with a sense of open perplexity. The sensory numbing of the spa had worked its charms on her sure enough. She didn't feel frustrated or anxious, or scared, or really anything in response to the sounds blaring from the speakers. She was just openly perplexed.

The Numbered Man's words rolled the way palindromes feel. When Jenn first learned about palindromes, she thought they were neat, but then in the hearing of much longer palindromes, ones longer than Dad, Mom, and Wow, she had this slightly skeptical feeling about them. It was as if, somewhere deep down, Jenn didn't actually believe that "A Santa Lived As a Devil At NASA" was a palindrome. Somehow it was breaking the laws of word physics, and it shouldn't be! At the end of the day, though, however its voodoo works, it's such a dumb thing that no one should actually care how it runs its trenchant chicanery.

In that same vague way of listening to unending palindromes, Jenn hearkened her attention to talk of her lost hand.

The Numbered Man was still rattling on. "If you make a certain choice, dare I say the right choice, then you and I will sink our talons into this mortal toil, and you shall have your hand anew. See? It's so simple.

"Okayokayokayokayokay! Onto the show. Your options, if you please. And your decision, I greedily await.

"I can make my dreams come true on this island, but I've no one to share it with. I want, nay, I yearn for a co-ruler. A goddess among the living. A wife."

A shiver ran down Lex's spine and would not abate.

"I've said I'd give you three options. This is option one. You give me one of the two women as a bride, and I'll let the other two go. Simple. This is the option I prefer. I understand, people can't make love happen, you can't will yourself to meaningful submission and love, so I offer you option two. The three of you join our ranks. You'll be experimented on. I've used humans before... it doesn't always work to plan. But, fear not, or maybe fear slightly less! We're getting better all the time. There's a good chance I'd get things right with you and you'd be so so so so so thankful to me for having improved you so inconceivably. That's option two. You become my specimens for further experimentation."

154

"I've never worked on an unwilling client before... agh, scratch that, there was the thing with number 014... and then the 702, 703 twins... oh! And 169 wasn't exactly something I'd call mutual. Ah... well, the point is I won't force you to be my little experimentees either. I am, at this place and time, unwilling to go that distance. You see, I don't need you. I can make my manifestations come to life, come to complete, apple-plucking-luscious fruition without you. So. It's just an alternative option.

"And of course, who could forget? There's option three. You refuse option one, you refuse option two, you get option three. That's the option I'd like to call 'the Nuclear Option.'

"You won't like what happens next. You won't. I love you, and so I need to be honest with you; option three is a bad deal for me, for you, for everybody. And let's face the facts here, choosing option three would be the least loving thing for you to do. It would, in a word, be hateful. HATEFUL! Full of venom. Miserable ingrates, you'd be! I'd hate you, I'd hate you so bad.

"This world runs on hate, you know that, right? That's why my creation, my plan, my great dream realized is just about the best thing possible for the world, and the only hopeful destiny left for planet Earth.

"Let's summarize, shall we? I despise people who aren't clear and concise, don't you? Oh, and lest I forget! As soon as you choose, I'll let you into my little secret... my realm of ideas, my plan and my cause. That's a promise... a trustworthy promise.

"Summary: Here it is. Option one: one of you beauties takes me as your wedded groom. Don't worry, we can make you a marvelous dress. And when you say, I DOOOooo! then your friends will be given a rowboat and an exit plan. And we all live happily ever after! Perfect! You should choose this option, hooray!

"Option two: you can't summon up the lovey-doveys, so rather than take the dreadful path of option three, you give yourself freely to be my experimentees. AnnDD-ddd-dd-dd, most likely end up with marvelous superpowers. Though I want you to choose option one, who's to say what wonderful mysteries will unfold if you choose the second option. In fact, over the years, you'll undoubtedly fall in love with me and may even choose to marry me after all is said and done. You see, the bittersweet pill of option two isn't the end of the world. You get your bitters, I get my sweets. And never two, or three, or four shall part!

"But lest I be a bad host, option three remains: that is, the end of the world. Your world. Choose that abomination, and I'll end you. And just so you understand the STAKES, my lovelies, oh the tormented stakes! Don't choose three, I beg you, don't you dare choose it. But, sigh, if you choose to be urchin haters, I'll have no choice but to end your souls. Understand, I can't just kill you. No, that'd be too easy. Many men have had courage when faced with death. Some folks even prefer death. Suicide is a real threat, people! I know that demon's knocked on my door more than once.

"Choose option three, and it'll all happen so slow. You won't believe how slow. Remember, my friends, the isles of imagination know no end, and they go both ways; both towards light beautiful manipulations and stories, and towards doomed, hollow dread. Trust me, I know both routes, I've created things that—I can barely speak of them—they were horrid. Abominable things. A darkness that cannot end...."

A long, uncomfortable pause set in.

"Go, have a pow-wow. Sleep on it. Give your answer in twelve hours."

Some hedgeys gave Miles and Jenn towels. They marched back to their chamber silently. Once alone, or at least, free from the listening ears of the hedge-minions, Miles wrote in the ashy Earth beneath them.

He wrote these words: *Investigate. Meet in 1 hour.*

"Make sense?" Miles said.

"Each separately?" Jenn said.

"Yes," Lex answered authoritatively.

So here it is that we must briefly depart from Jennifer Dash. Miles, Jenn, and Lex turned towards the seemingly endless tunnels, each hoping to find a way out, or at least some ammunition to make a wise decision.

Miles followed a dark gray trail. When one thinks of rays of light, one does not envision gray being on that scale—and this very strangeness attracted Miles to follow the certain strange underground path.

He weaved left and right, marking his trail back by smudging some of the illuminated stones with his hand print. He was careful to mark the rocks with his fingers pointing forward, that way, upon his return, he'd know to follow the smudge of his palm back to their allotted chamber.

Miles came across several alcoves, chambers almost identical to the one where the hedgeys had led the group. He reckoned that there were plenty of inlets and grottoes to hide in, when the time came to play a high stakes game of hide and seek.

Twenty minutes of wandering led Miles to a particular ditch. At first it looked like a dead end, but upon further inspection, there was an ash colored ladder attached to the wall. And so Miles Faa ascended. It went twenty feet up or so before Miles climbed reached a path illuminated by brownish-yellow stones. He felt he must be close to the surface, maybe just ten or so feet below. Perhaps if he dug at the ceiling. The roofing was just low enough that Miles had to bend his head at the neck to walk. He went no more than twenty feet when the ceiling bloomed in front of him. A fork in the road presented itself. Forward was no longer an option. He could go left or right—both ways looked identical and unending. Just at his back, however, was a spiral staircase. He followed the stairs up with his eyes. It spiraled up and up. How was that possible? Where was the surface? Curiosity got the best of Miles Faa, and he chose the stairs. Plodding up and up, round and round, he couldn't help but feel trapped in some hideous M.C. Escher painting. Was it possible he was descending? Like when you're caught in a strong wave or current, and think you're swimming up for air, but you're actually swimming down to your doom. Was that happening?

No.

The spiral staircase ended. Just stopped. It seemed as though the staircase ascended to nowhere. But then Miles caught sight of it: a small hole, at shoulder height, completely black. Fitting into the space took an act of desperation, for it clearly wasn't made for the proportions of a full grown adult.

Claustrophobics beware: the space Miles smuggled himself into was akin to pushing through a birth canal. The sides of the hole smashed and compacted as Miles wiggled through. The walls were caving in.

In complete dark, Miles Faa pushed on, searching for a revelation in the pitch black.

As for Lex, she followed the purple stone road that broke off from the blue trail Jenn chose.

Lex's methodology was simpler than the others. Go straight. Never turn. But she did turn. Life changes, throws us for a loop. Lex was thinking about the infernal options the Numbered Man had given them, when she heard it.

A loud voice, speaking in... some language.

Although Lex was only fluent in a few languages, she'd taken several courses in linguistics, and felt confident she could identify almost any language group on Earth, save for some African, Amazonian, maybe Polynesian tongues... and apparently Pacific-islander languages, as she had no idea what sort of language she was hearing.

It was blurting out loud and bark-y, like that of a teacher or disciplinarian parent. The sounds weren't getting closer, so Lex stood still listening, trying to place the new intel. She couldn't. Though the noises astonished Lex, there was no momentary danger, so she slowly, carefully, followed the sounds.

Lex described the smattering of language to herself as a kind of rhythmic chortling. And, as if to confirm Lex's earlier suspicions, there were various responses to the leading voice. What a wonder this all was. Since falling down the hole at the center of the island, Lex had felt she'd lost her personal verve. She was a freakin' cryptozoologist, for Pete's sake! She'd already seen two new, extremely distinct species of animals since landing here. How many of her colleagues would die, would straight up murder for the chance to see and hear and touch the things she's encountered here? Probably all of them.

First the fanny-pack sporting hedgeys—which appeared to

be remarkably intelligent! We're talking an intelligence on the level of Sasquatch!

And then there was the completely mystifying beaked-thing. It was funny, Lex had to actively focus on the memory of that thing to picture it. As bizarre as it was, and apparently as healing as it was, the image of it didn't stick very well in her mind. She wondered if there wasn't some evolutionary element to that. Maybe all cryptids have that ability. Maybe the beaked-thing produces some fashion of pheromone that causes memories of it to be hazy. A forgetful haziness. Maybe if Lex wasn't a cryptozoologist, a specialist of the weird, she would have been taken in by the pheromone and totally forgotten the beaked-one in full by now.

Maybe.

And now, there was this classroom of chortlers.

Lex walked closer and closer, the chortling getting clearer with every step.

Wait.

It's not some new tongue, not some foreign, backward people's language. The chortling was in English, just barely recognizable.

The stone colors went from purple to a smooth, crisp, white as Lex neared the room of sounds.

So close now. She was maybe ten feet away from the chamber of secrets and sounds when Lex decided to get down on hands and knees and crawl the rest of the way. She was going to see this thing through. The cryptozoologist mindset in her was finally snapping into place and it felt so good. After months on the *Orion* playing nice with others, Alexandra Keitel was finally in her comfort zone, and she was going to, at the very least, capture with her own eyes what these native chortlers were up to.

Jennifer Dash found steps. Not a ladder. Not a spiral staircase, but steps carved out of the ground leading straight down. She counted the steps as she descended: *1, 2, 3, 4, 5, 6, 19, 29, 39, 45, 67, 78, 89, 100, 130, 150, 200, 299, 300, 400, 490, 500, 600....*

When Jenn first came to the steps, following the baby blue

stones that looked so very, very pretty, there were walls on either side of her. As Jenn descended, however, the walls stretched away from her. They crept so far out of reach, in fact, that Jenn now felt that she was descending into a great cavern of hell, with the only options being up, down, or falling into utter darkness.

780, 890, 950, 960, 970, 980, 990, 995, 996, 997, 998, 999, 1000.

On the 1,000th step, Jenn reached the base. A pile of white glowing stones gleamed up at her. They were, Jenn realized, smooth and laying free from the Earth around them. This didn't happen organically. Besides this pile of stones, the base of the steps led unto a pitch-black realm of unknown proportions. What to do now was obvious; Jenn picked up a glowing white stone, and walked around.

Jenn couldn't quite handle how bright her stone was. It wasn't just bright like the stones in the rest of the subterranean universe. No. This stone shone like the day, like the tip of Gandalf's staff. Jenn found herself unable to stare directly at the rock.

Jenn stood at the base of a magnificent cavern, the ceiling looking to be a hundred feet up, at least. Around her jutted stalactites and stalagmites. Unlike the tunnels above, this place seemed more natural, untouched by mankind's hands. Jenn walked about, unsure of where to go, as there was no path, per se, no flight of stairs paving the way onward. So Jenn doodled about, hemming and hawing at the dribbly stalactites and mites, suppressing all fears that there were goblins or gadflies down here in the deep. She'd come so far, Jenn wondered if this was the deepest cave on Earth, the center-most point anyone had ever naturally traveled.

A flash of light.

Movement.

Something caught her eye. Jenn cowered in worry that it was someone or something down here with her, but a quick scoping of her surroundings, white stone far outstretched, revealed the truth at hand.

She'd found an enormous cave painting, a great mural to the unknown viewer, at least twenty-five feet tall, maybe double that in width.

The image was likely painted with ground-up glow-rocks. It glowed, but not brightly; it almost hummed, its visage and likeness so mysterious.

It depicted a grim portrait, the perfect facade for a perverse Sistine chapel.

There they were, dozens of children, skipping along a path. All the children were of the same general age, maybe six or seven, but some were fat kids, round kids, black kids, white kids, brown kids, Asian and African, and European kids. Not only were the children from all tribes and tongues, but from left to right they appeared to be from all time periods. The kids at the far left wore animal skins, heavy ridges above their brows. The kids in the middle wore togas and then bright medieval uniforms. The kids in the front of the line, at the far right, they wore t-shirts and blue jeans and held cell phones in their hands. One kid stared at a tablet in his hands as he marched. All of them, the children of every age, the offspring of every loving parent, they all frolicked and followed the man in red.

The Pied Piper.

Lex stuck her head through the chamber entrance. She was now lying down, as near to the ground as possible. She was certain now she was listening to a classroom. She could hear distinctly now the fidgets of bored and anguished listeners, as well as the chortling commander-teacher's chalk scribbling against a wall.

Be brave.

Lex snuck her first and only look at the classroom. Six rows with five desks in each row. Every seat occupied. A teacher lecturing at the front of the class. This was a classic schoolroom; only the room was filled with ghouls. Mercifully for Lex's eyes, the first two rows facing the teacher were filled up with the hedgehog-y creatures. They sat upright in their small seats, but they looked very uncomfortably folded in. They held pencils in their paws and made marks on paper, just like regular students. Ahead of them, their teacher was made of something else entirely.

It stood awkwardly at four feet tall, its back badly hunched

161

over. It looked to be fighting the very natural urge to stand on four feet instead of two. Lex thought it to be some cruel mixture of donkey and werewolf. It chortled and chortled and chortled on.

Behind the hedgeys were all sorts of unidentifiable creatures. Lex could confidently say that these were not alien beings. They all had humanoid, or at least Earth-like parts. No little green men. They were genetic mutations, genetic freaks. Someone went crazy with their Mommy and Daddy's genetic conveyor belt.

Trying to piece the memory together in later days, Lex would associate the classroom with the movie *The Fly*, wherein a man gets mutated with a fly. All the bastard creatures in the room looked like sad exploits of a Nazi experiment gone horribly awry. She saw a horse with no legs and no eyes. A walrus with a human-esque mouth and tongue. Several rows of fish-like dogs. Or dog-like fish.

In the back row, at the far corner, Lex recognized the bird-frog-woman. She sat, her fat rolling over the desk, motionless. Lex questioned if there was any brain inside the repugnant drooler.

Four sentences were written not on a chalkboard, but seemingly, on the walls of the chamber itself. The four sentences gave Lex as many bad dreams in the coming days as any of the schooled monstrosities.

It read:

Numbers are our freedom.
When we sin we dishonor our number forever.
Sin takes away our freedom.
Too much sin takes away our number.

Lex had enough. As silently as possible, she rose to her feet, and hurried to her chamber. She was the first to return, and so had time to sit and think on what she'd just seen.

Most disturbing was not the Pied Piper showing his face in this dark place in the bowels of the Earth. No. It was what was painted above him. Looking down upon the Piper and his legions was a floating, giant ghost, spanning almost the entirety of the sky above the scene. The shape of it was not

162

dissimilar to that of the ghosts from the old Pac-Man games. The ghostly form looked like a gelatinous dress with a face.

And the face of the ghost smiled down upon the Pied Piper.

Jenn understood intuitively; it was God, and he was happy with the work of his son. The artist envisioned a god that delights in the accomplishments of the Pied Piper, and his song of many sirens.

Jenn had enough. She abruptly made an about face, poised to begin the long 1,000-step climb back to her chamber and her friends. But behind the stairs, hidden in the shadow of its ascension, there was another set of steps, descending yet further. These steps were much narrower, smaller, descending 180 degrees in the opposite direction of the larger steps.

These steps oozed with ominous fervor.

Jenn had gone this far... she might as well march to the very heart of the Earth.

And so she descended onward.

Miles suppressed fear as he wedged himself onward through the dark. He didn't know why, but he felt important in that moment. Maybe it was that he felt like an old-timey explorer, unsure of what lay ahead in the same way that Magellan and his crew must have felt chills of excitement conquering the unknown high seas.

Pause. There was a sound. Faint, very faint. Miles didn't hear it at first because he was too busy scooting along, scratching the walls and making all manner of noises. But now, as he lay sandwiched in that small pipeline, he heard...

Water. Running water.

Miles pushed himself through the darkness with double the fervor. If there was running water, there was a way out, right?

Follow the water!

The noise got louder and louder. This was a sizable amount of running water! A venerable river wild.

The ashy ground below Miles turned wet. A few more feet inching along and Miles began to sink in ashy mud.

Panic.

Miles couldn't turn around. That was impossible. The

dimensions of his little crawl space barely allowed for wriggling, let alone a full turn-around.

Two options presented themselves: go forward, praying that the space opens up before the mud deepens and turns into a shrewdly constructed coffin; or, option two, smash backwards little by little.

The obvious answer was to wriggle in reverse. It would be frustrating, painful, and slow going, but Miles Faa was confident he could survive this night and utter blackness if he dedicated himself to backing up. It might take an hour or more, but it could be done. Miles could live to see the sun yet.

But the hope of what lay ahead embodied the hope of freedom. *Escape from witch mountain!*

Miles Faa pushed on.

He wedged his elbows below his stomach to create a wedge between the mud and his mouth and nose.

He had to keep his face as high as possible.

Above. *Stay above.*

He squirmed on.

The mud sank him deeper.

He was confined now, trapped in the pitch black up to his chin in mud.

Jenn tipped-down and down. She tried to count the steps as she did on the first flight, to keep her mind occupied on an objective, if nothing else. But the surmounting fear and memory of that celestial ghost smiling down on Piper blasted through the corridors of Jenn's mind. She couldn't keep track of the numbers, and by 27 was already utterly off course.

There was moaning. Far below yet.

A deep, cosmic groan.

No reason to go on.

Jenn couldn't see anything, but the groan, the monstrous echo solidified the fact that Jennifer Dash was not alone in this deep dungeon.

Is it getting louder?
Is it coming for me?
Does it hear me?
Run.

Jenn sprinted up the skinny stairs, back to the open cavern of Piper and God. She didn't give the portrait even a faint moment of glance. *Just keep going. Don't look back.*

Jenn catapulted herself up the 1,000 steps. Back. Back to friends as quickly as possible. Back to humans. Away from the deep moaning.

Rushing back into the chamber, Jenn embraced Lex. The two hugged and coughed out sobs of relief. Until this moment, each woman had harbored doubts that this perverse underworld had eaten the others. What a relief this was. Feel. Touch. There are still other humans in this world.

After collecting themselves, the two ladies waited in silence for Miles Faa to return.

An hour later, the once-harbored doubts returned.

Two hours later, and Jennifer Dash chose to retreat into the dream world, wherein there was always peace. The god of Jenn's dreams didn't care for riches or gems, and he didn't smile upon the great deceivers of the world. Her god didn't love the Pied Piper's fife.

The women woke up to a wild-eyed, muddy from head-to-toe Miles Faa.

They embraced him and said prayers of thankfulness for the return of their own.

Just like that, all of Jenn's anger at Miles sifted away. Here was a man that was just as desperate as she was, just as hopeful for a better future, just as stretched as she was. He was just like her. He made quick and sometimes disastrous decisions, but that's what people have to do who don't hold all the cards. They improvise. They make the best of what they've got left.

Miles motioned for the women to follow him. He led them, not to the spiral staircase, not to birth canal that led to muddy water, but to another chamber, just like their own.

"Maybe he's listening here too, but at least it's something."

"What happened to you?" Jenn asked.

"What happened to you!" Miles responded.

The three swapped stories and visions. Each took as long as possible in their retelling of their solo journeys, trying hopelessly to avoid the inevitable. They remembered and remarked on every detail, every jot and tittle. Maybe they could talk their troubles away.

But it wasn't to be.

Eventually, all the stories dried up... and there was no more to tell.

Now it was time to make a decision.

Now it was time to face the Numbered Man, and choose one of his wretched options.

~~~

Jenn and company have now seen the ghouls of Pishtaco's island. There's no camouflaging what's going on. Jenn's seen with her own eyes the connection between this dark place, and her dark follower, the Pied Piper.

Wherever there's the Piper, there's trouble. Jenn has set her heart against him, and against his schemes.

Soon, Jenn and Lex and Miles will fix their destiny.

The Numbered Man's true aspirations will be revealed.

Chapter 32: True Mythology

J.P. Kourage, a doctor of social studies from the University of Denver, sent this editorial to every major newspaper published in English. The essay was written in response to a popular movement, and in greater particularity, a paper published by the psychiatrist and politician, Dr. Braylen Cooling. Through the sands of time, the contents of that editorial are shared here:

Insofar as Dr. Cooling has used eloquence and sophistic language to woo sheep to his peculiar fountain of faith, I write to you today to combat his rhetoric with the strongest words I know how to leverage. I intend to confront Dr. Cooling's conclusions by rebutting, in order, the three arguments he so craftily dictated. I fully intend to publish a greater work in the coming months for peer review. Because of the medium by which I intend to reach you, I am forced to be brief and appeal to emotion, that is, appeal to your emotion.

As I understand them, a summary of Dr. Coolings three points may be read as:

1. Charles (C.C.) Clovis' life experience led him to his work

2. Gene extraction and imputation was C.C.'s invention, but fated by evolution

3. His Number theory was a great societal construct and should be experimented and implemented

Dr. Cooling argues that Charles Clovis, the eccentric scientist known to history as The Numbered Man, or, as he was continually referred to until his internment on that god-forsaken island, C.C., had little option but to do the incredible things he did. He argues that C.C.'s harsh childhood left the boy feeling a deep sense of loneliness and an unquenchable desire to construct for himself deep relationships that would, for him, fill the trench where paternal and maternal love and fondness should have been. Dr. Cooling even goes so far as to say that C.C.'s (I refuse to refer to him by his devilish self-

assigned numeric name) whole life was a search for a "divine hug". This language most assuredly displays Dr. Cooling's intentions. He is not writing a thesis to be scrutinized for truth; rather, in the like manner of the Pythagoreans, he is meddling into Spiritual terminology in hope that his transcendent (rubbish) dialogue would seduce the reader. Sadly, this seduction has indeed taken root. This is, of course, why I have taken cause to write you today.

Here are the facts that we know: Charles Clovis (C.C.) was the only son of Mormon missionaries Henry and Tilda Clovis. Charles was born in a Salt Lake City hospital, but being that the Clovis family moved to the inner desert jungles of Peru when C.C. was just ten months old, it is unlikely that C.C. has any memory of living with his parents in the United States. Yes, journal evidence from Henry Clovis undoubtedly paints a portrait of a Father consumed with his work and not his wife or son. This, it must be said, may or may not explain why Tilda would never again get pregnant. We have no medical records. It may well be that Tilda or Henry had medical complications that would make bearing a second child particular difficult or unfeasible. We just don't know. The dastardly rumors that Tilda was a virgin when she conceived C.C. have no validity whatsoever. I will remind the reader, that from the over four-hundred hours of audio tapes we have of C.C. recording himself, a self-diagnosed ego-maniac, he never once stated or even implied that he came from "unsoiled loins". Never once. Surely that would have been a point of profound boasting for such a man. But it is simply not there, and therefore, we may correctly assume the logical: Charles Clovis was born by traditional means.

Dr. Cooling likens C.C. to an orphan. Having myself been orphaned at age four, early enough to say with confidence that I never knew my parents, I find this comparison detestable. The so-called divine hug that C.C. was searching for was not a mystery that C.C. was solving "for the sake of humanity." Whatever void he felt, whatever sorrow he carried, there was nothing in it that had (or has) universal relevance. Dr. Cooling has ascribed Messianic motives to C.C., but he cannot point to any historical incident in C.C.'s history that would attest to this.

168

*What Dr. Cooling does quickly leap to is the fable that C.C.
read from* The Croatoan. *The cult of our generation is to mold
all the events of the 21st century into one narrative. We know
that Lillith Babbit believed she found the book called* The
Croatoan, *and that she commissioned the exploration that ran
amok onto C.C.'s island. That's the end of our knowledge. The
video reports of her so-called usage of the book are
unsubstantiated. There are a million reasons to doubt the
validity of the YouTube movie, but that is not the reason I write
you today. The point is simple: the book, if it was ever a real
manuscript, is lost to history, and we know of no intersection
between that book, its contents, and Charles Clovis getting his
dirty hands on its pages.*

*I am in the remarkable position of being one of only a
handful of people alive on this Earth who has interviewed
Alexandra Keitel. Here pasted are the direct questions I asked
her in my interview many, many years ago, as well as Ms.
Keitel's responses:*

Q: To your knowledge, did the Numbered Man ever read
The Croatoan?

*A: The first I heard of that book was from Lillith, after we
reunited in Peru.*

*Q: There's a theory circulating that the Numbered Man
based his genetic techniques off of secret knowledge found in
part one of* The Croatoan, *while your employer, Lillith Babbit,
used information found in part two. Can you confirm or deny
those rumors?*

*A: I never read the book. Not a single page. Lillith wasn't
exactly sharing its contents with the rest of us. If you want an
answer, Jenn would be the only person I know of who could
provide it.*

Q: Do you know where Ms. Dash is?

A: No.

Q: Do you believe she is alive?

A: I don't know.

Q: She hasn't reached out to you?

*A: As far as I know, she died in the glass house as
everyone supposes.*

There is scant evidence that C.C.'s life experience destined him to do the outrageous things he did. There is absolutely no evidence, none, that C.C.'s life prepared or destined him to be the agent of history that he has become.

Dr. Cooling's 2nd point is remarkably stupid. In the space of one breath he invites you to believe contradictory claims. On the one hand, he wants you to buy into a belief that C.C. was a titan of science, that his experiments were a magnificent leap in scientific knowledge. He wishes you to remember C.C. as a kin of Sir Isaac Newton and Albert Einstein. Simultaneously, he calls you to remember that C.C. was only an instrument of evolution. This repugnant claim is wholly soulless, as it treats death, disease, and tortuously-slow demise as something that some mystical evolutionary agent is wonderfully procuring out of nature through the expanse of time.

Do you really wish to believe that C.C. was directed by a secret will of evolution? That his paths were marked by evolutionary destiny? This is a perilous assumption to follow. Furthermore, I wish to remind you that C.C. was not standing light years ahead of his scientific contemporaries. Have you forgotten Banfield, Doudna, Feng Zhang, and legions more microbiologists and scientists that were doing EXACTLY what C.C. did? These contemporaries all did their genetic mods more than a decade before C.C.'s island of Dr. Moreau! The difference is that they knew the dangers at hand. That's why they only experimented at a viral and bacterial level. These prudent innovators, the true geniuses of the 21st century, performed their experiments with ethical sensibilities. They worked on amoebas long before contemplating such a heinous ruin as to experiment on large mammals and men!

C.C.'s scientific prowess has long been pondered over. Read Pritesh Zarathura's book The Awful Prize of Life Alteration if you desire the gritty details of C.C'.s scientific manifestations. Another worthy read is Leslie Pandarlocks' exhaustive work Genetic Cut-and-Paste in the 1st Half of the 21st Century.

Finally, Dr. Cooling, and far too many of you, accept C.C.'s *harebrained societal theory as gospel. These numbered patches and tattoos, how fruitless are your efforts!*

Do you not realize that numbers would be bought and sold, that there would still be a social hierarchy? Only with regimented numbers, there'd be no social mobility! It's a caste system, people!

Don't fall for the lies! And when Dr. Cooling asks for your vote come November, you cannot vote for a man who's white-washing history, a man who says the vilest person on the planet should be sainted. He calls C.C. our antecedent, our forefather. NO!

This cannot be the way!

Vote Mira Yin for W. Secretary!

"I'll do it. I'll marry him," said Jennifer Dash to Miles Faa and Alexandra Keitel.

"No, Jenn. I will. You've been through enough. Plus, I'd get the chance to examine all the cryptids I could ever hope to encounter! This place was made for me," Lex argued.

Lex was selling too hard and Jenn saw right through the veil. The Numbered Man made Lex's skin crawl. There was no way Lex had such a change of heart. Only hours ago Lex was refusing to wear the bikini the Numbered Man had delivered. No, the classroom of beasts had not changed Lex. There was no way.

Jenn, on the other hand, actually, truly, accepted the arrangement. Or so she told herself.

Her logic progressed simply enough. Options two and three were unacceptable. Jenn didn't want to be experimented on. She didn't want to turn into one of those chortling beasts Lex had described. Dying a martyr's death would be a better end. But the Numbered Man promised that death would come slowly—torture. Jenn had already experienced the excruciating agony of a severed hand. The thought of going through any brand of physical pain like that again was just about unbearable. No, come hell or high water, that was not okay. Jenn had heard those moans from the deep and had no desire to become intimate with the cause of such guttural utterings.

So then, the only thing left was option one. Once upon a time, Jenn might have hoped for Miles to save them with some sort of mental gymnastic, some option #4. But no longer. Not after weeks of living in the hole. Jenn Dash saw the end of Miles Faa's wisdom, and that end was a machete. A sharp point was the best he could do.

By default then, marriage was the only choice to make. Sure, letting someone else marry the King of the Island would make things easy, but Jenn knew the cost was too high. Lex was untarnished. Lex was whole, still herself. To let Lex marry the Numbered Man meant letting this island misfigure, misshape both Jenn and Lex. One mangled girl was enough. Jenn was already a used substance. Let her go to him.

Let Lex be free, let Lex live long, live for herself. Jenn's life, as she knew it, was already over. *Did it ever really start?* She wouldn't have to worry about solving the world anymore, she could just take care of this little perverted underworld. Better a queen of the damned than no queen at all... *right?*

"Look at me, Lex. I'm broken here. I've got nothing to fight for, no one to come home to. This makes the most sense. Let me do this. For you. For both of you." Jenn looked to Miles for affirmation. Convincing Lex to give up her spot on the good ship wedded bliss was not going to be a problem. But Jenn wasn't so sure Miles would so easily succumb.

"Wait wait!" Lex blurted out. "There's got to be another way! There has to be!"

"There is no other way," Miles said calmly.

"Yes! There is!" Lex's voice was tipping on the verge of crazy. "We can... we can fight! We take the illuminated stones, sharpen them, use them as weapons. Whoever comes through our hole, we stab! It's easy! Eventually, he'll have to let us go."

"Even supposing you're right, that we can fend off intruders, we still die. We still starve down here."

"We eat the bodies! The hedgeys! Just like Merkyl said we should!"

"And when there's no more left?" Miles slowly answered, the calm grand inquisitor.

"We'll have more time. Time to search out every nook and

cranny of this place! We'll find a way out!"

"There are too many ways we lose."

"How? How do we lose?"

"If at any point we're caught, we'll be fully at his mercy. Now is the only time we have to make a real choice, a real decision. After we choose, everything's set. There won't be a chance to redeem ourselves."

"At least we'd go down swinging! Do not go gentle into that good night! RAGE! Rage against the dying of the light!"

"Shut up!" Suddenly aggressive, Miles struck Lex. The pummel blew the sleek Lex down instantaneously.

As if watching the scene play out on daytime television, Jenn asked oddly, "Why did you do that?"

Before Miles answered, Lex bounded up, spat in the man's face, and thrashed at him. She grabbed his shirt and yanked. He didn't resist. Lex wept bitterly and hit him in the chest repeatedly. Then she stopped.

"Are you done?" Miles said condescendingly.

Lex was done. And Miles hit her again. Just as hard.

Jenn, finally moved with compassion, got up to do something. To do what, she didn't know, but this moment was playing out unpredictably and dangerously.

Miles, seething with anger, pointed at Jenn, "YOU SIT DOWN."

Jenn sat.

Then Miles clenched his fist, bracing to hit Jenn in the face. But he flinched, turned his attention to Lex, and hit her once more.

"What are you doing?!" Jenn cried out, completely aghast at the scene.

"You would both prostitute yourselves to that beast! NO! You will not do that! You whores!"

A silence fell and remained there in that hole many agonizing moments. Jenn sat there, reflecting and crying silently. Miles, Miles, Miles, what had become of you? Why did Jenn only see evil all her days? Where was goodness? Where was kindness? Why was the world full up with suffering? Even faced with an impossibly harsh decision, the world dipped itself yet deeper in the bath of pain and cruelty. Why? Why

173

was everything, every little aspect of life so dark? Where was the sun? Where was mercy?

Jenn knew where these things were. She had left them. Back in the Pelican State. The Further house, that was the one ray of sunshine.

Why had Jenn ever left?

"There is a 4th option. It comes to me now as I stare at you pigs." Miles breathed slowly. There was something in his delivery... something... staged. "You kill yourselves."

"What?" Lex mumbled, still holding her bruised face in her hands, her swollen eyes peering up between her fingers at her betrayer.

"Go. Silently walk to the spa. Drown yourselves like a good boy and girl."

Why had Miles just said that? In that way?

"We're not doing that," Lex said defiantly.

Miles sneered at Lex, then got up and momentarily left the chamber. He returned with an illuminated rock in his hands. He held it up violently, "What did you say?"

"Are you going to hit me with that?" Lex said, her point firm, but her words coming out more cowardly than she wished.

"This is your decision. You do it, or I do."

"And what about you?" Jenn asked.

"I will be his. He'll carve me up and make me some monster, but I'll be his."

"You already are," Lex stammered.

"Why can't we go with you?" Jenn said. "Why can't we all choose Option #2?"

"Because you already showed your cards. You told me your heart. We'd get there and you'd throw yourself at his feet. You'd marry the freak. He loves you too much to let that happen."

A pause.

"Walk silently. Don't say a word. Miles remembers the way," said Mr. Faa. "Go. And drown yourselves in the spa. Be careful to say nothing. That's the only way you two can be together forever."

It was a plan. Why else would Miles tell them to go quietly? It was a plan. He was going to work something out! They'd

174

go, Jenn and Lex, and before they died under that water, Miles would solve the equation, figure something out—set them free. That was the only logical explanation for this insane behavior.

"Come on, let's go," Jenn said and outstretched her hand to grab Lex's. Amazingly, Lex took hers, and the two women left the chamber.

Jenn wanted to lead, to be strong and decisive, but she really had no idea in what direction the spa lay. Lex knew and wordlessly led Jenn towards their supposed doom.

As Jenn walked to her own personal gallows, she couldn't help but think of dark things. She wanted to dwell on Atticus and little Scout, and even the kind train conductor Mr. Further.

She couldn't.

First, her mind drifted to Antonio D'Anconia. The illuminated rocks lighting the way to her death reminded her of the veiled new attraction at Magical Kingdom that Antonio had snuck her into. She remembered the peace of drifting into space followed by the shock and fear of being touched. D'Anconia was a devil in a knight's shining armor, just as these beautiful stones paved the way to final darkness.

Then Jenn thought of Thomas Flusher O'Malley and Tiff. Flusher left this world not unlike Jenn was about to. He was caught between rival gangs, rival ideas, rival men, and whatever choice he wound up making was going to end in his death. He simply wasn't smart enough to survive. Tiff, however, thought she was smart enough, thought she was cunning. Jenn ended her. Jenn the murderer. Smarts don't get you anywhere if you're not strong enough. Might makes right. That's what kept Jenn alive until now.

To survive in this world you have to be the smartest and the strongest. Jenn was neither. That's why she walked silently to the underground spa. That's why she lost. But maybe... just maybe... Miles Faa was the strongest, maybe he was the smartest.

They arrived at the precipice.

Jenn went first. Fully clothed, she marched down the ladder with little hesitation and no fanfare.

The water was warm. Really warm. It hurt. Jenn's stump

burned brighter and fiercer than the rest of her body, and she was reminded of her so recent loss.

She waded over and pulled a string releasing ice down upon the water. She then made her way to another string, and another, and another. Meanwhile, Lex stepped down the ladder. She was moving slower than Jenn. More deliberately.

There were no more strings to pull, and Lex was fully immersed.

Jenn couldn't bear it. She smiled at her friend and said aloud, "Ready?"

Lex waded over to Jenn, smiled, but put a finger to Jenn's mouth. They weren't to speak.

Suddenly, fear set in. Was this really it? Did Miles and Lex really expect her to drown herself? Right here, right now!

No way! *This can't be happening!*

Jenn thrashed, and like a drowning elephant, flopped towards the ladder. She had to escape, she had to flee!

Then... underwater.

Lex had grabbed her, pushed her under.

Jenn clawed up at Lex's face.

LEX IS KILLING ME LEX IS KILLING ME!

No.

Lex pulled her up, held her up with her arms around her.

Just then, the speakers rattled.

"Why hello, you two! Going for a little swim! I do thank you so much for letting Lex come to me. Did you know she's the one I wanted? Of course, I would have accepted Jenn as my bride, but gosh, who wants to marry a one-hand-Jill? And Alexandra Keitel is going to look so beautiful in her dress! I've got the others preparing one for her now...."

Miles had tricked him.

Somehow.

The Numbered Man thought Lex was there with him... Miles must have pretended....

"She told me that perhaps your little bath in the spa wasn't as innocent as you want me to believvvvvvvvvveee. Why is that? Why would you take your life? Lex tells me you don't trust me! You think I'm going to experiment on you? That I won't let you leave? Well take care, look up! Those ones you call hedgeys will lead you to a boat. That boat sits on a little riverbed. Untie the boat and it'll spit you out at the base of my island.

"That's it. You are free. Sorry for not seeing you out, but I have a date with my new number. Please pray for us to have a long, long, long happy marriage."

Jenn and Lex got out of the spa and followed the hedgeys. They walked for quite awhile, until they came upon a river carved in the underground. And strapped to the side of the river, a small motor boat. A hedgey hopped aboard, roared up the engine, and hopped out. The two women got in the boat as the hedgey untied their rope.

Jenn and Lex floated down the dark river.

Jenn, nearly delirious from the turn of events, couldn't believe this was real, that escape from the awful mountain in the sea was upon them.

There, in the distance, a speck of light... growing. Not a stone. The sun! The sun was there, just ahead.

The speakers! They rattled and came on once more.

"Oh! One last thing! Number 500 is my biggest creation. She's a monster that swims around and protects this island. My own personal leviathan."

The light speck was growing with every syllable. They were almost to it now, almost free.

"If she eats you, remember this, I let you off the island, that was our deal. I didn't say anything about the water around the island. You see, I'm trustworthy...."

The small boat passed the last speaker, and sunshine drenched Jenn and Lex.

Come what may.

Somehow, Jenn had escaped Pishtaco's island.

~~~

Miles has sacrificed himself. He played the villain and conjured up the right feelings and beliefs from all known parties to successfully extract his two friends.

It's time to leave the island.

It's time for hope again.

No more darkness.

The physically trying times are over for Jenn, at least for the time being. Now we must sift through the myths and return back to our most central theme. Jenn must wrestle with her experience and decide, in light of what she knows about this world, in light of just how very dark it can be, who she wants to be, who she chooses to be.

Identity is everything, isn't it?

Chapter 33: Eden

"We made it, Jenn! We're free! Miles got us out! Jennifer Free, you're free! You really are!"

"That's not my name! Don't call me that!"

That moment, which should have brought a rush of relief, did the opposite. As the motor hummed and took the small boat away from the horrible island, Jenn stared at her hand, what used to be her hand. Leaving meant a return to reality, but reality still included a Jennifer with no hand. And if life outside of Pishtaco's island still meant Jenn suffered with a painful stump, then maybe it also included a Leviathan.

But it wouldn't be the Leviathan of that Rabbi, the man who once counseled Jenn to scream in a dream—he wasn't describing a sea monster made by the Numbered Man! No. That couldn't be what Jenn was after all this time. It couldn't be that. It couldn't be. It couldn't be.

Whatever swam in the deep, whatever circled the depths around that numbered hell, that place with more than a 1,000 steps into the abyss, that thing wasn't a guardian. Jenn had striven for so long now to find Leviathan because that meant meeting a creature formed to protect the truest purposes of life. Rabbi Itamar Levi had spoken to Jenn's heart when he depicted three monsters fashioned by God at the beginning of time: Ziz, a flying monster to protect the skies, Behemoth, the great roamer of the fields, and Leviathan, the unsearchable one of myth and majesty.

This Leviathan, if real, would be the oldest living creature on Earth. She would know every secret. If the Earth had keys made to hide its knowledge behind old doors, Leviathan knew those keys, was intimate with them.

But this devastation, this perversity—what if the Leviathan Jenn was destined to find was the one the Numbered Man cocked-up in his wicked mind?

Silently and desperately, Jennifer Dash prayed. She didn't know who to pray to—to God or Zeus or Atticus Further. The only power that Jenn knew was real, the only supernatural event in her life, was the prophecy Rabbi Itamar Levi gave to her when she locked herself in the bathroom, hiding from the terrors of Tiff. The Rabbi saved her once, gave her a key to unlocking a certain future. Maybe he would aid her again.

Rabbi, I know. I know, it feels like all I've ever wanted was to see Leviathan. But don't you forget; you did this to me. You put these thoughts in my head! You got me excited for something I never knew existed. But not now, Rabbi, please, not now, not like this. Save me from seeing her now. I can't bear it. Is there nothing beautiful in the world? Leave this pure, for me. Come on. Please.

Jenn repeated the prayer in her mind over and over, until, at great last, the island was out of sight.

I made sure there would be no Leviathan that day.

There wasn't much to do in the boat. Neither lady had much appetite for conversation. There wasn't much point in debating which way to steer the raft. East was the only option. If the little boat had enough gas, it could maybe make it to the west coast of Peru. Aside from the motor and two oars, there were two large cylinders of gas. They'd at least be able to make a shot at it. There was however, no food or water. Just happy to be away, neither Jenn nor Lex worried about that specific concern.

Both women did worry about the only other artifact left in the boat: a tape player.

Three hours into the journey, Lex summoned the courage. She pressed play.

"Helllloooooooooooo--"

No more courage.

Lex pressed stop and threw the tape down.

"We should destroy it," Jenn said.

"No. We don't have to listen to it, but it's proof—evidence that what we experienced was real."

It had never occurred to Jenn that people might not believe their story. What's not to believe about an island made up of underground tunnels and mutants led by a mad scientist?

The sun went away. Jenn shivered. Night had fallen.

180

Darkness returned. But it wasn't the same darkness, for the whole host of heaven was on display. The caves had no stars. Darkness without stars is a terrible thing. Jenn stared up at the stars, sighing with a feeling of both relief and regret.

"What do you think he did?" Jenn asked Lex.

"Miles?"

"Yeah, how do you think he pulled the veil over the Numbered Man's eyes?"

"I don't know. He's Miles Faa. He does stuff like that."

"You're really okay not knowing? Lex, Miles punched the crap out of you!"

"I'll take a beating any day of the week if it gets me out of weird, trippy, solitary confinement world."

"Seriously, you have no idea?"

"I don't know. The Numbered Man knew our names, but I don't think he was wiretapping us. I don't think there was any electricity down there at all."

"But the speakers?"

"Classic megaphone—just like playing telephone with cups and strings."

"So how did he know our names?"

"That must have been what Miles knew that we didn't."

Jenn tried to put the pieces of the puzzle together, but they didn't fit. The only thing that kept circling around in her brain was what Miles said.

"Walk silently. Don't say a word. Miles remembers the way," said Mr. Faa. "Go. And drown yourselves in the spa. Be careful to say nothing. That's the only way you two can be together forever."

Why did he speak in third person? Miles didn't go with them to the spa, so what did it matter that he remembered the way?

"Should we go back for him?" Jenn said meekly.

"And do what?" Lex answered, "We're no help until we first help ourselves."

Later in the night.

"Lex, is your mother really a selkie?"

"I'd like to think so. I'd like to think she didn't just abandon me for no reason. I'd like to believe that although men create horrible things like that classroom, there are things at the other end of the spectrum. If there are things this gross, then shouldn't there also be things on the other side, pure things, good things, extraordinary things?"

Around dawn, Lex eyed a spot on the horizon. They motored towards it and within an hour, it was apparent what it was.

Another island.

Jenn's stomach churned. They had to go. They needed to be brave. The island might be small. There might be no one on it, in which case they could hunt for coconuts or fruit, or scavenge for anything that might help them live longer. Or, the island is bigger than they expect and there's actual help there. Or! It's just another lair, another hole with another Pishtaco.

Even from afar, it was clear this island was different. It was lush. Green. So green.

Unlike Pishtaco's island, this one looked exactly like every remote tropical island paradise where every John Q. Cast Away got lost.

Except, as they neared land, there were people waiting. Dozens, hands up, staring at them from the shoreline. The sun was bouncing off those people harshly... they were so bright... and white.

A little closer now.

They weren't people.

They were statues. Lex and Jenn glanced at each other, each entranced with something between fascination and fear.

"Hola, hola!" A little girl's voice bounded out towards the small boat. For the quickest of moments, Jenn entertained the fear that it was the statues themselves that were calling out to them. They'd seen so many unexplained phenomena, why not talking stones? Hell, a friggin' griffin had snatched Jenn's hand. A griffin, for Pete's sake!

But no, the statues were not singing out to the sea-bound nomads.

It was a little girl. The girl's dress was primitive, sporting a reed-based skirt. But it looked clean, and the girl appeared well fed and happy.

The statues too, they were happy. Every fifteen feet or so in either direction on the sandy shoreline, statues of men, women and children stood cheering the newcomers. They were welcoming statues!

As they set foot on dry ground, the little girl grabbed Lex's hand and at once the two were speaking.

Jenn couldn't pick up on it, it was all in Spanish, but the girl and Lex were smiling and laughing as they spoke. The girl led Lex past the jungle line of the island. Lex smiled back at Jenn and motioned for her to follow.

She did.

What follows was a miracle.

Swiss Family Robinson was Jenn's favorite film. Riding ostriches around always seemed fun, but it was the architecture of island life that caught Jenn's imagination. And that, friends, is exactly what Jenn found on this new island: Pulleys and suspension bridges, tree houses and conveyor belts, a mansion on a forgotten island. More than just that, you could just feel the love. It was palpable. Love overflowing from the footbridges and cabinets carved into trees. The nooks and crannies shouted out, "We belong to a loving world, a careful world."

The little girl led Lex (and by proxy, Jenn) to a little amphitheater that seemed to be at the center of the architectural community.

"Mama, Papa, Hermano, Hermanas!" The little girl squealed out with joy.

Doors opened. Doors high above Jenn. Doors that the sun smiled down on. Homes built under the sun's loving care.

A few minutes later and Jenn and Lex were being welcomed (read: kissed on the lips) by the inhabitants of the island. A quick count revealed 3 little kids (including the girl whom they first met and her two sisters), an older girl, maybe 13, and a boy, probably 15. Then came someone who Jenn supposed was the mother of the kids, a beautiful woman, a breathtakingly stunning lady, perfectly formed and glistening in the sunlight. Last came an elderly man Jenn suspected was the woman's father.

They spoke in the round, with various introductions coming fast and heavy. When Lex could get a word in, she tried translating for Jenn, but when the food came, a coconut mush on top of lettuce salad, the two sailors munched and listened.

It was kind of comforting for Jenn to not understand what this family was saying. The unfolding situation allowed her to relax, to breathe in the luxury of the moment. And to top it off there was so much smiling. Oh, how good to see smiles, to hear laughter, and to work the muscles in her face as she beamed back at the Peruvian Family Robinsons.

A few moments later, the old man spoke to Jenn directly, in English, grinning.

"Hello, Jennifer."

"Hi. Thank you for your kindness."

"In this place, in our home, it is easy to be kind. Would you take a walk with me? I have something I'd like to share with you."

Jaded by the recent events of her life, a hesitation welled up inside of Jennifer Dash. What did this old man want from her? Why did he want to "share something" with her? What sort of demonry was he concealing?

"It is okay. Your friend will be at ease in the company of the rest. She will be more relaxed not having to translate for you. Come, I will speak to you in your language."

Lex laughed glancing over at Jenn. She was at the center, both physically and conversationally, of the family.

These were joyous people, people who needed nothing. Not urchins. Not vampires that suck the life out of you for their own amusement. If it was a trap, then it was a better one then the Numbered Man had ever dreamt up. If there was any romance left in Jenn, any hope that the world could be made right, or better yet, was right in certain places, she needed to trust this old pater familias.

She took his hand, and let him lead her.

As he slowly led her through the dense jungle, Jenn chuckled to herself. Before she set out to solve the world, Jenn had never kissed anyone on the lips in her whole life. That's what made the seduction by D'Anconia so painful—it was her first. Since then, she'd been kissed by Robles. Though it was passionate, Jenn instinctively knew then, and clearer still in retrospect, that Robles' kiss was a goodbye serenade to the world. Jenn was merely a placeholder for the world. She could have been any woman. Jorje Robles had a never ending romantic Don Quixotic view of the world, and knowing he was about to climb aboard his own doom, he had to embrace romance one last time. He'd have kissed Lizard if she was the one jammed in that stall with him. But now, now!—here on this isolated island, Jenn had just been smooched on the mouth by, count them, 7 people. It was nice. These islanders were kinesthetic welcomers. Their love was dissipating the perverse memories of Antonio D'Anconia.

The old man took Jenn to a wood-and-string ladder hanging against a vertical cliff. It was a flimsy thing, flopping around like those ladders thrown off the sides of helicopters. Still, the old man had a dexterous touch, and ascended with relative ease.

Jenn followed, three or four notches below him. It was hard work climbing a loose ladder with only one hand. Jenn quickly learned to use her mouth as a stabling device whilst ascending.

She counted the rungs as she climbed.

One.

Two.

Three.

Four.

Five.

Six.

Seven.

Eight.

Nine.

Ten.

Eleven.

Twelve.

Thirteen.

Fourteen...

Twenty-one...

Thirty-one...

Forty-one...

Forty-five...

Fifty-three...

Sixty-six...

185

Seventy-seven...

Eighty-eight...

Ninety-nine.

One hundred. Exactly. One hundred rungs. The old man helped Jenn onto the top of the cliff. The height made one nauseous. Don't look down. The mount was skinny, and didn't allow for more than two people to sit.

"We call this the philosopher's stone."

"Why?" Jenn asked.

"Because we only come all this way up to think on life, or to see who's coming... to see what the future brings."

"Oh." Jenn realized she didn't know the name of the old man who brought her here. "What's your name? Who are you, anyway?"

"Who are you is a much better question than what my name is. Long ago, I was known as Aaron Amaru."

"How long have you been on this island?"

"Oh, many, many years now."

"How did you find this place?"

"I was searching for Eden."

Jenn didn't know how to respond to that landmine.

"Before man followed the call of the serpent—you know of whom I speak, I believe—before he put his trust in those who spoke to him, he lived in a garden in a place called Eden."

"Did you ever find it?"

"Jennifer, where do you think you are?"

Jenn took a big breath, and looked out from their eagle's nest view. The ocean stretched 365 degrees out and away from Jenn, pushing itself against the borders of the horizon, maybe hundreds of miles off. Nearly limitless was the view here. Jenn thought it then a good idea to look up at the heavens, but doing so brought on a great deal of vertigo, and she momentarily tried to grab onto the old man for comfort, but she grabbed with her stub arm, and managed to lose her balance even more so. Aaron Amaru took hold of her with both hands, steadying her with care.

"This is Eden?"

"Why not?"

"So, Eden is an island."

186

"I found out long ago that Eden can be almost anywhere. Before I came here, I was a vigilant member of the *Movimiento de la Izquierda Revolucionaria* or, M.I.R; a communist organization. I believed that until everyone on Earth was free, until every last one of us was equal under the eyes of God, then none of us could ever get back to Eden. So I fought. I was a good fighter, too.

"But in the end it always finishes the same. The lion pride always falls to the newest, youngest fighter. You cannot be the strongest, bravest, fiercest forever. There always comes another.

"I was ousted by my own people. Had the enemy captured me, had the capitalists obtained me, then I would have been M.I.R.'s biggest champion, a martyr for all seasons. But I was trapped from inside."

"Why are you telling me this?" Jenn asked.

"It is good to share your story with others. You learn who you are by the details you choose to share.

"I was exiled. I came to this island in 1978. For many years I was very sad. Lonely. I thought, if the world is full of wicked men, then I will not be a part of it. I spent all my time carving these horrible gargoyles. I wanted them to keep watch for me, to scare off any possible intruders."

"Then, I started coming up on this rock, every morning, to watch the sunrise. And I started talking to God. And guess what?"

Jenn assumed the question was rhetorical. It wasn't. "What?" She finally asked.

"He talks back!"

Jenn didn't know how to process this. "What did he say?"

"Oh, he says lots of things, but the first thing he said to me was, 'Aaron, you are not important enough to have a name.'"

"What?" This was not what Jenn would have supposed a God-believer would think God said to them. "Why did he say that?"

"For a long time I didn't know. I think I do now, but it's a secret I don't wish to share."

Then why did you share at all? Jenn thought.

"Over time, God changed me. He helped me to see that it is

187

not people that are evil. No, it's a person. Here. There. It's in their decisions, in their thoughts. But people, no! People is just an idea. Only a person is real.

"So I carved at the statues some more. I carved a happy child, a happy father, a happy mother. I tried to make the statues as welcoming as possible, the opposite of what they once were. Did you see them?"

"Yes, right away. They're lovely," Jenn said.

"Did you feel welcomed by them?"

"Most certainly!"

"Good. I am glad to hear it. They do their job well, with honor."

"So when you came here, you brought your daughter?"

"No, no, you see how young my children are! They were not yet even a dream when I first landed here."

"Oh, then..." Jenn trailed off.

"I was on the island many years alone. Even though I enjoyed the company of God and the sunrise and sunsets, I was lonely. Then, one day, God saw my loneliness and said it is not good for man to be alone. A boat of travelers came to me, came to my island. There were many, twenty in all, I think. And one of them was so lovely I could hardly bear it. The rest decided to leave, but God moved her to stay with me. We married each other in the sight of Him right here on this philosopher's stone many years ago. And God has blessed our marriage with five beautiful children."

"But you're so old."

"Ah, now you're getting to what I have to share with you."

"That you're old?" Jenn said, "I can see that just fine."

"Ha. You are a funny child. No. Two weeks ago, I was sitting on this very stone, talking to God, and he said to me that a girl was coming. He said I would know right away that this girl was the one I was supposed to talk to because she would be carrying a deep burden in her eyes, though she'd be very young. I petitioned God, I did, I said, use one of the children, my daughters perhaps. Or maybe, God, this is the answer to my son's prayer, that you would bring a wife for him. I said to God, 'I am very old, it would be better to use my children for this task.' But God said that it must be me."

188

The old man was silent for a duration, looking perplexed, as if he forgot where he was going with the story.

"Did he say why?" Jenn offered.

"No, but when I saw you, saw that you recently lost your hand, and that I alone of my family speak English, the reason seemed easy to decipher."

Jenn was starting to become a bit dismayed. She wanted the old man to get to the point and share whatever it is he was going to share. And all the while Jenn couldn't help but spot and keep her eyes fixed on a spec in the sky near the horizon. "Well, what is it? What do you have to share with me?"

"Just this: and he gave me these words. They are his, not mine."

When the old man said "his words", Jenn thought of the Rabbi once more. He had found her once in her sleep, maybe he found her again through this old man on this island of Eden.

"Because whatever we are, we become more of that over time."

"What does it mean?" Jenn asked.

"In your case, only you can know, but I can tell you what it means to me."

"Okay," Jenn answered now only half paying attention. That speck had grown. It was coming their way.

"Back when I first came to this island, I was angry at the world, angry at everything. I thought in isolation I'd get better, I'd naturally become the person I wanted to be... take away the things that trouble me and I should be all better. But that didn't happen. I got worse. Meaner and more sullen. That is, until I talked to God and he told me I wasn't important enough to have a name. After that I realized my decisions and my thought-life made me. Not the outside world. Everything is in motion, Jennifer. You never just are, you are always becoming more of something. Therefore, the older you are, the MORE of that thing you naturally become.

"Thankfully, God has taught me gentleness, patience, and happiness instead of anger, violence and stubbornness. Instead of being a man of stubbornness, I get to be more and more a creature of kindness, goodness, and faithfulness. And

189

I'll be more like that tomorrow than I am today."

That speck was no mere speck. It was a helicopter.

Upon identifying it, Jenn chose to race down the ladder, through the forest. She caught Lex, who shared a wide-eyed expression.

The helicopter levitated above the sands on the beach. A man threw a ladder down to them. Lex climbed it up gingerly, yelled out some words at the pilot, then signaled down to Jenn with a thumb's up.

On her way up the precarious ladder, Jenn was thankful she had learned that the use of one's mouth is necessary for swinging ladder-ascension. It was a difficult task.

Once on board, the two women smiled and waved down at the family Amaru. As they flew off Jenn spied the old man still seated at the top of the island. He smiled at nothing atop his philosopher's stone.

"Who are you?" Jenn shouted at the co-pilot.

"We were sent here on the orders of Mrs. Babbit."

"How did you find us?"

"Just following coordinates given to us from Mrs. Babbit."

"Where are we going?" Lex asked.

"Just a few miles onto the mainland."

"Peru?"

"Peru."

Lex turned to Jenn. "What did the father want to share with you?"

"I'm not sure... but I'm sad to leave. What a place."

"I know," Lex responded, "But they should never have had children," Lex said.

Jenn pondered Lex's cynical response as she anticipated reuniting with her rich mentor, Lillith Babbit.

~~~

The island hopping days are behind us.

Jenn and Lex are destined to reunite with what's left of Team *Orion*. There, along with Lillith Babbit and her consortium of lawyers and bodyguards, the group will make a plan for the future. Will the *Orion* set sail again? Will the team try to rescue Miles Faa? What have Captain Alf, Godard, Lizard, Sir Isaac, and Father Thomas been up to all these weeks?

The Second Great Debate is nearly upon us. The only thing missing is an ancient book of secrets.

Let's add that in.

Chapter 34: The 2nd Great Debate

Off the helicopter.

The women were quickly corralled into what looked like an elementary school. There wasn't much time to take in the surroundings, but what Jenn did see looked like a minor, dusty settlement; a small town at best.

Jenn and Lex were being marched through corridor after corridor, briskly traversing the whole structure. The co-pilot behind them gently pushed at the small of Jenn's back to point her towards a relatively large meeting room. Jenn didn't care for him touching her there. Not polite. Not polite at all.

A long metal table presented itself to Jenn and Lex. A smattering of papers, binders and maps lay strewn across the table, giving the impression that great decisions had just been made in this room.

Across the table, some familiar faces, some not-so familiar faces. Four men stood at attention dressed in some sort of military garb. Jenn couldn't place what branch. One of them, an older man, looked to be the most decorated and wore a mean face. Beside the military personnel was Mark Janner, Lillith Babbit's lawyer and Jenn's first grand inquisitor back on the grounds of Magical Kingdom. Janner looked tired... and nervous.

At the other end of the table, already seated, were five men who, Jenn surmised, were local officials. Their mannerisms betrayed a certain cultural distinction from the others. Maybe this was the Peruvian F.B.I. Or was it the Peruvian C.I.A?

At the center of it all, dressed exquisitely, standing robustly, not betraying any hint of tiredness or deterioration, Lillith Babbit. Here she was, the former CEO of Magical Kingdom, and present patron of the *Orion* adventure schooner.

The room itself was almost windowless, save for two rectangular small windows at either corner. White iridescence cascaded down on this, what should we call it, let's say War Room. Jenn took note that having artificial light shine down from above felt extra unnatural. Weeks in the hole got Jenn acclimated to illuminated floor stones shining up into her eyes. Not this downcast whiteness. It felt surgical. Emotionless, like the faces staring at her.

"So, no shower or anything?" Lex asked in disgust.

"Hello, Alexandra. Hello, Ms. Free," said Lillith Babbit, "I'm sorry, but time is against us currently. We got you as soon as we could. Your rendezvous on that island made things easier for us."

Jenn wondered if Lillith was referring to Pishtaco's island, or the second island where they recovered them.

Jenn opened her mouth to speak, to say something, to say hello back to Lillith, it's nice to see you, but nothing came out.

"Please, be seated," Lillith said.

The ladies took the nearest seats available. Jenn was glad she wasn't near the mean-faced General guy.

A door from the other side of the room opened and through it walked Captain Alf, Godard, Sir Isaac, and lastly, Lizard.

Jenn and Lex leaped to their feet, joy at reuniting with their friends welling up inside.

"Where's Merkyl?" Godard asked flatly. "Miles?"

Lex responded with a shake of the head and a touch of her face, as if to say her bruises explained enough. The real answer to Godard's question was a tale that still hadn't come together. Jenn wondered, *how are we going to explain what happened to the rest? How do we account for the banishment of Merkyl... and then his disappearance? How do we explain Faa's sacrifice?*

Following Lex's bruised-face touch, Jenn lifted her stump. She noted that Captain Alf grimaced. Isaac diverted his eyes.

"Please everyone, take a seat. There will be time for welcomes and hugs later." This time it was the lawyer Mark Janner piping out orders.

Lex leaned over to whisper to Jenn, "Our next great debate."

The others sat on the opposite side of the table. Jenn stared at each of them one by one. The usual bubbliness that floated off of the Captain was nowhere to be found. No energy at all emitted from the four remnants of the *Orion*. What had happened to them? They didn't seem outwardly happy to see

193

Lex and Jenn.

"Thank you all for coming. I know the last few days have been trying for many of you. I know you all would like to get a good night's rest. Jenn, Lex, I'm sure you'd like to indulge yourselves with a long bath, maybe some wine. And you both look to need medical care, maybe some new clothing as well. I promise, as soon as we finish here, we'll see to those things promptly. We're glad you're back.

"Let me briefly explain why we're here, why we've been here, and then we all very much would like to hear your story, hear what happened. It's vital we extract every detail we can from you. So when you tell us the events of the last few weeks, leave no stone unturned; be as thorough as possible. If it takes all night for you to tell us everything, so be it. We're ready."

Jenn really didn't know how to make sense of the experiences of Pishtaco's island herself, so trying to depict it for others was devastatingly intimidating. She shuddered in her cold metal folding chair.

Jenn stared at her missing hand. Wasn't that story enough? Couldn't they see? Why did they need details?

The details are inhuman, unreal.

Janner picked up where Babbit stopped. "After the *Orion* sank, the rest of your team was rescued and taken to mainland Peru. At that point, they made a reckless and frankly stupid decision of not notifying us, or any of the authorities, about the plagued ship, the right triangle, pi, and the loss of comrade Jorje Robles. They instead sought out the renegade cult known as the Pythagoreans. The base of their operations originated just a few kilometers from where we are now."

Janner suppressed a mild cough. Jenn took note that Captain Alf, perhaps because of being publicly ridiculed, lowered his head. Janner cleared his throat and continued, "The team discovered that the whole tribe was infected with the disease, the same you witnessed from the ship. At that point, they did the right thing, realized the potential danger this infection held for the ENTIRE human race, and gave us a call. We brought our men in, such as Major Brennelhoff," the mean-faced man nodded slightly, "to investigate. We

194

concluded that to faithfully suppress any chance of an outbreak, we had to exterminate the tribe." Janner hesitated.

"The Pythagoreans are no more," Lillith Babbit said.

Janner picked back up. "This has been done in accordance and agreement with Peruvian administration." Several of the local men nodded in approval. "And now we'd like to hear your story. I think you can understand why such information is relevant to everyone in this room."

The full force of Janner's speech took awhile for Jenn to comprehend, but it made sense. It explained why Alf, Godard and the others looked so sullen. They were, at least incidentally, responsible for the deaths of probably dozens of people.

Then a question occurred to Jenn, and she blurted it out before thinking better of it, "Does anyone know what you did?"

"No," Janner answered resolutely. "The Pythagoreans were remote. Some neighboring tribes may notice their absence, but this isn't the type of story that does the public any good to be aware of. It would only cause panic and residual fear."

"So, is what you're telling us top secret?" Jenn said smiling, trying to make light as best she could of the situation. "Are you going to kill us if we tell anyone?"

A smug grin on Janner's face. "No one would believe your story. Tell whomever you like."

"Jennifer, Lex, please, tell us. What happened?"

Jenn put her (one remaining) hand over her mouth. She didn't know how to tell this story. It wasn't at all warm in the room, but Jenn was sweating.

Lex picked up the pieces. She started slow. Talked about ascending the island in the dark, how the ground was warm and the island seemed barren. Told how Merkyl went ahead. How they fell. She even told them what she remembered from their conversation in the webbing. Then Merkyl's heroic return. Then the waiting. Starting to starve. The way they slept in the hole. The hedgeys. The bite on Merkyl. Faa's decision to banish him to the squatter's hole. Then the big one—the griffin. The machete. Followed by another fall. The underground. Hedgeys carrying Jenn. The beaked woman. Codifying saliva. The bountiful food. The piles of grub. Next,

195

tapes from the Numbered Man. The spa. Three options. Splitting up. Lex and the horrid classroom. Miles and the ladders and mud. Jenn's steps. One thousand of 'em. Pied Piper mural. More steps. Moans from the deep. Miles' anger. The beating. The suicide pact. Then, release. Boat ride to freedom. No leviathan sighted.

"And," Lex concluded, "He left this in our boat." Lex took out the tape player from her lap.

"What's on it?" Janner asked.

"Don't know," Jenn finally piped up, thanking Lex with a smile for carrying the burden of the story, "we started to play it, heard his voice. That was enough for us."

"Play it now," Janner said cruelly.

Lex followed orders.

"Helllooooo.... how are my little farewell puppies? You know you'll never make it. Don't you know the horrible things down there, in the depths? Let's say I'm Grendel... you know, from your perspective... Daddy, he makes awesome creatures, better than God ever imagined. He's the god of the post-modern world. Kill 'em, daddy, kill him. Yes, since you've chosen to give me my bride and escape-you coward, Miles—I must assume that you think I'm a Grendel monster. But if I'm a monster, the sea, the sea herself, she's my Mother. And my mother is soooooooooooo much worse.

"Anyway, pretty good of me to make up this tape before you've even made your decision, am I right? Of course I am! I'm the master of preparation. So, don't come back, okay. Don't find some people. Don't do that. I'll be ready for that. I'm always ahead. And my wife will tattle on you. You won't blindside me. Grendel isn't blindsided.

"Ahhhh... I don't mind playing the villain. I don't. I really don't. Kinda fun. But here's the thing, friendos. I'm not the bad guy. I'm the revolutionary. I'm the necessary push. Or, to say it in a way that you Earthlings can understand; I'm the good guy. I'm the one that takes this world to its next stage, its future era of evolutionary development. It's zenith upon a zenith! HUZZAH!

"I realize, however, you don't see that side of me. Again, I'm just mean old Grendel to you. Boooo! Here's who I am. Here's

196

my M.O.

"My kingdom will not have names. No. All will have numbers. Numbered 001 to 999. Just that. Sounds simple. And it is. But it is a revolution in a box. Because done correctly, your numbered association will reign over you, comfort you in your sleep, soothe you in a way that even the best-est Mommy-dearest never could.

"Imagine it. You're born, given a number by the state. Now, you know mother, father, sister, brother, all by their numbers. Your brother idolizes that great football player, 129. Your sister wants to be a ballerina in the form of 577. Your mother wishes she looked as good as 903, and your father dreams of 896's wife.

"The first great accomplishment will be that immediately, racial, national, social orders will fall away. If you want to know someone, you'll have to get to know them. You can't just say, Oh, did you hear 304 is having an affair—because that might be three different people that you know personally, as well as two or three celebrities with that number. Our minds have been trained by language. Stupid, stupid, language. Math is much closer to perfection. So we adopt numbers as our shelter instead of names that imply heritage, race, social class, blah-blah-blah. Take it away.

"The trick, friends, comes with time. Give it a generation or two. 999 is the perfectly balanced amount. Not too frequent, not too sparse. You're at the drug store, and you learn that the cashier is your number. Suddenly, you have a friend. A RARE friend.

"With your number, you'll never be alone. Jennifer and Miles. I'm sure my lovely Lex isn't with you. Surely you're not sticking me with ol' one arm. All the pretty ones get their hands chopped off, don't they? Sigh.

"People will start forming cliques based off number. JUST random numbers, but they'll come together. And then they'll be the stereotypes. Everyone will know 614s are slobs. 093s are great musicians, yadayadayada. This can't be helped. But you see it, right? How beautiful it becomes? People can't judge you like they do now. They won't look at your skin color or your last name or your nationality and sum you up. They

197

won't have the tools to do that anymore. Because although society all hates 504s, they can't tell who IS a 504.

"With my numbers you are both hidden, sheltered from the evils of society, but also cocooned and loved. Feel lonely? Sad? You'll reach out to a fellow 440. You will. And it will feel sooooooo gooood. God forgot to give us purpose. So my numbers will.

"This is the future. The future you're betraying. And when everyone is different, when we all have genetic super powers, you two will be left out. When they teach my biography at grad schools, when they place me above Marx and Plato and Jesus, they'll mark you as the derelicts. Sure, you'll tell my story. But just because you're in it doesn't make you any good. University students will scribble your non-numbered names in their essays as those stupid knuckle-draggers that betrayed me.

"I love you. And you leave. How do you think that makes me feel?

"You will never fit in. You'll never feel loved. You'll never find shelter in another. I curse you....

"Oh, by the way, just so you remember. What's my real name? It's not the Numbered Man. That'd be silly. My name is simple, for it's the number of man. I am 6-6-6."

The tape clicked to a stop.

The room was silent. If ever there was suspicion, if anyone in the room couldn't quite swallow the events Lex had just described, the Numbered Man's speech, Number 666, just removed all doubt.

Mark Janner spoke up, "Ms. uh, Free, just so we have your perspective, do you think Miles and Merkyl are dead?"

"What? No. Why... why would you ask that? Why would you presume they were?"

"So you believe they're both alive?"

"I don't like to think that people are dead unless I know otherwise."

Lillith Babbit spoke. "Thank you, ladies. You've been a great help. Do you have anything else to share?"

Jenn said, "How did you find us?"

Mark Janner responded, "You had GPS units inside you.

198

You know this. We presume the signal couldn't reach us from underground."

"What?" Jenn was incredulous. Once upon a time she thought she was injected with a GPS unit by the men and women in black of Magical Kingdom. But Lillith or anyone on the Orion never injected her with any sort of needle.

"It's okay, Jenn," Lex put a hand on Jenn's.

"We..." Captain Alfred Bacon spoke up, "Knowing where you had came from, knowing the trauma you endured, we thought it best not to tell you. We injected you in your sleep."

A vision of Godard and Merkyl surreptitiously working on a monkey's brain in the middle of the night crept into Jenn's mind.

"No. NO."

"Jenn, this is hard, but I think you should know," Lillith began. "Remember, I've always been direct with you. I'm not going to change my position towards you now."

Jenn felt light-headed. "You betrayed me. You lied to me. And you killed those people. All those people."

"No. I didn't know they wouldn't ask you first before injecting you. Mark that among the many errors your Captain has made in recent weeks."

Emmanuela Godard found her voice, and wanted to say something. "Jenn, listen. When we went into the tribe, when we searched the Pythagoreans paddock. we found two creatures in cages. Jenn, these were the real Pishtacos, the ones people were writing about in the newspapers. These creatures caused the scare. And they were the ones transmitting the disease. They were giant, very pale white creatures, like white werewolves. The Pythagoreans, they'd dress them up, march them into a town or city. They fit the fabled description, Jenn. That's why they did it. They wanted the whole Earth to fall victim. They were an evil group."

"Why are you telling me this?"

"We tested the creatures. They were locked up in cages, so before we exterminated the village, we got blood samples. They were the contagions."

Jenn's mind raced trying to find relevance to the story. Why was Godard directing all this at Jenn?

Lex spoke up, "So what? Maybe all the mutants carry the disease."

"The disease, it takes awhile. The cellular degeneration takes many weeks. Maybe months. The story that the crew of the *Known Triangle* told you, the timeline doesn't line up. We suspect that the members of the boat were all infected and that's why they were at sea. The tribe made them quarantine themselves. We think they were the first test subjects."

Janner butted in, "We believe this Numbered Man, he is or, was, their chief engineer. They experimented on the island, and then were carrying these Pishtaco creatures back to the mainland to infect the whole country."

Lillith again, "This Numbered Man, he wasn't a rogue agent. He was no Judas. He was their pride and joy."

Jenn was stoic. She refused to let this get to her. "You're saying I was never infected."

"We think it's highly unlikely."

"But if I was, if Miles didn't take my hand, would you have been able to cure me?"

"Not at this time. Once the macro-degeneration starts, we can't stop it from running its course."

"And you don't know for sure that the griffin didn't carry the disease?"

"No. We don't. But we suspect—"

"You don't know," Jenn's resolve was firm.

"No."

"Then save your words for someone who cares."

"Okay, good meeting. Adjourned," Janner said.

And that was it. All the bigwigs stood, dusted themselves, and made their way out.

Where was the debate? Where was the heated discussion about what to do next? What now?

Janner motioned toward Lex and Jenn. "Ladies, we have rooms prepared for you both. There'll be time to meet with your crew-mates later, but we think you should wash up, get some medical aid, and have a good night's sleep before you spend the extra effort to reconvene with your friends. Tomorrow or the next day we can all talk about what still lies in the future for the crew of the *Orion*." Janner said that last part

200

with too much enthusiasm. He was laying it on hard. Jenn didn't approve.

"Can we at least say hello?" Lex said.

"Of course, of course," Janner said, but before he did, Lex was already hugging the Captain, and moving on towards Godard and the others.

Jenn was more reticent. She shook Godard's hand. "I'm sorry about Merkyl," Jenn said to her.

"That's okay," Godard responded in monotone.

Jenn hugged Lizard—or at least, tried to. "You taking care of yourself, Liz? Any songs of innocence?"

Lizard didn't say a word. Jenn found that strange.

Jenn went ahead and hugged Sir Isaac, even assuming that Isaac would disapprove, but he seemed eager for it, and held her firmly. While hugging, he whispered into her ear, "I'm still going to Mecca. Will you come with me?"

"What?" Jenn said and tried to read his eyes.

"I'll give you my number, so you can call."

Then onto the Captain. He didn't make eye contact, just swayed away from her to avoid any chance of a hug. He held out his hand, but in it, Jenn spied a note. The two shook hands, and Jenn tried her best to disguise the note as she put it in her pocket.

That was that.

Jenn showered. She thought about a bath, (they had a large one with turbo-powered jets) but Jenn didn't want to lie down and contemplate life, as she would be apt to do in such a position. Post-shower, she was welcomed into some sort of medical quarter of the school. A kind doctor and assistant examined Jenn's stump as well as some minor cuts and bruises here and there. Looking at her rounded stump, the doctor blurted out, "I'd like to get my hands on the material that sealed up your wound here. Excellent stuff. Really excellent. Never seen anything like it."

While the doctor's assistant continued questioning Jenn about her health while scribbling down on a form, acting as if it would be revered and read by many others, Lillith Babbit strut in.

201

This was the first time Jenn had spoken to her outside the wandering ear of Babbit's lawyer.

"Jennifer, I have a recommendation for you, for your future, if you'd like to hear it."

"Okay."

"I know a center. It's a special place. In Europe. They can help you."

"Like give me a prosthetic hand?" Jenn had already started hoping that such an option would be available to her at some point.

"No, Jennifer, something better than a prosthetic."

"What then?"

"A new hand."

"What?"

"They can give you someone else's. They've perfected a way to give patients new body parts."

"How?"

"Well, a patient dies, for whatever reason. Maybe a car crash, something like that. Something not related to disease. And this office extracts the pieces of the person's body and saves them for people like you."

"Is that legal?"

"Legality is relative. You'd have to chat with Mr. Janner to get a good answer. I think the paperwork is tricky, yes, but if you want it, I can get it done for you."

"Yes," Jenn said without hesitation. She yearned for the chance to be whole again. "I want it."

"Great. I need to leave in the morning; I'm headed to Europe myself. You can accompany me if you like and then take a plane to the office in Europe."

"Where is it, exactly?"

"Zurich. Switzerland."

"Oh, okay. You know, I can't pay for any of this."

"I know, sweetheart, I know. Money's not much of a thing for me. You'll be taken care of. You never have to worry about those issues."

"I'm sorry I was rude before. You didn't betray me. Why are you so nice to me?"

Lillith leaned in.

"Can you not see how special you are, Jennifer Dash?"

Lillith smiled and turned away to leave, but suddenly paused.

"Jenn, would you like to maybe be my assistant?"

"Uh, I don't know. What would that entail?"

"Not what you might expect. I just need another set of eyes with me. Clear eyes, young eyes."

"I have clear eyes?"

"Can I tell you a secret?"

"Sure."

With a little brush of her hand, Lillith shooed off the doctor's assistant.

The two women were alone.

"While going through the Pythagorean village, we came across a book. A very old book. It's something of a book of secrets. I've been hoping to find it, or something like it, for years. When you told me you wanted to find Leviathan, that's when I first knew you and I are very much alike. We're both searching for the spark of life."

Jenn's thoughts fell to this ancient book. "What does the book say?"

"We don't entirely know yet. It's tough to translate. That's why I have to go to Europe."

"Okay. I still don't know what you need me for."

Lillith kissed Jenn on the forehead, and headed out of the room.

"I'll see you tomorrow. I'll have someone wake you."

"Okay."

If Lillith Babbit meant anything to Jennifer Dash, she meant instant change. Instant, radical change. And once again, Jenn felt the desire to run away. To run away back to a place where she could forget about her captivity, forget that she almost drowned herself in an underground spa, forget that a mutant eagle took her hand. Lillith Babbit was once again going to be Jenn's savior.

An hour later and Jenn was in a comfy bed, sporting new, silk jammies. There was even a stuffed animal doggy on Jenn's bed for snuggling.

203

Jenn had slipped the note from Captain Alf into her silk pockets. She had almost forgotten about it when she finally pulled it.

It read simple. One line.

"Don't believe Babbit's lies."

~~~

Is Lillith really Jenn's savior? Why were the Captain, Godard, and Lizard so cold to Jenn and Lex? What's really in the ancient book? And why is Sir Isaac still so intent on getting to Mecca? Why, why, why? So many questions.

To Europe

<u>Main Cast</u>
Jenn
Lillith Babbit
Ludwig
Robin

Chapter 35: The Book Croatoan

Jennifer from Louisiana.
Jenn the Dreamer.
Jenn the Optimist.
Jenn the Searcher.
Jenn the Cleopatra.
Jenn the Killer.
Jenn the Informant.
Jenn the Deckhand.
Jenn the Prisoner.
Jenn the One-Handed.

All these words. All these actions. So far, Jenn's attempts to solve the world had been action oriented. That's the through-line of all the names. It seemed that above all, Jenn was a doer. She was an active body. Perhaps a busybody. But maybe action was only half the formula. Now, it appeared, what was needed most was research.

Sitting on a luxury airplane 40,000 feet in the air, headed to an old continent on which she'd never set foot, Jennifer Dash had decided now was the time to become: Jenn the Researcher.

Across from Jenn, reading from a pile of papers Mark Janner had just slapped onto the desk by her, reclined Lillith Babbit. In the hours leading up to their departure from Peru, Jenn had learned a few things about her personal patron. After reading his note, Jenn managed a late night rendezvous with Captain Alf before takeoff. It was a revealing conversation. The results Jenn chronicled in her mind as follows:

1) Lillith Babbit is cutthroat and capable of doing bad things.

2) Lillith Babbit wants something.

3) Lillith Babbit doesn't want others to have (or know) the thing she wants.

4) Lillith Babbit believes the ancient book points her to the thing she wants.

5) Jennifer Dash should not be chummy with Lillith Babbit.

She should say no to Lillith's request to become her assistant.

Reflecting upon the list, Jenn added one more herself.

6) Lillith Babbit may be useful. Don't alienate her.

The simple fact remained that Lillith Babbit had rescued Jenn twice over. And now, she was paying for, in full, a renewal of Jenn's body. She was taking time and allocating money for Jenn to get a new hand. There was no external reason, that Jenn could figure, which would compel Lillith Babbit to do such a thing. She was either doing it out of kindness, friendship, or some other reason Jenn couldn't yet see.

She said Jenn was special. What baloney was that? Jenn recalled that moment when Lillith had smiled knowingly at Jenn, saying, "Can you not see how special you are, Jennifer Dash?" Was Jenn Neo from The Matrix?

Jenn knew this much: she was no prophet.

She was no orphan princess.

She had no ancient Midi-Chlorians in her; she was no Jedi. She knew what sort of blood ran through her veins, and it was closer to that of a Sith Lord's than a Jedi's.

She was not the one destined to rule them all.

She was, Jenn confessed to herself, nothing more than a bored girl with a bubbly ego.

Somehow, her ego had led to all this. So, if not some sort of chosen one prophetess, what attracted Lillith to Jenn? Was it friendship? Could it be?

No.

Jenn didn't have any friends. That was made blatantly obvious just a few hours earlier. As she prepared to jump aboard the plane to Europe, she woke Lex to say goodbye. Jenn didn't feel right just up and leaving without saying adieu to the person with whom she'd spent so many days in excessively close proximity.

The conversation went something like this:

"Hey. Lex. Wake up."

"Jenn. Don't wake me."

"Lex, I'm leaving. Babbit's getting me a new hand."

"Oh. Good."

"So, I gotta go. Get on a plane to Switzerland or

something."

"Yeah, that makes sense."

"I just wanted to say goodbye. Do you know what you'll be doing next?"

"Sleeping."

"Sorry, I know it's early."

"We haven't slept in beds forever, Jenn."

"I know. I just wanted to say goodbye."

"Yeah. See you around."

And Lex closed her eyes.

Some friendship, eh?

Come to think of it, besides the Further family, which, let's be honest, she'd only spent a day with, Jenn hadn't made any real friends on her adventures.

Once she might have thought Tiff was a friend. But not really. That was wishful thinking; from the beginning Tiff was weird. Too weird. The only other candidate would be Miles. Jenn quickly brushed the thought aside; Miles only seemed like a friend. That's what he wanted her to think. There was no real connection.

Friendship was hard when you were changing so often and so quickly. Any friend Jenn had before setting out to solve the world, old Redjeb, none of them knew her anymore. Old friends didn't know the Jenn Dash of the present, the Jennifer of the now.

Maybe Lillith Babbit was like Jenn after all. Maybe she reached out to her because she sensed a kinship in Jenn— maybe they're both changing so often that friendship isn't really a reality. Maybe no one knows the true Lillith because Lillith is always changing into the new Lillith. Even so, once upon a time Lillith fell in love. Got married. That's more than Jenn had even been.

Jenn stared at Lillith as she contemplated the woman. Maybe she wasn't evil—yesterday a monster, today a new Lillith. Everyday someone new. Everyday, Lillith needs to be learned again, an ever-evolving creature. That's what makes her so mysterious. And so powerful.

Jenn spoke up, "What are those?"

"Come here, take a look," Lillith invited.

Jenn moseyed over to Lillith, grabbing several of the papers on her desk.

"They're photocopies... of what?"

"These are the precious, copies of the book I told you about."

"What language is that?"

"That's the tricky part. Here, follow me."

Lillith arose and walked back towards a secondary cabin of the private jet. Lillith and Jenn were alone in the front. In the back, Janner and four others—including two military men from the "great non-debate" meeting—huddled over a desk strewn with stacks of papers, laptops, sticky notes everywhere, and, at the center of it all, two bound sheepskins, the one on top much thicker than the one below.

Without saying a word, Lillith grabbed the book and caressed the cover before sharing it with Jenn.

"This is, we suppose, the first found, complete transcript of *The Croatoan*."

"What does that mean, Croatoan?"

"We don't know."

Lillith opened the book. Jenn expected to see CROATOAN written somewhere in big bold letters. She was mistaken. There didn't appear to be any title at all. The book just started with no header, no paragraphs, no punctuation. It did use readable letters though, not the strange markings that were on the photocopied page.

"This is the first section. There are six sections. We've found some of the sections before, but never all six."

"Can you read this?" Jenn asked.

"Well, let's see, all this takes some explaining." Lillith peered down at the discombobulated table. The six peered up at Lillith in obvious servitude. "We're going to peruse this for a little while," Lillith said holding up the sheepskin-covered book.

Lillith marched back to the front cabin. Jenn followed obediently.

She was Jenn the Researcher now.

Jenn the Knowledge Obtainer. The world was built on information. If Jenn wanted to solve it, she needed to slow down. She needed to hear what the world had to say. Enough running around. Here, in these ancient pages, what did the early generations of homo sapiens learn? Did they hold secrets? Did they lock them away somewhere? In some book, perhaps? In this "Croatoan"?

As long as Jenn was just a listener, just a fly on the proverbial wall of knowledge and life, she need not worry herself with whether Lillith was evil or not. It didn't matter. Lillith was kind to Jenn and presenting her with worldly knowledge. That's all that mattered.

Lillith sat back in her comfortable recliner, "Go get a stewardess to get you a folding chair."

"Is that allowed? Don't we need to be in chairs with seat belts?"

"I own this jet. If we crash, no seat belt is going to save you."

So Jenn meandered around until she found an attendant to fetch her a small folding chair. As the stewardess brought the chair, Lillith ordered her to bring her a double-scotch on the rocks.

Once Jenn was seated, and Lillith found comfort with her spirit in hand, she began.

"There's two categories: what we know, and what we've heard—call that tradition. There are myriads and myriads of traditions surrounding Croatoan, many of them diametrically opposed to each other.

"The mainline tradition holds that the gods of Greece and Rome and Iceland and the demon gods of the Mayans, all of them, everywhere, were real. At least in some way.

"I've encountered certain events in my life that I simply can't explain except to admit that there are forces at work beyond our capacity to understand. Today, I'm not so confident that what the ancients called 'gods' really are. I think..." Lillith hesitated, looking to choose these words carefully, "I believe that the gods are as natural, as opposed to supernatural, as you or me. You and I are natural creatures, products of the rules of the natural world, but the ancients perceived very natural things as supernatural. Sometimes, those beliefs led them astray. And sometimes it led them to certain scientific fruits. Do you understand me, Jennifer?"

"Will you tell me what you experienced that made you believe this?" Jenn the researcher, Jenn the investigator on the prowl.

"Belief isn't the right word. This is not about religion."

"Then what is this about?"

"Knowledge is ethereal, Jennifer. We tend to think it's sturdy... our modern generations think that once a thing is known, it becomes firm, it becomes eternal... but that's not how it works. Knowledge can very easily be lost. Sometimes it even changes its form."

"*The Croatoan* has lost knowledge," Jenn suggested.

"Did you know that almost every religion and every old culture has a variant on the flood myth; a moment when the waters of the world overran the Earth? If you know where to look, there's a thin line of knowledge, of truth; behind every myth, behind every god is a reality."

"*The Croatoan* is the thin line?" Jenn ventured.

"For hundreds of years, there have been reports, biographies, whispers, that a man called by various names, but most often referred to as 'The Mad Arab' had a document written in the original language of mankind. This is part of the tradition now... not the part that we know, but it helps inform the parts we do know."

"Okay. Go on."

"Have you heard of the Tower of Babel?"

"Maybe... sounds familiar, but I couldn't tell you what it is about."

"It's most widely known as a Bible story."

Jenn's heart revved up. Leviathan was a Bible story. Maybe all this would get back to the eternal guardian of the sea.

Lillith continued, "The story goes that at one time, all of man spoke one language, and during those generations man was accomplishing untold feats. One of those feats was a magnificent tower, Babel. According to the book of Genesis, God looked down on Babel and grew nervous about man's reach. So, he confused the people, made them all speak different languages. But God had mercy; he didn't confuse man's tongue entirely. If no one could understand each other, then there would just be chaos, and we homo sapiens would

211

be just as every other creature on Earth. In his mercy, it is believed, he created 72 languages at Babel. And from those 72 languages come all the languages on Earth. The biographies of the Mad Arab say that he had found fragments of the original tongue, and greater still, using the original writings, he could decode any tongue on Earth. His piece of the original language worked as a cipher for the future. He had to have been a sensational man, brilliant. And he used his brilliance in the cleverest of ways. He traveled the world, all his days, collecting secrets from every tribe and every tongue. He gathered them all together, and bound them in one book."

"*The Croatoan.*"

"Yes. This is what tradition says. It all makes for a fine story, but without any proof, it's just a story to tell children as they fall asleep. Like the story of the Pied Piper."

Piper? Piper!

Why had Lillith just said the Piper's name?

Why did she do that?

Jenn tried valiantly to obscure her momentary panic, and it appeared that Lillith took no notice, being too wrapped up in her own story.

"Then, from time to time, starting in the 1500s in Europe, these little manuscripts started showing up. Often, the people that came to obtain the manuscripts had no idea what they had. Tradition also holds that the Mad Arab bounded all this world knowledge in a book written in many old tongues. He did this to conceal the secret knowledge. Someone would have to work diligently, translate all the pieces in order to understand his great work."

"Or find the original cipher, the original language document."

"Yes, that's true, but tradition also holds that the Mad Arab, after completing *The Croatoan*, burned the original language."

"Why would he do that?"

Lillith shrugged, "He's not called the Very Sane Arab."

"Okay, so, the Pythagoreans in Peru found the original, *The Croatoan* he wrote?"

"You'd think so, but it doesn't all quite line up... another tradition says a rich Venetian got hold of the book, and,

212

wanting to understand it, tore it into its pieces—some say he tore it into 3 parts, some say 5, and a few, just a few, say he tore it into 6 parts. He sent the six pieces to six different nations, hoping that his friends in those nations would translate it for him, and each would separately send back their portion translated. Those people then made copies, sent them to their friends, and from there more and more copies were made. This explains why there are different sections written in different languages in different countries all over the Earth. *Croatoan* searchers like myself usually find just one section at a time. But here, these Pythagoreans, this copy, it has six parts written in six languages."

"What languages?"

Lillith pointed at the first page, "This here, the first section, it's written in a Romanized version of Chinese. This particular Latinization of Chinese is called Wade-Giles, invented so Westerners could pronounce Chinese, so there's no chance this section is based off the original. The Mad Arab would have had to live at least a millennium before the Wade-Giles system was invented."

"Bummer," Jenn said, "So does that mean it's a fake?"

"Actually, no. Quite the opposite. It rather proves it."

"Proves what? How?"

"I've been searching for *The Croatoan* for a long time and before this trip, I had found, collected, two full sections, and pieces of a third section. I found this first section already, this section here that's in Wade-Giles Chinese. But the copy I found was written in Coptic."

Jennifer's blank stare betrayed her ignorance.

"Coptic is the Egyptian language written using Roman letters."

"Oh, okay. So how does that help?"

"This section one in Chinese reads just the same as my Coptic version. They're two translations from an original source. So, they verify each other. Whoever put this collection together at least got the first two sections right."

"First two?" Jenn asked.

Lillith flipped to a later page in the book. "This is written in Ancient Greek. It's identical to a section I found in Crete. Both

213

are in Ancient Greek. Both are identical. So, this *Croatoan* is two for two."

"You said you had found two and a half sections before this? What's the half?"

"In here I found pieces," Lillith flipped to a page covered in scratched, crazy vertical lines, "of the fifth section. It's Vedic Sanskrit, one of the oldest languages in the world."

"What languages are the other sections?"

"That's what makes this so fun!" Lillith's eyes were beaming.

"I know of one tradition that speaks of 6 sections—that belief seems to be reflected exactly in this manuscript. The tradition says that all the sections are 'How and How-To' books. Book One is 'How the World Began', and, this here, this Wade-Giles Chinese, tells exactly that, a beautiful creation narrative! Tradition then says that section two is a 'How to Create' guideline. Both my copy and this tell of how to create new species. It's gross and bizarre, a lot of crossbreeding with certain monsters and spirit creatures... but it also has these hints, these descriptors that seem to require a backdrop of understanding DNA and modern eugenics. Then the third section, according to tradition, is 'How the Change Happened', supposedly telling a story about how history changed traumatically at one point. I'd never seen this section until now. So, we've supposed that it had to deal with the flood narrative, but..."

Lillith flipped to the third section, which was very geometric, filled with triangles and slashes. "This is Assyrian cuneiform, another ancient language. We've just started our translation." Lillith lifted the photocopied pages. "A professor sent me these documents, also written in Assyrian Cuneiform. So far, it seems it tells of the fall of the gods, not unlike the story in the Bible and elsewhere of the fallen angels, or the Greek myths of the binding of the Titans. But there's a catch. It suggests that all the gods come from two firsts: a first creator, and a first emulator. The creator made the emulator, and the emulator betrayed him. Fascinating material."

Lillith turned to the next section. Jenn recognized it immediately. "Elvish!"

"Very good. It does comes from that part of the world. The language is called Manx. Haven't started translating this one yet, but it should be easy enough... I just don't know any Manx scholars."

"Where," Jenn thought about her question, "where and when did people speak that language?"

"It originates with the Isle of Man, a tiny little island between Ireland and England."

Jenn thought of the Numbered Man's island and reckoned that the Isle of Man was probably bigger than that island.

"Next is the one in Vedic Sanskrit. Tradition says it's a how-to guide for escaping Earth, or, at least, for escaping this plane of existence. I'm very excited to translate this one. The last section is supposed to be titled 'How to Release Dragons,' or 'How to Unleash Monsters', something like that. And that, Jennifer Dash, is why I'm headed to Budapest. We can't even figure out this section's language. One of the eggheads back there," Lillith motioned toward the back of the plane, "thinks it might be some form of Uralic, from which the Hungarian language branches off."

"Wow. So that's that."

"Yes. When I'm not trying to get secrets out of you about Magical Kingdom, this is what I'm searching for. I've spent the better part of my life yearning to find this book. It actually..." Lillith paused, floating off into memory before reconstituting herself in the present, "is how I fell in love with Mr. Babbit. We found each other searching for *Croatoan*." Lillith was lost in her thoughts. "Jennifer, we've never been closer to unwrapping the *Croatoan*'s secrets. Never. This is a great day to be alive."

Mark Janner stepped into the front cabin, standing small as he always did, dressed to the hilt in three piece suit and nerdy glasses.

Clearly annoyed, he said, "Can we have it back? We've got lots of work to do and precious time before we touch down."

Wordlessly, Lillith handed him the sheepskin. "Get Roger in here."

"Yes Ma'am."

Janner left. Lillith sat up and leaned in towards Jenn. "Why

215

don't you get comfortable, rest up." She motioned for Jenn to sit back in the recliner as opposed to the noticeably uncomfortable metal chair Jenn's bottom had taken up residence on for the duration of *Croatoan* story-time.

One of the military guys, Jenn supposed Roger, walked in holding a briefcase.

"Jennifer, I know that trusting me might be difficult after all you've been through," Lillith nodded at Roger. He sat in the metal chair, opened his briefcase on his lap, and investigated the contents.

"I want you to trust me. Anything that I can do to re-earn that trust, I'll do it."

Roger pulled out a wand device and motioned towards Jenn.

"Roger here is going to find the GPS unit in your arm. Please hold out your arm."

Jenn did so. Roger hovered his wand over Jenn's arm like a metal detector. A red dot on the wand appeared. Roger pressed a button and a mist sprayed out on a particular spot over Jenn's forearm. Then Roger grabbed a pocketknife from his pocket, flicked it open, and, not stopping to listen to Jenn's rebuke, plunged the tip of the blade into Jenn's arm.

"It's painless, Jennifer. Don't fidget."

She wasn't wrong. It was painless. There must have been something in the mist. A moment later, and a little fleck of metal rice was out.

Lillith stood up as Roger applied a cotton-ball to Jenn's arm. Lillith pulled out a black credit card, handed it to Jennifer.

"With this, you can purchase whatever you need, catch a flight to wherever you want to go. You'll need to stay around Zurich for six weeks. The doctor will explain it better than I can, but they'll need to keep an eye on you, just a check-up every few days or so. There's always a chance that your body will reject the new hand. We'll be in the clear after six weeks. Use this card to purchase food, go to the movies, go out with boys, whatever you'd like. After you're given the green light, I'd like you to come and join me... join my team. Help me uncover the secrets of *The Croatoan*."

Jenn took the credit card.

216

Soon after, Jenn dosed off, but before she did, the conversation she had with Captain Alf replayed in her mind.

After reading the note, Jenn snuck off to Godard and Alf's room and found them both awake on a bunk bed. Godard lay on the top bunk staring at the ceiling while Alf sat on the edge of the bed smoking a pipe.

"Glad you came," he said. "Let's take a walk."

Captain Alfred Bacon led Jenn outside. Jenn felt a little vulnerable walking outside in just flip flops and silk pajamas, but the content of the conversation, and the Captain's spooked voice captured all of Jenn's attention.

"What did your note mean?"

"Babbit's a liar."

"Yeah, I got that. How do you know?"

"We called her when we got to the Pythagoreans' camp. She was uninterested, said she'd send someone to get us back to the States. While we waited, we thought, might as well get to know these people. They did show us the white werewolf creatures. Two of them. They said this guy, Charles Clovis, he was a member, but got involved with some crazy stuff written in one of their books, and used it to start this genetic mutation business. When the Pythagoreans found out, they banished him, said the book was a warning, not a guide. Well, we called Lillith again, just trying to find out who was going to pick us up and when. It came out in conversation that the Pythagoreans have an ancient book. I had no idea at that time it was the *Croatoan*. But, as soon as Lillith heard about it, she was here the very next morning with a whole hell of an army. Jenn, no one was infected. That story about the whole tribe being infected with the virus, the leprosy thing, that never happened. No one checked anyone for anything. They just came in. They wiped out the village."

"They shot them all?"

"No. I don't know how they did it. They came in, all these military guys, they scouted the place, Lillith found the *Croatoan*, and within a few hours, everyone, except us of course, was dead. Then they came with flame throwers, burned the whole place to hell."

"Why would they do that? Why would Lillith want that to happen?"

"She wants something."

"The book."

"Something in the book."

"She wants me to go with her. Alf, she wants me to be her assistant."

"I was wrong about her. You can't trust her. You can't go with her."

"She said she's going to get me a new hand."

"You didn't see the dead bodies. Little children. They were alive, playing soccer, hanging their clothes in the sun, regular people. Babbit killed them. Don't align yourself with her. She's a cold-blooded murderer."

The conversation went on, but the recliner on the jet was so comfortable, it collapsed as Jenn leaned back on it, so as to let her completely lie down.

Jennifer Dash the investigator, the aggregator of knowledge and truth, drifted off to that kingdom of jewels and diamonds in her dreams.

~~~

Jennifer believes Lillith Babbit is onto something. There may just be ancient secrets locked up in this fabled *Croatoan* book and Jenn can't resist the desire to figure out those secrets. But finding out means continuing to side with Babbit, a woman of power Jenn now knows is a certifiable mass murderer.

Worry not. Jenn's not making any brash decisions. She's Jenn the investigator now, and there are more clues to be found before any judgments are reached. All she needs is a helping hand.

Chapter 36: Connections

A hundred hours after touching down in Zurich, Switzerland, Jenn gripped in her hand something she'd never had before: a mobile phone.

Though her other hand gripped nothing (it was under a thick cast), it was nevertheless a new hand. But Jennifer had already had a hand attached to that wrist, so, the new replacement was not quite as awe-inducing as the mobile phone.

After Lillith and co. sans Roger and Jennifer exited in Budapest, the plane rerouted to Zurich. Once on the ground in Switzerland, Roger escorted Jenn directly to what looked like a hole-in-the-wall amidst the otherwise gorgeous Swiss town.

There really wasn't much to it. Roger and Jennifer bid their time for maybe an hour in a drab waiting room. Two TVs in the room both played the Nicolas Cage action flick *Face/Off* on mute. Jenn had never seen it and found the plot rather difficult to track without any sound. A nurse came in to have Jenn fill out some paperwork. She handed Jenn a clipboard, but Roger immediately snatched it out of Jenn's hand, filling out pages upon pages of forms, finding answers to the questions asked on his smart phone.

Finally, the nurse asked Jenn, in English, to follow her. She escorted Jenn through a long hallway, and plopped her down in an even smaller room that also had a TV, but no *Face-Off*. The nurse ordered Jenn to remove her clothes, put on a hospital gown, and wait. Jenn did as she was told. Peering down at her paper-thin gown, Jenn noted it was covered in dancing unicorns. Jenn reminisced about the fast food joint where she first overheard the Rabbi explaining the existence of unicorns to his daughters. Simpler times.

The nurse came back, took a blood sample from Jenn, asked her to stand on a scale, and finally noted Jenn's pulse. The nurse left, but returned within a minute.

"This is Dr. Nanamudi. He'll be your anesthesiologist today."

"Hello, Jennifer."

"Hi."

"I'm going to inject this into you," the doctor held up a needle. "Are you scared of needles?"

"No Sir, not really."

"Good."

He stabbed her.

"Please count back for me from 10."

"10, 9, 8, ..."

A bathtub filled with ice cubes. From the elbow all the way down, a white cast. Jenn was freezing in the ice water, but her cast arm was bent outside the tub and dry. At the end of the cast, bluish-purplish-black fingertips protruded.

A new nurse waited outside the tub to comfort Jenn and tell her the surgery was a success.

In retrospect, it was rather odd how little Jenn knew about everything that went on. She was never told why she awoke from surgery in a bathtub, never given any details about the procedure. But there appeared to be evidence, in the form of oddly colored, bruised fingers, that Jennifer Dash was rejoining the world of the two-handed. For the next several days, however, no extra evidence mounted. Her fingers remained unnaturally colored and she didn't seem to have any control or feeling of her new appendage.

As Jenn left the office, she was given a few specific instructions. Roger had left, but he'd taken the liberty of checking Jenn into a motel three blocks from the doctor's office. Apparently, Roger had delivered Jenn's things there.

Most importantly, the nurse commanded Jenn to return to the office in five days. On her return, they'd knock her out again, open the cast, check up on the new hand, and re-cast it before Jenn would wake up. Jenn asked why it was necessary that she sleep through the procedure. The nurse responded by saying that it was absolutely crucial that Jenn not move her arm or hand. The only way to ensure no movement was to put Jenn to sleep. That explanation made sense, but Jenn wondered if it didn't have more to do with making sure Jennifer never saw the doctor's face.

Jenn had strict orders to never get her arm wet. The nurse

220

packed with Jenn an ugly plastic sleeve she was to wear in the shower. Complete immersion underwater was absolutely off limits—beyond the bounds entirely.

Anyway, that was all old hat.

The thing now was the phone and what it possibly meant.

Jenn had wandered the streets of Zurich by foot, by trolley, and by water-bus looking for ways to utilize her unlimited black credit card in the days following her procedure. Jenn had never been the type of girl enamored with clothes and fashion, but Zurich was fancy, and Jennifer wanted to fit in. She bought several ensembles, including a full length, powder blue gown, the likes of which suited Cinderella much more than the arm-casted Jennifer.

After a perusal through an Armani boutique, and subsequent purchasing of a blinging gold chained purse (whose price tag was a whopping 1200 Euros, by far the most expensive thing Jenn had ever purchased or owned in her life), the thought arose in Jenn's mind that she needed something to go inside her ornate arm candy.

It just so happened that the first store Jenn passed after this thought was a candy store. And so it came to pass that Jennifer Dash came to fill her Armani purse with fancy suckers. Growing up, one of the few luxuries kid Jenn had were lollipops, which now were one of the few consistent elements of her childhood. And they were great! They lasted far longer than other candies. On a few occasions, Jenn's neighbor Redjeb gave her Twix bars. But the momentary glee that such an intoxicating sugar, chocolate and caramel rush brought forth was quickly and viciously erased by the fact that the Twix was gone so fast. It seemed a cruel trick; to enjoy something so much, only to have it be gone so swiftly. So here in Zurich, Jenn's inner-girl chose lollipops, a whole bag full of them, to suck on and enjoy all-the-live-long day. As a child, Jenn wouldn't stop once the Tootsie Pop itself was eaten but went right on sucking at the paper handle, sucking every last ounce of pleasure from the experience, until, at final last, the paper too dissolved away.

Jenn was sucking on a latte-flavored pop when she purchased the phone. She'd never owned a phone before, and she wasn't entirely sure how to use one—but the idea festered in Jenn's mind that she could call two specific people if she found the right digits.

So she purchased one. A half-hour later, at an internet cafe, Jenn found the two numbers she was hoping to obtain.

The first was much easier to find: the office number of Miles Faa. Jenn had hoped that maybe he'd been saved in the end. Maybe Lex would lead the remainder of the *Orion* to Pishtaco's island, the Numbered Island, Clovis' island, 666's island—whatever that crazy monster called himself. Maybe Lex had already saved Miles. Maybe he was safe and sound. Or maybe he had saved himself somehow. Maybe he used his mental telepathy to get out of the grotesque marriage contract. Or he just beat the snot out of every hedgey until they let him go. Who knows? But oh, the peace it would bring, knowing Miles was okay.

Jenn was living with shame. And anger. Frustration. She didn't want to be the girl who left her colleague behind. She didn't want to carry that burden. As long as he was still there, held in captivity, the burden would remain heavy. If Miles was out, Jenn was free, free once more.

One simple call and it could all be put to rest.

The second number was a bit trickier. There were no computers in her home growing up, so for Jenn the internet and social media remained something of an mystery. She felt secure in her ability to relate to her surroundings, to mold herself and be charming in whatever environs the world threw at her, but she knew she lacked the thumb skills of her generation. It was a big ol' gap in her development. Nevertheless, with the help of a nerdy guy at the internet cafe, Jenn found Atticus' number.

She saw his face once more.

What would she say if she called him? What would they talk about?

How could she explain how much Atticus had come to mean to her? How could she do that without coming off like a boy-obsessed weirdo? For goodness sake, they'd spent one evening together!

This would take some thought. One couldn't just walk into

that phone call. It required a high degree of forethought. Jenn's conversation with the one and only Atticus Further had to be premeditated. She would think through every possibility. Every question Atticus could conceivably ask, she'd have anticipated it. She was not going to be a floozy. She needed to come off self-confident, cool, collected. Could she some way manipulate Atticus into calling her first? If Gimli were around, she'd have him surreptitiously drop her number off at his house, or better yet, the convenience store when only Atticus was working. How cool would that be if this big ol' gull waddles in through the automatic sliding doors, only to deliver a message to Jenn's boy wonder?

That'd be romantic, no?

Building off of that fantasy, Jenn envisioned Atticus calling her, Jenn acting nonchalant about the whole thing, Jenn twirling her hair (this was a fantasy, so Jenn imagined herself as she was when she first met Atticus, long-haired, two-handed and cast-less). They'd talk for hours while Jenn meandered through the beautiful streets of Zurich at dusk. She'd describe to him in detail everything she was seeing, touching, tasting, while he'd laugh and add his geeky knowledge of the Swiss people as insight into the conversation. She'd continue to talk as she prepped herself for bed at the motel. Neither of them would want to hang up. Finally, as the sun would crest over the horizon, Jenn would yawn, and Atticus would suddenly, in a vibrant burst of inspiration, announce that he was going to take the red-eye to Zurich. He'd be at the airport before the sun went down.

Jennifer would go to meet him at the airport. He'd come off the plane with a teddy bear in one hand, a dozen roses in the other, but when he finally sees her, he'd drop everything, sprint to her, caress her face in his hands.

And kiss her.

That moment would never die. It would never age. They would stick there, eternal fixtures of united love, in the Zurich airport, until the sun turned dim at the end of time.

All this. It was so simple. The only thing Jenn needed to figure out was how to get hold of Gimli.

This daydream kept Jenn afloat for days. If nowhere else,

Jennifer Dash could live there, in the little fantasy she'd so carefully constructed. It was just big enough for her to live there.

In the midst of Europe, Jenn found a world of her own creation, a sham-reality, much worthier of her time than the real world. Solving the world was proving perilous and impossible. Why not just journey off into a land of make-believe?

Sunday morning and Jenn was due back at the secretive surgeon's office. For whatever reason, Jenn had been waking up earlier and earlier each morning in Zurich. She wasn't conscious of it, but the reason was this: with nothing to do, with no immediate cause for concern in her days, Jenn found that fantasizing about Atticus was a hobby more intoxicating than sleep.

This morning was proving to be a little different, probably due to paranoia about the doctor's visit. Jenn's thoughts on Atticus kept swimming away from the Pelican state, away from the darling of her dreams, towards the thing attached to the end of Jennifer's arm. It'd been five days, and she still couldn't feel it. At all.

It looked dead... all blue and purple. It reminded Jenn of the way people looked in movies after turning into zombies. Was her new hand a zombie hand? What if it attacked her? What if it had the infection? The *Known Triangle* infection?

At 6:15 Zurich time, Jenn dialed out. She wasn't sure of the math, but she figured that it had to be the middle of the night at Faa's office. If someone answered, that person would be less likely to be some receptionist with a pre-programmed response concerning the whereabouts of the venerable Miles Faa.

Jenn's heart stopped as she waited for someone to pick up. "Hello?"

"Hello, Hi. I'm calling for Miles Faa."

"He's not taking any clients at this time."

"Yes, I'm aware of that. I know..." Jenn faltered, she knew so much. What was safe to divulge? "I'm an associate that planned on joining him on the *Orion* adventure schooner, but

I... I was unable to join the ship's crew. I thought maybe Faa would be back by now."

"Excuse me, who is this?"

"I—I... I work for Lillith Babbit."

"Miles Faa is dead."

Dial tone.

Jenn couldn't believe it.

Dial again.

Ring. Ring. Ring.

No answer.

Hang up. Try again.

Rinse. Repeat.

Jenn refused to let any thoughts in.

Just.

Rinse. Repeat.

Ring. Ring. Ring.

"Stop calling!"

"How do you know he's dead? I want to know for sure!" Jenn yelled.

"For sure? Who are you? I'll take the battery out of my phone!"

"I just need to know!" Jenn's voice was too loud.

"What do you want from me!?" The voice was as pained as it was angry.

"Who are you?"

"I am... I was—Miles' girlfriend. Please leave me alone."

Miles never mentioned a girlfriend. Not once. He never wrote anyone on the boat. Never made a phone call. Never talked about a girl while they waited in the hole. Nothing.

Be brave, Jenn thought. "I don't believe you."

Dial tone.

Miles is dead and he had a girlfriend.

The revelation should have devastated Jenn. Her burden of guilt should have increased ten-fold. But Jennifer Dash refused to believe any of it. Miles wasn't dead. And he didn't have a girlfriend. It wasn't true. It wasn't true. It wasn't true.

The thoughts were stuck swirling in Jenn's mind as she walked to the doctor. The appointment was for 9am. She strolled in maybe ten minutes late. The TVs showcased on this Sunday morning Nicolas Cage's bomb of a horror-remake, *The Wicker Man*, once again sans audio. They put a cage of bees over Nic's head. He was screaming, but Jenn had to smirk. Without the sound, it kinda looked like Nic Cage was shouting for joy. He was so happy to try on the bee helmet!

"I like bees!" said the only other soul in the waiting room, a little woman who looked to be the size of a large doll, but had a face seventy years old.

"Excuse me?"

"I said, I like bees!"

"Oh, good," Jenn said trying not to sound to patronizing.

"Do you wanna know something?"

"Is it about bees?"

"One of the nurses stole a little boy."

"What?"

"I heard her in English say there's a missing boy."

"Oh."

"And the way she talked, I can tell. She stole him."

"How can you tell?"

"I'm telepathic."

"Really?"

"Yes. I know you miss your boyfriend, and you don't like your job."

Jenn didn't have a boyfriend. She didn't have a job. She pulled a sucker out of her purse, key lime pie, and jammed it into her mouth, non-verbally signaling that she wasn't interested in conversation.

"Don't you think you should do something?"

Jenn didn't want to respond. So she didn't.

"I said, don't you think you should do something?"

Jenn crunched down on her sucker. She immediately regretted it as it shattered into a thousand tiny candy swords in her mouth.

"I said, I SAID, don't you think you should do something?? Listen to me!"

The persistent question broke Jenn down.

"What am I supposed to do?"

"Investigate."

"Why me? Why not you?"

226

The nurse-receptionist walked in, clipboard in tow. "Jennifer Dash?"

"That's me!" Jennifer said with relief.

Within minutes Jennifer Dash was knocked out, floating in a dreamless void.

She awoke. Jenn was glad to discover this time she was not floating in an ice bath.

A nurse stood beside her.

"Okay. Jennifer, everything looks good. We expect you back Friday, 9am."

"Uh, nurse?"

"Yes?"

"Is there a lost boy... somewhere?" The haze of the anesthesia was still clearing.

"Oh, I'm not Lara."

"Lara?"

"One of the other nurses, her nephew is the one who's missing."

"Can I speak to her?"

The Not-Lara nurse escorted Jenn to another small room. Jenn didn't have to wait long. "Yes, I'm Lara."

"Hi. I'm Jennifer. I heard about your nephew from one of the other patients. I was just wondering if there's something I can do."

"Your Lillith Babbit's friend, yes?"

"Uh, yeah, I guess."

"She sent you here?"

"Umm... yeah."

"Did she tell you to talk to me about this?" The nurse sounded angry.

"No, no! Really, I don't really even know what's going on... I just... I'm here for these six weeks, and I don't have anything to do, so I thought maybe I could pass out flyers or something. I don't know."

"Meet me at Shamrock tonight, 10pm."

"Shamrock?"

"The Irish pub."

Jenn went into town to stall until evening. She thought

227

about shopping, but mostly just wandered. She did end up buying a pink skin for her phone.

She got to the Shamrock pub an hour early, ordered a shepherd's pie (it was gross) and waited around for Lara.

Lara came, ordered a stout beer, and held a tablet up in front of her eyes.

"I am from Liechtenstein. My little sister married the mayor of Vaduz, our capital city. He owns several hotels in the country. My sister, she didn't want to just be a mayor's wife, so she worked at one of their hotels. She died last year, found in the back room of the hotel, the room where they kept the safe. They say she died of acute, sudden spontaneous asphyxiation. I've always wondered. My sister had a son before she married the mayor. This is him, Robin. He's eight.

"Here is what the newspaper said, I'll translate as I read. *Yesterday, in Eschen, a man was found in Hotel Eschen, that had apparently suffered from sudden asphyxiation. Of note, this morning, a boy, Robin, was reported missing. The boy, Robin is the son of the mayor, and was spending time at the hotel visiting a friend. At this time there is no indication that the asphyxiation is linked to the boy's disappearance.*

"That was three days ago. They are calling him the Lost Boy of Lichtenstein. Everyone's looking for him, but he can't be found. This is what the paper said this morning. *The manager of the hotel Eschen had asked Robin to spy on the man who was later found asphyxiated. The manager thought the man was suspicious so he paid young Robin to hide in the man's closet. No word yet on whether the hotel manager will be prosecuted for child endangerment. Meanwhile, voices are rising that the mayor of Vaduz should be prosecuted for criminal neglect, as he had no idea where his stepson was on the night of his disappearance despite the mayor being his step-father.*"

Lara dropped her voice just above a whisper, "I think Robin found out something. Maybe he found out who killed my sister. I think he's hiding, and I think he's hiding because the mayor is the one to blame."

"Wait, you think the mayor of Vaduz killed your sister, his wife, and then a year later randomly killed some other dude, and your nephew found out, so he's hiding."

"You know Lillith Babbit. I'd like to ask you for her help. I believe I know where Robin is."

"Where?"

"My sister and I, we grew up very poor. Our parents died on a trip and we were raised by our grandparents. They were very cruel and didn't feed us much. We didn't have much to play with, or to eat, so we hunted in the sewers. Even after we had food and welfare, we still went down there. It was like this big secret world she and I had. I think maybe my sister taught Robin about our adventures."

"You think he's in the sewers."

"Where else could he be?"

Jenn left the Shamrock perplexed. She wanted to help Lara. She wanted to do something good for a change, but she really didn't know how to help. For one thing, although she had Babbit's credit card, she didn't actually have a way of contacting her favorite millionaire. Roger left her without a word on how to reach Lillith. Secondly, Robin, this Lost Boy of Liechtenstein, he was supposedly in the sewers. Jenn had already had a long adventure in the sewers under Los Angeles, the working space of the Patriot. She wasn't exactly riveted to get back into the underworld.

Jenn couldn't sleep that night. Thoughts of the Lost Boy of Liechtenstein and the hot and bothered girlfriend of a deceased Miles Faa kept bobbing to the surface.

Jennifer Dash once again had to be a woman of action. She couldn't bear to be alone with her thoughts.

She dialed the number.

It rang for what seemed an eternity, and then, finally, like fresh air after years holding one's breath:

"Yello?"

"Atticus?"

"Yeah, who's this?"

"It's Jenn. Jenn Dash."

"Oh my gosh, Jenn! How are you? Where are you?"

"I'm in Switzerland."

"Wow! Your adventures have really taken you far! How'd

229

you get this number?"

"I looked you up... I don't know, the internet or something."

"Wow, I thought you didn't know how to use the internet."

"Yeah, well, I've learned a lot since we last talked."

"I bet, I bet. Hey look, is this your number?"

"Umm... yeah?"

"Are you calling from like your own phone, or someone else's?"

"Oh, right, yeah, this is mine."

"Okay great, I'm gonna save your name in my phone. But uh, can I call you later?"

"Oh."

"Yeah, sorry. I'd really love to catch up, but, I'm at this recital thing, and it's gonna start like any minute."

"Recital?"

"Yeah, it's like a piano thing, uh, my girlfriend's little brother's thing... um... yeah, I... sorry, I know that's... uh, I feel a little awkward. Can I call you back? I really would love to talk more. But, they just dimmed the lights. I gotta go."

"Oh, okay."

"Okay bye. Great to hear your voice!"

"Great to hear your voice too."

~~~

The Lost Boy of Lichtenstein needs to be found.

Chapter 37: The Lost Boy of Liechtenstein

Doubt leads to paralysis. Sometimes this paralysis manifests itself in the form of physical lethargy, sometimes as indecisiveness, or sometimes as emotional detachment. For Jennifer Dash, paralysis amidst doubt meant all the above.

She had tried her best not to be downtrodden by the news that Atticus Further had a girlfriend. Jenn had been a million miles away for months now. He's a strapping young man, why wouldn't he go out and get himself a nice girl? Jenn had no say over his life, no direct influence.

A stream of potential maneuvers rushed into Jenn's mind. She could show up on his doorstep, once again homeless, beg onto his generosity. Sleep on his couch for a week. Win over Scout, Atticus' little sister, get her to push for Jenn being a presence in the family. Or, better, impress Joseph Further, the pater familius of the household. Impress him with all she learned from the book he gave her. Lie to him, tell him how she kept sacred every one of his ten rules.

But Jenn wasn't good at lying, especially when it came to things like the death of Tiff. Any thought of the "Guidelines" brought with it the searing pain of fighting Tiff... and all that blood, the blood that even now coursed through Jenn's veins.

And then there was the book. All the lessons Jenn had picked up from it were now foggy. She could barely recall one of the fifty pitiable ones. Something about Dr. Seuss? Some painter guy who made up a new color? Amelia Earhart? Jenn had left the book back at Pishtaco's island. Plans of a drowning suicide don't leave much time to remember to grab all of your things before exiting through the gift shop. Maybe one of the hedgeys picked up her book. Maybe the Numbered Man, 666, was reading it right now.

More than all these potentials, Jenn fantasized about wooing back Atticus. Showing up around town, all dolled up, maybe wearing that Cinderella gown she just bought in downtown Zurich.

231

She could buy a plane ticket back to the States right now if she wanted. She could use that black card of Lillith's....

But showing up all mascara-ed and eye liner-ed up wasn't going to cut it. Atticus wasn't available. So, Jenn shouldn't be either.

It struck Ms. Dash that she should show up with some arm candy of her own—an older, rich, beautiful man. At this, she vomited from her mind the idea of Antonio D'Anconia, the trophy boyfriend. No, only one man would fit the bill. Miles Faa. He'd make the perfect fake-suitor, playing the part in spades and winning the day for Jenn once more, her salvation in time of need.

It couldn't happen. Miles Faa was dead. Worse still, he was dead and had a girlfriend. Double blow.

Reality being what it was (hard and inflexible), Jenn did nothing.

She waited in her motel room. For days.

Atticus said he'd call her back. Why hadn't he? Did he lie? Was he just trying to get rid of her? Out with the old Jenn, in with the new girlfriend and her snotty-nosed, piano-recitaling brother. If only Jenn had a little brother. Then he could have piano recitals. Then maybe none of this stupidity would have happened.

A burning sensation had started to develop under Jenn's cast. That was probably a good sign, but it sure didn't feel good.

Why, why hadn't he called?

Three days, and Jennifer Dash had just about lost her mind.

A large aquarium glowed in the motel lobby. Countless times various staff had asked Jenn if she needed something, for she appeared to be waiting for someone or some service as she stood there, for days on end, staring into the fish tank.

It occurred to Jenn that all this waiting, this burning, this remorseful, fiery contemplation, it could all go away. All Jenn had to do was drop her cell phone into the fish tank. She wondered if Biggie, her name for the big puffer-like fish that swam aimlessly from end to end all day, would try to eat it. The phone waterlogged and damaged beyond all repair, Jenn wouldn't have to worry herself with the likes of Atticus Further any further. She wouldn't be doting on his call. It'd be over. Atticus could return to being a blithe fantasy at the center of Jenn's mind. No longer would pesky reality get in the way.

But then the awful price of treason; what if Atticus did try to call her? Then she'd be selling out a perfectly blissful reality for her sham imagination works. Gah! No good, none of it.

Stuck in the nether world of doubt and indecision, Jennifer Dash watched TV. For being in Switzerland, essentially the heart of mainland Europe, Jenn was impressed with the vast array of English-language TV channels her motel room received.

Saturday morning, amidst a commercial break during a very strange end-of-the-world flick, *Knowing*, Jenn flipped through some channels until a news story about the Lost Boy of Liechtenstein caught her attention. The news was in German, but the images carried the message well enough.

The boy was still lost. That much was clear. Thousands gathered the night before for a prayer vigil. Many held up signs with the boy's face. He was so small, such a skinny little thing. But such a big smile. And eyes. Deep blue eyes of wonder and awe.

Jenn's heart bounced out for the boy. He was probably just like her, being tossed and turned in a sea of adventures beyond his comprehension. Right now, he was probably hiking through unknown turns in the vast metropolis of Liechtenstein's sewers. Jenn could help him. She was just like him: a person no longer tethered to the economy of the world, no longer fixated on family ties and geographical inter-connectedness. He was a boy of the world just as Jenn was now a young woman of the world. She could lead him. Robin could be her sidekick. Robin, a sidekick. Well, that just about sealed the deal. Jennifer Dash as Batman, with the Lost Boy in tow as Robin the Boy Wonder? Yes, please.

Screw Atticus. Screw Miles. Screw their girlfriends too. Jenn was going to do some good on this Earth. She was going to save the Lost Boy of Liechtenstein.

But this wasn't Jenn's first underground rodeo. If she was to traverse back into the underworld, this time, she was going to

233

go prepared.

Jennifer Dash needed three things. With Lillith Babbit's everywhere-you-want-to-be black credit card, all Jenn's needs were attainable.

Thing One: a backpack. A large one. Jenn picked out the darkest black backpack she could find. It reminded her of the one on her back when she had left her Louisiana home. But this one, being brand-spanking-new, hadn't lost its deep blackness yet. That was good; camouflage for the night.

Thing Two: heavy-duty clothes. The winter in Europe, now just beginning, had thus far been unseasonably warm, so warm that today it was warm enough to be raining rather than snowing. Jenn thought of the sewer water, and, even in this moderately warm temperature, how cold it could be. Jenn bought several layers, and many bundles, so that she'd be cocooned in a water-resistant, warm jacket.

Thing Three: night-vision goggles. Hey, she had all the money in the world right now; why not splurge? Plus, uh, sewers are dark, yo! Who knows who's hunted for the boy already and came up with nothing because Robin hid in the shadows? The intimidatingly buff dude who sold her the goggles asked if she would be in a low-light setting or a no-light setting. Jenn wasn't sure. Since she wasn't exactly sure, the man recommended new, state-of-the-art, heat-sensing goggles. They wouldn't pick up depth very well, or form, per se, but this particular outlet didn't have army-grade, no-light night vision, so this was the best they could offer Jenn if she found herself in the pitch black. These would do the trick just fine.

And while she was there, Thing Four: a reasonably small grappling hook. No real reason for the purchase, besides the idea of being Batman. Batman always had a grappling hook... and a utility belt, but Jenn wasn't willing to go quite that far.

On her way out of town, Jenn filled her backpack half full with suckers. Robin would surely be hungry, and what child, when hungry, wouldn't think a lollipop the most desirable thing in all the world?

The motel ordered Jenn a taxi. The fare would be outrageously expensive, but what did Jenn Dash care? After some dialogue about which place would be the best to start if Jenn wanted to see every single city in Liechtenstein, the cabby and Jenn decided on the humorously named Liechtensteinian town of Balzers.

Still unsure of the conversion rate, but thinking it wrongly cheaper than the dollar, Jenn tipped the cabbie 100 Swiss Franks. That man had a good day.

Liechtenstein, even in the rain, is a pretty place. Wedged in the hills, the petite nation gives off a constant breezy feeling of "Everything's going to be okay. Troubles may come, but they won't linger." Jenn marched around the small town for some time before parlaying in front of a manhole.

Balzars, as well as modern Liechtenstein as a whole, is wondrously clean. There are, in fact, more companies registered within the borders of the landlubber nation than there are natural citizens. As a European country, Liechtenstein is replete with wealth, natural geographic beauty, and just the right amount of citizenry. Unlike Los Angeles or Las Vegas, Liechtenstein does not present to the passerby an overwhelming mass of humanity.

Jenn remarked to herself that this little slice of heaven would be a fantastic country to retire to. A vision of herself, seventy, holding the hand of an aged yet ruggedly handsome Atticus, flashed in Jenn's head before venom seeped into the fabric of the image, changing Jenn's face, her body, her hand, into some unknown girlfriend. Atticus Further, old and happy, bumbles about the streets of Balzers, Liechtenstein with his mate of fifty years, some unknown wench. What a pity.

Wishing for herself an escape from the daydreams, Jenn studied the manhole at her feet. It was the middle of the day, but with the cold sting of just-above-freezing rain puttering down, Jenn wasn't worried anyone would catch her descent into the underworld. What did worry her, however, was how to open the manhole itself. With just one small hole at its center, it looked mighty heavy. And that's when Jenn gleefully patted herself on the shoulder. It hadn't once crossed her mind back in Zurich that opening a Liechtensteiner manhole would prove difficult, yet something in her must have intuited the situation. Why else instinctively purchase grappling hook? She pulled the hook out of her backpack, slid one of the sharp edges into the hole, and with relative ease pulled back the manhole.

And now, a ladder back down, into the unknown.

Perhaps as a force of habit, she counted the steps down.

One.

Two.

Three.

Four.

Five.

Six.

Seven. Seven and that's it. What a relief!

The sewer emitted no light. Jenn was right to buy the night vision goggles; they came in handy instantly upon her descent. Unlike the catacombs under LA, which the Patriot filled with false phosphorescent light, the passageway under this landlocked nation offered no illumination.

Jennifer wasn't alone. She knew instantly, as soon as she donned the heat-sensing goggles.

Rats. Lots of rats, scurrying all around. And what Jenn supposed were spiders held themselves in air at various degrees to either side of Jenn.

The rats and spiders kept Jenn strictly marching north up the center of the tunnel. Unlike many women, Jenn had no extraordinary fear of either rats or spiders. Actually, much to her own surprise, she found them inviting. This purgatory hadn't yet been subsumed by the wit and power of human will and imagination. There were no spiders in the Patriot's lair. Critters meant regular old nature, not the Numbered Man's genetic-freak island. These revelations soothed Jennifer.

There are 250 km of paved roads in the fourth smallest nation in the world. It felt like Jenn had traversed half of that (in reality, it was much less than half) when her goggles shone red—the figure of a small human.

The image was frightening at first. Jenn threw her goggles off to try to see in real life what the goggles presented. She feared, upon first inspection, that she'd stumbled upon a sewer troll or a gremlin of some sort. But that was no help; the sewers went pitch black.

It was maybe sixty paces in front of Jenn, a little thing, huddled over itself. Even from a distance and using the infrared goggles, Jenn could tell the thing was shivering. The poor boy, he was probably freezing down here.

"Hello!" Jenn called out, trying to sound as chipper and welcoming as she could.

The huddled mass froze. It pivoted freakishly. Could it see her? Jenn stopped in her tracks. What if it wasn't the boy? It could still be a gremlin, some sort of night monster, an abomination of the dark—like whatever it was she heard in the bowels of the Earth on Pishtaco's island?

"Hey! I won't hurt you. Come here," Jenn said bravely.

The huddled mass evaporated, sprinting into the distance as fast as his little legs could take him. He was no gremlin. He was the Lost Boy of Liechtenstein. He was Jenn's Robin.

Not knowing what else to do, Jenn sprinted after him. She was tired, sure, but she hadn't gone all this way just to lose him.

"WAAIIITT!" She called to the boy.

She was nearly on him. He was so skinny... and small.

"I have food."

The boy collapsed. He froze, seemingly defeated.

"It's okay..." Jenn neared the boy, trying to reach out a loving, warm hand, "it's okay, it's—"

A horrendous scream. Jenn grabbed at her ears. It was shrill, terrifying.

"LEPRECHAUN!"

Jenn hurdled back. The boy shot up and darted up, somehow renewed in his terror.

Jenn was dazed. Before she could collect her thoughts, the boy and his red heat-sensored form... were gone.

He said Leprechaun, didn't he? Why did he shout that? He must have thought she was one. Why would an eight-year-old boy suspect that the thing that was chasing him in the sewers under Liechtenstein was a creature from Irish myth?

As Jenn trekked on, once again trudging through the underground in search of her Robin boy wonder, she sucked on a mint chocolate-chip sucker and racked her brain for what she knew about leprechauns.

237

They liked rainbows and pots of gold. They're small. They wear green suits. They have red hair.

That's it. That's all Jenn could come up with.

Why was Robin scared of little green suited men?

Jenn trudged on, but to be honest, she didn't much care for the mint-chocolate-chip flavor, and this particular sewer, besides going on and on and on... was boring. Jenn was tired.

Tomorrow, she'd figure out a new way.

She found a ladder, climbed up, pushed off the manhole, and returned the world under the sky where it was now dark.

Jenn was in Vaduz, the capital city. That was good news. The first motel she tried to check into asked to see her passport. Jenn didn't have any such thing, so she slipped out as the Maitre De turned away to grab some paperwork. She then made her way to a snazzier, upper-class-looking joint. This time she made sure to flash her black limitless credit card at reception. No one asked to see any paperwork.

In the morning, Jenn set out on foot to search for reinforcements, which she found in the form of a brute of a man, Ludwig.

Jenn established three criteria for the person she was going to hire to help her recover the lost boy.

1)   The person had to speak English as well as the local dialect of German.

2)   The person needed to be strong and fast. Jenn was looking for a "bodyguard." She wasn't going to market herself as a sewer-wanderer in search of the most wanted person in the country. Asking for a bodyguard seemed like a reasonable request. People could believe that, right?

3)   The employee had to be discrete.

Jenn's first thought was to go to a tourist shop and ask around for a tour guide, but upon reflection, how was that going to work? "Hi, I'm looking for someone to give me a tour of the sewers below your city?" No, tourism wouldn't work. And tour guides aren't exactly known for keeping their yappers shut.

That's when, by mere coincidence, Jenn passed by a gym. Ludwig was doing lunges with 100 kilo weights when she approached him.

What she liked best about old Ludwig, besides the fact that he was available immediately, was that he was a quiet man.

When she told Ludwig they were going underground, he grunted. No questions asked, just a mild manner grunt that Jenn interpreted as, "Is that what body-guarding is about these days?"

Back below, in the darkness, Jenn had to make some quick decisions. She only had the one pair of goggles, so either Jenn or Ludwig was going to have to trudge blindly.

Solution: Ludwig wears the set. Jenn holds his hand.

The next internal debate: does she come clean with Ludwig about what they're doing down there?

No.

"Ludwig, I have to be honest."

"Yes?"

"I didn't need you as a bodyguard."

"No?"

"No, Ludwig."

"Lood-vig."

"Right, Ludwig, I... my husband hit my son, and he ran away yesterday. I found him down here, but he ran away. I need you to catch him."

"Okay."

That was it. No questions. Jenn loved this big lub!

It didn't take long walking in silence before...

"I think... I see him. Stay."

Jenn listened to the big pounding steps of the gym rat chasing down the small pitter-patter of Robin.

No scream this time. Jenn couldn't see it, but Ludwig had wrapped an arm around the boy like a vice, carried him nearly horizontally, and covered the boy's mouth with his hand.

He returned, Lost Boy in arm.

"Up?"

"No. Not yet. I need you to ask him a question for me?"

"Me?"

"Yes, Ludwig. I told you, discretion. Don't ask questions."

"What do you want me to ask him?"

"Tell him my name is Jennifer, your name is Ludwig, and

239

we aren't going to hurt him."

"Her name is Jennifer, my name is Lood-vig, and—"

"Knock it off, Ludwig, this isn't the time to be silly. Tell him in your language."

Ludwig followed Jenn's orders.

"Now... here, hand him this!" Jenn pulled a sucker out of her pocket, and handed it to the darkness. Ludwig grabbed it, said something to the boy. Jenn smiled as she heard Robin's little fingers unwrapping the pop.

"Okay, now ask him why he's hiding here."

Ludwig again obediently followed directions. But no answer came.

"Tell him I can give him anything he wants."

No answer.

"He is too scared, I think."

"Okay. Ask him... ask him why he shouted out 'leprechaun' yesterday."

"Leprechaun? The little green men?"

"Yes, Ludwig, the little green men."

There was silence. Then... the boy whispered softly.

"He says the leprechaun came out of the Golden Boos' backpack."

"Golden Booze?"

"This is an old legend in Liechtenstein. This boy is Robin, everyone's been looking for him."

"Don't you think I know that, Ludwig... jeez, what do you think I hired you for?"

"You said...?"

"Why you ever listen to me, Ludwig, I'll never know."

"You are a confusing woman."

"It's a confusing world. Tell me about the Golden Boos."

"Long ago there was an old, big, fat woman that would come into hotels in Liechtenstein. She carried a big box. She'd ask the motel keeper to keep the box in a safe place. In the middle of the night, a small man would pop out of the box, and steal whatever gold or jewelry was in the safe place."

The boy began to feverishly whisper something. Ludwig responded. Jenn could hear compassion in his voice. He was now following in Robin's manner, whispering just as the boy did. Maybe Jenn had misjudged her golem. The boy was now whispering back to Ludwig, the two having an entire conversation without Jenn being let in, in the slightest.

"He says, whatever we do, if we're good people at all, we can't let anyone know he's here. He says his father will kill him."

"Why does he think that?"

Ludwig whispers. The boy responds.

"He says that the Mayor, his stepfather, made sure that his mother was killed, and he tried to have Robin killed the same way."

"Did someone try to strangle him?" Jenn asked sadly.

"No. Robin says a man saved him. His best friend's father saved him."

"How?"

"He was there with Robin in the room with the Golden Boos and the Leprechaun. Jennifer, I don't think we should give this kid up to the authorities. They'll just return him to the mayor."

"You don't trust the mayor."

"I've had my own dealings with him. He's not a good man. I believe the boy."

Robin began whispering feverishly again.

"What's he saying?"

Ludwig paused, then said, "He wants to know if you are a good witch?"

"Why does he think I'm a witch?"

"Because he saw the Golden Boos... he thinks she's a witch."

"Does he think all women are witches?"

"I don't know. He says if you can do anything, there is one thing he wants."

Jenn smiled. She was in a unique position to grant any request the boy would have.

"He wants you to bring back his mother from the dead."

~~~

If Jenn's adventures on the Numbered Man's island gave her a lesson in the limits of biology and science on this Earth,

241

she's about to experience first hand, the other side of the coin.

What's in store for Jennifer Dash?

Magic. Real. Bona fide. Magic.

Chapter 38: The Witch and the Leprechaun

Liechtenstein is a peaceful place. Like her larger neighbor, Switzerland, when the powers of the Earth erupted into war for a second time in a generation, Liechtenstein remained neutral. So peaceful is Liechtenstein, that in 1989 they officially outlawed the death penalty, despite the fact that no criminal had been executed in the country since February 26th, 1785.

Jennifer Dash and her bodyguard Ludwig huddled together in a closet, completely silent. Any squeak, rattle, hum, heavy breath might cost them their lives. Jenn couldn't believe it.

It was happening.

Robin, the Lost Boy of Liechtenstein, was right. He was dead right. And perhaps, about to be just dead. He was lying in the king sized bed of the room where Jenn and Ludwig hid. Jenn could see through the blinds that he was shivering under the covers. His eyes looked closed, but Jenn knew he heard and felt her presence.

The motel room was quite small. Quaint, one might say. To the right of the front door, as you entered, was a bathroom just large enough for one to squeeze in and shower just beside the toilet. Besides that, there was just the one room with the large bed, which looked *Alice in Wonderland*ishly big when just tiny, little Robin lay in it. Directly across from the bed was a small TV on a stand, and a seven-foot tall closet, from the grooves of which Jenn and Ludwig now purveyed the ghastly scene.

After a long talk with Robin down in the sewers, after Ludwig popped above ground to get food for the threesome, a plan was hatched.

Robin was a bright boy. If you could get him to calm down, he had quite the noggin above his neck. In the calm moments, if you could gain his trust, get him to slow down his breathing (at which Jenn and Ludwig were remarkably successful), then the youngling was even quite brave. This night's plan was all his initiative. Jenn could not doubt now, in this moment, the bravery it took to put himself in such harm's way.

The last state-operated execution in Liechtenstein, nearly 250 years ago, was of the infamous thief, Barbara Erni.

Erni was a hulk-like woman, as brawny as she was busty.

Over the course of several years, Barbara Erni, along with an unidentified accomplice, managed to pull off seventeen successful heists in hotels across the Liechtenstein region. When she was caught, the courts found Mrs. Erni guilty of being the infamous Golden Boos. Her prize was death by beheading. No one in Vaduz or the surrounding region had ever executed anyone, so the humble people called upon their blood-drenched neighbors to borrow an executioner.

That was 1785. The executioner cut Barbara Erni's head off in front of over 1,000 entertained spectators.

All that was true, yet here, defying logic, now creeping up on the supposedly sleeping Robin, was the Golden Boos herself. Barbara Erni resurrected, stood like a monolith above the quivering boy.

Jenn and Ludwig knew what came next. Robin had coached them through it—told, in scrutinizing detail how his encounter with the Golden Boos went.

Of course there are no photos or realistic paintings of the original, historic Barbara Erni. Liechtenstein didn't think the mug of their infamous prisoner something to be chronicled and remembered for all time. So then, quite naturally, neither Robin, nor Ludwig, nor Jenn or anyone else in the 21st century could identify this witching Boos as the actual reincarnation of the original.

They had waited three hours. That was quick. How did she know the Lost Boy was here? Earlier in the evening, Jenn returned to the fancy hotel she'd slept at the night before. This time, however, she registered along with her quote 'hubby', played sparklingly well by big ol' Ludwig. The two held hands at the receptionist desk to try to imprint that idea on any onlooker. In Ludwig's non-Jennifer-Dash's-hand-holding hand he carried a duffel bag. To make it look like a normal duffle bag of clothes and such. They stuffed the top of the bag with some real clothes, in case, for whatever reason, someone decided to inspect the bag.

Lying below the layer of clothes, little Robin was smuggled into the room.

Robin believed that the Golden Boos and her leprechaun were out to kill him. Hunting specifically him. He came to this conclusion after long days in the dark sewers. As things would later turn out, Robin had done a pretty fine job of putting the pieces of the puzzle together. He pretty much had it right. The only variable he missed was why exactly Robin's stepfather had called upon the Golden Boos to murder his wife and her son. Motive. What was the Mayor's motive?

Robin, being a still young and impressionable little boy, couldn't get past "He just doesn't like me." He had assumed the mayor of Vaduz, his brutal stepfather, had simply wanted to get rid of Robin and his mother. He assumed the motivation was one of lovelessness. Daddy doesn't love me, that's why he hurts mommy and me. Sadly, this was the logic imprinted onto Robin's psyche.

Once inside the hotel room, Jenn, Ludwig, and Robin wasted no time. Robin ran to the bed while Jenn and Ludwig hunted for the perfect hiding spot.

Waiting those hours in the closet, Jenn wondered what they would do if no Golden Boos showed herself. If they went the entire night with no sighting, the boy's theory would certainly not be disproved, not in the slightest. His stepfather could still have contracted this menacing woman and little friend to kill Robin. In that scenario, the assassin simply wouldn't have been aware the boy was above ground. Come to think of it, the logic of the whole operation was hairy.

If, as Robin intimated, the Golden Boos was magic, and magically could find him anywhere, then why was he safe underground?

If the morning had come with no sighting, Jenn wouldn't know what to do next. It's quite possible that in the eyes of the law, she'd be considered a kidnapper. She'd be keeping a mysteriously vanished child not only from his rightful parent, but from an entire (though tiny) nation that was praying for his peaceful return.

Those worries vanished when Jenn heard the doorknob

turn. They locked it hours ago. When Jenn first heard the slow jangle of the handle twist, she thought maybe someone had just come to the wrong room. They would try their key, realize it didn't work, and move on to the right room.

Not so.

Sharp but subtle clicking noises were followed by the slow creaking of the door as it opened.

From their position behind the closet door, Jenn and Ludwig had no line of sight to the front door, or the golemic shadow that passed through it.

When the frame of the Golden Boos came into Jenn's view, she couldn't believe it. This woman was enormous, and yet, her footsteps made no sound at all. The Golden Boos hung there, in the room, standing maybe seven, eight feet tall. It seemed to Jenn that the monstrosity was just as wide as it was tall.

Ludwig couldn't help it, he swallowed, trying to calm his nerves and mount his strength. His Everest stood hulking in front of his eyes. Ludwig was a big man, and big men aren't used to feeling dwarfed.

With its back turned to the closet, Jenn and Ludwig had a keen view of the thing that crept out of the woman's backpack. To call it a backpack conjures up the wrong image. The woman had a mass of cloth, maybe sheepskin, ladled over her back and strung up at the top. It resembled a grocery bag knotted at the top more than it did any modern backpack. Over the skin-cloth pack, the Golden Boos' long hair overhang. One could say it was golden, yes, but it was a rusty gold, deep and reddish. It hung to the center of the woman's back, and amidst the vivid golden strands were white and gray stalks. The resulting image was completely stupefying. From the back, this woman was ageless—or rather, age-ful. She looked both young, with her thick long, deeply colored hair, but simultaneously old, as white and gray strands seeped through the picture as a whole.

The hair wasn't the problem.

The problem was the thing that slowly spun out of the sheepskin.

Robin had tried to prepare them for this. In the traditional story, the tale of Barbara Erni and her thievery, the large-scaled woman carried a chest from hotel to hotel. She'd tell the lodge owner that all her worldly goods were kept in the box. She'd ask that the hotelier place the chest in a safe room. The owner would do so, and once inside the hotel's room of safekeepings, a little man would sprout out from the chest and steal everything he could get his hands on. Then the twosome would disappear in the night, hands full of whatever jewelry or treasure the other hotel guests had asked the owner to keep safe.

The 18th-century Golden Boos used a chest to sneak in her little thief. The 21st-century iteration skipped the chest in favor of this weird, antique rucksack.

The creature that slithered out from the bag was just as Robin described him. Jenn understood instantly why it was the little one Robin feared, not so much the Golden Boos. *"LEPRECHAUN!"* he had shouted. Jenn suppressed doing the same now.

He didn't wear a green three-piece suit as artists often depict leprechauns. But he did have a blossom of bright, laser red hair atop his head. He climbed out of the bag and slithered his way up towards the Golden Boos' shoulders. Through the slats in the closet door, Jenn could make out a demon-smile at the corner of the thing's mouth. A cold shiver pulsed through Jenn's veins.

Robin's first encounter with the Golden Boos and her evil friend apparently began this same way.

Robin said he and his best friend, along with their father, were staying in a motel. Robin and his friend Lukash were in one bed. Lukash's father was in a twin bed just beside theirs. They had all fallen asleep after watching some late night movies.

Robin said he woke up when he first heard the door unlock. Robin had a terrorizing fear of hotels since his mother mysteriously died in one a year before. It was for this very reason that Lukash's father came up with the idea of having a slumber party at a hotel—to get Robin over his fear, to help him see there was nothing evil in hotels, that no one was out to get him, that he wasn't fated to suffer the same mysterious end as his mother. Except, as it turned out, Robin had every reason under the sun to beware of hotels.

His worst nightmare had come to fruition.

He had woken up as the Golden Boos floated above the ground into the room. Robin had watched, absolutely petrified, as the smiling leprechaun slithered out of the backpack.

Robin had managed to nudge Lukash as the creature took a seat above the Golden Boos. He was probably at least three feet tall, but on the Golden Boos, the leprechaun looked to be no bigger than a pinprick of blood. He wasn't small in the same way that little people or dwarves were. He looked proportionally normal—just diminutive, like a child stunted by a gallon of coffee every morning.

Lukash had opened his eyes to catch the leprechaun entity leaping from the Golden Boos onto the bed. It had landed with precision, crouched over Lukash's body, staring directly into the boy's eyes.

It had smiled a wicked smile. Robin had been too terrified to move. He knew he should, knew somewhere in the back of his brain that what was happening was evil, and that not moving would only allow it to continue. He was only a boy, and so phobia, great all-consuming terror, ruled Robin to paralysis. The leprechaun had brought its left hand to Lukash's eyes, the fingers horrifically overlong and pointed, the fingers of a witch, protruding and dangerous. The leprechaun had twirled these fingers slowly in front of Lukash's eyes.

A second later, the leprechaun had leaped to the other bed, where Lukash's father still slept. Lukash too slept, Robin's friend hypnotized by the fingers. It had been clear to Robin that the leprechaun was aiming to do the same to Lukash's father, a hypnotized coma.

Why hadn't the leprechaun hypnotized Robin? Because Robin was the Golden Boos' business. From her side, she'd pulled up a long stick, a skinny, shrimpy little stick. She'd snarled and pointed it at Robin.

Gagging.

Robin couldn't breathe. He'd grabbed at his neck, his body wretching, searching for air. She was asphyxiating him.

Dying, dying, Robin was dying!

He'd managed to cry out while the leprechaun was still working on Lukash's father. The cry awoke the man who instinctively flung the little creature across the room.

"Robin!" he'd cried. Golden Boos then had pivoted her attention, moving her stick away from Robin towards the father.

Robin didn't think. He didn't even bother to breathe. He had run out the motel room door, sprinted down the hall, past the front door, into the dark, cold night where he had found a storm drain that he could squeeze through. There, in the underground sewers of Liechtenstein, Robin had waited, and abated his enemy.

When Robin retold the story to Jenn and Ludwig, he ended it by asking if Lukash and his father were okay.

Ludwig slowly, and with as much grace as one can possibly muster in such miserable situations, told Robin that Lukash's father was found dead of spontaneous asphyxiation. The good news was that Lukash himself was okay. Lukash had told none of this to reporters or the police. It was only in the last 48 hours that police had even connected Robin to Lukash and his father. Lukash had emphatically claimed to have no memory from that night—no memory of being at the hotel at all, or spending any time with Robin that evening.

From this intel the plan was hatched. Robin was convinced that the Golden Boos had come for him, that the horrible leprechaun was merely her henchman, putting to sleep the ones who weren't supposed to be there.

They planned for it to go down like this: Jenn and Ludwig would hide, wait for the Golden Boos and the leprechaun to come. When they did, and they saw the boy alone, they'd begin to choke him. That's when Ludwig would sack the Boo Monster from behind.

Jenn was in charge of the leprechaun. She'd pin him down somehow—just be careful not to stare in his eyes or at his fingertips. If all went to plan, they'd tie up the evil twosome with some rope Ludwig had bought and walk them over to the police station, telling the authorities everything that went down. Sure, the story would still sound ludicrous, but a tiny, slithery leprechaun and giant wand-pointing woman would make the whole thing palatable.

From there, they'd request asylum for Robin in the form of his moving in with his aunt Lara in Zurich. That would do, at least until the fog cleared on the whole situation.

It might not have been the best plan, but in the dark, damp of the sewers, it sounded reasonable enough. When push came to shove, it really was Ludwig that made it all possible. If he'd have wanted to turn Robin in for a reward, neither Jenn nor Robin would be able to best him, especially while he donned the infrared night vision goggles. But as it played out, Ludwig was the plan's biggest supporter. He listened emphatically to Robin's story, never once hinting that he was skeptical. Jenn thought this remarkable; after seeing fanny-pack sporting hedgehogs and being healed by saliva from a beaked woman, Jenn had had enough interesting experiences to suspend judgment at least until further notice, but ol' Ludwig here, what experiences did he have to call upon that led him to be so empathetic and believing? Jenn didn't know, and Ludwig wasn't sharing.

But now, with all skepticism thrown asunder by the sudden appearance of witch and leprechaun, all that was left of the plan was its practical application.

The leprechaun now sat on the Golden Boos, his long fingers resting atop her head.

"Go! Ludwig, now!" Jenn whispered into Ludwig's ear. He had to make the first move. Jenn couldn't take down the behemoth on her own. She'd be asphyxiated before she laid a finger on the demon-woman.

He shook his head.

The leprechaun's clothes were peculiar, more suited for Peter Pan than a figure from Irish myth. It pulled out, from somewhere, (Jenn couldn't see where) a mason jar. Uncapping the jar, it pointed the open side towards the boy, and began to cackle. Jenn could see the terror in Robin's eyes. He trembled under the sheets.

Jenn smelled the fear. Robin had lost control of his bladder. He was petrified by fear. No one could blame him. Jenn couldn't imagine what it must be like to be at the receiving side of that hideous cackling above the behemoth.

The witch raised her stick at Robin. More of a busted up old twig than a staff or cane, not something magical the likes of which Harry Potter would use. No. This was wood encrusted with muddy Earth.

The Golden Boos shimmied closer to the boy, concealing him from Jenn and Ludwig's vision.

But they didn't need to see Robin. They could hear him. He was choking to death.

"Ludwig. Now!" Jenn whispered desperately.

Ludwig didn't budge. Was he somehow hypnotized? Why wasn't he attacking?

"Ludwig!" Jenn said too loud. The cackling leprechaun heard her. It stopped its hideous laughter. Slowly pivoting its scrawny body towards the closet, the leprechaun stared directly at the hidden two. Jenn watched stunned as the little thing's eyes grew big.

He saw them.

"Ludwig! NOW!" Jenn yelled.

Nothing. Jenn pushed him through the closet door.

Like a bowling ball powered by a locomotive, the beastly Liechtensteinian bum-rushed the wicked witch. The force of his weight slammed the witch to the ground. The leprechaun, impossibly spry, leaped off and landed on the bed, positioning himself not towards Ludwig, but Jenn.

The stick wand had been flung out of the witch's hand, hitting the wall. Jenn saw that Robin was breathing, though he appeared in hysterics. The boy wasn't in the clear yet. The trauma might still do him in.

The witch and Ludwig tumbled on the ground grappling, pushing limbs, scraping to gain control and dominance over the other. The witch, much broader and bigger than Ludwig, caught his left leg in a vice between her two trunk legs. She thrust herself against the direction of Ludwig's body, causing his knee to invert. Brutal. Jenn heard it snap.

"AAAHHHH!" Ludwig gasped in wretched pain. The brute of a man brought his two huge arms together and pounded the Boos in the chest as hard as he could in blind vengeance. The thud was booming, as though Ludwig shattered her chest cavity; but she made no howl, no complaint. The two continued their deadly duel.

Jenn didn't know what to do. She knew she had to contain the leprechaun, but how? She didn't know what to do, so she took a lesson from Ludwig and rushed towards the little man. He easily jumped over her head.

"The wand! Get it! Get it!" The leprechaun said in an otherworldly, high-pitched shriek.

"What?" Jenn said astonished. Was it talking to her?

"Get it!" it squealed.

There was no time to worry about intent. Jenn ran to the wall, grabbed the wand, and pointed it at the leprechaun.

"Break it!"

"What?" Jenn said.

The witch, now sitting up, had a hand on each side of Ludwig's head. She pressed in hard. She was breaking his skull. Shards of his skull were beginning to splinter.

"AAAHHHHHHHHHHH!"

"Break the wand!"

Jenn took the little stick in both hands.

She snapped it.

The witch's strength went out from her. Her hands fell to her side, her head drooped... and then... it rolled off onto the floor.

Jenn stood stunned, not believing what she saw.

And then, just like that, a puff of smoke, and the witch was gone.

Ludwig looked up at Jenn, breathing painfully, unsure if the evil was over.

BANG, BANG, BANG.

"Open up in there! Open up now! The police are on their way!"

Jenn looked to Robin. To Ludwig, "Can you stand?"

"Yes, but I can't walk on the leg."

Jenn ran to Ludwig, to help him to his feet. Next she grabbed Robin like a rag doll, threw the boy onto Ludwig's back. A lamp on the nightstand—Jenn crashed it through the room's window. They were on the first floor. That was good. Jenn put her arm around Ludwig, and the three together hobbled out the window, headed back to safety, back into the sewers.

The leprechaun stood dumbly on the bed, staring at Jenn and her two new friends as they fled from the authorities for their lives.

~~~

Was it real? Did Jenn, Ludwig, and Robin really just encounter a witch armed with a wand of potent power? Or was it some sort of mirage? A trick of the night?

One note here, as the hotel manager knocked on the door, he of course, did not yell in English, but rather in Swiss German. His words have been translated and written here in English because in the moment, Jennifer would have understood his words no matter what language was shouted. The intent was clear to her, and so for your sake his words have been translated.

But I ask again: was it real? If it was, what does that mean about our world?

Chapter 39: Where You Need to Go

What do you do?

Heavy, fast, uncontrollably breathing.

You're underground, in the pitch black.

You've got a little boy with you. You don't speak his language. He's curled up in a ball, hyperventilating. You can't blame him.

You've got a bodyguard whose pain tolerance appears to be dropping. His kneecap was just smashed into a million pieces by a behemoth-sized witch. A witch who, after her wand was stolen, lost her head. Literally. She then evaporated into a momentary smoke.

The cops will no doubt be looking for you now. All the commotion in the hotel; Liechtenstein had already been on full watch because of the recent death and disappearance. They'll go crazy now. Probably lock down every hotel in the micronation.

All because of you. Not to mention your cargo; little hysterical Robin, the lost boy on everyone's list. What happens next? What do you do?

Topping it all off, whatever it is that's under your cast burns. Badly. It feels like a hot coal is smoldering a hole through your skin, veins, blood, and bones. You were told by the secret hospital not to get the cast wet. But everything in a sewer is wet. The air down here is a bath. The cast had gotten numerous full-on splashes when you chased Robin the other day, back when you had the night vision goggles. Maybe the water has soaked through. Maybe your new hand is ruined. Maybe it's rotting.

Maybe it's rotting.

Between the busted bodyguard, the hysterical boy, and the pitch black, you're unable to go anywhere. You're trapped.

What do you do?

Jennifer, what do you do?

"Help. Help. Heeeellllllp!" What are you doing? Why are you calling for help to no one, to nothing in the black underground

254

of Europe? You're not sure, but you can't help it. "Help. Heeeelllllp! Help!"

"I can help."

Jennifer knew that voice. It directed her earlier in the evening. Jenn's blood ran cold as she tried to convince herself that it wasn't what she knew it was.

"Who's there?"

"Jenn, no!" Ludwig managed to protest, his attention momentarily taken away from the stifling pain spiraling up, out of his knee.

"Who are you? Tell me your name!"

A regular person would have answered Jenn's question. People like to say their own name. But not this one.

"I can help you."

There was no doubting it now, no doubting who was speaking.

"I don't want your help. Go away."

"I can't. I'll be caught."

"I'll kill you if you come any closer." These were the scariest words that had ever come out of Jenn's mouth. Who had she become? I'll kill you if... That wasn't Jennifer Dash. That's not who she wanted to be. Maybe it wasn't. Maybe it was the thing under the cast speaking. Maybe.

"I'm already dead. I can help you."

The voice was getting closer. Jenn could hear the pitter-patter of small footsteps.

What do you do?

"The boy's ours!" Jenn yelled, assuming the leprechaun, (that's what he was, right?) wanted to get his witchy long fingers on Robin's neck. "You can't have him!"

"I don't want him... I... can help."

"Uussghh—aahuuann." Ludwig wasn't doing so well. He had to get to a hospital.

"I can heal him."

"Jenn, no!" grunted Ludwig.

"No, you can't," Jenn said passively, confidently, as if to dare the little red-haired man.

"It won't take long."

"How?"

"I know how."

"How do you know how?" Jenn pressed.

"I need to get somewhere. You can take me."

"I'm not taking you anywhere."

"Trade?"

"Trade? What trade?" Jenn said angrily. "What do you want?"

"I fix your man, you take me."

"Where do you want to go?"

"No. You make deal. I heal him. Then you take me. Deal first."

"I'm not making a deal in the dark just like that. I need more."

"I stay with you."

"No. You don't."

"I stay."

The leprechaun's logic was simple, but solid. He had all the cards. Jenn didn't have many moves to play.

She could risk taking Ludwig to a hospital, risk getting taken in by the police. Even if Robin stays in the sewer, she'd have to answer too many questions if authorities suspected Jenn. What if they made her take a lie detector test? Jenn had an abnormal fear of lie detector tests.

Jenn didn't see a way out of this thing... and didn't see a way to get rid of this stupid little man if he belligerently chose to hang around.

Here's a good one: a lost boy, broken knee-capped bodyguard, a girl trying to solve the world, and a leprechaun walk into a bar....

Was this really going to be Jenn's posse? Her new outfit, her newest clique? It appeared so.

"I need more. How can I trust you? You and your witch just tried to kill us."

"Not kill—tether boy's identity."

"Aaaaa... tether the what now?"

"Don't listen... Nothing goo--" Ludwig passed out from the pain in the middle of his chortled warning.

"I tell you. What you want to know."

"Good, yes. Tell me."

"We make deal."

"No. You tell me first."

"Deal. Then I say. I tell the mysteries."

"Why do you need our help getting to this place, wherever it is?"

"You take me, and I won't be captured."

"Captured by whom?"

"ANYONE!"

"Oh, I forgot, everyone's out hunting for leprechauns these days!" Where did Jenn's sass come from? Was it a product of pretending to have more cards, more moves on the table than she actually did? Or was it something else? The hand under the cast?

The little guy was silent in response to Jenn's snark.

A moment passed, each side unwilling to make the next move. Jenn's mind replayed the scene in the hotel. Perhaps she could figure out what was really going on....

"You took out a jar, while Robin choked, you took out a jar. Why?"

"Catch."

"Catch what?"

"Had no choice. Was imprisoned. When got the wand, I got free. I didn't want to do it."

"You were laughing when you were doing it."

"Not laughing. Had to do it."

"I don't believe you."

In the dark, Robin crawled up to Jenn, he curled up in her lap and hung onto her, his body shaking, but his breathing was now more controlled. She stroked his hair to calm him as she continued to interrogate the leprechaun in the darkness.

"Tuatha De! Take me to Tuatha De!" The leprechaun shouted.

"What's that? Where's that?" Jenn would soon come to find that the leprechaun's shout of Tuatha De referred to an ancient burial ground in Ireland, about 30 minutes outside Dublin. Not far. It's known today as Newgrange. The burial tomb site looks like a giant mound. It's believed that locals built it in 3200 BC. 200,000 tons of loose stone were

257

assembled to construct the underground passageways and recesses that make up the mystic building. Like so many ancient sites, each year, during the Winter Solstice, the light of the sun illuminates the passageway in a manner that is only seen on that one day. This creation, built in an era when Ireland yet had no written language, predates Stonehenge by 1000 years, the pyramids by 700. It is a mystery too few of us know... and embrace.

"Tuatha De! Take me to Tuatha De!"

"Okay, okay, good!" Jenn said, "That sounds like a place. We can go there. We can go there... if you fix Ludwig.... and answer every question I ask."

"It's deal! It's deal!"

There was scurrying in the dark.

Jenn couldn't see anything. In later days she'd recreate the scene in her mind, imagine what it must have looked like. In time she'd even come to believe that she did see it, just because she envisioned it so many times as to confuse her imagination of the event with the actual pitch black memory of it.

The leprechaun healed Ludwig.

There was almost no sound to it. Just a few scurrying little noises.

Then, just like that.

"Finished. Better. He better. He is better. Now we go."

"Ludwig? Ludwig!"

"Yes."

"Are you okay?"

"I... I think so."

"Is the pain gone."

"Yes."

"Can you walk?"

"YES! YES I CAN! What happened?"

"He fixed you."

Jenn didn't have to say who; Ludwig knew. The little monster healed Ludwig.

"Now we go," said the healing critter.

"Where are we going?" said Ludwig.

It took awhile to come up with a plan, but a plan they did come up with.

The four of them—Ludwig, Jenn, Robin, and the leprechaun—would hike up the sewers until they got out of Liechtenstein. Once they were confident they were in Switzerland, Jenn alone would go above ground. She'd use her black credit card to book a personal plane to Dublin.

Jenn worried about the details... worried that people would ask too many questions, worried that she wouldn't be able to find a private jet. But everything went off without a hitch, far easier than Jennifer Dash could ever have imagined. Money, or specifically in this instance, a limitless credit card, cures a litany of ills.

When they boarded the jet, Ludwig strapped Robin to his chest, and then wore many, many layers of clothing, so as to seem like just a large-and-in-charge fat man. The leprechaun was smaller, and thus much easier. He fit into a carry-on bag.

There was no flight attendant, and thankfully, a large door separated the pilot (and presumably a co-pilot, though Jenn never confirmed this) from the passengers.

Once high above the earth, the questioning of the leprechaun began.

"I've lived up to my side of the bargain. I'm taking you to the druids. You've made good on half of your deal. Ludwig's not complaining. Now's the time to answer my inquiries. For starters, why Ireland? Catching up with your pot of gold?"

"I'm no leprechaun."

"No? Then what are you?"

"I was boy once, just like him!" The long, twisty fingers of the little man stretched out towards Robin.

"I don't believe you," Jenn said. "Why are we going to Ireland?"

"I lived there."

"Because you're a leprechaun. That's where leprechauns come from."

"No. Please. I am... I was human."

"What are you?"

"I lived. Don't remember it well. Very long time past."

"How long ago? How old are you?"

259

"Don't know."

"How do you not know?"

"Time... isn't same on this side."

"On this side? On this side of what?" Suddenly, Jenn thought of the Croatoan. Did it describe creatures like this irkiddy-erkaddy leprechaun sitting before her?

The leprechaun couldn't stay still. He bobbed his scrawny legs like a kid hopped up on sugar and coffee. He twitched. He constantly creaked his back, as if trying to pop a bone back into socket.

"Dead."

"What?"

"That's the side I'm on."

"Jenn. Don't talk to him."

Jenn turned to her adventurer buddy. "How can you say that? Your kneecap! It was shattered. He healed you, Ludwig. This creature, he's magic! Aren't you curious? Don't you want to know how he did that? By what power he healed you?"

"No. I don't want to know."

"Why not?"

"He does what he does either by the powers of goodness, or the powers of darkness. I don't think the good guys try to strangle children."

"Didn't want to!" the thing protested.

"Just because you healed me, doesn't mean I like you."

The leprechaun jerked back in his seat, reacting as if Ludwig's words physically slapped the little guy in the face.

"Sorry, so sorry."

"Don't worry about Ludwig here, Mr. Leprechaun. Remember, we have a deal. You have to answer my questions."

"Know. I told you."

"Told me what?"

"That I'm dead!"

"What do you mean by that?"

"Hehehe..." The thing cackled in a manner that seemed like nervousness to Jenn. "When lived... In community, there was sick boy. Didn't like boy. Son of great man, he. Because of his father, was going to grow big, be a great man himself. I

260

wanted to be big man, but father, my father, my father, my father, my father, he was not big. He was normal. When boy sick, wished, I wished, I wished, I wished, I wished, I wished he would die. Wished every day. And he did! He died. Then it happened to me too."

"What happened to you?"

"I sick. Same way other boy did."

"What was the boy's name?"

"Don't remember."

"How long ago was this?"

"Don't remember."

"What's your name?"

"Lost my name."

"How do you lose your name?"

"Died, I died. Sickness got me. I floated up. My body out of. Floated into sky. Up, up, up, up and up."

"What like, your soul?"

"Just me. Meeeeeeeeeee. Identity mine."

"I think that's pretty much what they call a soul."

"No. Soul is different. Know soul. It's different."

"Okay, then what happened?"

"He caught. He caught, he caught, he caught me."

"Who?"

"The Shining One."

Jenn's mind flashed: the mural, children from every tribe, every tongue, following the song of the Piper. With a great god smiling down. As big as the sun.

"Who is it?"

"He's a great. Hate him. I hate him."

"Why?"

"She give me option. He eats me, or I become his. Come back to work for him."

"Wait, she? Who is she?"

"She, he. Does matter? No. Shining Man is her. Shining One is he, he eats me."

"You were dead. How could he eat you?" Ludwig asked, finally interested now in the conversation at hand.

"Eats identity. That's what makes great. Eats and he eats."

"So he's a fat man," Jenn joked.

"No, she's a great man, legion of one."

"Legion?" Jenn asked, but the leprechaun ignored him. The little fella kept squirming, as if he wished to wriggle out of his skin.

"So why are we going to the land of druids?"

"I hear, I hear, I hear. I listen and hear, I hear. They have secret."

"What secret?"

"Secret of how to die again."

"Huh?"

"Want, I want, I want, I want, I want to be free... and don't want to be eaten."

"You have to die twice to be free?"

"Freedom is..." The thing thought for a long time. "not being a slave. Say... they say druids know how kill the identity. Want, I want, I want that. Want them to kill me. Then Shining One can't eat me, eat me, eat me, eat me, anymore."

The realization of what this sad little thing wanted slowly washed over Jenn. What he wanted wasn't money, wasn't fortune, wasn't even food or shelter... he wanted nothing. Literally. He wanted to become nothing.

"Leprechaun, when I die, will the Shining One eat me?"

He shook his head vigorously. "I not leprechaun. Refuse, I refuse!"

"Okay, it's okay... answer me. When I die will the Shining Man/Woman eat me?"

"Don't know," the little thing confessed.

"What do you know?" Ludwig added.

"She makes identity catchers. Some catch when you alive. Some catch you when die. Was, I was, I was, I was, I was caught because wished for friend to die. I did it, I did it, I did it. I tethered myself to him... BUT I DIDN'T KNOW. I DIDN'T KNOW. NOT FAIR! NOT FAIR! WANT, I WANT, I WANT TO BE FREE!"

Robin the Lost Boy, unable to understand English, still managed to be unsettled by the shouts of the leprechaun. A shiver ran through his body and didn't stop. Did it ever?

"Why do you look like a leprechaun?"

"The Shining Man."

"He... she made you look like a leprechaun?"

"Because from the island—Ireland, made look this way, me, me, me. When work him, you to be an identity snatcher." The little guy pulled out the glass mason jar from seemingly nowhere.

"This," he held out the jar. Ludwig grabbed it. Examined it.

"It's just a regular jar," he said.

"In this place," the little critter said.

"Why couldn't you go to Ireland yourself? Why did you need us?" Jenn redirected the conversation to more practical matters.

"Get trapped. So easy. That's how she got me."

"Who?"

"Golden Boos."

"Who was she?"

"Just like me, like me, like me... but different form."

"I don't understand." Jenn threw up her arms.

"You can't understand."

They continued to question the nameless thing, but his answers became increasingly incoherent. It's not worth our time to examine the contents of the thing's words. Useless and pointless. Jenn kept pushing and pushing, question after question, searching for a rhythm, some sort of sense to it all. She figured that if only she asked the right question, then everything would fall into place. She made a thousand inquiries about this 'Shining Man/Woman'. Jenn was convinced, beyond any doubt, that this had to be Pied Piper. He was the monster under every bed, the vision beyond every dream. He was her nemesis, and Jenn knew it. It would only make sense that even in her running, she'd fall back into the Piper's snare. He was everywhere. He was in everything. He was the cook behind every death, every mystical fantasy.

While Jenn plugged away at her leprechaun inquisition, Ludwig spoke to Robin, explaining all that he had learned to the young lad. Robin took it all in with solemn pride.

When the jet landed down in Dublin, everyone was exhausted.

Thankfully, now out of Liechtenstein and mainland Europe, the group felt confident that Robin was safe. No regular passerby on the street would suspect him. Of course, the leprechaun was another story. He smashed himself back into the luggage.

Before any further adventures, the crew needed to rest up.
    They booked themselves into a Dublin hostel and slept.
    Jenn dreamed her altogether lovely nightly dream. That is, until Ludwig awoke her.
    "Robin has something he needs you to hear."
    Jenn went to Robin's bed. Ludwig sat at the foot of the bed while Jenn got on her knees. She leaned over towards the boy who still cowered under his covers.
    "Hey there, what's up?" Jenn asked.
    Ludwig translated.
    The boy responded.
    "He says that he had a dream."
    "Okay, it's okay. We all have bad dreams."
    "He says a man came to him in his dream, told him that it was important..." Ludwig paused, thinking about his choice of words, "...imperative that you join the druids."
    A man came to Robin in his dreams. Was it the Piper?
    Jenn cleared her throat, "Who was the man, Robin?"
    Ludwig translated: "He said he was a nice man."
    "Was he the Shining Man, Robin?"
    The boy shook his head.
    "Was he playing an instrument? A flute? A fiddle?"
    "He says there was no music, no instrument, but the man was very nice, and he said that you have to go join the druid group, Jennifer."
    "What else, sweetie?" Jenn said to try to keep herself as much as Robin calm and comfortable.
    "Nothing else."
    Jenn went back to sleep. In the morning, Jenn got help from the receptionist to rent a car.
    Once in the car, Ludwig drove. Jenn sat in the back with Robin. In the passenger side, the little sad leprechaun sat and squirmed.
    They arrived at a commune a few kilometers outside the Newgrange mound. A long building covered in windows

264

reminded Jenn of a Summer camp retreat. Jenn admitted that it looked comfy.... Green hills rolled behind the building surrounded by patches of trees and several teepees, like those of the Native Americans.

A parking lot sat empty in front of the resort, but for one dirty truck and a black SUV.

"This is it!"

Before everyone could unbuckle, a man and woman, both in their mid-thirties, beat on the front windshield.

"Hey!" The woman said.

"You need to come with us," the man shouted.

Ludwig got out and looked ready to slam his fists into the man's face. Both the man and woman wore black suits, which reminded Jenn of the security at Magical Kingdom. Jennifer Dash instinctively feared them.

Jenn eyed the front door of the resort opening. Five monk-like elders stepped out slowly making their way towards the rented car. As they stepped outside into daylight, they pulled the hoods of their long brown robes over their heads.

The leprechaun wheezed, swung his door open, and at once pranced towards the hooded ones. When he got to them, two of them immediately outstretched welcoming hands accepting him as if anticipating his arrival.

"Don't go in there! Stay away!" The woman in black said to Ludwig.

"We do what we want to do," Ludwig said stoically.

Two monks were still headed towards the vehicle.

As Ludwig began to step towards the resort, the man in black put his hand on Ludwig's chest, then immediately removed it, feeling the ripped Liechtensteinian and realizing the folly of his ways.

"Please, you have a child," the man in black said as he looked at Robin, "This place is not safe for anyone, especially children."

Jenn thought it odd that the two well-dressed provocateurs spoke in American accents.

Ludwig looked to Jenn, then to Robin. He hesitated, and the group stood still—an unnatural standoff.

The two, apparent Druids, Jenn guessed, reached the car.

265

They were both old men, both bald. They smiled at Jenn and company.

"We'd like to see your facility," Ludwig nodded at Jenn, "she might want to join."

"That would be a terrible mistake," the woman said.

The older of the two men smiled again at Ludwig and said, "We call this couple 'The Controllers'. They're on something of a campaign to stop our work. But they won't hurt you. And they won't stop you." The two robed men took a couple steps back. "Since today they've gotten the jump on you, you must go through them before you come to us."

The man turned his attention to the man in black. "72 hours. If they still want in after that, you let them go. Yes?"

"Of course, same as it always is."

"Good."

The two robed men walked away.

"Would you please come with us," the woman in black said, motioning towards their black SUV.

"What about the—" Jenn stumbled not knowing what to call the leprechaun. "What about our little one?"

The woman in black shrugged, "We are where YOU need to go."

The leprechaun was already in the resort. With the druids. Out of sight.

~~~

For the next 3 days, Jenn, Ludwig, and Robin will submit themselves to the "Controllers."

These people will do their best to convince Jenn that she doesn't need to join the Druidry. If Jenn and company can withstand the mental onslaught, in three days they'll be given access to the Druid community.

Is it worth it?

266

Chapter 40: 72 Hours

Transcript of the encounter between Jennifer Furth and Controller Yasmine Stormach on day one of Jennifer's subjugation.

Yasmine: Jennifer, thank you for coming to us. I speak for our community when I say I'm thankful you're here and looking forward to spending time with you the next couple days.

Jennifer: Where are my friends?

Yasmine: The gentlemen is with my companion, Pavel, and we're waiting for a German speaker to come in before we start our line of questioning with the boy. Understood?

Jennifer: I'd like to be with them.

Yasmine: I can assure you, they are fine. No one's going to hurt them. They're in good hands, our hands. Here's what's happening, Jennifer. You want to go to the Druidry. My community, our community, focuses much of our attention on dissuading individuals from joining this, what should we call it... neo-cult. We have an agreement with the Center and the local government; if we physically encounter potential joiners once they're in the parking lot, which remains publicly owned, then we may question them for three days before those individuals may enter the Druidry Center. I want to be clear with you, Jennifer. If, at any time, you wish to leave, you may do so. We are not holding you against your will. But, if you desire to enter the Center, you'll need our certificate of completion, which we'll dutifully present you after you've lodged 72 hours with us. Any questions?

Jennifer: Will I see my friends again?

Yasmine: We've spent many, many seasons sculpting the next 72 hours for you, to provide you with as much multi-sensory information possible. Our studies have shown that until you've reached the decompression point, that is to say, the point at which you need to verbally process all the information you've taken in, it's best to not have the distraction of peers about. Therefore, it generally falls that we'll reintroduce you to your comrades on the evening of the second night... but if the decompression point isn't reached, reunion with peers doesn't happen until after the 72 hours, if necessary. Understood?

Jennifer: *(no response)*

Yasmine: Let's get started. Here's how today's Socratic session works. I'll ask you a series of questions. You answer them. Once you've answered every question on my list, we're done. We also want to be open, honest, and compassionate with you. We don't want to ask you anything that we wouldn't ask ourselves. So, at any point if you have questions for me, I'll do my best to answer them, and if, during any question, you'd like to hear how I'd answer the question, then I'd be tell you. If you feel uncomfortable with a particular question, you may say *pass*, and we'll return to it at the end of the session. If you decide to be confrontational and not answer any questions whatsoever, well then, I'll just repeat myself until you decide to answer.

Jennifer: Have you ever had someone never answer any question?

Yasmine: No. We had a lady once, much like you, but older, maybe in her thirties. She came in here with the thought that she'd just give us the silent treatment. I believe she lasted fourteen hours... something like that. But you know what? The beautiful thing was, that once she finally broke down and started answering questions, this remarkable, intelligent, thoughtful, dare-I-say, vivacious woman came out. And guess what? She left us after 40 hours, went back home, decided that Druidry was not for her. A happy ending. Alright, here we go. My name is Yasmine Stormach, I am your Controller today. Shall we begin?

Jennifer: *(no response)*

Yasmine: Shall we begin?

Jennifer: I've been tortured before. I don't appreciate being held against my will.

Yasmine: But you're not being held against my will. You can leave any time you'd like.

Jennifer: You won't let me see my friends.

Yasmine: Have you ever been to a theme park, Jennifer?

Jennifer: Yes.

Yasmine: When you go on a ride, let's say the best, most popular ride at the park, you have to get in line first, right?

Jennifer: *(no response)*

Yasmine: Of course you do... and the more popular the ride, the longer the wait. Think of these three days as the line to get onto the ride, except, the ride is horrible. It might kill your body. And it will most definitely kill your mind.

Jennifer: What's your question?

Yasmine: My first question is: what's your name?

Jennifer: You know my name.

Yasmine: I'd like it to be on the official transcript. What's your name?

Jennifer: My name is Jennifer.

Yasmine: Last name?

Jennifer: Pigly-wigly.

Yasmine: Are you being serious with me, Jennifer?

Jennifer: No, no I am not.

Yasmine: Did you just tell me a lie?

Jennifer: Yes, yes I did.

Yasmine: *(sigh)* Okay, can we get Cole in here please?

Jennifer: Who's Cole?

Yasmine: He's our lie detector test operator... Ah, that was fast work, Cole.

Cole: Yeah, well, the others are going better, so I was listening in on this one.

Yasmine: Already?

Cole: Smooth operation. Looks like you picked the short straw today.

Yasmine: Great. I'm up for the challenge.

Cole: Would you please raise your arm so I can apply this?

Jennifer: What if I say no?

Cole: Then both of us have to work longer hours today.

Yasmine: People often come here and they think it's a fence they have to climb over. It's not, Jennifer. You'll get way more out of this then you put in. We've done the research. Later, you'll see a video from people that have been through this process, have come out the other side. Nine times out of ten the folks thank us for our work. We're not doing this for us.

In fact, no one pays us to be here. We raise our own financial support. And listen, there's no special something we're trying to boil out of you. You've said you were tortured? Tell me how this is similar to that?

Jennifer: *(no response)*

Cole: Lift your arm one more time for me... Thank you... Now, can you state your name so I can get an initial recording?

Jennifer: Jenn.

Cole: Good, good. We should be up and running, Mrs. Stormach.

Yasmine: Thank you, Cole. Jenn, when people are hooked up to lie detectors, they're three times more likely to tell us the truth. We know it's hard, on day one, to gain your trust, so we're trying to speed up the process. The lie detector helps us get to our destination sooner. Now, would you please tell us your last name?

Jennifer: It's Furth.

Yasmine: Furth, spelled F-I-R-T-H?

Jennifer: F-U-R-T-H, like in the word Further.

Yasmine: Ah, thank you. Jennifer Furth, where are you from?

Jennifer: Louisiana.

Yasmine: How old are you?

Jennifer: Seventeen.... no, wait, I guess I'm eighteen now.

Yasmine: You're not sure.

Jennifer: Birthdays weren't a big deal in my household.

Yasmine: Do you know when your birthday is?

Jennifer: *(long silence)* Yes.

Yasmine: Would you mind telling me what day it is?

Jennifer: Pass.

Yasmine: Okay, good, that's fine, that's fine. Thank you for your honesty. I appreciate that you have boundaries you're uncomfortable crossing. Would you like to tell me something about your parents? Their names? Professions?

Jennifer: Pass.

Yasmine: How about school? What was the name of the high school you attended?

Jennifer: Pass.

Yasmine: Aunts, uncles, any relatives you'd like to talk about?

Jennifer: Pass.

Yasmine: Are you interested in Druidry because you're trying to escape your past, Miss Furth?

Jennifer: No. I'm not escaping anything. Coming here wasn't even my idea.

Yasmine: Who's idea was it?

Jennifer: The little man's.

Yasmine: The little man? And what is his name?

Jennifer: Ummm... pass.

Yasmine: These passes are piling up, Jennifer. But that's okay. We've evidently started with a delicate subject. Let's talk about beliefs: do you believe in God, Jennifer?

Jennifer: Are you some kind of church or something? Is that what this is about?

Yasmine: Would my answer change yours?

Jennifer: No, it would just explain a lot.

Yasmine: Can you answer the question?

Jennifer: Do I believe in God? I don't know. Do you?

Yasmine: I didn't for the first twenty-nine years of my life.

Jennifer: Then you met Jesus?

Yasmine: No, then I met the Devil. Do you believe in the Devil, Jennifer?

Jennifer: I believe there are bad people. Maybe one of them is the Devil.

Yasmine: Do you think these bad people may be possessed by the Devil?

Jennifer: How would I know something like that? Doesn't the Devil work in mysterious ways?

Yasmine: I believe that sentiment is usually attributed to God. Do you believe in karma?

Jennifer: Like when good things happen to good people, bad things happen to bad people?

Yasmine: Yes, that's a very, very good definition.

Jennifer: Then no, I don't believe in karma.

Yasmine: Why not?

Jennifer: Because I've seen bad things happen to good people.

Yasmine: Are you thinking of someone in particular?

Jennifer: I knew this girl... uh, Taryn. She was born on the streets, I think pretty much an orphan. And she kept getting caught up in all these schemes. All she wanted was to be wanted, you know? To be important. And... and the world didn't want her. No one did. I know I didn't.

Yasmine: That sounds like a hard situation. Do feel some shame about that?

Jennifer: Yes.

Yasmine: In general, would you say that you have a lot of regrets in life?

Jennifer: I used to think no, I didn't. But lately... I guess if I'm being honest, I do. Yeah, I do have a lot of regrets.

Yasmine: What's your biggest?

Jennifer: Pass. Can't make it that easy for you.

Yasmine: Do you fear making bad decisions?

Jennifer: Not really. If I did, I think I wouldn't be doing what I'm doing.

Yasmine: And what is it that you're doing?

Jennifer: Solving the world.

Yasmine: Don't you think that's a little precocious? How does one go about doing that, 'solving the world'?

Jennifer: That's two questions.

Yasmine: Why not answer both?

Jennifer: Fine. It doesn't have to be precocious. That's just bad marketing.

Yasmine: Excuse me, what do you mean?

Jennifer: Shouldn't we all be doing what I'm doing? I think everyone should be trying to figure out this place.

Yasmine: I think everyone is.

Jennifer: Really? What's the point of life?

Yasmine: That's a big question.

Jennifer: Too precocious for you?

Yasmine: No, it's just, I could go a lot of directions with it.

Jennifer: Choose one.

Yasmine: Okay. I think the point of life is to follow the right boss.

Jennifer: That sounds like a philosophy of fear to me.

Yasmine: Does it? How so?

Jennifer: You're assuming that there are these powerful bosses controlling everything... and that one of them is going to win.

Yasmine: What does that have to do with fear?

Jennifer: You're scared you'll be caught on the wrong side!

Yasmine: It sounds like you're the scared one.

Jennifer: That's not fair.

Yasmine: How is it not fair? You asked me a question, I answered it, and you criticized me.

Jennifer: I wasn't criticizing.

Yasmine: No, not really, you were just being defensive. Shall we move on?

Jennifer: *(no response)*

Yasmine: Who do you love?

Jennifer: Ummm... pass.

Yasmine: Why?

Jennifer: That's personal.

Yasmine: Maybe, but it is usually a question people like to answer.

Jennifer: Well, not me. Pass.

Yasmine: How about the opposite, who do you fear?

Jennifer: Wouldn't hate be the opposite of love?

Yasmine: Not necessarily. Who do you fear, Jennifer?

Jennifer: There was this neighbor guy, he came over a lot when I was a kid. And he was always so insistent. He really badly wanted to get me to fear, or hate, whatever, Communists. He'd go on these long rambles about reds and pinkos and Soviets. But, I don't know. I liked hearing his ideas and his speeches made me smile... but it didn't really stick. I don't think I have the type of personality to really hate someone.

Yasmine: This neighbor, what was his name?

Jennifer: Redjeb.

Yasmine: Do you love Redjeb, Jennifer?

Jennifer: I guess, sure. Why not?

Yasmine: So this man wanted you to hate the Communists?

Jennifer: I don't know. I don't think he'd say it like that.

Yasmine: Do you fear the Communists?

Jennifer: No. I don't fear anyone.

Cole: Lie.

Yasmine: Everyone fears someone... it doesn't have to be someone big or tough. Just someone that, if they showed up right here, today, you might be afraid of what they would say or do to you. For instance, my husband, you met him in the parking lot, Pavel. He has an identical twin, Barnabas. They do everything together... always have. When Pavel and I were courting, it became clear to me that Barnabas didn't really like me. I knew that if he didn't come around, if I didn't win him over, then Pavel and I would never get married. So, every time I was around Barney, I froze, I choked up. I was petrified of what he'd say or even think of me. Who do you know that if they walked through this door and started listening to all your answers, you would be petrified, just like me with Barney?

Jennifer: There's... there's some people that don't like me. I wouldn't want them to be in the room with me.

Yasmine: Maybe... but that's not really it, is it Jennifer? You're holding back.

Jennifer: I... nevermind.

Yasmine: What about Taryn?

Jennifer: Who?

Yasmine: The girl you said just "wanted to be wanted". What if she were here now? Would you fear her?

Jennifer: No.

Cole: Lie.

Jennifer: It is not!

Yasmine: Have you ever had a boyfriend?

Jennifer: No.

Yasmine: Ever kissed a boy?

Jennifer: Yes.

Yasmine: Did you like it?

Jennifer: Eww!

Yasmine: Sorry, believe it or not the question's on my paper.

Jennifer: So, I have to answer it or listen to you ask me again later?

Yasmine: That's pretty much how these things go.

Jennifer: Yes, I liked it.

Yasmine: How many different people would you estimate

you've kissed?

Jennifer: Oh my word! Why is that a question you care about?

Yasmine: The questions are built to make you feel uncomfortable with yourself as well as break down whatever current lens you have of the world.

Jennifer: Why would you want to break my lens? You mean, my outlook on life?

Yasmine: Precisely. Our goal is to convince you not to join the Druidry. Our assumption is that your current convictions about life make the Druidry appealing. We're trying to cause you to self-reflect, get you to recall what got you here, and then to accept that whatever you're looking for, it won't be fulfilled at the Druidry.

Jennifer: How do you know it won't?

Yasmine: Because I'm a former member. I'm in recovery.

Jennifer: Recovery?

Yasmine: Yes. Think of it like alcoholism. You can be sober for 30 years, but you're still an alcoholic in recovery.

Jennifer: Listen, I don't care about the stupid Druidry.

Cole: That looks to be the truth.

Jennifer: You're darn right it is! The only reason I came was because a leprechaun healed my friend in return for us taking him here.

Cole: Lie.

Yasmine: If that was the case you would have left him and gotten out of here hours ago.

Jennifer: When people tell me not to do things, I want to do them.

Cole: True.

Yasmine: Maybe so, but you would have thrown in the towel already once the questions got tough. You're in this to win this. Why?

Jennifer: Is that question on your sheet?

Yasmine: I have permission to go off script when the situation merits it.

Jennifer: And this is a merit-able situation?

Yasmine: Figuring out why you're here is of utmost importance.

275

Jennifer: Not that I just told you a leprechaun healed my friend?

Yasmine: Is there a reason that should be important?

Jennifer: Ah, for starters, that the woman you're interviewing believes in leprechauns apparently, that seems a teensy-weensy bit important. And secondly, she believes that at least one leprechaun has magical healing abilities. So, not just leprechauns; magical leprechauns.

Yasmine: How is that relevant to figuring out why you're here?

Jennifer: I told you exactly why it's relevant!

Yasmine: No, you told me how it is you came to Newgrange and the Druidry Center, not why you're here, right now.

Jennifer: Because you're making me sit here!

Cole: She's off the charts.

Jennifer: What does that mean?

Yasmine: Jennifer, you know what it means. You're lying to us, and you're probably lying to yourself. You can leave whenever you wish. You know that.

Jennifer: Then I wish to leave.

Yasmine: That's fine... as long as you under—

Cole: Please, let me take that off before you get up, you could harm the equipment.

Yasmine: You understand you will not be given access to the Druidry.

Jennifer: The boy I'm with... he had some sort of dream last night. Said that I needed to go to the druids. Join them.

Yasmine: That doesn't explain anything.

Jennifer: I... I trust dreams.

Yasmine: Is that true, Jennifer?

Jennifer: Yes.

Cole: True.

Yasmine: Why do you trust dreams?

Jennifer: Because there's no one else to trust.

Yasmine: No one? Really?

Jennifer: People just want things, right? Isn't that what this place is all about? We want things, and if we find people that want the same things we want, we fight them or join forces.

Yasmine: What about God? You don't trust him?

Jennifer: I told you already, I don't know anything about religion.

Yasmine: Look at it this way...

(phone vibrating, ringing)

Jennifer: That's my phone!

Yasmine: Yes, I kept it in my pocket in case someone decided to call... let's see... caller I.D. says someone named Atticus.

Jennifer: Give it to me!

Yasmine: You can have it right now, just give up. Don't go to the druids.

Jennifer: That's blackmail! It's mine! Give it!

Yasmine: Doesn't matter what it is. Do you want the phone or not?

Jennifer: Yes, I want it!

Yasmine: And you want go to the Center?

Jennifer: —uh... I ...

(phone stops ringing)

Yasmine: Oops. Too bad. Maybe Atticus will leave a message.

Jennifer: —

Yasmine: Who is Atticus, Jennifer?

Jennifer: No one. Just a friend.

Yasmine: A boyfriend?

Jennifer: No... just a regular friend.

Yasmine: But you don't have any friends Jennifer.

Jennifer: Yes, I do.

Yasmine: If you can't trust anyone, if the world's made up of just different people colliding when they want stuff, then true friendship can't exist.

Jennifer: That's not fair, you're twisting my words.

Yasmine: I'm helping you to see the obvious implications of your manifest beliefs.

Jennifer: I have friends.

Yasmine: Who do you trust, Jennifer?

Jennifer: Ludwig, I trust Ludwig. And Jorje Robles.

Yasmine: What if Ludwig chooses not to go to the Druid Center?

Jennifer: That'd be fine. That's his prerogative.

Yasmine: You'd feel betrayed.

(phone buzzes again, then rings)

Yasmine: Unlisted number. You're popular today.

Jennifer: Of course, I haven't gotten any calls for days... now they all come when I can't answer.

Yasmine: Is that how you view the world? Ironically?

Jennifer: No!

Yasmine: Then tell me, what's the world about?

Jennifer: I don't know! If I knew the answer to that question I wouldn't be gallivanting in Europe!

Yasmine: Tell me about the leprechaun.

Jennifer: No.

Yasmine: Tell me about the leprechaun.

Jennifer: No. That question's not on your page. I don't have to answer it.

Yasmine: Jennifer, tell me about the leprechaun.

Jennifer: *(no response)*

Yasmine: Ms. Furth, tell me about the leprechaun.

Jennifer: There's no such thing as leprechauns.

Yasmine: You don't believe that.

Jennifer: Yes, I do.

Cole: She's lying.

Yasmine: Thank you, Cole, for stating the obvious. Jennifer, tell me about the leprechaun.

Jennifer: *(no response)*

Yasmine: Do you believe in any other myth besides leprechauns?

Jennifer: I want to believe in Leviathan.

Yasmine: Tell me about that.

Jennifer: At the beginning of time, God created three immortal creatures: a bird, a land monster, and a sea creature. An evil man killed the land monster, the behemoth. Then the bird went away when God called him home. But the Leviathan stayed. The Leviathan... I'm so tired. Can we stop now?

Yasmine: It's okay. Everything, Jennifer, everything's going to be okay. Do you know how I know that?

Jennifer: No.

Yasmine: Because I know how the world is solved.

Jennifer: I don't believe you.

Yasmine: Why not?

Jennifer: Because you're too cruel.

Yasmine: I don't know your story, Jennifer. I don't know what you've been through... but, it seems, for being still so young, you've had a lot of life experience. I'd bet you've seen what, unfortunately, we all see sooner or later.

Jennifer: Seen what?

Yasmine: The world is broken. It's been broken for a long time now. Nothing works like it should. And so friends, who should always be trustworthy, betray us, hurt us. Our family, who should love us unconditionally, burden us with years and years of baggage and expectations. Our leaders, who should be fearless zealots for righteousness, are proven time and time again to be sham-artists. And when we finally find goodness, a sense of awe, an experience of wonder, maybe in the form of a tender hug or a kind word, when we finally think we're secure with a good thing, we're hit in the face, beaten black and blue. There's no justice in this world. And there's no mercy. I'm here because I've seen the pits of hell. I know how beautiful that wild green flame looks at first, but it turns so sour, Jennifer, and burns brutally, without remorse. I work tirelessly here for people like you, because although I don't know you, I love you. I love you enough to do everything lawfully in my power to get you to not taste the fires of hell in that place. The Druid Center is not just the next stop on your world tour. It'll be the end of you. And you may think I'm being cruel, but honest to God, I'm being as loving and merciful to you as I know how to be.

Jennifer: Prove it.

Yasmine: Prove what?

Jennifer: Show some mercy.

Yasmine: You want your cell phone?

Jennifer: I don't know what I want.

Yasmine: Okay, okay. Cole, I think we're done for today.

Cole: What? You didn't even get to the questions about—

Yasmine: Cole, I think we're done here for today.

Cole: Norman won't like this.

Yasmine: He's given me the authority to make judgment calls. This is my call.

279

Jennifer went right to bed, exhausted. It was just passed 3 pm local time. That didn't matter. She escaped to sleep. To the kingdom of her dreams.

Jenn slept for something like 16 hours. Because of the length of rest, her dream story ran out of plot. It played out as it always did, with the boy, now an old man, making it into the kingdom at the top of the mountain. But Father Thomas hadn't dictated what happened next, once the boy was in the kingdom in the clouds. So Jenn's mind filled in the gaps. Not with story, there were no plot twists or third act surprises. There were just these shades of feelings... and color. Smells and variations on smiles. It was the imagination's feeble attempt to comprehend heaven in shadow-form. The taste of it, the small breeze of it, the wink of its presence left Jenn renewed when she woke.

Renewed in form and vigor.

Yasmine Stormach was right: Jenn always had a choice. The choice in front of her was to abandon going to the place that dreams were urging her towards. She didn't know why Robin dreamed that it was Jenn's destiny to go to the druids, but the fact that that came to him in a dream was a more compelling reason to go there than any scare-tactic not to.

When Yasmine called her into the interrogation chamber, Jenn was fully armed with her personal security system.

Yasmine found easy enough ways to wriggle under Jenn's skin yesterday, just with a few forceful questions. The problem was Jenn's tongue. It stirred the conversation, it fed Yasmine's arsenal, gave her more ammunition.

Jenn had survived day one, even got off easy once the waterworks came. Now was the time to buckle down, show this institution the balls this teenage girl had.

Jennifer Dash grit her teeth and her soul.

She'd outlast 'em all.

Yasmine began, much in the same way as the day before. Question on top of question. Cole was back, the lie detector fitted onto Jenn's good arm. But it didn't matter. Jennifer Dash shut her mouth, and kept it so.

Question after question, hour after hour, she didn't budge, she didn't break.

Five hours in, rather than asking for a bathroom break, she peed herself. She thought nothing of it, but it sure scared off Cole! All the while, Jenn stared at Yasmine with dead eyes and a smirking grimace. This was a game. Jenn had a choice. The spoils go to the one who endures.

After 10 hours, Yasmine brought in Pavel, her lunatic husband. He played good cop, and Yasmine bit down, went full screamer bad cop. By that point though, Jenn smiled in her heart of hearts. They asked a lot of questions about her past, fixating especially on the *Orion* adventure schooner. But Jenn saw the ruse, was able to anticipate every pressure point the mad couple tried. Jenn wondered if this was how Miles Faa saw the world all the time... like a series of chess moves.

Transcript of the encounter between Jennifer Furth with Controllers Pavel and Yasmine Stormach. Day three of Jennifer's subjugation.

Yasmine: Congratulations, Jennifer, it's 1 pm. You've officially made it 48 hours. You're on the home stretch, just 24 hours of silence to go.

Pavel: But some exciting things are in store for you in this, your last full day with us, Jennifer. We've got a couple different movies we'd like you to watch.

Yasmine: The plan was for you to watch the movies yesterday... but since you wouldn't answer my questions, we've been stuck in limbo.

Pavel: But not today: we've got some special guests for you that we hope we'll break your silence.

Jennifer: *(no response)*

Pavel: Okay, McGwire, show Ms. Babbit in please.

Lillith: Hello, Jenn.

Jennifer: I didn't think someone like you would subjugate yourself to these people.

Lillith: I've worked with one of their proxy institutes before. We're on the same side. Mostly. I wasn't thrilled to pick up the bill for the private jet. That was a costly exercise. I expected the cell-phone, thought a rented car was likely. I must be honest with you—you really pulled one off with the jet. I didn't see it coming.

Jennifer: You didn't give me boundaries.

Lillith: That's true. And I don't care that you took that liberty. I tried calling you... but then these people returned my call in your stead.

Jennifer: Are you here to convince me to stop?

Lillith: In a way, yes. My motives, however, are different. How's your new hand?

Jennifer: I don't know. It hurts.

Lillith: You missed your last appointment in Zurich.

Jennifer: I know.

Lillith: It's not the sort of thing that you can put off.

Jennifer: *(no response)*

Lillith: I'm taking Robin with me.

Jennifer: Why? What for?

Lillith: I told you before, I need a helper. Robin's untied to family, friends. He's like you in that way.

Jennifer: He's not going to the Center?

Lillith: No, I talked with him. He's coming with me.

Jennifer: What about Ludwig?

Yasmine: Let's bring him in too. McGwire, would you fetch him for us?

Ludwig: Hello, Jennifer.

Pavel: Tell her what conclusion you came to, buddy?

Ludwig: I'm not going.

Pavel: Where exactly?

Ludwig: I'm not going to the Druidry.

Jennifer: Why?

Ludwig: I've got a girlfriend and kids back home. I can't leave them.

Jennifer: You have kids? You never told me that!

Ludwig: You never asked.

Lillith: Come with us. I found the key. I can translate the *Croatoan*. It'll all start happening fast now. I don't want you to be left behind... but if you go to the Center, there's no predicting if I'll be able to get you when you're ready.

Jennifer: I'm going to that Center. I have to.

Lillith: That's your choice.

282

Pavel: Thank you both, Ms. Babbit, Ludwig. McGwire will walk you out.

Yasmine: We've got one more person that would like to talk to you... come on in.

Father Thomas: Hello, Jennifer.

Jennifer: Oh, hi.

Father Thomas: How are you?

Jennifer: I've been better. I lost my hand on Pishtaco's island, but, uh, I got it back.

Father Thomas: I know. I heard.

Jennifer: The boy, this little lost boy, he had a dream that I was supposed to go to this Center.

Father Thomas: I heard. I got on a plane as soon as they contacted me.

Jennifer: Why?

Father Thomas: Do you know why the rogue waves stopped, Jennifer?

Jennifer: No.

Father Thomas: I stopped them.

Jennifer: How?

Father Thomas: Robles had left an idol, a carved image on the *Orion*.

Jennifer: So?

Father Thomas: Its god was angry with us.

Jennifer: What are you saying?

Father Thomas: There are angry spirits, powerful beings just under the covers of this world. We can't see them, but they're there.

Jennifer: I don't know if I believe that.

Father Thomas: Search your heart.

Jennifer: I don't know.

Father Thomas: The people at the Druidry, they worship the bad spirits. They'll harm you, Jennifer.

Jennifer: I'm not religious.

Father Thomas: Okay. I just came to say that. You make your own decision. But I wanted you to hear it from me.

Jennifer: How can I believe, unless I see for myself?

Father Thomas: Yes, that makes sense. But also, actions have consequences. Sometimes those consequences are not

283

what you expect. Once things are in motion, they can't always be stopped.

Jennifer: Are you okay, Father?

Father Thomas: I've never been better.

Jennifer: Why weren't you in Peru with the others?

Father Thomas: All that matters now is that I'm okay, and you're okay. But please, don't go. Nothing good will come from it.

Jennifer: I can't just take everyone's word. I need to solve the world myself. I need to see, to feel things for myself. I can't trust your experience. I only have this one life, Father.

Father Thomas: I know. Don't waste it.

Jennifer: I liked you better when you doubted everything.

Father Thomas: I'm still that person.

Jennifer: I'm done talking. You can take him away.

Father Thomas: Jenn. Please, don't cut me out. Jennifer....

Jennifer: *(no response)*

Father Thomas: Jenn?

Jennifer: *(no response)*

Father Thomas: Please. Don't do this.

Jennifer: *(no response)*

~~~

Jennifer Dash is going to the Druidry. She wants to see it for herself. She will.

To the Center

<u>Main Cast</u>
Jenn Dash known as Ne Ime
Lourna Von Schloss known as Lourry
Marshall Winston
Momma Beck
Fater Beck
At-tila

Chapter 41: Conversion

"Hi, Jennifer."

"Hi, Atticus, sorry I didn't answer the phone when you called... things have been... crazy."

"They always are with you."

"Yeah, I guess so. So, did you want to talk to me about something?"

"Yeah, Jenn... I really like you, liked you."

"Oh."

"I felt like we had a real connection. I don't know. I hadn't felt anything like that before."

"Me too."

"Sure, but it was really hard not hearing from you. I was ready to fly to California for Thanksgiving—I just needed to hear something from you. Some affirmation."

"Atticus... I...."

"And then I met Betty."

"Betty?"

"Yeah, and, I don't want to do anything to screw this up, you know? So, like, I think Betty's worth it. I gotta give this my all, give it the best chance for success. I'm falling in love with her."

"Yeah?"

"Yeah, but then you call out of the blue. If it was another time, then sure, I'd be super excited just to hear your voice, just to talk, not even talking about a relationship or anything, just to talk. But now, with the emotions I had for you... I talked to my dad about it. He gave some good advice. I just don't think it'd be right, for you or me, or Betty especially, if we keep talking. You see what I'm saying?"

"You don't want to even talk to me?"

"Look, when I got your letter, and you told me you kissed that other dude, that kinda broke my heart, Jenn."

"Atticus. It wasn't like that. That was just an accident."

"Was it though? And... and... it doesn't matter. I'm sorry I brought it up, it doesn't matter who you kissed or didn't kiss. I guess I'm just saying that as closure. That's not fair. Sorry. I'm sure you'll find someone who's perfect for you. Right now, for me, I'm betting that person is Betty. Gosh, I'm sorry, this conversation went way better in my head."

"I... don't know what to say."

"We'll keep in touch."

"Will we? Because I think you just said that even talking on the phone is too much."

"Yeah..."

"What do you want me to say, Atticus? I'll miss you."

"I'll miss you too, Jenn. Goodbye."

"Bye."

.Click.

Welcome to the Druidry.

You're welcomed by the eager leprechaun, excited you're here. He pulls you by the hand like an excited kindergartner on the first day of class.

He explains to you that tonight they're going to "UNDO IT", whatever that means. He promises you'll get a firsthand view of... of the process of "UNDOING IT".

The center itself is something of a marvel. Past the front doors in the parking lot, your first thought is on how it feels. Physically. The floor below your feet is not wood laminate or carpet or any sort of common flooring you'd expect at a welcoming center.

It's mulch. Ground up tree bark. It feels odd underneath your feet, but you have to admit, the woodsy scent wafting up is delightful.

The building sprawls out into five or six different wings and bubbles with activity and a general sense of life. All sorts of people mull around. You spot at least a dozen white-collar American-looking businessmen who appear more ready for a big merger meeting than a hippy cult gathering. There's also tribal-looking people—you think one gentlemen, sparsely clad in a lion skin, must be Zulu. Another pod of people could very well be real African pygmies.

There are others too—uncategorizable entities. You try not to focus on them.

Your hyper leprechaun buddy takes you to an outside foyer.

It's something like an amphitheater, but rather than a stage, at the center-most point, there's a large, many-tendrilled tree.

"That's where we UNDO IT, tonight!" it screeches.

On closer inspection, the tree isn't just a tree... it's a tree growing out of a massive stump, which, at first glance you assumed was a platform. No, ma'am! The tree has sprouted, grown out of a stump. A massive stump. The stump had to be twenty-five feet in diameter... maybe more. The tree that this once was, that lurched out of this humongous base, must have been the largest tree on Earth. The fully formed tree that now shot out of the base stump was maybe eight feet in diameter, no slouch itself. You wonder if the tree is on steroids.

The leprechaun takes you past the amphitheater, past a large chicken den and chicken yard, past rows and rows of vegetable gardens. You suspect the people at the center live off the land, off the chickens and vegetables now in full view. You think that's noble.

There's a barn, and beside it, a fenced yard. In the yard a few dozen goats, sheep, and cows roam, mingling about with no particular agenda. Your attention is fixated on what appears to be a yak lying in the shadow of the barn. Such a hairy, large thing. The leprechaun has a specific path for you two, and he's not dilly-dallying. You follow the fence-line until you reach a goat tied to it. It's a young thing, surely no more than a year old with a brown spot on top of its head, between its two eyes. Why do goat eyes always look so evil? Besides the brown spot, the creature is perfectly snow white. The leprechaun pats its head with its skinny, pointy digits. The goat pushes in on the hand, clearly enjoying being pet.

It squeals, "This one's for me."

"What do you mean?" You reply.

"My sacrifice. It gives its life for me."

"What?"

"Tonight. You'll see."

"You're going to kill it?"

"Always a cost."

A few minutes later and you're back in the welcome center.

There are still bundles of people walking to-and-fro without any real sense of direction or purpose, not wholly dissimilar to the yard of sheep and goats and cows, you think. Everyone, man and beast alike, just idles along, passing t me here aimlessly. That thought should bother you, should get under your skin, but it doesn't. Not now. Not today. Not after Atticus Further.

While you're thinking of Atticus, a little girl walks up to you. She reminds you of yourself, though in truth, you don't much recall what you looked like when you were six or seven years old.

"May I see your mobile, please?" The little girl asks you.

What manners! You think.

"You may," you respond, and hand your junk phone to her.

The little girl grabs it out of your hand, puts both her hands around it, and, just like that, hands it back to you. The girl walks away, dissolving into the crowd. You look at your phone. She turned it off. That's weird.

What an odd place. Your leprechaun friend has disappeared, and you're left holding the phone in your hand, trying to comprehend what just happened.

"She's anti-electronics," a good-looking man says to you.

"Excuse me?" you say, peering into this handsome man's chocolate eyes.

"Ever since she was born, if she touches electronics, they short."

You look up at the tall man, at least five inches taller than you, with non-understanding.

"You can throw it away. It's dead now."

"I don't..."

"If you're going to stay here, Momma Beck doesn't allow electronics anyway, so it's just as well."

"My phone won't work?" You jam your fingers on the screen, trying to get the phone to light up, turn on. Nothing. That little brat killed your phone.

"I'm Marshall Winston, resident skeptic."

You shake Marshall's outstretched hand. It's ridiculously cold, yet still strong and inviting. You momentarily flinch with bashfulness, realizing your hand is clammy.

"It's common practice to introduce yourself."

"Right, yeah, sorry, I just, I can't believe that little girl just freaked out my phone."

"Your name?"

"Jennifer—Furth"

"Ah, so it's your first day!"

"How'd you know?" You look around among all the passersby in the busy corridor trying to spot a general difference between you and everyone else, trying to see if you're distinctly different.

"You have a normal name. Level Ones and higher tend to have weird names."

"Your name is normal," you say bluntly.

"That's because my role here is, as previously stated, Resident Skeptic. If I'm recalling correctly, I'm the only one around here that has a first and last name."

"So, you get assigned a name?"

"That's part of the Level One initiation. You haven't met Momma Beck yet, have you?"

"No, who is she?"

"Momma Beck and Fater Beck are the only Level Sevens right now."

"What does that mean?"

"We expect Fater Beck to graduate to Level Eight sometime next year—Level Seven is the highest plateau you can have here at the Center."

"You believe in all this?"

"Of course not. You're a little slow, aren't you?"

"Umm... no?"

"I told you twice, now thrice. I'm the Resident Skeptic."

"Yeah, but I don't know what that means."

"A skeptic is someone who practices skepticism. Merriam-Webster's defines skepticism as 'an attitude of doubt or incredulity either in general or toward a particular object.'"

"Did you really just quote the dictionary at me?"

"I have a photographic memory. Come."

You follow Marshall Winston through a maze of lives as you beeline past a partially-outdoor sanctuary. You push past a door that enters into a coliseum-style classroom, fully

290

furnished with levels of chairs facing a large chalkboard. Beside the board, two people stand at the center of a mob, twenty or so weirdos hanging around them.

You follow Marshall Winston to the center of the weirdos.

"Jennifer Furth, this is Momma Beck."

Momma Beck looks to be of Indian heritage, her features dark, her cheeks round and red, and her hair brown and long. But the most immediate feature of Momma Beck is her size. She stands seven feet tall, and without being noticeably overweight, stands nearly as wide as she was tall. Upon being introduced, Momma Beck opens her arms to you.

You fall into her, your face smashed into her large bosoms.

A collective, "Awwww" echoes through the classroom. The freaks surrounding Momma Beck are watching you, exhilarated.

Momma Beck, wordlessly, brushes the back of your head while you embrace.

You can't help it. Your eyes water. You don't know why. You don't feel emotional. A tear rolls down your cheek silently.

After a moment, Momma Beck pulls you back from her bosom, far enough to inspect you, to stare into your eyes. She has glistening hazel brown eyes. She smiles at you. Broadly. The smile makes her round cheeks somehow even rounder, like spheres waiting to be pulled off her face like taffy.

A little man standing beside Momma Beck speaks up.

"Hello! I'm At-tila!"

He shakes your hand. He looks the polar opposite of Momma Beck. Short. Skinny. He's wearing blue goggles, as well as a pair of reading glasses on top of the glasses.

"Hi, I'm Jennifer Furth," you say.

"Not for long, I bet! You're Timpantan's friend?"

"Who?"

"The leprechaun. We named him yesterday."

"Oh. Yeah. I came to see his ceremony or something."

"Good, well, you're just in luck. Momma Beck tells me we've been waiting for you. There's a temporary Level One class that's starting, oh, probably right now. Marshall Winston, would you take the young lady over to the Temp Hall K4?"

"Yes, Ma'am."

You follow Marshall out of the room, back into the milieu of the marauding corridors.

"Why did you say 'Yes Ma'am' to that man?" You ask Marshall as the two of you walk.

"Hold my hand, would you?"

You do so. You hold Marshall's cold hand as you walk. It's comforting, nice.

"You'll get less eyes if you're holding my hand."

"What? Why would that be?"

Marshall ignores your question, instead answering your previous inquiry. "When At-tila speaks, he speaks for Momma Beck. So, I was answering her, not him."

"Oh, does Momma Beck not speak?"

"Supposedly, she speaks through the power of the mind. Everyone, mostly Level Twos and higher, hears Momma Beck speak in their heads. At-tila follows Momma Beck to speak to newcomers like you."

"Oh, and you said there's a Father Beck."

"Fa-ter. Not Father."

"Oh," you say, not sure how to respond.

You're back outside, walking through very tall but very uniformly groomed grass. You walk past some of the teepees you spotted the other day from the parking lot. You can't help but try to sneak a peak into one of them with its entrance partially draped open. A fire pit is just barely smoldering, and five feet up dangles a hammock with what appears to be a person sleeping in it. You wonder how that person isn't dying from the heat of the fire embers.

"Fater Beck is rarely seen," Marshall Winston says, "And almost no one hears from him. He's too busy."

"Busy with what?"

"The Druidry would have you believe he's constantly in touch with his true identity... what you might call his soul."

"Oh. Is that what this place is all about? Getting in touch with the soul?"

"I thought you'd know more than that, seeing that you came here palling around with a leprechaun."

"Umm... well, I don't."

Marshall lets go of your hand. You admit to yourself that

you like the physical contact, the physical touch. He pushes a swinging door on what looks like a cheap portable trailer.

You walk into what looks like an A.A. Meeting, a dozen or so people sitting in a circle on cheap folding chairs. There's a stand in the corner of the room with a coffee jug. Every single person around the circle is holding a Styrofoam cup.

"Hey Volva, this is Jennifer. She's here to get temp Level One status so she can attend tonight's thing."

"Of course, Momma Beck, just let me know you were coming. Please Jenn, have a seat," the woman Marshall Winston called Volva says. You can't help but think that Volva's skin tone has a hint of blue in it. Besides that though, she looks normal. Mostly.

You take a seat next to a large-and-in-charge Russian babushka woman on one side, and a large-and-in charge Mongolian lady on the other. You feel dwarfed by the severely strong heroines flanking you on either side.

"Hi, Jennifer Furth. Let me catch you up," Volva says. "This is a quick micro-study so that everyone here can get Level One status so as to be able to witness tonight's events. Please, grab a cup of tea. It'll help calm your nerves."

So the coffee isn't coffee. It's tea. Okay, you think. You like tea well enough, and you prefer to keep your coffee drinking in the mornings anyway.

You grab some tea from the back and return to your seat.

"Elder Smackinsoot, you were about to give your reason."

A sun-tanned cool kid, the type who ten years ago was the captain of the football team and still tried to get by on that persona, spoke up, "I'm here because I'm a bad person. I don't want to be a bad person anymore."

The tea tasted pretty good. It sure went down the throat easy. It tasted like roses baked in sugar. Sweet, light, fragrant, and slippery, that's how you describe the tea to yourself. You've never tasted anything quite like this. You figure they probably make the stuff here at the center. That's why it tastes so good. It's fresh.

"I want to see things... the middle of people, their insides. I hope the Center cures me of that."

"If you stay with us, it very much will."

Others share short little testimonials. Apparently, people tend to come to the Center, as Volva and others short-handedly called this place, because they needed help. Like a mystical self-help asylum.

You note that almost everyone takes spontaneous turns returning to the jug at the back table and refilling their styrofoam cup. You want to do the same, as your cupeth no longer runneth over.

You casually get up and do so.

Meanwhile, a woman with extremely spiky hair soliloquies in a squeaky voice:

"I fear ceramic mugs. Thank you for not having ceramic mugs. I love styrofoam."

"That's good," says Volva. "We chose styrofoam today when we heard you were coming. Why, Lady-lee-lore, are you afraid of mugs?"

You think to yourself, for this place being so nature friendly, it does seem awfully odd that they'd use non-biodegradable styrofoam. Haven't you heard somewhere that styrofoam is one of the worst things for nature?

"Ceramic handles always break in my hand."

"Any other reason?" Volva asks non-judgmentally.

"My ex-broke up with me over coffee."

"And you were holding a ceramic cup?"

"Yes. Holding it with two hands, because all the mugs in our house had already broken handles."

"I'm sure we can help you. Who's next?"

"I'm Jake McBitterson. Everyone calls me Bitters."

"Why are you here, Bitters?" Volva asks smiling.

You've returned to your seat, fresh hot tea in hand. This Bitters was one of these American businessmen lookieloos.

"I'm a stockbroker. I've had a bad year. A really bad year. Someone told me you guys could help me."

Bitters shoots you a questioning eye—as if to suggest that normal people came here for special abilities, not to remove already set psychosomatic maladies. You look normal enough. That must be why you caught his eye.

"At Level One, you'll be given a name, a work position, and a destiny here at the Center. Once you fully embrace your destiny, you'll receive certain insights beyond the veil of this mortal toil. I cannot guarantee that you'll be able to use that for financial success in the stock and trade markets, but I can certify that it'll help you live your life in a manner worthy of eternity," Volva says to Bitters.

"I have no idea what you just said," Bitters responds.

Volva smiles. "That's fine, that's fine. Knowledge comes with time." Volva adjusts her smile from Bitters to the entire circle. "We require little of you today. All we ask in return for temporary Level One status is your trust. You must trust that we are on your side. That's it," Volva says as somehow her smile grows. "As long as you accept that we're on your side, and your side is the right side, then everything is fine. It's heaven, actually!" Volva says, almost in a full scale cheer. She turns her embarrassingly huge smile your way. "And you. What's your testimonial? In brief please, we'll have ages to dig deep in coming days, weeks, months, maybe even years if you so desire."

"Gosh," you say, "I guess I'm just here to see the leprechaun I came with go through the UNDO process. Whatever that is... or means."

Volva's smile goes flat. "That's not good enough. We don't embrace people who are just here to watch. We want participants, not tourists." Her smile re-emerges. "Try again, sweetheart."

"I want to solve the world," you blurt out.

"That's more like it."

After three more refills and a weird word-association game, you wonder why you don't feel the need to use the bathroom. You stare at the tea. Maybe you were dehydrated and didn't realize it?

"I've got some good news," Volva says. How long has she been speaking? How long have you been here? "You've all been accepted and are ready to be given your temporary Level One status. You'll stay at the Center tonight and tomorrow start Level One orientation and speculation. Understood?"

"Yes," everyone says in unison, including you. How did you know to do that?

Volva starts calling out names. People stand up, walk to where Volva is now standing (at the center of the circle), and Volva, from somewhere, pulls out a hard round pin with each person's name and the declaration Temporary Level One Status. You can't believe it. For one, these are real, hard, metal pins. Like the type that presidential candidates have their followers wear. How did the Center get these made so fast? And Volva, she seems to be pulling these pins out of thin air. She raises her left hand into the air, and with some weird flick of her wrist, some sort of sleight of hand, she pulls down the person-specific pin. How was this happening? In some way, you reckon, this is far more mind-boggling than the beheaded witch and the evaporating mist. And not just once! Again and again. Are your eyes playing tricks on you? You wonder. You look down at your tea. The milky colored rose sugar water is spinning slowly counter-clockwise. You lower your face to stare at the tea more intently. How is it doing that? Wait. Is it speaking? You raise the cup up for closer inspection. It's whispering to you, isn't it? What's it saying? What's the message?

"The one who was formerly known as Jennifer Furth, please come and receive your acceptance," Volva says at you. You forget about the cup and walk to this, your smiley leader.

Left hand up. Flick of the wrist. And now a pin. "Your name has been chosen. Nevermore are you Jennifer. Now, here at the Center Infinitum, your name, Level One and beyond, is Ne Ime. Do you understand?"

"I do," you say, smiling for some reason.

"Do you accept?"

"I do." You hear cheering, but no mouths around the circle are open. You find yourself at the amphitheater. It should be cold. It's the middle of winter after all. But it's not. You feel very warm, in fact. Your spot in the amphitheater is less than prestigious. It's midnight, the ceremony is beginning. You're so far away, you can barely see the massive stump at the center from which the tree grows. As it turned out, seating was based on Level (I say seating, but everyone stood for the whole ordeal). Level Sevens—just Momma Beck and Fater Beck— stand on opposite sides of the tree just feet from the epicenter.

296

Fater Beck is not much like Momma Beck, except, you surmise, that Fater Beck looks to be of Indian heritage just like Momma Beck. Besides the ethnic similarity, you are hard-pressed to see a resemblance. Fater Beck stands clutching not one, but two canes. One for each hand. He is very well just as tall as Momma Beck, but he leans so heavily on the canes it's hard to get any sense of dimension. And most remarkably, while Momma Beck is humongous in every physical way, broad-shouldered, big-hipped, and bow-legged, Fater Beck appears horrendously emaciated, skin and bones. Maybe with some meat on him, he'd have the same blooming cheeks that Momma Beck shined with, but it's impossible to tell, the way he presumably refuses to nourish himself.

The next ring after that are the Level Sixers. They all wear red caps. You can't make out any of their faces.

Level Fives all stand on wooden stilts, which looks uncomfortable, not to mention a little goofy.

Another row back, and a good measure higher so as to be able to see over the stilted ones, are the Level Fours. They wear brown hoods and capes. You surmise that the old men greeters you saw that first day in the parking lot were this level.

Looking about, you can't help but feel compelled to want to be a higher level. Level One sucks! Bleacher seats! Worse still, you are Temporary Level One status. That means you are a full section behind the actual, true Level Ones.

"Ne Ime," the person next to you says. It's the guy who was named Bitters, the stockbroker. His pin says his name is Fimafeng. "Ne Ime?"

You realize that's your name now. He's talking to you.

"Yes?... Fimafeng?"

"How many people do you see here?"

You start counting. You guesstimate that there's roughly 50 or so people per level. Six major levels times 50... "I'd say somewhere around 300."

You take another sip of the tea. There's an elderly Level Two woman going around with a jug filling up all the Temp Level Ones' styrofoam cups.

"Ah, yeah, okay... and how many people have long ears?"

297

"What?" you say bewildered.

At first you don't see it. You stare and you stare and you stare, trying to make sense of Fimafeng's words. Ears? What ears?

You down your tea. It's not so hot anymore, more tepid. The Level Two woman spots your empty cup and moseys over to fill it.

You thank her and sip again.

Things start moving down in the center. You see your friend, the leprechaun, appear! He's on the tree! And the goat, the goat he showed you this morning, it's in the tree too... is it, is it levitating?

You take another sip of the sugar rose.

Yummm....

Then you see. Between every regular person are two or three long, shadowed, rabbit-eared witnesses.

"I see them," you say to Fimafeng, "I see them all!"

~~~

Jennifer Dash has become Ne Ime at the Center near New Grange, Ireland.

We've got to walk this path with her now, for there's so much to take in.

Come with Jenn, fall deeper and deeper down the spiraling levels of the Druidry Center. Find out what truth there is to be uncovered.

And get out while you still can!

Chapter 42: Center Life

The girl formerly known as Jennifer Dash, now known as Ne Ime, didn't sleep the night of the leprechaun's ceremony. Entranced by the ordeal, and the mysterious shadow bunnies, Ne Ime and Fimafeng, formerly called Bitters, wandered about the various groves of the Center trying to gesticulate with their arms some sort of understanding of what they just saw, all the while nursing their tea. Somewhere before dawn, they perched below the long limbs of a particularly large tree, blathering on about their lives.

When Fimafeng and Ne Ime departed, meandering about the grounds in separate directions, Jenn realized that although they spent hours together, often bearing their souls to one another, she didn't feel particularly close to Fimafeng. He was just another character in this place. No better or worse than any other soul traipsing about the Druidry.

In that thought, that blithe recollection of relativity, days floated by.

Jenn, now spoken of as Ne Ime, slept in a large, ceiling-less room, with levels of hammocks. Hers in particular hung at mid-height, meaning she had two hammocks above her, as well as two below. One might surmise that it's better to be in the center of a hammock bunk when it snows or rains, but one would be wrong. The winter continued to be uncommonly mild, and sleet seemed to be the most common form of nightly mischief. Pools of water would aggregate at the base of the hammock just above Jenn, before splashing down on her wholesale. It was unpleasant... unpleasant, but the constant warmth of the local variety of tea kept Jenn at least bearably warm from the inside out.

The process of going from Temporary Level One member to an official Level One extraordinaire was pretty simple: just go to a handful more meetings in the A.A.-like trailer. The meetings were led by At-tila, the googled and spectacled man who spoke for Momma Beck. Except, after that first temp meeting, Momma Beck didn't stick around much. At-tila often repeated that he spoke for Momma Beck, that he transcribed her thoughts for the masses. The group waiting to be initiated into the company of permanent Level Ones was smaller than the temp group Jenn, or should I say Ne Ime, joined on day one. What happened to them? Ne Ime found it strange that these people, these little lookieloos, would watch the gobstoppingly incredible leprechaun night and then choose to go back to their normal, commonplace lives. Why? And just as strangely, why would the Center be comfortable with them leaving? Wouldn't they go back to their homes and tell their friends and families about this international oddity? Wouldn't the press come buzzing around, hungry journalists looking for their big break, wanting to capture the truth about the tree-loving, ancient Irish cult? The fact that there weren't gossip predators floating about was slightly alarming.

After a few days, At-tila scheduled "sacred walks" for Fimafeng and everyone else in the circle. Ne Ime was assigned a time last of all. She found this a little confounding too, but then again, she was a latecomer on the day of the leprechaun ritual, so maybe it was all natural.

When Fimafeng, formerly known as Bitters, got official Level One status, Ne Ime asked him about his sacred walk.

"It was fine," he said.

"Just fine?" Jenn aka Ne Ime asked.

"Yeah, I guess I expected more. I got the job of chopping down trees."

"Chopping down trees? They do that here?"

Fimafeng raised his foot off the ground, showcasing the mulch sticking to the bottom of his heel. "Where do you think this comes from?"

"Oh. So, did At-tila ask you any questions?"

"No, I don't think so. I'm not sure, actually. Maybe. Yeah. I think there was a question or two. I can't really remember all that well. It's kinda foggy."

"Don't you think that's a little weird?" A little spark of the old Jenn the Questioner jumped off the page, submitting the new girl Ne Ime to her thoughts momentarily.

"Everything's a little weird here. I think that's part of the

300

deal."

"That makes sense," Ne Ime said.

"There's too much to take in. We're like infants again."

"Yeah, I guess."

On the day that At-tila and Ne Ime were scheduled to take a walk, Jenn's casted hand hurt horribly.

The pain, an overall burning that would start at the base of her wrist and flame up into her skin all over, had been slowly getting worse day by day. The reason was easy enough to surmise. She'd missed multiple appointments with her doctor in Zurich. Her cast was getting filthy. She'd gotten it wet. She'd been given no medical anesthetic... it was quite foreseeable now to imagine that her whole arm was rotting.

As a source of nourishment and somehow as a fairly effective (apparently natural) pain reliever, the girl Ne Ime, sipped and sipped and sipped and sipped her aromatic home brewed tea.

"Hello, Ne Ime," At-tila said to her when they first met.

"Hi. Are we going on our sacred walk?"

"It is that time, yes."

They walked out fifteen minutes away from the main building, past the amphitheater where Ne Ime watched the leprechaun depart from this realm, past various teepees and gardens and chicken coops. They found themselves traipsing calmly under the shadows of a natural dirt path with branching trees spindling to-and-fro on either side.

"This is your day, Ne Ime, your day, says Momma Beck," At-tila spoke.

"What do I have to do to become a true Level One?" Ne Ime said.

"Is that all you want, to become a Level One?"

"I want to be a Level One and then a Level Two and then a Level Three...."

"You'd like to live here forever?"

The question took her by storm. She hadn't thought much about time while being here at the Center. The 72 hours at that interrogation place flashed in her mind. If that was the choice, to live years in small, windowless rooms, or here out in

301

the open, out in nature, then it was no choice at all.

"I guess I do, although..." Ne Ime scratched at her cast, "I have these pains. This cast hurts."

"Don't fear. Your pain will soon depart from you. Tell me, do you remember why you came here?" At-tila asked non-confrontationally.

"I want to solve the world."

"Do you know how many people come here wanting to do just that?"

"No," Ne Ime said, ready to be surprised by whatever answer was to be given.

"None. You're the first."

Ne Ime smiled. It was good to be a one-and-only.

"That's what makes you special... you see this tree?"

"Yes," Ne Ime said staring at the specimen in front of them, a deeply green tree with a dagger stabbed into it at shoulder height. From the dagger, a trail of dark red sap, much thinner than Jenn would normally think sap to be, drained down to a basin at the foot of the tree.

At-tila pulled what looked like a wooden spatula from his back pocket. He dipped it into the red sap, grabbed Jenn's casted arm, and generously splotched the stuff onto the cast. He dipped the spatula three times into the red sap lake to get an adequate amount of the stuff smeared onto her plaster protective.

Ne Ime stood in wonder. What would happen next? The Center was the best place in the world for asking that question. Every time you anticipated something, it seemed that the very opposite came to occur.

At-tila placed the red-sapped wooden spatula in his back pocket, and the couple returned to their traipsing about in the grove. Ne Ime figured she'd let the red sap do whatever it was going to do; she contented herself with not dwelling on it.

"There's a reason you're here, Ne Ime. A very important reason."

"Yes?"

"Yes, but we're none of us confident yet on what that reason is. Not me, not Momma Beck, not anyone."

Ne Ime ventured to ask, "What about Fater Beck?"

302

"He may know, but he hasn't spoken of it. Not yet."

"Could we ask him?"

"No. He is not one to ask questions of. If he wants to speak to you, you'll know."

"He's magic, isn't he?" Ne Ime said playfully after finishing her cup of tea, crumpling up the styrofoam, smashing it into her pocket.

"He's just like you or me, only more in tune with the universe. Ne Ime, do you know why Momma Beck gave you that name?"

"Umm... no."

"It means 'No Name'. Can you guess why she chose that for you?"

"Ummm... no."

"Because she doesn't want you to be noticed by a certain someone."

"Who?" Even in Jennifer's drug-addled brain, the Numbered Man came to mind... and then, briefly, Merkyl. Jennifer Dash, the real Jennifer Dash, conscious mind already locked away under a layer of ever-thickening haze, knew that Merkyl was a man she wished to never see again. Someone she never wanted to be noticed by ever, ever again.

"Momma Beck didn't say exactly, but I think she must be referring to the one we don't speak of here."

"Who's that?"

"We don't speak of him. If we did, then well, we'd tell you who he is."

"Please! Please, please, At-tila!"

Ne Ime reached out to grab At-tila as a token of affection, but she did so with her casted arm. She saw now that the sap had completely hardened on the cast.

At-tila grabbed Ne Ime's cast.

"It looks ready." He marched her over to the nearest tree. "Swing it at the tree. Go on. It won't hurt."

Ne Ime swung her arm at the tree. It hit with a thud, and then a crack, like an earthquake, sprawled up and through the cast. At-tila took the cast in his hands and peeled it off like an egg to reveal...

a Frankenstein hand.

303

Ne Ime gasped.

It was ugly.

It still hurt.

She could move the digits slightly, but God almighty was it ugly.

Jennifer was a darker-skinned girl. This hand was not her shade at all. It must have come from a Swedish or Finnish or Norwegian person, so pale in tone as to be almost completely devoid of color. Who had offered their hand, an albino?

At-tila dropped the empty cast down, like a piece of litter. Catching Jenn's concern, he said, "Oh, don't worry, these woods are very hungry. They'll eat that cast with its amber right up!"

"Oh..." Ne Ime said, "Okay."

"Momma Beck says that she sees two paths before you. Either you will rise and be the Center's brightest star, conquering our primitive system of Levels faster than anyone thought possible. Or, you'll turn sour. You'll use what you've learned here against us. You'll seek out the other side."

"What's the other side?"

"It's the side where the one we don't speak of is."

For some reason, maybe it was that she'd not had a sip of tea for a full two minutes now, or perhaps due to the shock of seeing this albino appendage attached to her arm, Jennifer Dash's mind was working properly. Her memory banks were stirring. She remembered Mrs. Moose and her precious words to Jennifer. The old cartoonist believed that all of life, all of history, was a flaming hot war between two rival factions: Order and Entropy. According to Mrs. Moose, the only way for peace was for both sides to be held in each hand.

No side should win.

"Maybe..." Jenn needed to be careful with her words. She'd state her reservation in the form of a question. Questions usually came off as less argumentative. "How do you know that the Center is on the right side? How do you know you don't have everything reversed? Or! Or maybe what's right is for neither side to win!" Jenn got a little carried away.

"Those are fair questions and wonderings. You're still young and innocent. You haven't come into the greater knowledge yet. Once you have access to the limitless depths of Momma Beck and Fater Beck, you'll know for yourself that there's a right side and a wrong side."

At-tila took Ne Ime's hand in his. Her albino-y hand. "Evil is a real thing. Come, we're almost there."

The rows of trees were coming to an end. A large brick wall lay in front of them with a clumsy wooden ladder leaning against the wall. "Climb this ladder."

Ne Ime climbed the ladder, now fully focused on the now, invested only in the minutia of the moment. She didn't take time to reflect on how this ladder was similar (or dissimilar) to the one on that Edenic island Jenn and Lex stumbled upon once upon a time.

On the wall, Jenn had a perfect view of what lay beyond. Suddenly, Ne Ime got a bad case of vertigo, and found it necessary to crumple down and hold onto the wall for safety.

On the other side of the wall was a round hole.

On all sides of the hole, a dozen or more large ropes extended out. Following the ropes with her eyes, Ne Ime saw that all the ropes were tied around various trees surrounding the hole.

The pit itself was dark and black. Ne Ime couldn't see the bottom of it.

At-tila pushed himself up on top the wall after Jenn.

"This is our trench, our great hole."

"Why is it here?" Ne Ime asked.

"We take all of our Level One initiates here. Do you know how deep it goes?"

"No. I can't see the bottom."

"Of course you can't. What if I told you it was endless?"

"What?"

"What would you think?"

"I'd... I'd think that was impossible."

"Why?"

"Because the... because... because that's just not possible."

"What if I told you that if I pushed you..." At-tila opened his arms, gesturing violently. Was he about to push her in? Was that why he brought her here? Was this where the Druidry took applicants who failed their tests? Did Jenn fail? "...down

305

the hole? What do you think would happen?"

"I'd die," Ne Ime said stoically.

"Why would you die?"

"I'd hit the bottom and... and that would kill me."

At-tila extended his hands to embrace Ne Ime around the waist. He was hugging her. At least now, if they were going to fall, they were going to fall together. This calmed Ne Ime.

"There are so many facts about this world that the common man or woman just can't accept. This pit is one of them. I'll tell you what would happen if I pushed you.

"You'd fall, of course you'd fall. You'd fall straight through the Earth. And you'd come out the other side. Gravity on the other end would slow you down, so you'd come up just right at ground level."

"Where?"

"The other side of the Earth! The world is a sphere after all... well, a slight oval."

"Oh."

"Ne Ime, you are to be one of our chief rubies here at the Center. We are excited for you. You are now a true Level One. Hear me closely. You have a job to do. It takes a lot of work to keep the Center going, and so we all must do our part. Momma Beck has assigned you the job of 'Mulcher'. You will work five hours a day, from 10am to 3pm in the mulch department."

"What's that?"

"You'll grind up trees for our feet."

"Oh."

"But that's not the fun part. Are you ready for the fun part?"

"Okay," Ne Ime said as she gazed once more into the endless pit just beyond her feet.

"You've been given a position. That position is: drum roll please.... TALL."

"Huh?"

"Your position is Tall."

"I don't understand."

"Oh, you make me sigh. New Level Ones never understand when they're given their position. You'll see in time. It'll come to you. Your position will assert itself within you."

306

The two slowly made their way back down the ladder, through the sacred grove, and back to the main Center.

Ne Ime was quick to hustle over towards the tea jug. She was parched.

At this moment, someone, somewhere, is reading Jenn's copy of 50 People Whom I Pity.

#49: Anton LaVey

It is only right for the penultimate pitiful one to be the father of modern Satanism. My problem with Mr. Anton LaVey is not what you suspect. So what, the guy invented a religion celebrating the inverse of god and the things that most normal people worship. No biggie. Good on him if it gets him anywhere. The problem is that these spurious made-up religions never actually lead to anything new. Ironically, the Church of Satan has a list of nine Satanic Sins. On that list are notions like: Stupidity, Pretentiousness, Self-deceit, Lack of Perspective and Counterproductive Pride. Anton LaVey most assuredly, my friends, is guilty in no small amount of every single one. He's a satanic sinner, no doubt. Not unlike televangelists or Charles Manson, Anton LaVey's whole success in life was built on the foundation of his cult of personality. Translation: he's a huckster. His religion gets you nowhere. You want to join the dark side, be a Darth Vader? Fine. Darth Vader could actually strangle people with his thoughts. That's power. What power does the Church of Satan have? None. They die, just like all the rest of us. They have no power over this Earth, no freedom from the general sweat and toil of existence. Add to that, Anton LaVey wasn't very good at life. He was a domestic abuser, a drug abuser, and he screwed up every one of his children. By what measure, any measure, could that be considered success? If you want to thumb your nose at God, or you want to rattle people's cages, fine! But don't act like you're accomplishing anything of significance. Why add lying to your bevy of impurities?

REMEMBER REMEMBER: Rebellion, no matter how noble, is always reactionary, and therefore, has no creative power. Rebellion can only ever be destructive, and no matter what anyone else tells you, destruction is the antithesis of creation.

I shouldn't have to tell you this.

The reader of this little book placed it down on the coffee table, and considered the author's point.

Jennifer Dash should have left the Druidry Center the day they got the leprechaun to the parking lot. She never should have withstood the Controllers' 72-hour harassment. Once she had some awareness that the sugar rose tea was some sort of opiate, she should have left. She should have left when she saw the shadowy bunny ears. And above all, she should have left when she witnessed the murder of the leprechaun.

The goat that you first thought was levitating, is suspended in the air by six ropes. Four ropes around each leg, one around the neck, and one holstering the entire goat up, down the middle of the its underside.

The leprechaun isn't crouching on the limb of the tree like you first suspected, either. He's also held in place, suspended if you will, by a rope—just one rope, as far as you can tell, around the leprechaun's waist.

Drums. From where? You can't see. They are deep, hollow, and menacing.

The sound of monks chanting.

A strong wind.

Something's about to go down.

You think you can see, you're not sure, but you think the leprechaun is grinning. Or is he grimacing?

A yell. A man's yell. Who? Deep throttle. Like someone kicked up the bass twelve notches. Could it be Fater Beck? "The Sacrifice!"

Cheers from the crowd, in unison.

Panic. You realize that the loudest shout, the ear-piercing cheer, it's bursting forth from your own lungs. Why are you shouting? Why are you joining the bunny ears? Why are you here?

The drums.

Again, the voice, "The Sacrifice!"

Drums.

308

"NOW!"

The ropes must have had metal blades on them. Someone tightened them. The goat falls to pieces.

Blood splatters onto the pinned leprechaun.

The crowd goes wild.

Fimafeng beats his hands on his chest like an ape, hollering with righteous glee at the night wind.

The leprechaun, was this what he wanted? Grinning or grimacing?

The goat was gone, torn to harrowing bits by the ropes.

"LOWER!" the scary voice shouted.

A cauldron comes into view, lowered from the top of the tree. You think it's a cauldron, a deep, black cauldron, until you realize what's in it.

"BURN THE HEART OUT OF HIS SOUL!" the voice bellows.

Now Momma Beck is standing up on the stump. She pulls out thick gloves from a purse. Raises the gloves up to the crowd. More cheers and jeers. She slips the gloves on each finger.

The black cauldron is no cauldron at all. It's a pot, a black pot of gold. It hangs just a few feet off the ground. Momma Beck leans in over it. With her gloved hands, she pulls out a round, gold coin.

You don't know how you know, but you do. The coins are smoldering hot, nearly melting.

With the gold coin, Momma Beck makes her way to the little creature.

Then she does the horrible thing.

She uses the coin. She places it on the leprechaun's chest. She is burning the heart out of the leprechaun.

He screams.

You watch.

The crowd roars.

Before it's over, Momma Beck, upon instruction from the voice that you still assume is Fater Beck, melts the worthless creature's tongue out, as well as his eyes. The gold coins, like a warm knife through butter, cut their way through the eyes into the sad, skinny sack's brain.

309

How Ne Ime didn't leave the Center after witnessing that atrocity, Jennifer Dash will never know.

~~~

Adam and Eve were kicked out of Eden after tasting the fruit of the tree of the knowledge of Good and Evil. Jenn has found her fruit and decided, for good or for ill, that in order to solve the world, she'll have to eat whole, that forbidden fruit.
    Knowledge comes at a price, doesn't it?

Chapter 43: Center Death

Admitting that it is an overwhelming and ultimately futile exercise to try and encapsulate six months of experience, I nevertheless have decided to take a stab at explaining Ne Ime's time at the Druidry Center near New Grange, Ireland.

Again, it's an impossible task, and undoubtedly I will exclude important moments and crucial conversations. There's just no getting around it. To tell the story perfectly, to embrace Jenn's time immaculately, we'd need to spend six months relishing every minuscule detail. So, seeing that few of us have six months by which to relive Jenn's life at the Center, I have taken it upon myself to organize the events into pods of experience. Henceforth we'll refer to them as "labs". Every second that went by in the Druidry was to be taken captive by education. Everything was meant to be observed and recorded as a merited measure of time built to bolster your understanding of your surroundings, yourself, or the game of life at large. Therefore, as I'm sure you can surmise, Ne Ime survived, endured, and underwent many, many, labs. What follows is my personal assemblage of those "labs", in no particular order.

Empathy Lab

"What we have here is a failure to communicate," Volva told the classroom. Ne Ime sat in the back beside Fimafeng, the closest thing she had to a friend at the Center.

It was better to be at the back of the room. There was a certain steam-machine that wafted most strongly in the back. No one told Ne Ime this, she figured it out on her own; the steam contained some sort of drug, a sort of hypersensitivity drug. She noticed that when she was in the classrooms with the steam, she felt a heightened sense of awareness. She didn't just hear the words the teachers taught—she felt them. The words floated out from the speakers' mouth, out, like a balloon, and hung in the room, so much so that by the end of a lecture, Ne Ime often felt crowded. The room was stifled by an overpopulation of floating words. The benefit, however, was obvious. Rather than just hear words, she could feel them, see them, really internalize them and take them to heart. If only real college was just like this, Jenn might have wanted to attend.

"What should I do?" Volva said in a near falsetto, wringing her hands as she played through this operatic drama. On the table beside her, in a small fence, was a toddler goat, brown with a white spot on the top of its head. Grown-up goats are weird with their staring and their evil, demonic eyes, but the babies, oh my! So cute!

Under a glass jar, beside the fenced-in goat on the table, a small wasp flew around angrily.

"This world is full of life... and death. At the Center, we have learned this deep truth, a truth I'll begin to impart to you now. Since we cannot speak to the animal kingdom, we are forced to make a decision. We must be empathetic, or... we must not begin to allow ourselves to feel any sort of emotion towards these creatures at all. Do you yet understand? Of course you do not... not yet.

"Every choice we make, whether that's a conversation, or deciding where to take our next step, it affects someone, something. Maybe that step squishes an insect's home. Maybe that conversation hurts someone's feelings. Everything hurts someone.

"So the deep truth is this: you have two options. Some at the Center are pacifists, absolute empaths. They will try to harm no one and no thing."

Volva opened the glass jar, the wasp flew voraciously up and out the window, hurting no one, being hurt by no one. Volva smiled. "You won't find many like this here at the Center. They are almost eternally in the sweat-house or in counsel apologizing and praying for forgiveness. Living the life of an empath is hard. But it is LIFE, it is LIVING. You feel for everyone, everything, always, in a constant state of vicarious living."

Mulch Lab
Ne Ime worked in the mulch department a few hours a day

with Lourna Von Schloss, a beach bum from the sands of San Diego, who, on her 18th birthday, convinced her parents to fly her and her friends out to Europe as a graduation present. Lourry, the nickname she went by, heard about the Center during one of her yoga meetings. Though a hippie by nature, when Lourry showed up and, just like Ne Ime, had to go through the 72-hour conditioning by the Controllers, she bit down. She didn't like being told what to do, and her short life as the wealthy daughter of two real estate tycoons had taught her that if she dug her heels in, she could upend any authority. There's a good chance Lourna Von Schloss would never have ended up at the Center had the Controllers not shown up in their manipulative fashion.

The bummer was that as Ne Ime and Lourry smashed tree limbs into a wood chipper, they weren't allowed to talk to each other. The rationale for this decision, as At-tila had described, was so that they could hear Momma Beck's telepathic instructions during the course of the day.

Ne Ime, for many weeks, heard nothing, and the hours mulching went by slowly. Painfully.

There's something to be said here about familiarity. Besides both being American, Lourry and Ne Ime didn't have much in common. Despite their differences though, they ended up spending much time together. After work, they'd attend the same lectures, eat dinner together, and generally hang out until lights out. In this way, the Center played out just like any summer camp, with the campers falling into cliques and not intermingling much after the first couple days of introductions. Fimafeng also joined Ne Ime and Lourry after work hours. Ne Ime began to suspect that Fimafeng and Lourry were more than just friends.

One day during work, Ne Ime heard a voice. A deep, soothing voice in her head. The voice said, "You know that I love you." It said it twice, and then it was over. After work Ne Ime asked if Lourry heard anything.

"Nope. Just like, you know, every other day."

Self-Knowledge Lab
Ne Ime sat alone in a sweat room, one of the taller teepees

313

and it was blisteringly hot. Her instructions were to wear several layers of clothes, clear her mind, and sit there for six hours.

She did this twice a week for six months.

Most of the time, the sweat lodge was uncomfortable. Ne Ime would get incredibly dehydrated and the resulting headaches wouldn't go away for a good day or two.

But twice, on two separate occasions, some real insight came. I shall only mention one insight (perhaps we'll visit the other another time).

Ne Ime had been in there a good four hours when suddenly she pictured Momma Beck in her mind, talking to her.

"Ne Ime, why don't you have a name?"

"I do have a name," she replied, "actually, I have several names."

"You say this, but it's not true."

"Sure it is."

"Without a name, you have no identity."

This startled Ne Ime. Identity was hugely important to the Center.

She defended herself, "I do have a name."

"You have no name, because you haven't decided who you are. Until you do, you're stuck."

That was all. After that, all Ne Ime could think about was a cold, wet glass of water.

Or tea.

Religion Lab

The only class that At-tila, via Momma Beck, taught was a comparative religions class. Ne Ime enjoyed the class very much, as she didn't know much about history, and the class opened her up to the bigness of civilizations and world history.

"Geography," At-tila said, "plays the biggest role in how we imagine the afterlife. The Egyptians had the Nile River. The Nile worked like a clock. Every year it flooded, every year the flooding evaporated. It created a system, a very logical system that the peoples of that time could comprehend. That's why the Egyptian afterlife, more than anything else, is built on order. At the root of their beings, the Egyptians saw the world

314

as clockwork, and so death must be an echo of that. Meanwhile, the Assyrians and other ancient Mesopotamian peoples saw no such systems, no such order. Life was hard. The landscape of Mesopotamia was barren and muddy. Life was schizophrenic. One day you live, the next you die, and the only order in the world was survival of the fittest. There was no justice in the geography, no gold, no treasure to mine out of the ground. And so the people envisioned an afterlife where everyone chewed on dust after death. It didn't matter if you were good or bad after you died—you chewed on dust. Think on it, you made the mud of the Earth with your dead mouth. Do you see how that works?

"So then, what would you say about us? In our modern world, how should the afterlife be reflected in our geography? Don't think about the Center, here, the Druidry, think of the outside world. The cell phones, the computers, the airplanes. What sort of afterlife does that foster? Anyone?"

Ne Ime raised her hand.

"Yes, Ne Ime," At-tila said.

"A complex one?" She said, doubting herself.

"Exactly!" At-tila said proudly, "The new afterlife is one of infinite complexity."

Levels Lab

Apparently, it was Marshall Winston who had commended Ne Ime and vouched for her to be merited as a Level Two. Ne Ime wasn't so sure about this, since she had noticed that no Level Two or higher ever drank the wonderful tea. It was already well known throughout the Center that you couldn't find a bigger fan of the hot rose water than Ne Ime, who was seldom caught without a fresh cup in hand.

But when it came time to be initiated into Level Two status, everything was made clear.

The tattoo itself (more like a branding than a tattoo, as the resulting image would remain abraised on her skin for all time) apparently contained within it the essence of the tea itself.

At-tila informed Ne Ime that if she ever missed the tea as a Level Two, all she'd need to do was touch her tattoo, or, in worst case situations, scratch it, and her withdrawals would go

315

away. The tattoo somehow continually secreted the essence of the tea into her blood stream.

Past Life Lab

A shadow stood beside Ne Ime's hammock. She had woken in the middle of the night only to doubt whether or not the shadow was real.

It held the outline of a boy. It was too dark to make out any features of the shadow creature.

Silently, it handed a note to Ne Ime.

She took it.

The shadow sighed. Creeped out, and assuming she was dreaming, Ne Ime turned her hammock, pocketed the note, and forced herself back to sleep. Her last thought before gliding into a visionless slumber was that she didn't care for shadows that sighed. Sighing implied emotion. She preferred her shadows to be emotionless.

In the morning Ne Ime was surprised to find a note in her pocket. The small shadow was real. It must have been Robin the Lost Boy of Liechtenstein.

The note read:

Jennifer,

The time is now. I don't expect you to come, but as it turns out, it's coming to a head near where you're staying. So, maybe you'll find a way.

On the Summer Solstice, at dawn, I'll be at Stonehenge. I've uncovered the last of the book's secrets, and my time is upon us.

If you don't come, then we won't meet again. I've left no will or living testament, but you are welcome to claim any of my fortune as your inheritance. Use this note that I've written in my own hand as certification.

I'm taking Robin with me. I'm so glad you led me to him. He's such a better helper than you could have ever been, but how could we have known at the time?

If you still care about your ambitions, you'll be there.

The secret, Jennifer, is this: Croatoan means more than just death. Death isn't enough. It never was.

Respectfully yours,

316

Lillith Babbit

Connections Lab

One day, after their mulching shift, and after Lourry had measured Ne Ime's height for a second time in the same day (Ne Ime thought that maybe she grew during the shift, since she felt her muscle tendrils stretching over the course of the day), the two women meandered to the lost connections corridor.

The room looked like an old telephone operator's workplace from the black-and-white fifties. Four women and one man—all Level Threes, Ne Ime noted—stared at old-timey switchboards and spoke into earpieces.

"Hello, hello?"

"Is anyone there?"

"Talk to me if you're listening?"

"Is there a word that needs to be said to arouse you?"

"Can you whistle or hum, anything that I could hear? Hello?"

Lourry was excited. She'd visited this room almost everyday for the past month. She'd been petitioning Momma Beck to let her be re-positioned to work here in the lost connections department. Lourry thought that daily visits to the workplace might establish good faith that Momma Beck would reward.

"So, how does this work?" Ne Ime asked Lourry.

"Like, okay. So, follow the cords."

From every switchboard in front of the operators, visible telephone cables bored through holes in the wall.

"Okay. Where do they go?"

Lourna Von Schloss smiled and grabbed Jenn's dyed new hand. They walked outside, to just the other side of the operators' wall.

"See? So, the cords come together and then they're encased in this blue plastic sheath." Ne Ime's eyes followed the plastic tubing where it continued off into the distance... towards an open grass field.

Lourry pranced about. Ne Ime tagged along as they followed the cables.

Past the field.

317

Past another forested area.

Over a babbling brook.

To a small cemetery. At the entrance of the cemetery the blue sheath opened up and the cables again split apart, each cord extending out and appearing freshly buried in front of a tombstone.

Skepticism Lab

"Will Fimafeng ever return?" Ne Ime asked Marshall Winston.

"Where do you think he is?" the resident skeptic replied.

"He had told Lourry and me that he felt compelled to go to the other Center."

"The other Center?"

"Yeah, you know, the one on the other side of the hole, on the other side of the world."

"Ah, the hole through the center of the earth."

"Why do you say it like that?"

"Have you ever wondered, Ne Ime, why there are ropes leading into the hole?"

"No. I suppose it's so skeptics like you can take a deeper look down."

"If that were the case they'd only need one rope. Not six."

"I don't know, then. Tell me, oh wise Skeptic man."

"Have you replaced me yet?"

"That's not how you say it. I replace an older character with you. And yes. Yes I have."

"Who am I?"

"Am I supposed to say?"

"You know our contract... you're allowed to speak with me in ways that aren't necessarily Momma and Fater Beck approved." Marshall Winston was right. Every Level Two was allowed to have what the Druidry referred to as a Doubt Broacher, someone with whom they were allowed to speak all doubts and frustrations, the idea being that everyone needs a release valve, a place where there would be freedom to vent. At-tila had told Ne Ime that they learned early on in the Center's history that without a Doubt Broacher, the Center was suspect to schisms and various breakouts of gossip. The insertion of the Doubt Broacher, the release valve, had

318

dramatically decreased that tension. When the prospect of finding said release valve was brought to Ne Ime's attention, she had no doubt whom she wanted as her Doubt Broacher—the man whose very destiny was doubt and skepticism: Marshall Winston. He seemed pleased to oblige.

"I put you into the place of Miles Faa."

Empathy Lab

"On the other hand..." Volva slid over to the goat and petted it with one hand. The cutey baby goat did the closest thing to purr that it could, cuddling up to Volva's outstretched hand as she, with her other hand, pulled out a curved blade. Her petting hand turned into a wrathful fist, holding the kid hostage.

She slit its throat. The little innocent creature quivered and gurgled a sad cry as it bled out. "Shhh," Volva said sweetly to the dying kid. "Shh...."

The thing collapsed into its own blood and died.

"Our other option, which I sincerely appeal you take up, is devoiding yourself of pity. It's hard, and it takes many years of work, but once achieved, once you're free of the burden of shame and empathy, then anything is possible. What you once never could imagine yourself doing now is graspable. Myriad obstacles between you and perfection fall."

Jenn couldn't help staring at the dead goat. It was so cute. Why did it have to die? Just to make a point? She looked over at Fimafeng. One tear after another rolled down his cheeks. The man was grasping the sides of his desk with tremendous force. It was amazing that the desk didn't crumble under Fimafeng's emotional pain.

"The enemy is wise, children." Volva said. "He will use whatever weakness he finds in you and EXPLOIT it. Empathy—let me remind you—empathy is not real. You're attaching emotions, feelings, to this baby goat that it never felt. You still, right now, are spiritually decimated by what you believe is the goat's pain. But I ask you, what does he feel right now? Much less pain than you! No pain, to be precise. He is free. You are not.

"The enemy uses your imagination, your created thought-life, as a weapon against you.

"Choose wisely. Class dismissed."

Anything You Want Lab

Any member of the Center, Level One or higher, was entitled to any claim they wanted to make, within reason. There was a general notion that no one should lack for what they so desire. Surely At-tila and Momma Beck denied some requests, but that was not the Druidry's reputation.

Ne Ime was terrified by her hand implant. Specifically, it's Scandinavian-white color.

She complained about it to At-tila (in front of Momma Beck, of course), and the very next day the Center brought a small pool of skin dye for Ne Ime. She waded her hand in the gooey stuff for about an hour.

The color wasn't perfect, (it was now a darker hue than the rest of her arm) but it soothed Ne Ime. Close enough. She felt that she could come to terms with this hand. She felt now that she could live with this appendage.

Past Life Lab

A night not too many days after Ne Ime had been silently handed the note by a sighing Robin, she awoke to the sound of a bird bellow—not a caw like most birds echo, nor a siren song like those of love birds. This was a distinct noise, coming from just outside the sleep den. Ne Ime fumbled out of her hammock, trying her darndest not to bump into the levels of hammocks below. As always, she failed at that enterprise.

Cognizant of how warm it was, even for the beginning of spring, Ne Ime tiptoed outside. She'd always thought Ireland would be cold. Her months-long stay at the Center had proven otherwise. It did, however, rain a lot, and the bare ground was wet and muddy.

What awaited her outside swept all thoughts of weather outside.

Gimli the gull fluttered his wings in anticipation. He'd flown long and hard to find Jennifer Dash. His birdbrain was overwhelmed with relief at the sight of his prize. He waddled over to her.

320

She grabbed a letter from out of his gullet and petted his wet head.

"Good bird," Ne Ime said in monotone, her heart focused on the words written in her newly arrived mail.

A small glimmer of hope sprung in her heart that it could be from Atticus. It'd been months now since they spoke. That magnetic girl had zapped Jenn's phone, so if Atticus broke up with Betty, well, he'd have no way of communicating that to Jenn, unless he somehow got in contact with Gimli.

The first words of the letter denied any hope of Atticus:

Report to your Captain immediately. The Orion has come back together. Reports have surfaced, too immeasurable to recount. The disease, the Known Triangle disease, the very death spell that Miles chopped off your hand to save you from, it's sweeping through the countrysides.

Rumors abound that a man, the Real Pishtaco, they call him, has unleashed vengeance upon the world.

Jenn, this is full-blown outbreak.

We've squashed the island. We had it bombed long ago. But we have reason to believe that it's Merkyl. He betrayed you. He betrayed us. He's betraying the world.

Help us find Merkyl and stop the infection... before it's too late.

Call us at_____(the number was written three times. Ne Ime supposed it was penned three times to make sure Jenn could read it clearly).

I'll get you further instructions once you contact us.

STOP WHAT YOU'RE DOING AND CALL NOW.

-Godard, First Mate of the Orion.

Skepticism Lab

"Ah." Marshall Winston appeared notably dejected.

"What? What's that look for?"

"I was hoping to fill someone else's shoes."

"Whose?"

"Doesn't matter. Fimafeng is gone."

"I know. He's on the other side of the world."

"You really believe that?"

Ne Ime scratched her dyed tan hand. "Why shouldn't I?"

321

"Of all the things to believe here... and there's many good things to embrace, the bottomless pit is just about the stupidest. Come, let me show you."

It was dark out. The two walked along the same path Ne Ime and At-tila walked the day she reached Level One status. On the trail, they talked more personably... but who can remember such shenanigans? Moments like that are too effervescent to recall. Dust in the wind.

The wall was gone.

They stood at the summit of the pit.

There was the hole, and in it, lights.

Shimmering lights, fading in and out, colored something between green and purple, almost flashing. Jenn heard, somewhere in the depths of her mind, sounds. High pitched, like echoes down a long, long corridor. What were they saying? Ne Ime's body shivered as a bad bout of vertigo swept over her.

She threw herself at Marshall Winston, relying on the tall, strong man's ability to hold her from falling into the sparkling depths.

"What are those?" Ne Ime asked astonished.

"Will O' the Wisps."

"Why are they there?"

"They seduce people to fall in."

"Why?"

"It's just a pit, Ne Ime. It has a bottom."

"So, Fimafeng..."

"He dropped down. He's dead."

"Why? Why do they lie?"

"To extract the worthy from the unworthy."

"That's horrible!"

"Why?"

"That's wrong! You can't do that!"

"Touch your tattoo."

Ne Ime followed the instructions. As she did, as she felt the grooves of the symbol at the small of her back, a peace subsumed her.

Connections Lab

"They're trying to talk to the dead?" Ne Ime said, aghast at the very words she found herself saying.

"Yeah, like, so, you get it?"

"Not exactly."

"The Center's looking for stuck identities."

"Yeah, I haven't really gotten lessons on that yet."

"Coolio, yeah, so, you know, like, how we all have identities?"

"Yeah. The leprechaun told me about that."

"SURE! Great! These identities in us, we're constantly sculpting them... and like, when we die, the identities have to go somewhere. They're like prized art treasures. At-tila told me—"

"You mean Momma Beck."

"Oh, yeah, right, uh, Momma Beck by At-tila... he said—"

"She said."

"Right, she said, like, she said that identities are like relics, reflections of our life."

"Everyone keeps describing this to me, but it still just sounds like the soul."

"No, like, okay, you know like, uh, buried treasure?"

"Yeah?"

"Or like Egyptians, or the guy who built the Taj Muhal?"

"Yeah."

"The pyramids, the Taj Muhal, they're like, the treasures of those people's lives. The physical treasures. They like, show off their wealth and stuff."

"Okay..."

"Identities are like that... but for the spiritual realm."

"If it's just treasure, why's the Center trying to talk to inanimate objects?"

"When you die, your work speaks for itself."

"Oh."

None of this made sense to Jenn, and it was creepy seeing those telephone wires dig into the cemetery graves. It was creepier yet to imagine the operators actually getting a response on the other side of the line. Still, the weird mystical stuff was forgivable, and Ne Ime didn't feel like she needed to understand it, or even really agree with it, in order to suck the marrow out of life and out of the Center. She could slide along without focusing on all the weird....

Right?

Levels Lab
She got the tattoo at a midnight ceremony. She was asked to bring her two closest friends as witnesses. Fimafeng and Lourry came and bore witness. Marshall Winston was there too. A cloaked person penned the tattoo into the small of Ne Ime's back. It stung a little, but it also felt good, like scratching an 18-year-old itch. The tattoo was a circle with two horns inside, its color a dark, burgundy hue.

Mulch Lab
"Nope. Just like, you know, every other day."

It happened again four days later. Only this time, the message was different.

It said, "You are ready. Level Three awaits." Ne Ime answered in her heart, "What must I do to get to Level Three?"

The response came two days after that.

"You must survive the Maze."

Skepticism Lab
Walking back to camp, Ne Ime asked one more question.

"You never explained. Why all the ropes?"

"Into the pit?"

"Yeah. Why so many?"

"Two reasons, one I'm certain of, one less so."

"Okay. Tell me both."

"They go down and clear out the broken bodies."

"How many fall in?"

"Lots. Remember that day you went in to the Temp Level One class? Remember how many people there were?"

"Sure."

"Remember how there were loads less the very next day?"

"I just figured they were creeped out by the sacrifice. I thought about leaving."

"No one leaves, Ne Ime. You either stay, or you fall for the Wisps. Now, enough talk. You need good rest tonight.

Tomorrow you're going into the maze, right?"
   "Yeah."
   "You nervous?"
   "No. Should I be?"
   "Probably."

~~~

Jennifer Dash is set to survive the Maze, whose victors get to taste the prize of Level Three. But before we get there, we need to take a trip away from Jennifer aka Ne Ime.

   Now, we return to the USA. The game pieces are in motion. We must keep track of the movements.

Chapter 44: Scourge of the Earth

Friendship Baptist Church
West Virginia
Sunday Morning

"Some of our friends, our loved ones, dear sweet li'l ones, they are suffering. Oh, how they're suffering. You've seen it on the television. You've heard it on the radio. You've read about it on the internet.

"God's big bowl of wrath is pouring out like tomato soup on our brothers and sisters. This plague sees no difference between color, no difference between Jew or Greek or Muslim or Hindu. It's taking down all of us, all of our brothers and sisters.

"But I'll tell you this, I'll tell you. I spoke to Brother Johnny. You know him and his congregation; they're on their knees night and day. They're just on the other side of those Sierra Nevada Mountains, out in Reno, Nevada. You think there's not a renaissance? You think every man, woman, child, and even little babies aren't night and day praying to the Lord Almighty that this plague upon the human race come to an end, halted by God's armored angels BEFORE them zombies crawl over those mountains? You know they are!

"Let me tell you this: I do not know if this is the end of days. I do NOT know if Jesus is fixin' to come down here and swoop us up and outta here. I DO NOT KNOW! But I'll say this, brothers and sisters, I KNOW THIS MUCH. The men, the government, those smarty-pants officers with their gas masks and hazmat suits, they'd like you and I to believe that everything's fine, that they've got the disease contained, and that no brain-rotting cannibals are scuttling over Mount Rushmore.

"But this much I KNOW: Unless we fall on our knees, grab our children, hug them as tight as we know how, filling them with peace and love, unless our knees bleed from being on the ground crying out to God, DELIVER US, SAVE US FROM

326

YOUR WRATH OH LORD, SAVE US FROM YOUR VENGEANCE! Unless we do that, in earnest, every single day for the rest of our lives, well—what do you think's gonna happen?

"You think God's gonna stop this flood? You think he gives a rat's ass about us unless we admit, unless we say we're sorry?

"We're sorry for not loving him more. We're sorry we haven't offered ourselves as daily sacrifices.

"We're sorry we've introduced our children to SIN! Don't you say you haven't! We've fallen in love with this world. We love it so very much. Maybe Jesus is trying to tell us something. Maybe he's trying to warn us that the true death, you know I'm not talking about being eaten by some diseased soul whose nose is crumbling off! I'm talking about the true death, the second death, spiritual death! Yeah, I'll say it, you know what I'm talking about: HELL. Maybe Jesus has been trying to warn us about that place—he's been whispering and whispering in our ears about it for years. Generations. SINCE ADAM BIT THAT APPLE! He's been whispering to us. Warning us. And now, judgment's a fallin'. And it's eating up the world. The Lord lost patience with us. He's not whispering anymore. No, Ma'am. No, sir! He's a shoutin'!

"If Friendly Baptist and all the other churches in all the other towns east of the Mississippi don't stop and repent... The gas mask men aren't going to keep us safe. Them dead bones are gonna creep straight through those great walls in the Sierra Nevadas. If this is from God, ain't nothing stoppin' them bones."

Radio
FM 90.9
The Breeze

"It's the top of the hour. Our non-stop coverage of the pandemic, Day 87, continues here at *90.9, The Breeze.* We're offering minute-by-minute breakdowns of what you can being doing to stop the spread as well as valuable insight from specialists in the field live 24/7. I'm Brent McGolligers and this hour, to take us through the most recent mutations of the disease, we're welcoming gene-splicing scientist Dr. Norwin Fliesht on air now.

"Dr. Fliesht, walk us through the evolution of the pandemic. At this point, is it possible to separate fact from mere rumor, regarding this horrible atrocity?"

"I can only go so far, Brent. The simple fact of the matter is, the only DNA we've caught of this thing was nearly 3 months ago, and clearly, the situation has evolved."

"And is continuing to evolve."

"Yes, that's right."

"Can you tell us, Doctor, how it's possible that this disease could mutate so fast?"

"This is speculation, but... "

"Wouldn't you say it's more than speculation at this point? It's clear now to us all that what we've seen, even in the last two weeks, is drastically different than the reports and research done in Peru months ago."

"Yes, well, the simple fact is we're in the dark on this thing. People like me—the best we can do is make inferences based on how we've seen other diseases work before, and how we believe life works here on Earth."

"Tell us about that. What inferences are you able to draw?"

"People think evolution always happens slowly, over millions of years."

"You're saying that's a wrong assumption?"

"It tends to miss the point. Genetic changes occur through mutation. That's not so much about time as it is about numbers."

"Numbers? What numbers?"

"Brent, if you wanted to grow wings, that would require a pretty serious mutation. For that to occur you'd need a series of mutations over multiple generations. For there to be change in humans, because our lives last roughly 70-80 years, and the average family has 2.1 children, that change is going to take, again this is generally speaking, millions of years. But when you're talking about mutations at the microbial level, as well as with viruses—their procreation, their genetic reproduction occurs at rates that are, say, maybe a billion times faster than we humans procreate as a species."

"What are you saying?"

"I believe that this disease, essentially, finds a host, reproduces itself several million times, and dies. This happens quickly. Each individual microbial carrier may only live a few seconds."

"So, the quickness of the change, from birth, reproduction, to death, is so rapid—am I understanding you correctly? That's what you're saying is causing the change in symptoms and variation."

"Exactly, Brent."

"With a pandemic reaching the scope that this one has, of course, there's going to be endless speculation and some pretty far out theories. We had on yesterday a researcher that believes that this is not in fact just one disease, but that it's two distinct strands that have now combined, interbred, if you will. What do you think about that theory?"

"Look, even if you just examine the way this disease attacks us, it seems highly unlikely that there's two separate demons out there."

"That's fair, but how do you account for such dramatic changes? Our first reports out of South America—"

"Which, we have looked at DNA from the disease at that stage, by the way."

"Yes, yes, we've all heard the stories of heroic doctors and scientists who decided to throw caution at the wind, give their lives so we could obtain those early samples. It does make you wonder, why haven't we heard similar stories of heroism in the United States? I've got numbers in my hand projecting 2 million currently with the disease, 4 million already dead, and likely millions more before this is all said and done. Why can't we even get a blood sample? That seems preposterous, no?"

"Brent, I think if we look at the evolution of the pandemic, we might find some answers. Can we walk this back?"

"Okay, but please get around to answering my question."

"Think Peru. What were the symptoms? The reactions? Slow moving necrosis combined with brain distortion. This all merged to reflect rabies-like symptoms. Fury. Cannibalistic tendencies. But the disease took weeks, if not months to lay

329

siege and ultimately kill its victim. Now, it seems the disease has mutated to become a more effective weapon."

"How do you mean?"

"If I see a man who's severely handicapped by necrosis, limbs breaking, appendages tearing off, I'm naturally going to run away from that man. What does the disease want? It wants to find a new home, another brain to procreate in."

"You're saying the disease uses our brains as a sort of fertilizer?"

"This is conjecture, but yes, we think the brain hosts the disease like a home, like a dark, wet cave for bats."

"Okay, yes, I see. Continue."

"In order for the disease to be most effective, the necrosis needs to stop. That way, the feral man can chase me if I run away. But, there's a compromise. If it's not slowly eating us, which is the primary cause of the necrosis, it has to eat what we'd call "the high fiber, the super-sauce"—the brain stem. It feeds off our brain stem, and the result is a much quicker fatality."

"That explains some of the changes—the lack of leprosy in newer victims, the astronomical rise in deaths. But what about the rabies symptom, the terrifying actions that many have described as turning people into zombies? Why has that gone away?"

"Go back to thinking what's best for the disease. The disease has always been spread the same way—saliva. That hasn't changed. But now its taken a much more insipid form. Victims are being described as being hysterically depressed as well as lonely. I will run away from a diseased, feral man, but if my infected mother knocks on my door crying, I'm letting her in, I'm hugging her to try and comfort her, and therefore, I'm getting infected."

"Does this explain the sudden stoppage of gut vomiting?"

"Yes. If my neighbor is rejecting internal organs, I'm staying away from him. If he's merely crying with a runny nose, I'm more apt to touch him, to want to try to comfort him. This disease seems to have deciphered our desire to empathize."

"It feels like this thing is going to keep changing itself until there's no one left. Can we anticipate its next move? Its next

330

mutation?"

"No. Maybe... I don't want to cause a scare."

"Tens of millions are already dead. We're already scared."

"If I were the disease, I'd go airborne."

Louisiana
Lake Charles

The doorbell starting ringing at 4am. It continued, and continued and continued. Atticus, his entrepreneurial spirit always at work, took floorboards out of the attic and used them to nail the windows on the first floor shut. Betty cuddled Scout. The two of them kept their focus entranced on Disney's *Mulan*. Atticus couldn't handle cartoons right now. He kept one ear listening to local radio news and the other on the doorbells and banging.

This wasn't supposed to happen. America, to her credit, had, for the most part, stayed one step ahead of the pandemic, cutting all transportation to and from Mexico and South America almost from the start. The recently-elected president wasn't worried about the US appearing xenophobic or unmerciful. A new terror was sweeping the world, and he was not going to let the blood-sucking demons of the Pacific into the world's only super power. Not on his watch.

But it did. The ides of March called it. The first reported case came to America's collective conscience on March 15th. There was panic immediately.

Within three days, the President, by executive order, quarantined essentially all of California south of Sonoma. And it was working. The terror was growing, millions of people were dying, but besides the unlucky souls trapped in Southern California, Americans were safe. For a moment, it was contained.

The President wasn't going to stop there. When things go bad, power belongs not to the authorities, but to those who are willing to do. This president was a doer. He had twenty-foot walls erected along the entire Sierra Nevadas.

The newest intel showed that the infected were not living more than 72 hours, and the last 24 or those were so

331

debilitating that the threat was severely reduced. That meant that if you could contain the infected for the first 48 hours after initial infection, you were okay. You'd make it. This wasn't over yet. This thing could still peter out. This 21st-century war for humanity could still be won.

All we had to do was build a wall.

So we thought.

Atticus Further and the two women trapped in his house would beg to differ.

Atticus had played out various scenarios in his mind of how he'd protect his sister and girlfriend in the event of a zombie invasion. But this was so different.

Yes, there were thoughtless meanderers in the street. But they didn't hobble, mouths ajar, chanting for brains. No.

They cried. Literally. They prayed to a god that wasn't listening.

Atticus watched an old lady get infected; Merriam Solace, their cranky neighbor down the street. She somehow didn't hear the noise. Must not have had her hearing aids. In her morning pajamas, she waddled out to pick the newspaper off the ground. When she got there, a young woman came up to her, tears streaking down her cheek. The girl collapsed into the old lady's arms. Atticus watched this from his bedroom window. He thought maybe it was okay. Maybe... they were hugging, the girl was sobbing, stroking old Merriam's aged face.

Then, the young girl got up, momentarily composed herself, and started back down the street, walking in the middle of the road, intermittently sobbing, calling out for someone to help her. Her cheeks had two streaks of dark purple painting her face—skin rashes from too many salty tears.

Merriam was catatonic on her front lawn for what seemed to Atticus to be several minutes (though in truth was not even 45 seconds). Then young Mr. Further watched as tears started pouring down Mrs. Solace's face. She was drooling profusely as well, and began scratching all over. Several times she yelled, with just one name on her lips: Henry. Merriam Solace called out for her dead husband Henry. Maybe he could appease the pain somehow. From beyond the grave, he'd take away this small, horrible moment. Somehow take away the shame.

Another difference between these infected ones and zombies: these people didn't travel in packs. Atticus saw. They didn't. When two were even in line of sight from one another, they'd work hard to distance themselves. More than once on that foggy morning, Atticus saw two infected walkers spot each other and simultaneously start walking in disparate directions.

Then, the fateful doorbell. The doorbells to end all doorbells.

No one answered. The girls were on their third viewing of *Mulan*—they had some sort of I-Spy game going on with it now. Atticus couldn't quite figure out how it worked. The radio exacted his attention too often to stay focused on the logistics of their game. After the doorbell was left to no avail, a yell. More of a yelp. But all three inmates sanctioned in the Further house knew the voice.

Joseph Further.

He'd come home. To his imminently maturing son and still innocent daughter. The Pater Familias was home. Why was he crying?

"Kids? Atticus! Let me in!"

Molly Further (Atticus and Scout's mother) had died shortly after Scout's birth. Joseph Further had raised his children all while off traveling the country on the Sunset Limited half the time. Such a warm father was he that his returns after long days and nights gone always came with cheers and hugs, kisses and squeaks of joy from little Scout. Not this time.

Scout ran downstairs, grabbed a stool, and peered through the front door peephole.

At first glance, Joseph Further, dressed in his conductor uniform, appeared quite respectable, but a loving daughter saw through the thin veil immediately. His eyes were bloodshot and his cheeks puffy, red, and wet. His nose ran disgustingly into his mouth and down his chin in two solid streams.

He looked scared. Scout had never seen fear on her father's face.

333

"Scout, get away from the door."

"But he needs our help."

"Just step away from the door Scout."

"Come here," Betty said to Scout, arms opened wide. "Let's get back down to business. We have to defeat the Huns... again."

"Scout?! Scout can you hear me? I can hear you, sweetheart. Open the door! Please!"

Scout examined her brother's eyes. They were unflinching, unforgiving, while Betty was opened-armed, doughy-eyed, and altogether condescending. Scout was a girl of action, taking more after her mother than her brother or father.

Before Atticus could stop her, Scout unlocked the two door locks and swung the front door open.

Fearing that his father would swoop in like a vulture, Atticus pounced on Scout, tackling her and rolling away from the door, all too fast for Scout to scream.

On the ground, Atticus looked up to see that his father still stood in the doorway, apparently hesitating, fully unsure of his next move.

"I just wanted to see you two," Joseph choked out through tears.

"Betty, would you give me a moment with my children? This won't take long."

"She's not going anywhere. You're infected," Atticus said, holding the now sobbing Scout in his arms on the floor. "You're not welcome in this house."

"This is. My. Household, son. And I'm coming in."

Joseph Further marched in. Filling with terror, never expecting that his own father would be the talking zombie that did him in, Atticus, on the floor, inched and scooted away from his Dad, trying pitifully to shield Scout from the oncoming doom.

"I'm... I'm going to sit on the couch. Betty, please move, I don't... I don't want to touch you. That's, that's not my job."

"Okay."

Joseph sat on his couch, the same couch on which Jennifer Dash had once slept.

"Scout? Scout, listen to me for a moment."

334

"She's not talking to you."

"I have had enough of your attitude, Atticus. I'm, I'm the man of this house, you will, you will know your place."

"I'm protecting her, Dad."

"I... I know... I can't... I can't, I can't think, I can't think, I can't think. Oh God, Oh God help us. Oh God help us."

He continued on like that a while. Atticus whispered to Scout. She sprinted up and ran into Betty's arms. Atticus slipped into the kitchen and further depths of the house. He returned prepared, baseball bat in hand, sharp kitchen knife jammed into his back pocket.

"Scout, just look at me. You stay there. Just look at me."

"Daddy?"

"Yes. Yes, Scout. Listen. Some bad things are happening. I'm not going... I'm not going to be around anymore. I want you to remember. Remember. Always say your prayers before meals and before bed and first thing when you wake up. Okay?"

"Okay, Daddy."

"Good girl, good girl. Remember, remember that I've loved you. Since the day you were born, since the time I first laid eyes on you when your mother was... when your mother was here. Betty?"

"Yes, Mr. Further?"

"I'm so thankful you're in my son's life. You be good to him. Say kind words, all the time. That's all you have to do. Just be kind to him. Say nice things. That's more challenging than it sounds."

"Yes, sir."

"Atticus, my only son."

For the sake of his tribe, Atticus said nothing to his father. He had to keep his cool. To stay calm in case of... if the worst case came to be.

"Don't you blame God for this. Don't you do that. He's a good guy. You can't turn your back on him. You cannot do this... I love you."

Joseph's head was shaking violently. He was suppressing strong desires. Everything within the train conductor's hell of a body was shouting at him, begging him, cursing him to

335

somehow touch his family. That's all. Just a touch. Just to rub his son's cheeks, to kiss his baby daughter's hair. To hug his son's girl. That's all his cursed body wanted. And with every ounce, every fiber, every will of his ultimate identity, Joseph Further resisted these deep urges.

"I'm going to go lay down in the bath. Atticus, in two minutes, I want you, you alone, to come into the bathroom. I want you to protect your family. Scout and Betty are your responsibility now. Do you understand me?"

Long pause.

"I can't... I... I can't do it myself. I need help. I need, I need help this one last time. I told Jesus I'd never do it myself. Do you understand me?"

Atticus was silent.

"Dear God, boy, answer me!"

"Yes, Father."

"And we're back live here on 90.9 The Breeze, you're safest and most reliable source for moment-to-moment news on the pandemic. I'd like to introduce to you today Captain Alfred Bacon. He was, so we're told, aboard the *Orion*, drifting off the coast of Peru some six months ago when he and his crew supposedly came into contact with an infected boat of Peruvians. This, Captain, was so long ago in the history of this disease. If your claims are correct, then you were in contact with essentially the first victims of this terrible pandemic. Can you walk us through your experience?"

"I don't appreciate the 'supposedly', Brent. But yes, I'd like your listeners to know the true origins of this devastating event."

"Okay, Captain, tell us your story."

"I was the Captain of an adventure schooner, owned and sanctioned for the seas by Lillith Babbit. Various investors, millionaires mostly, paid us to take them on certain vacations that otherwise aren't readily available to the public."

"What sort of vacations are we talking about?"

"That's not really what I came here to talk about today."

"Alright, continue on. What happened in the South Pacific."

"We got a distress call from a ship. That ship ended up

being a fishing vessel called the *Known Triangle*."

"Any significance to that ship name?"

"Not that I'm aware of. When we got near the ship, we found the crew to be nearly rabid, like vultures, trying desperately to get on board our ship."

"Would you say that what you saw was similar to the earliest reports of this disease?"

"Yes, quite so. One of our crewmen, Jorje Robles, he volunteered to go on board their ship and try to understand what was going on—you have to remember that at this point we had no reason to suspect that this was a transmittable disease at work. The crew of the *Known Triangle* attacked Jorje, and though he was able to battle them off, he was infected. Before... before we made our decision, he got the whole story from their captain. Their ship came close to an unidentified island and witnessed an SOS signal come from this unknown island. They went to the island and discovered dozens of diseased, mutant animals. They stayed long enough to meet a small Russian crew of scientists."

"I want to be clear here, so that listeners understand what you're saying. This has potentially fantastic—I mean that in the terms of huge, not wonderful—just fantastic ramifications. You're saying the mutant animals, the ones reportedly hunting locals in Peru, the original carriers—you're saying they were brought there by Russians?"

"I'm saying the Russians were using this island to do illegal gene-extraction and implementation."

"This disease that's ravaged half the world, almost the entire western hemisphere—the Russians caused it?"

"Yes."

"Oh, alright, I'm just getting word, Captain Alfred Bacon, we're going to have to get back to you, because this just in, some very urgent and troubling news. There are reports coming in, and apparently online videos are already surfacing that somehow, someway, the pandemic has spread.

"God be with us....

"We're getting reports that, and this is just conjecture I believe, but the belief at this stage is that somehow a ferry carrying dozens of infected landed on the coast of the Gulf of

337

Mexico. Earliest intelligence is telling us right now... it's coming in that the Louisiana town of Lake Charles has been hit. I repeat, the infected appear to have made landfall in Lake Charles, Louisiana. If this, my god, if this is true, what's stopping them? What's stopping this thing from taking the whole world?"

Atticus Further is a flawed human being.

Imperfect, and having never dealt with real pressure, with a genuine crisis, he was unable to do what had to be done.

His Father waited in the bathtub for forty minutes, an excruciating forty minutes.

Joseph Further waited for his son to kill him.

Mercifully, Betty came in, and Betty ended it.

~~~

Now we know the cost of Jennifer wasting time at the Druidry Center. While she imbibes on Momma and Fater Beck's strange rituals, the world falls to ashes.

Instead of facing a pandemic, Jennifer is about to face the labyrinth.

Mazes are made for monsters.

Chapter 45: Lord of the Labyrinth

The terrible horns blew.

"He must be fed. Just stay there. He'll get you. And he'll eat you! Because you've been such a naughty girl."

Jenn held her breath. She was traumatized. Nearing shock. Almost giving up.

As she lay, Jennifer Dash looked through the branch walls. Just on the other side, metal-tipped boots, the kind that a skinhead neo-nazi would wear. But that wasn't the scary part. Follow the boots up. Past the laces, past the brown leather-strapped trench coat. The shoulders, the head. The snout. The horns. This was a minotaur. And it was coming to eat Jennifer Dash.

Why do children smile? Jenn thought.

Perhaps the reason lied in their options, their more-or-less limitless choices. Life is like chess. Your first move is one of a dozen obvious choices. As an infant, you can cry, wiggle your limbs, sleep, or suckle. For a few months, that's about it, just as, in chess, you only have so many first moves. But give a child a few years, say, eight, and suddenly the olive branch of potential has sprouted into a full grown tree. Eight plays into a chess match, and the potential movements of player one border on the infinite. The eight-year-old has just as many futures. She can grow up to be an astronaut, the first human to step on Mars. She can study science and swim with sharks for National Geographic. She can study law and tell everyone what they can and can't do. She can skip studies and become a homeless bum. She can choose to bathe only in public fountains. She can become a mime, a retail salesperson, a con artist, a chef, a libertarian, a communist, a protector of the proletariat.

At the end of the chess game, usually a half-dozen or so moves after the climax, the death-rattle turning point, the options, the potentials, the choices, dwindle back to the point of origin. Available options are litigated down to the following: crying, wiggling limbs, sleeping, or suckling. That's it.

Jenn dreamt of being eight again. She dreamed not of her life as an eight-year-old, but of that potential. Instead, here she was, not eight anymore. She'd made choices. So many choices, directions, decisions. Now those decisions had come for their reaping. Jenn could only move her pawn one of two ways. She could stay down, embrace the horrible destiny that hunted her. Or she get up, try her hand at survival once more.

The day had started peacefully. At-tila led her to a room, gave her a microphone, and asked her to say the words, "You are very welcome here."

Then, shortly after lunch with Lourry and Marshall Winston, At-tila accompanied her to the outdoor maze's entrance. First, he took her to a wooden tower overlooking the entire labyrinth. It was a large maze, Ne Ime could see that much, but it didn't look unconquerable. Not by a long shot.

"Remember when you're in there: You've seen the entrance, and the exit."

"Yes, ma'am."

"Now it's time to begin."

At-tila walked Ne Ime to the entrance.

"Wait for the signal." Ne Ime didn't know what the signal was until she heard it: heard her own voice.

"You are very welcome here," Ne Ime's voice rang out through a speaker-system that looked built into the maze.

First steps.

Right at the beginning, there was a choice. The labyrinth led right or left. Ne Ime chose left. But before she took more than two steps, she smuggled out her secret weapon: a small knife.

Ne Ime couldn't sleep the night before. Marshall Winston had warned her about this labyrinth. He wouldn't divulge many details, but he said it nearly killed him, said it was the hardest thing he'd ever been through in his life.

Ne Ime recalled the initial conversation about this heart-sickening maze:

"No one leaves, Ne Ime. You either stay, or you fall for the Wisps. Now, enough talk, you need to get some good rest

340

tonight. Tomorrow you're going into the maze, right?" said Marshall Winston.

"Yeah."

"You nervous?"

"No. Should I be?"

"Probably."

"Why?"

"I didn't tell you my other theory."

"Huh?"

"I said that I thought there were two reasons for the ropes going into the pit."

"Oh, right. What's the second reason?"

"Thank you. I think they're digging—trying to dig—to the center of the Earth."

"Why would they want to do that?"

"Because there's something important down there. Something somebody wants."

"Somebody?"

"You'll see tomorrow. This place isn't just run by Momma and Fater Beck. It predates them. Souls have been seducing people into the center far longer than that."

"Who?"

"You'll meet some of them tomorrow."

"Promise?"

"Oh yeah. You know Jiu Jitsu, Karate?"

"No."

"That's a shame. Mine really came in handy."

With that in mind, Ne Ime knew she had to find a way to prepare herself, to defend herself. So, she tiptoed in the night into the forest, retracing the steps on the way to the Will O' the Wisps pit. Thankfully, despite the dark, she found what she was looking for: the tree that wept that crazy sap, the tree with a dagger.

And now, merely two steps in, she'd already thought of a great use for the sharp blade. She used it to notch a mark onto the branch-filled wall of the maze. She marked it with a single vertical line, signifying the number 1. If she got turned around and happened to stumble back this way, or if by some

341

measure she needed to escape, she'd read the 1 carved into the wall and know she was back at the very first start.

The walls were made of skinny branches bound together. They rose up well over Ne Ime's head, at least ten feet. They weren't perfectly straight, however, and one could easily see through the branched barrier to the other side.

After just a few minutes, a second turn left, a turn right, and a third turn left, dagger scratched 2, 3, 4 accordingly, some delightful classical music blared out on the surround sound speakers.

What was Marshall Winston talking about? This was a breeze... and super fun to boot!

It occurred to Ne Ime that maybe the labyrinthine experience was re-tinkered for every new Level Three hopeful. Maybe the Center thought Marshall Winston needed some humbling.

It was something to think about.

Thirty minutes later, Ne Ime was convinced she was almost free. She'd notched 14 numbers into the walls, and had yet to see one number repeat. As long as she kept covering new ground, she was bound to find her way out. The maze was only so big. She was only so small.

She'd just notched number 15 after a turn left when she came to her first dead end.

At the dead end, right in front of the intertwined branches marking 'no exit', there stood a seven foot tall white bunny rabbit.

One of those spectators Ne Ime saw the night of the leprechaun's sacrifice. Rabbits, when over-sized, don't give off the cute and cuddly feeling. It was frightening. Worse still, this one was staring right into Ne Ime's eyes, and it appeared to be smiling.

Then—POOF—the music changed. The rabbit was gone. Evaporated. In its place stood a tall, medieval garbed man. Smiling. Heinously smiling. Holding an old school fife in his hand.

This, after so long! The Pied Piper! Here. Now!

On the intercom speaker system; "What? Surprised? Don't be. And don't be afraid. We're all here!" Who's voice was that?

Fife music.

Ne Ime about-faced and sprinted away. She zigged and zagged, not caring whether she was going back the way she came or turning somewhere new.

It must have been somewhere new. Another right turn, and BAM!

Dead end. Another white rabbit. Ne Ime froze with fright.

Through the speakers, "Don't be shy!"

It evaporated too, then re-appeared. Not as the Pied Piper. Not leading generations of children to their doom. No. It changed into another villain. The Patriot. Big, fat, and old.

"Who did you expect?" The intercom shouted. The Patriot just stood there, smiling. The ineffable speakers spoke for him. "I am a king in my own right, but I have yet some ambition in me. For three years now, I've tried to gain a certain prize. Why? That's none of your concern, just as your whimsies are none of mine. Tiff here will work with you. Is that okay with you?"

Ne Ime ran. *Don't look back.* She feared what would happen next. She feared the ghost of Tiff.

She came anyway.

Ne Ime ran straight into another dead end and a momentary white bunny. Evaporation. And Tiff. Just standing there. Smiling, smiling, smiling, smiling.

Words through the intercom: "GUIDELINE NUMBER 1: DON'T KILL, DON'T KILL, DON'T KILL."

Ne Ime ran, collapsed, ran again. Found another dead-end. This one featuring none other than Flusher O'Malley.

After turning the corner, safe on a long stretch of maze that provided no deathly dead end with subsequent transmorphing white rabbit, Ne Ime collapsed into a puddle.

Get it together, get it together. Stay calm. Stay cool.

Big breath. Count to ten. 1, 2, 3, 4, 5, 6, 7, 8, 9, 10.

Okay, everything's okay.

Through the intercom: a gong. Then a siren.

What's that?

Ne Ime's own voice on repeat over the loud speakers: "YOU ARE VERY WELCOME HERE. YOU ARE VERY WELCOME HERE. YOU ARE VERY WELCOME HERE."

Close your eyes. Tight. Drone out your voice. Drone out every voice. Don't think about the grotesque smirking bunnies. Don't think about the Pied Piper. Don't think about Tiff or Flusher or anyone.

Keep your eyes closed. Go back to the kingdom, the kingdom in your dreams. Do it. Do it. Do it now. Escape in your mind.

Drum it out. Cancel everything. Be at peace. Climb the mountain to the everlasting king. Do it. Do it. Do it.

She couldn't capture it. Her peaceful dream, once instilled deep in her conscious by the combined forces of brain extraordinaire Miles Faa and the religious fervor of Father Thomas; it couldn't quite be imagined, remembered. Jenn imagined herself climbing that towering sacred mountain to the King's realm, but the rocks kept crumbling under her feet. She couldn't make any progress. Not with these dirt clogs surrounding her.

Ne Ime catapulted the dream out of her mind. What good was it if it couldn't' be used to calm her down?

As a back-up plan, Ne Ime furiously scratched at her tattoo.

1 – rhymes with fun.

2 – don't be blue.

3 – find the key.

4 – don't ignore.

5 – go for a deep dive.

6 – learn the tricks.

7 – there is no heaven.

8 – you're never late.

9 – you've done fine.

10 – your name is Ne Ime and you are a Level Two at the Center of the universe. You are loved by Momma and Fater Beck, and are devoted to the center's mysteries and magicians.

Ne Ime opened her eyes. Looked up. Scanned left to right. No sounds blaring on the intercom. Just calm labyrinth passageways. Nothing to be scared of. Nothing that Jennifer Dash can't muscle up and figure out.

Then he came.

344

His footsteps carried no weight as he walked towards Ne Ime, nearly floating. Smiling. She stared at his visage with an odd blend of kindness, love, and fear-laden anxiety. Like the others, his lips didn't move, his mouth never opened, but his words, for the first time ever in English, rang out through the speakers.

"Yesterday was the Summer Solstice."

"Oh," Ne Ime replied, "I lost track of time."

Through the intercom came Robin's voice, while his visage smiled. "Do you want to be like me?"

"Like you?"

"Yes!" Just for a moment, a flick of the eye, the image of Robin, the eponymous Lost Boy of Liechtenstein—like a light switch tapped from on to off, Robin revealed himself as white rabbit. The switch was flipped back to on, and the white rabbit returned to hiding underneath the visage of the nine-year-old orphan.

"Do you mean—like you, as in, a rabbit? Rabbity?"

"Dead."

"You're not dead."

"I died yesterday. And you'll die today."

No words. Ne Ime had no way to process this information.

"You'd better run, right now, or the minotaur will have you for lunch."

The boy/bunny evaporated and Jenn heard for the first time, the pounding of a six-hundred-pound half-man, half-bull-beast thundering through the labyrinth.

It roared. Horrible.

The monster turned the corner. Mace in its grip, it roared ugly, and pummeled toward Jennifer Dash at top speed.

Ne Ime froze. The beast rammed her.

Had the minotaur's head been smaller, his horns would have been closer together, ergo, Jennifer Dash would have been skewered, killed if not instantly, then in minutes at most. But it just so happened that the minotaur's horns were far enough apart that when he ramrodded the young woman, hitting her square with the middle of his overgrown forehead, no horn pierced her skin. As the beast hit her, he reared his head, sending Jenn flying twenty feet down the labyrinth

345

passageway.

Her body splashed against the back wall of the maze.

There was no time.

No time to reflect on damages. No time to pity yourself.

"YOU'RE A HORRIBLE PERSON, YOU DESERVE THIS," rang out as a hymn on the speakers.

The minotaur didn't break stride. He had gored her down the line, kicked the bucket as a toy, preparing to finish off his prey.

He stormed down the corridor.

Jenn tucked and rolled out of the oncoming locomotive. The minotaur couldn't react quick enough and slammed into the wall.

This bought Jenn some time. Four seconds, to be precise.

She ran. Left, Right. Left. Right. Right. Left. Right. Right.

Dead End.

Smirking white rabbit. Change. Jorje Robles.

"You have two options. It's the end of the game, Ne Ime. You can join me. You can be dead. You can. Lay down and die. Like I did. Remember when I died? Do you?"

Jenn turned and backtracked. Left instead of right.

No. She sprinted past a branch with the number 9 scratched into it. She was lost. How'd she get back to number 9? How could finding the exit be this hard?

"YOU'RE A FOOL, AND ALWAYS HAVE BEEN," chants the headless voice of the speakers.

The scratching reminded her—the knife. She could knife this thing. Stab it in the heart. She could.

Ne Ime paused, took out her blade, and waited.

"What are you doing?" Lillith Babbit appeared to Ne Ime.

"I'm going to fight him. If Marshall Winston could beat him with... with Karate, then I can win with this." Jenn stabbed at the air.

"Do you know how old this minotaur is?" The smiling, lip-sealed Lillith asked.

Jenn didn't have an answer for her.

"He's one of the old ones. You think he hasn't seen weapons before? You won't beat him with that."

A snort. He was coming. Just on the other side of this row.

Jenn got up. Babbit may not be right, but the fear was too gripping. Jenn got up and ran again.

The minotaur must have sniffed her. She could hear his boots tracking her, always just a turn behind. She picked up her pace. Thankfully, not running amok into more dead ends.

Can you imagine the misery? Jennifer Dash, Jennifer Calling, Jennifer Free, Jenn Furth, Ne Ime—one woman bombarded with the faces and names of her past, all while being chased by an unspeakable monster. Hell is often imagined as a depressed static place. Jennifer Dash knows better. It's constant misery imputed with manic desperation.

Hours went by in the maze. Jenn had at least two broken ribs from her one encounter with the Lord of the Labyrinth. She was running on fumes, and due to the near constant voice of doom spewing vitriol from nowhere, serenading her about her insignificance and her sins, Ne Ime was beginning to hate herself.

She wanted it to stop.

She needed it to stop.

A new horror at every dead end. A beast neverendingly catching up with her. She was drowning, and the idea of just sucking water into her lungs was becoming more and more appealing. Just make it stop. Anyhow. Anyway.

That's when she collapsed on the ground.

The terrible horns blew.

"He must be fed. Just stay there. He'll get you. And he'll eat you! Because you've been such a naughty girl."

Jenn held her breath. She was traumatized. Nearing shock. Almost giving up.

The shoulders, the head. The snout. The horns. This was a minotaur. And it was coming to eat Jennifer Dash. And Ne Ime was okay with that. Push aside fear to let the sweet relief of failure seep in. Just do it. Give in.

"Ne Ime?"

That voice. From so long ago.

"Ne Ime? Look at me."

She did.

Redjeb Heller. Jenn's neighbor growing up. He was, in all truth, the only person Jenn respected back before she stepped out to solve the world. Redjeb Heller, cranky old neighbor that feared the return of the Russian communists more than death itself. Redjeb Heller, how on Earth did he get here? All this way. The old snark barely ever left his mobile home; he'd never even consider stepping a foot outside Louisiana, let alone be an ocean away from the safe, capitalist USA.

"Redjeb? What are you doing here?"

"I've died."

"Why are you here? Am I dead?"

"You have a choice, of course, but more importantly, Ne Ime, you have a destiny."

"I do?"

"Yes. And that doesn't involve being eaten by a minotaur. Not here. Not now."

"What's my destiny, Redjeb?"

"You've already been told."

"I don't remember."

"Tall."

"How do I..."

"Just focus. Focus on it. Let it save you."

Jennifer never expected to see Redjeb again. Seeing him here in this hell was a miracle. Instinctively, she was going to do whatever he said. Whatever Redjeb told her to do, she'd do it.

The minotaur was here. The snarling beast stopped, spotted Jennifer, and picked up his mace. He began to swing it and march towards her. Ramming hadn't been a successful approach for the monster, so he was changing tactics. A slow march to mace bashing.

Tall. Tall. Tall.

Jenn stood up. *Tall. Tall. Tall.*

She thought of tall trees, of pictures she'd seen of redwood trees, ancient groves spiraling towards the heavens. She thought of Stonehenge, those tall stones. The pyramids, angling up to the gods.

Ne Ime grew.

The sensation was odd. Ne Ime didn't feel anything inside—no growing pains, no sense of getting larger. But suddenly, the walls around her shrunk. Ne Ime watched the minotaur high tail it, pounding the ground trying to get away. She was scaring him. Because she must be growing. She stared at her hand (her good hand, that is). As she stared, she caught the distance between her hands and the walls extending and extending.

The ten foot tall walls, Ne Ime could see over them. More and more.

Ne Ime appeared to stop growing when the walls reached only her chest.

Her destiny had saved her. Redjeb, again, had saved her.

Tall now, and without the haunting of the menace monster, Ne Ime saw the exit and walked the straight path out of the labyrinthine hell.

~~~

We've seen many amazing things in our travels with Jenn Dash. But never before has the epicenter of mystery and wonder come from Jennifer herself.

Now Ne Ime must try to wrap her mind around what's happening to her, and what this Center really wants from her, the goddess of height.

Chapter 46: At the Edge

There they were. Quite pretty. Illuminating the deep dark. Unusual though they may be, the colors that radiated were enchanting. Before seeing the Will o' the Wisps, if you'd asked Jenn to imagine a phosphorescent light that emanated in strictly pastel hues, she would have been hard-pressed to conjure up such an image. But down there, in that deep, deep hole, these bodiless orbs sparkled pastel. And were they whispering, whispering, whispering. "Jump."

It was midnight. Maybe a few clicks past.

The magic trick that was solving the minotaur's labyrinth by way of sudden personal growth did not have the accompanying reaction of satisfaction that one might surmise.

When Jenn, as Ne Ime, asked At-tila, Volva, and whomever else she could how she was able to grow, she was uniformly laughed at. Ceremonially ignored. When she tried to dig, tried to not let the subject at hand go by willy-nilly, the result from At-tila and his colleagues came out thus:

"You should be happy, Ne Ime. You've found your destiny! It has taken others ages to discover theirs. You found yours in near record time. Keep up the good work, continue to strive here at the Center, and before you know it you'll be replacing Momma Beck as queen of the palace."

That was not the answer Jennifer wanted, precisely because it wasn't an answer.

By the way, when Ne Ime was finally leaving the maze, when she was on the final straight-away, she apparently shrank back down to standard size, so that when she past the exit, she was normal once more.

Deep in her soul, Jennifer needed an answer to this question. Long ago, when Jenn had set out to solve the world, she began under the impression that it was the outside world that was a mystery to her. This was permissible because she could trust herself. She knew herself. When she walked down the road away from her front screen door back in Louisiana, Jennifer Dash knew she was good at walking, fair enough at running, and maybe adequate at dodging. If you'd had asked her, she'd also be very confident that she was NOT able to grow exponentially, just by focusing on the letters "T-A-L-L". Now that this was, apparently, a weapon in her personal arsenal, Jennifer Dash was having a crisis of self. Who was she, this woman who could do the extraordinary? Was this ability always something she had locked away inside? Or was it something that the Center planted in her? Ne Ime didn't know which answer was worse.

She stared down at the supposedly unending pit, just past her feet. The sparkling night wisps, whatever they were, made the idea of just letting go, jumping in, all the more seductive.

Jump.

On this night, truth be told, Jennifer Dash hated herself.

As she walked to the pit, trying to think rationally, she enumerated her grievances against herself.

1) The guidelines she was given—given by one of the few trustworthy persons she'd met on her long escapade—she'd broken almost all of them. Most notably among them, guideline Number One: don't be a murderer. Worse still, an orphan murderer.

2) With her silly dalliance with that moral crook, Antonio d'Anconia, she'd scared off Atticus, the person she cared about the most in the whole world. And even if she forgave herself for the actual encounter, she was stupid enough to blurt out the story to Atticus, thus sealing her fate and turning the boy against her. What a stupid slut she was.

3) Robin, the lost orphan whom Jenn tried to rescue, appeared to her in the maze and told her he had died. In her heart of hearts, whatever the vision was, Jennifer Dash knew his words were true. Robin was dead. Robin was dead; a sweet, smart, abandoned little boy who needed and rightfully deserved someone to look after him, to protect him. And what did Jenn do? She gave him over to Lillith Babbit. Lillith Babbit, who Captain Alf begged Jenn not to trust. Lillith Babbit who, apparently, torched an entire Peruvian village just to get her hands on the *Croatoan*. If Robin really was dead, he was dead because he ended up with Lillith. Why didn't Ne Ime return him back to his aunt in Zurich? That was the whole reason she

351

went to Liechtenstein to begin with, to bring Robin back to his aunt Lara. How could Ne Ime be so cruel? So blind?

4)   This horrible other hand. She hated it. Hated it. Hated it. She wanted to rip it off. Better to have one hand, but know in your spirit that you are what you are, than to have two hands, but one of them is against you. Why did Ne Ime think the hand was in revolt? No reason, really. But she believed it, hook, line and sinker.

In the morning, Jenn had come to the conclusion that the hand had to go. She'd kept the dagger with her, and she naively suspected that since her hand transfusion was so new, maybe it would cut off easy.

When she put blade to skin, she started hyperventilating. Then the blood came (*Tiff's blood*, said a voice in her head). The blade fell out of her hand. It was too much. Jenn was a coward, a coward who couldn't do what needed to be done.

But there remained one way to get rid of the hand; a much easier way. Jump into the pit.

Jump.

There would be one of two outcomes. Either At-tila, and therefore, the Center as a whole, was built on lies and the pit ended with the unmerciful thud of hard earth. Or... everything Ne Ime saw and experienced here was true. She'd pop up on the other side of the world and continue her training amidst a new backdrop. That might get her out of the doldrums of despair. It might.

Jenn conceded to herself that Marshall Winston had to be right: the pit had an end. She'd go splat. The wisps would feed off her dead blood, high-fiving themselves on another successful body heist. There was no tunnel through the Earth. Jenn had once been to the very depths, one thousand steps down. Besides finding the Piper painting, she heard the cries, the moans. There was something down there, deep and big and in pain.

Jump.

Through depressed eyes Ne Ime saw the world as it was: a place that held a tortured giant (a true giant, not a tall giant like herself) at its epicenter. That was life, misery at its most specific.

352

"Don't you go jumping on me now. You're the only one around here I like."

The voice was Marshall Winston's.

"How'd you find me?" Ne Ime responded.

"I was told to keep an eye on you today. You're not fooling anyone. You've worn your emotions on your sleeve, Ne Ime, since the first day I laid eyes on you."

Jump.

"I can't solve the world," Ne Ime said staring at the beckoning, pastel-laden wisps below.

"Who ever gave you the idea that you could?"

"I'm going to jump, Marshall. It's the best thing for everyone."

"Okay. If that's what you feel you have to do. But can we talk first?"

"I don't want to talk."

"For my sake. If you jump, if you leave me, then I'll have this sticky remorse stuff to deal with. If I have to live with that I at least want to know that I said everything I could. Please, just for a moment. Sit."

Jenn submitted to Marshall Winston's suggestion. She sat on the edge with her feet dangling over the infinite edge. Marshall Winston followed suit, sitting right beside her and offering an arm and a shoulder to lean on.

"I told you I almost died in the maze, right?"

"Yeah. You said you had to use Karate to get out of it—beat the minotaur, I presume."

"Nah, the minotaur serves one purpose: cause panic. The misery of the maze comes from the Pookahs."

"The what?"

"You see any giant bunny rabbits in there?"

"Yeah, just for a moment, then they'd turn into people I knew."

"What people? Tell me about it."

"No. You tell me what Pookahs are." Ne Ime's voice was timid, but inflexible.

"They're spirits."

"What sort of spirits?"

"I don't know. Mischievous ones, I guess. They show up

353

sometimes for ceremonies, but mostly, I think, they stay in the labyrinth."

"And they can change into any person they want?"

"I don't think so. I think they're limited. They read your brain and project your thoughts. When I was in there, they turned into my parents. Just around every corner. Oh, look over there, to my left, there's my father yelling at me for wetting the bed. Oh, to the right, mother's tattling on me. Oh, come again, now both of them are telling me how much of a disappointment I've turned out to be."

Marshall Winston's face was lit pink from the wisps as he smirked. "It sounds so cliché now, but at the time—man, I wanted to rip my ears off to make it stop."

"How'd did you make it stop?"

"Still seeing 'em, eh?"

"No. But I can't forget."

"I attacked them. I karate chopped them!"

"And that worked!?"

"Of course not, but it felt pretty good. Therapeutic after awhile, really."

"How long did you spend in the maze?"

"Three days."

"Three days!"

"Yup. Like I said, nearly killed me."

"I can't imagine. How'd you get out?"

"Who'd you see that bothered you so much? Why am I out here in the middle of the night?"

"I saw an old friend."

"And he condemned you. Called you names."

"No. He acted pretty much like he always acts. He's always been nice to me."

"So, what's the problem?"

"I grew, Marshall. That's how I got out. My friend told me to focus on my destiny, TALL, and so I thought about growing. And I did. Like a magic beanstalk. I must have been 13, 14 feet tall."

"No."

"Yes. That's exactly what happened. Redjeb told me to be tall. I became tall."

Jump.

Marshall Winston smiled woefully, "No, Ne Ime, you didn't grow."

"I did. The minotaur ran away."

"Oh, I'm sure he did."

"I grew taller than the walls! That's how I could see out, find the exit so fast!"

"Whatever you do, and, really, ultimately, if you want to jump into this pit, and die with the same ker-splat that thousands already have, that's your choice. I won't stop you from being you. But do me a favor, don't die because of a trick."

"It wasn't a trick."

"Everything's a trick!"

"The minotaur? You think the minotaur's a trick?" Ne Ime lifted up her shirt. This was an unexpected surprise for Marshall Winston. The young girl's skin remained in view for several seconds. Due to the dark, as well as the strange illumination from the floating jellies below, it took Marshall Winston quite awhile to see Ne Ime's point. The right side of her body was black and blue, her broken ribs on display. "Some trick."

"No, the minotaur was real," Marshall Winston sighed, tired. "All the best tricks in the world meld real with unreal. If the pookahs didn't show, if the minotaur didn't destroy your body, you'd never accept this 'GROWTH' as real. But, fused with those things, they work. I'm going to be blunt with you. The reason you managed to get out of the maze so fast, the reason you lasted only a few hours, while I lasted three days, is because the Center takes you to your breaking point, however long that takes. Everyone who goes into the maze comes out. Honestly, you proved that you're too fragile right now. That's why we're having this conversation. I was able to shake off my labyrinth experience. You're considering suicide. You're too weak. I think that's the real reason you're here right now. You are ashamed of yourself. And for the first time, maybe in your whole life, you believe you're not strong enough. You came here with a lot of self-confidence, nothing on Earth you had more faith in than yourself. That's what the

Center is trying to break you of... even if it costs your life."

Jump.

Ne Ime paused, then found the question she wanted. "Everyone makes it out of the maze alive?"

"Don't you think that if the minotaur wanted you dead, you'd be dead?"

Ne Ime knew why she was alive. The minotaur's horns were too far apart. That's why she wasn't skewered. Her body just so happened to line up to fit perfectly between the eyes. It was dumb luck, not predestination.

"Tell me this," Marshall Winston continued, "you say you grew over the walls. Did you notice the minotaur's height after you grew? Were you taller than him, or were you still looking up at him?"

"He was running away. I couldn't tell."

"Ne Ime, you didn't grow. The walls shrank. The whole thing's rigged up—when they thought you were broken, they pulled the branches down. There's a walking path underneath the maze so they can mess with the maze's victims in all sorts of ways. With you, it was so easy. They just pulled the walls down. You thought you were growing. You didn't doubt it because you were somehow expecting to grow."

Jump.

Jenn shimmied her bottom closer to the edge. Both hands on the edge, ready to breathlessly, seamlessly, eloquently, nudge herself over the edge, into the wisps. End the game. End the world right now. Atticus hates you. No one loves you. And the ghost of Redjeb Heller, your ancient friend, is lying to you. Jennifer Dash, it would have been better if you were never born. You are a plague on this Earth. You'll never find Leviathan. You'll never be with Atticus or anyone you care for. And the Piper will always haunt you. Follow his fife call. Fall into it. Into the blackness. Into the hole. Let the wisps take you. Now. Push. Just a little. Simple. Push.

"One last question," Ne Ime said.

"Listening."

"I've seen the shadows of the Pied Piper, everywhere, in all my travels—"

"And he showed up in the maze."

356

"Who is he?"

"You really should talk to Momma Beck about him. I don't know much."

"But you know something?"

"Yeah, I know something."

"Tell me."

"You were telling me about this Mrs. Moose—the old cartoonist in California?"

"Yeah."

"And she said that the world is split between two warring factions."

"Yeah."

"The Center would be against a woman like her."

"What? No! Why?"

"Because if you're not with us, you're against us."

"I don't... I don't understand."

"The Center, and what the Center stands for, is on one side of the war. This Pied Piper... he's on the other."

Jump.

"I hate him," Ne Ime said, and she never felt surer of anything in her life. "I hate the Pied Piper." There was strength in saying those words. Suddenly, Ne Ime didn't feel so aimless, so helpless.

"There's gonna be casualties. That's why they teach us not to have empathy. This is war, and if we stop to cry for every lost soul, then we're gonna be beat. The Piper and who he stands for, they're gonna demolish us." Ne Ime's eyes went big. She pulled herself back, off the tip-top edge of the pit.

"But you don't have to be evil to beat evil."

"Ha. Well said. You know why I'm still here?"

"You told me no one leaves."

"That's true. And as scary as it sounds, it's necessary. But think—or just... look at those wisps! Yes, they serve something of a diabolical purpose. They lure people to their death. BUT! There's an important difference here. They don't kill. The minotaur, he doesn't kill. No one kills here. They make it easy, they allow for death to be a choice, but it is always volitional. That's why I'm okay with this place. There's a war, and if you only look at one side, no matter which it is, it's going

357

to look bloody, and there's going to be things that don't make sense, and yeah, even things that seem evil. But once you know the other side, the Piper and his sort, once you know them, you'll see how reasonable our side really is."

"If I stay, I'd get to fight against him?"

"Who? The Piper?"

"Yeah."

"You betcha. Absolutely."

"Thank you. I think I'm okay now."

"Glad to hear it. You wanna walk with me back to camp?"

"Okay."

The two got up and moseyed on back to the Center. Along the way, Marshall Winston said, "I'll see if I can't arrange a one-on-one with Momma Beck. She'll be able to scratch that Pied Piper itch for you better than I ever could."

"Thank you, Marshall."

"You bet, Ne Ime."

Jennifer Dash was back from the brink, back to being Ne Ime, through and through. The Lost Boy, Tiff, even Atticus; maybe they were all just casualties in a war behind the veils. She never really understood the The Patriots vs the Parrots, the proxy fight between the CIA and the FBI. That always seemed like two sides of the same coin. This had a different feel. The Druidry, a place of real magic, real awe-inspiring stuff, against the wicked Piper, a figure that steals children, over and over again. Generation after generation. Ne Ime could be a fighter, finding her sense of self in a war against an eternal child-knapper. Life made sense again. Everything could be weighed in a vice calculating the true cost of war. Ne Ime, formerly known as Jennifer Dash, born again as the true angel of the battleground against the Pied Piper and as his venomous minions. Ne Ime had already met one: that insane truck driver Dolores Burden. Maybe Momma Beck would let Ne Ime take her out. Maybe Ne Ime was ready to go on mission. And maybe the Rabbi had the narrative wrong. If everything's a battle, then maybe Leviathan is on the wrong side. Saint George was a saint, after all. If God himself was on his side, the side of the dragon killer, then it had to be good enough for Ne Ime herself.

In the span of just a small conversation, Ne Ime had gone from no hope, no mission, to signing up for the front ranks of God's army. This was good. This was hope. This was now.

Ne Ime slept better that night than any prior at the Center.

The next morning, a man finished his mandatory 72-hour stay with the Controllers. Once again, the Controllers' efforts were proving to be utterly futile. The man even convinced lie detector operator Cole to quit his job and leave Ireland entirely.

This man showed up to the Druidry Center with one motive in mind, and he was not going to be duped by anyone trying to sidestep him.

This was a man who was used to getting his way. He was a mole, the finest there ever could be. As he met Momma Beck, At-tila, and the general welcome committee in the morning, none of them, despite all their supposed mental powers, sniffed anything afoul about this man.

This man, this mentalist, had come to the Druidry by New Grange to escape it, and to do so with Jennifer Dash in hand.

This man, very much not dead, was ready to play the game, this Miles Faa.

~~~

Just as Jennifer Dash doubles down and bets her chips on the sworn enemy of the Pied Piper, old friend and companion in dark places, Miles Faa has come to upset that balance.

Do you trust him?

Chapter 47: Momma & Fater

His haircut was what his stylist referred to as the "Prime Executive".

His suit: pinstripes armed with a silver tie fashioned in a classic Eldridge knot.

His watch: Rolex.

His cufflinks: Phoenix by Givenchy, valued at $70,000 dollars. He entered the Druidry with the name Tadashi Ozu, playing up his one-quarter Japanese heritage to convince the powers-that-be that he was Asian James Bond incarnate.

As is custom, the Center took his clothes, of course reciting the fable that he could receive his valuables back whenever he so chose to leave the Druidry.

When it came time to meet At-tila and Momma Beck one-on-one, he made it clear, without showing cock or bull, that he was a man of considerable capital who chartered international leverage; leverage that, as of now, he was offering unto the Druidry as a gift, an homage, a sacrifice of goodwill. An eternal truth of humanity remains obvious, but utterly undeniable in every setting, every generation: Money speaks. Evil and good alike are attracted to it, usually in equal measure.

Miles Faa (Tadashi Ozu), rebranded by the Center as Uznay Vraga, was initiated by At-tila to Level One status before going through nearly any of the proper procedures. His money and his class spoke. The Center saw him as an instrument to be played, an extra accessory to be exploited and mined. Miles Faa foresaw this, and was merry to play whatever part would get him close to Jennifer Dash.

It was a Monday. Faa had been sentenced to evening duty, patrolling the heritage room. As of yet, Faa was not privy to what occurred inside the room he was to safeguard. But what did it matter? He and Jenn could be gone by evening.

On this morning, Miles Faa (aka Tadashi Ozu, aka Uznay Vraga) had an explicit mission. He would never admit it, but the plan had two objectives. The obvious, manifest goal would be apparent soon enough. The second, much more latent goal, of being with Jennifer Dash, being her beau, her new Atticus, her lover—well, a man's gotta dream. He'd played the sacrificial goat already, rode off into the sunset, dealing himself up to the wicked emperor 666 in return for Jenn's freedom. That had to have bought him some passion, right?

Miles was not a man quick to believe in prophecies, but so many were coming to pass. So many signs that his mentor had hinted at were showing up. Maybe this intricate design was all part of a divine plan. Whatever the case, Miles was never against a push. The truth was, whether Jenn recognized it or not, her love language was touch. That was the only way to explain her bizarre attachment to that Hester the Molester, Antonio d'Anconia.

Through some adroit spying, Miles saw Jenn enter the mulch mill a wink before 10am. He assumed she'd be working for at least four hours, so he decided to wait. For this to work, Jenn needed to be tired enough to not be on guard. He needed her walls to be laid down by physical exhaustion—that'd help his cause a good deal.

So Miles waited... until a hair before 2.

He was sweating, nervous. Once upon a time Miles had convinced the Lord of the Underworld to marry him, and he hadn't even broken a sweat in that scenario. But this, this was stomach churning! Miles Faa had spent months in hiding, in expectation, and he'd absolutely fallen into that old timey cliché: absence makes the heart grow fonder. He'd dreamed of Jennifer... or rather, tried earnestly to dream her dreams, just to feel close to her. He tried his best to recount Father Thomas' weird Jewel King story that he fed Jenn. Miles focused on the details every night, in hopes that he'd somehow, mystically, end up in the same dream space as Jennifer Dash. That may sound weird, but if you knew the things Miles Faa knew about the world, you'd be slow to judge. Stranger things have happened. Just ask Faa's mentor.

Prophecy or not, Miles yearned for union with Jenn. He wasn't above forcing fate's hand. Two details sideswiped Miles as he entered the Mulcher department, two details that completely derailed his plans.

For one, two days prior, Lourna Von Schloss, affectionately known as Lourry, Jenn's mulch-side companion, had, in a sudden bout of conviction, turned to asceticism. She'd decided to do away with her attachment to the material world. Most importantly for Lourry, this meant doing away with her love of self, her obsession with her own image. Her whole life, she had managed to get by on her inheritance and young beauty. She'd spent thousands of dollars on hair products. So, what better way to prove that she's no material girl than to do away with her Rapunzel-ian blonde locks?

Detail #2: To Miles' anxious heart, Lourry and Jenn, at a glance, looked similar. Now, this seems insane. Lourna Von Schloss didn't look much like Jennifer Dash at all! Besides skin tone differences, if you stood the two women side-by-side, you would immediately notice that Jenn was at least five or six inches taller than Lourry. That being said, with his heart beating as fast as it was, and sweat dripping into his eyes, smearing his vision, Miles' comprehension of what was in front of him never went beyond *Girl, bald*.

Please recall, when Jenn had first met Miles, she had recently been buzzcut by the men and women in black of Magical Kingdom. The weeks spent underground on Pishtaco's island only showed off a Jenn with G.I. Jane length hair.

Maybe part of the reason Miles was off his usual insular and controlled game was that he was no longer in charge of his wardrobe. The Center's attire for him was certifiably lacking in the department of suave.

So now you know the context.

It happened like this: at 1:59pm, Miles strutted into the Mulcher room. Through blurred eyes, he grabbed the bald headed woman in front of her, spun her around, and kissed her squarely on the lips.

Lourry didn't mind. She closed her eyes, sent caution to the wind, and fully embraced the oncoming tongue.

Miles was sky high. Not only had he pulled this thing off, but Jenn was really energetic about kissing him. He flicked the

362

note into her mouth with his tongue, and continued to add Faa-like nuance to the smooch. Extra savory.

Ne Ime, whose eyes were not sweat-stained, stood at the other end of the room when Miles had streamed in, but that didn't keep her from instantaneously recognizing him.

"Lourry, what are you doing?" Ne Ime asked astonished.

Miles heard Jenn's voice, but that couldn't be right. The data didn't compute. His tongue was halfway down Jenn's throat, so she couldn't be speaking.

Lourry let go of Miles, opening her eyes to take in the look of her new lover.

"You!... are something else," Lourry said, looking deep into Miles' wide-eyes. Wide-eyed indeed, Miles realized what he had done. Weeks of searching and planning had led to this. So quickly he had spoiled it all.

Lourry's look turned, twisted. She drew her hand up to her mouth. She'd found the note! The note Miles had intended for Jenn.

With no other option, Miles swooped back in—round two. Lourry flew up her hands. Miles nearly knocked her over with the force of his lip-smack. He worked vigorously with his tongue, trying desperately to snatch it back, use his tongue as an engineer's weapon, twirling it here and there in the dark depths of Lourry's mouth in order to come up for air with note enveloped in tongue.

Because Miles is naturally good at all athletics, this too he was able to conquer. He smirked once he'd freed his note, quite literally from the jaws of Lourna Von Schloss.

"Thank you," he said.

"My-my-my..." Lourry shimmied her body in satisfaction. But then she started to form an idea about what was happening when she became aware that the foreign object was now missing from mouth. "Hey, what did..." Lourry trailed off.

Miles made eye contact with Ne Ime. With longer hair now, she was more beautiful than he could have ever imagined.

He hovered to her. She crinkled her brow, not knowing what words to share, what question to ask, what to say, what to do.

Miles was close enough to kiss Jenn, and, like a puppy, he pushed in, offering Ne Ime the best of his sloppy seconds.

Nope. Ne Ime would have none of this. She pulled back, twisting away.

Denied, Miles had to think quickly. He shot her what he thought were meaningful eyes, trying to transmit the idea that this was important business without coming out and saying it, but the eyes were accomplishing nothing. He noticed Jenn had a back pocket. He could reach and like he was wanting to smack that, and in so smacking insert the note into her pocket. He took a seductive step towards Jenn.

"Who do you think you are!" Jenn said scornfully.

"Yeah, you can't just have both of us willy-nilly!" Lourry added.

Miles knew he wasn't to say a word. The more he spoke, the more he'd come under suspicion by the Center's powers-that-be.

"Well, what do you have to say for yourself, Romeo?" Lourry demanded.

Out of a plan, Miles slunk out of the room. He got two steps out and second-guessed himself.

U-turn. Miles marched back in, spied the bald girl, and plugged her with another Don Juan kiss, this one with a romantic full-tilt and no mysterious note.

Lourry was swept off her feet once more. Miles hoped he had finished with enough good faith that the bald one wouldn't report him to At-tila.

Maybe.

With that maybe, he left.

A moment later Lourry smiled at Jenn and said, "I'll take that any Monday!"

Ne Ime wanted time to process what had happened during her work shift. Miles' supposed girlfriend had told her over the phone that he was dead. The letter sent via Gimli had said the *Orion* was hunting down Merkyl, but had said nothing about Miles—they'd taken the island out. That was the story. Miles and Merkyl should have been on the island with Mr. 666. So, either it wasn't true, or the man she saw today wasn't Miles after all. That was always possible. If Miles had a secret girlfriend, maybe he also had a secret identical twin. Or maybe

364

the pookahs were working another number on Ne Ime's mind. She'd been taught to replace old memories with Center members. Marshall Winston was the new Miles Faa. Maybe the Center was playing with that.

Who's to say?

Having time to think through these things, maybe to come up with a plan of attack, would have been stellar. But that wasn't to be. Following her shift, around 3:15, Ne Ime was to meet with Momma Beck. Alone. Without At-tila.

Ne Ime crawled into the sweat lodge. Momma Beck was already waiting for her. The big Indian woman was liquid pouring a greenish on top of hot coals. The teepee smoked, and both women were forced to suck it all in. It tasted like the tea... Ne Ime figured there were tea leaves in the coals, or the liquid, somewhere.

It was a challenge to blank her mind, but Ne Ime, reformed soldier of the republic of Druidry against the evils of the Pied Piper and his army, had a role to play now. She had a mission, and Faa's being in the picture didn't change that.

Clear head.

Clear mind.

"Hello, Ne Ime." Momma Beck said in Jenn's mind.

"Hello."

"You've done well. I am proud of your progress."

"Yes, thank you. I am trying hard."

"No. This isn't about trying, it's about succeeding."

"I apologize."

"Tell me, why do you seek my counsel today?"

"I've had visions of a certain... a certain character."

"I see him in your thoughts. You dwell on the one you call the Pied Piper, or is it someone else? Someone... Faa?"

"Pied Piper! I dwell on him alone!" Ne Ime urged defensively.

"And why do you bring him to mind? To me?"

"I hate him. I want him dead."

"Which one?"

"The Piper!"

"You believe the world would be a better place without him?"

"Yes, yes I do."

"You are right to say so. He is the face of the enemy."

Ne Ime pushed in, "Who is he, Momma? What power does he have?"

"He is the night. He is the darkness that hides the day. Do you believe the Center is good?"

"Yes, I do."

"No. You're not sure. You have doubts."

"I'm sorry. I believe. Help my unbelief."

"Before we can talk of the enemy, we must master ourselves. What's holding you back, Ne Ime? Is it this Faa? Whoever he is remains hidden in your thoughts."

"No, Ma'am. It's... it's the way the leprechaun was killed."

"It appeared to you to be brutal, no?"

"It frightened me. I liked the little guy. Why did you kill him?"

"We gave him what he wanted. Listen closely. Are you listening?"

"Yes, of course!"

"You're listening is drek. Listen better, and you'll hear."

"Hear what?"

"All leprechauns are slaves to the Shining Man."

Ne Ime's mind lit up, "Yes! It told me about this person."

"The Shining Man is the Pied Piper."

Ne Ime's heart grew bold. This made sense. All doors led this way. "Why is he called that?"

"He stole that name. He takes all good things and twists them. He is the blackest of night. He's the very opposite of shining; he's a black hole."

"Who is he, really?"

"Your mind is not yet open enough to know the full truth. But I can tell you aspects of who he is. I can feed you milk today. Later, when you are farther along, I will feed you meat. You've heard of Rasputin?"

"Russian mystic?"

"He helped topple the Russian monarchy. An agent of chaos, this is who he is. Through space and time always the same role, never the same face."

"Yes. I understand."

"Not yet. This is piecemeal. He's not just the Pied Piper, nor

366

Rasputin. He's the vampire of so many generations. So many deaths. The leprechaun was a slave of this creature. We performed a ceremony, yes. Brutal but necessary: to free him from that enslavement."

"What can I do to stop the Piper?"

"Do you trust me? Do you trust the Center?"

"Yes."

"Then be patient. In time we will use you. You will not be forgotten."

"Yes, Mum." Ne Ime said. She'd heard others refer to Momma Beck as just Mum, so she was trying it out. It felt nice to say, but not wholly true.

The meeting was over. Momma Beck left the sweat hut. Ne Ime stuck around a little bit. She needed the quiet to think. To listen.

So... the Pied Piper was a spiritual being, an eternal demon, tempting and destroying humanity at every turn. And to think, even back in Louisiana, that truck ride in the middle of nowhere—even there, this demon was hunting Ne Ime.

Fascinating.

Where a moment ago she'd had only scorn for the fife player, now she was beginning to think of him as an arch-rival, a nemesis, make no mistake, but the type of villain whom you have a certain degree of respect for. If Ne Ime could see the day that her enemy was destroyed, that would be an extraordinary accomplishment. Something to live for.

Now, however, Ne Ime's task was to grow in strength and knowledge. She had to bide her time. She was just a seedling, and she needed to be powerful, like Momma and Fater Beck, before she had a chance to face the Piper. Mum told her to be patient. She would be so, so patient. People everywhere would look at Ne Ime and say, "Now there's the patron saint of patience."

Swept up in these conquering thoughts of grandeur, Jenn left the teepee with nary a thought about Miles Faa. And as it turned out, ol' Jenny Dash didn't have to wait long for her patience to pay off.

As soon as she slipped out of the sweat lodge on that Summer's Day, Marshall Winston was waiting for her with a solemn look on his face.

Ne Ime smiled up at her resident skeptic. Without him, she'd never have made it. She owed her life and her place at the Center to Marshall Winston.

"Did something happen?" Marshall Winston sounded concerned, even scared.

"Yeah, I just had a great meeting with Momma Beck."

"No, I mean, before. Are you in trouble, Ne Ime?"

"I don't think so. Never been better, actually."

"At-tila sent me. You are to report to Fater Beck immediately."

"What? One on one?"

"Yes. Ne Ime, no one has personal meetings with him."

"I'm sure it's nothing. Where is he?"

"He's waiting for you in the Heritage Room."

The Heritage Room was scrubbed white, bottom to top.

As Ne Ime walked in, passed security, she saw that the windowless room was laden with white tile squares, the lights on the ceiling radiating almost no orange or yellow in their brightness. Pure white.

Diminutive Fater Beck stood, his hands crossed behind his back, facing away from Ne Ime.

"Fater?" She said innocently.

"Hello, Jennifer Dash."

The voice didn't sound like it was only in Ne Ime's head.

The little Indian turned and smiled at Jennifer.

"There's no need for us to use silly names. You are Jennifer, I am Joshua."

He was talking! With his mouth.

"You don't have anything to say?"

"I'm sorry, Fater, I mean, Joshua. I didn't know you talked."

"I talk. Come, sit." He motioned towards a couch and chair in the corner of the room. Jenn sat on the couch while Joshua stood upright, with pristine posture, in his decorative chair, a king on his throne. Or a god. "I received some news today. I believe you were involved in the incident."

Jenn racked her mind. She'd been so caught up with her Momma Beck meeting that she'd completely forgotten the smooching Miles Faa.

"Oh, do you mean—"

"Your coworker, you know her as Lourry, she came to us, informed as that a man kissed her this afternoon."

"Yes."

"What do you know about this?"

"Uh, a man came in, kissed Lourry, then he tried to kiss me, but I wouldn't let him. Then he left. Oh! But he came back again and kissed Lourry a second time."

"Did you recognize this man?"

Jenn tried to answer right away, but her tongue caught in her throat. Finally, she clawed it free. "No."

"You've never seen him before?"

Pause. "No."

Fater Beck sighed, "Jennifer, Jennifer, I had such high hopes for you. This is a big step back." The man who called himself Joshua stood up and began to pace the room with his arms still tied behind his back. "What am I going to do with you?"

"Sir?" Ne Ime's knees shook.

"Why do you lie to me?"

"I'm not lying."

"I'll repeat myself. I won't ask again. Did you recognize this man?"

"No.... Maybe. I'm not sure."

"You are sure. I can see that. But whatever your reasons for lying, you're doubting yourself. You know what I had planned for you? Do you? No, you don't. I was going to make you a recruiter. You would have loved it, marching the globe looking for great candidates."

"Candidates?"

"Yes. There's a war on, Jennifer. I wanted to use you. It's a cold war, rarely any bang-bang battles. Everything's under the surface, one soul at a time. Excuse me, I mean identity. One identity at a time."

Ne Ime was gobsmacked. She had no idea what to say.

"You know this man. He came to us with the name Tadashi Ozu. At-tila advanced him quickly to Level One. He now goes by the Center-given name Uznay Vraga. Tell me, what's his real name?"

"Miles Faa."

"Good girl. And how do you know Miles Faa?"

"He was with me on the *Orion* adventure ship financed by Lillith Babbit."

"Ah, Lillith Babbit. She's quite the celebrity of late... but you wouldn't know about that. So, Miles Faa came for you?"

"I don't know."

"You're telling the truth. Good. I'll tell you what, there may be a second chance for you yet."

"Please, I'll do anything."

"Will you?"

"Yes sir."

"Tonight, I want you to take this Miles to the pit. Convince him to jump in. If you can't convince him, push him. The Wisps will work with you."

"You want him at the other Center, the one on the other side of the pit?"

"Come now, Jennifer, put the fantasies aside. We don't have to pretend, do we?"

"No?"

"Lourry could also be suspect. She brought this information to us, but I am wary she's a spy. A double agent. It's hard to say."

"No. She doesn't know anything."

"That's nice of you to protect her, but there's no way you could know that. Tell me, do you still hate this Pied Piper?"

"Of course. I hate him." The one thing Ne Ime didn't doubt.

"Good. Then destroying those who work for him makes sense, no?"

"We don't have to kill people."

"Oh yes, yes we do. We've tried being peaceable. It doesn't work. War costs. Every time we lose a match, people die. We have to kill for peace. Sometimes it comes to that. So here's what's going to happen. You'll meet with Faa tonight. Lourry will follow. If you can't convince him to jump, or if you fail to push him, her job will be to take you out. Push you into the depths."

Ne Ime's eyes grew big.

"And then we'll have her killed. Just a little internal maintenance. If you hate the Piper, and you care for your friend Lourry, then you do this right tonight. Be a good soldier. That's all. The future is yours, Jennifer Dash. Do with it what you please."

~~~

Jenn is faced with an impossible decision: kill Miles, or be killed. To imbalance the scales further, if she doesn't push Miles, she'll die, as will Lourry. Two for the price of one.
What will Jenn do?

Chapter 48: Injustice Must Be Served

"Good afternoon," the President of the United States began his address to the nation.

Because, ultimately, I do not value this President and the things he's about to do, I'd rather not inform you of his name. By some measures, he was a great man. If he'd received the position of president in a time of peace, his decisiveness, and surely his gutsy-ness, may have aided the nation, or even the world. As it stands now, can anyone rightfully speak in his defense? I think not. On this day, we take time to listen to his bully pulpit not so much because of the new initiative he is about to outline, but because of one particular set of eyes standing behind him. Reader beware.

"These times are troubling. Never in our history have we faced a pandemic on this scale. Never before has our resolve been tested to such an extreme. But in these dim hours, I think of the nation's dark night of the soul, when President Roosevelt waited to hear whether our boys would be victorious on the sands of Normandy. I think of the 18-year-old boys running up the sands of Iwo Jima, the heroes flying over Tokyo, Hiroshima, Nagasaki. They fought not for themselves. I think of our brave soldiers who nearly froze to death in the forests of France awaiting oncoming Nazi storms. They fought not for themselves, no. They fought for hope. They fought for the hope that there would come a day when they could live in peace. They fought for their children. They did not die in vain.

"Behind me are 18 of our children. Each one of these young souls has lost their parents. The world has spat at them, and they grieve. We grieve with them. Their pain is ours. I say again, we grieve with them.

"But it is up to us, just as it was up to our forefathers who valiantly fought, struggled, and defeated the enemies of the world during the Second World War, to do more than grieve. We are scared, there's no denying it, and there's no reason to be embarrassed. Our time is a frightening time.

"This is Tarrick." A boy, no older than eight, marched to the President's side. He put his arm around the stoic youngster. "Tarrick did the unthinkable. As his own mother fell on her knees in front of him, pleading her only son to come into her plague-marked arms, he killed her. No child should have to do this. Nevertheless, it had to be done, or Tarrick wouldn't be here today."

Without eye contact, the President brushed the boy aside. Tarrick stepped back, falling in line with the 17 other children standing behind the President of the United States.

"Tarrick will have troubles. He will have nightmares. We don't live in a world without nightmares.

"Today, I've signed papers authorizing an executive order. We will use every resource we have to make sure we do our part to keep Tarrick safe. He's already sacrificed so much. He and millions of children like him deserve to live. Let's give them that. Let's make sure that no child in our wonderful country is an orphan. Operation No More Orphans is in place.

"Operation No More Orphans, ONMO for short, will begin now with the 18 children you see behind me. Later today, centers in Washington, in New York, in Chicago, Houston, St. Louis, Seattle and San Francisco will open their doors. In the coming weeks we will expand our operation with hopes to open a center in every town of over 50,000 people in the nation. We must protect the next generation. If you know a child without parents, take them to one of these centers. If you want your child to be safe, no matter what, take them in. Any child, no matter the situation, between the ages of 4 and 14, will be protected. Our nation, America, will provide and keep our children safe. There are no orphans in this nation any longer. Each child is our son. Each child is our daughter.

"When a child is brought to an OMNO Center, that child will be transported to an undisclosed location. The location will be safeguarded night and day, safer than Fort Knox. No disease will get in there. Every power under the sun will be employed to keep our children safe. Because safety is our first and last priority, until the disease ravaging our nation is purged, until the last infected tear is shed, the children will remain safe and secure at the OMNO safe haven.

"Parents, if you give your children to us, know this, they will live. They will thrive. America will nurse them and bring them up in manner worthy of your honor. However, because of the intense nature of this operation and our situation, no contact with any child within our care is authorized. You will have to say goodbye.

"I pray for a day when these children may be safely returned to you, to your loved ones. But until that day comes, we must survive, and we must protect the next generation.

"Thank you." The President paused to take a drink of water. He would be remembered for this. These moments outlive us. These moments endure. Drink up, Mr. President.

"Remain vigilant, and stay tuned to your local broadcast about where you can find an OMNO Center near you. God bless America. I stand with you. Your nation stands with you. You are not alone."

Behind the President, second row, third from the left, little Scout Further stood silently, wondering what her future would bring her. As soon as the broadcast ended, Scout and her new tribe of 18 were caravaned to the undisclosed OMNO safe haven. Her new home.

A child of southern Louisiana, Scout Further was not prepared for the cold.

Before he ever met Jennifer, Miles made a promise to himself; he would not use his mental arsenal to win over the eponymous Jennifer Dash. If she was to like him, even grow to love him, she'd do it on her own accord. He wasn't going to go up into her brain and mangle things up for his own gain. She wasn't to be bandied about like the rest. This was a promise that he'd nearly broken once before, but then, way down in the hole of Pishtaco's horrible island, he found a way out. He devised a plot that omitted any mental strong-arming Could he do the same here? This place was drugging Jenn. Could he overcome the intoxication sprawling through her veins with a hand tied behind his back? Was it worth it to stay true to his own promise?

No one would know. Jenn would never know. No one else would ever think to ask. Only Miles himself would carry that

374

burden of knowledge. Even that, he could probably plop the memory of his personal betrayal out of his noggin if it bothered him badly enough. Maybe he'd already broken his vow and erased the thought of it. Maybe everything was just a repeat. Maybe he was stuck in a memory loop. Maybe....

So what was the point in tempting fate? Miles mulled these self-conversations over and over as he waited for the clock to strike 11:30 pm. He'd received a note at dinner from someone he didn't recognize, a man that bore some resemblance to himself. Some stud named Marshall Winston. The note said that Jenn would meet him outside the sleeping quarters 30 minutes before midnight. The scribbled words ended with the ominous sentence, "I have a plan." It was signed, *J.D. Known as Ne Ime.*

Leaving the Heritage Room, Ne Ime was a mess. Thankfully, her pal in all times of trouble, Marshall Winston was waiting for her.

"You okay?"

"No."

"What happened? What'd he say?"

"I have to do something. Tonight. Something I don't want to do."

Ne Ime walked briskly. Marshall Winston struggled to keep up while still maintaining his always suave, always not-caring demeanor.

"If you don't want to do it, then don't do it."

That stopped her. She froze in her tracks, spun around and stared Marshall down. Ne Ime's eyes were poised and strong, yet filling with water, "How can you say that?"

"Calm down."

"I don't need to."

"Just. Just scratch your tattoo a little. That'll help."

"No. It won't."

"It'll make this moment more endurable. Trust me." As he said it, Marshall scratched the space between his two shoulder blades, the place where his personal intoxicating tattoo burned deep into the skin.

Like a pole, Ne Ime stood unblinkingly, waiting for Marshall

375

to say something inflammatory that she could scoff at. Above all, she was angry right now. She needed someone to direct her anger at.

"Tell me what happened."

"You said..." Tears rolled down Ne Ime's cheeks, "you said the Center never kills. Did you lie to me?"

"No!" The timbre of Marshall's voice rang true. He believed his own words. This wasn't the person to direct Ne Ime's rage at. He was still one of the good guys.

Miles flashed in Jenn's mind. Marshall and Miles had played similar roles in her life. Could she really do this? What choice did she have? "Come. Let's take a walk, where noisy ears won't hear a lick of our conversation. Let's get somewhere safe."

"But? Don't you have your work shift?" Ne Ime stared up at Marshall's chiseled jawline.

"Screw it. I'm with you." This was not Center-speak. Marshall Winston and Ne Ime were not taught to empathize like this, to self-sacrifice. That wasn't how one gained knowledge.

They walked into the woods. While they meandered through nature, Ne Ime did her best to recall everything Fater Beck had told her. Marshall took it in silently.

"I can't do it. I can't kill Miles."

"You shouldn't have to."

"But you said?"

"Yeah, well, maybe I was wrong... still, what do you think Faa's doing here?"

"To get me, I guess."

"Why would he risk all this to get you?"

"I don't know... maybe to help hunt for Merkyl?"

"Do you know where Merkyl is?"

"Of course not. I don't know anything."

"So why would you be necessary to retrieve?"

"I... I don't know."

"That's what we need to find out."

Without realizing it, Ne Ime was giving in, scratching her tattoo. "What if he's with the Piper? Faa and the Piper, one and the same. Maybe Fater Beck is right."

"That's certainly a possibility. How would you find that out?"

"I don't know."

"Ne Ime... there's, well, there's no way out of this. Maybe before we could figure something. But now, I just don't see a way out. Someone's gotta die."

"I can't kill Miles."

"Even if he's an agent of the Piper?"

"I can't kill Miles."

"Even if he's Satan incarnate?"

"I can't kill Miles." Jenn was a broken record. Her thoughts flipping back every time she got to the end of the sentence. "I can't kill Miles."

"If you don't do it, Lourry's dead."

"And she'll kill me."

"No. I'll wait in the dark. First sign of her, I'll take her out. She'll never touch you."

"Why would you do that?"

"No empathy, right?"

"But Lourry's a good person."

"No one's good, Ne Ime. That's why places like this exist."

"Wait. The ropes!"

Marshall gave an unknowing twist of the head.

"Miles is athletic. If we set him up at the edge, right next to the ropes, we can put on a play."

"Huh?"

"Lourry'll be watching. So, we just have to play-act. I'll tell Miles what's up. I'll push him, and he'll grab the rope. He'll just have to hang long enough to convince Lourry he fell." Ne Ime smiled. She'd outsmarted the box she'd been thrown into. She solved the puzzled. Solved the Center.

"And then what?" Miles said. "When they don't find a body at the bottom of the pit, they'll know you lied."

"Miles will figure out something."

"I don't like this. Too risky."

"Everything's risky, and this is the only way no one dies. It's perfect, actually."

Marshall still looked unconvinced. Now it was time for Ne Ime to comfort and console.

"It'll work out, Marshall. Things always do with Miles. He's good like that. But, I need you on my side. You won't say anything, will you? I can trust you, right?"

"Of course. I'll follow behind just in case something goes awry. I'll make sure Lourry doesn't do anything stupid."

"Okay. Then we're set."

"Okay," Marshall confessed, sighing, "We're set."

Because murderous plots always take place under full moons, a bright and eerie light shone on the Center that evening. At 11:30, the moon rose big, the thick forest using its rays to cast deep shadows. Ne Ime was a bit bothered by the moon's brightness. The more light there was, the more chance Lourry might see something—like tension on the pit rope, or a body clinging to said rope just over the lip of the deep drop.

So, count your tears, this was it. This was happening. A great show... sans fatalities. No one had to die, as long as all went to plan.

Ne Ime's heart beat fast.

Miles Faa, aka Uznay Vraga, stood in the moonlight watching her silently as she made her way to him.

"Shh..." Ne Ime said, still a good deal away from Miles, "don't say anything. Walk with me. Let me do the talking."

Without touching, shaking hands, kissing on the cheek, without anything, the two turned and walked into the night forest towards the pit and the Wisps.

They marched in silence for a long while before Ne Ime felt secure.

She spoke in a low, deep voice, "You really screwed things up today...."

Miles said nothing. Then, along the path to the pit, past the now dagger-less tree, Ne Ime told Miles the entire plan for the evening. She left out no detail... no detail, except that Marshall Winston would also be waiting in the shadows.

"Do you understand?" Ne Ime asked.

Miles was silent, being true to the letter of Ne Ime's law.

"You can answer me."

"Yes. I understand."

"There it is," Ne Ime pointed to the pit, sparkling from below in yet still the distance with the ever-glow of the Wisps. The last paces were made in silence. Everything silent. Everything fine.

On this particular night, the Wisps were no longer pastel hued. No. They burned deep red, purple, and somehow, black. Any other occasion, this truly black-in-color light would have been a thing to behold, to ponder, but now, in these delicate moments, they sent a shiver over Ne Ime's mind.

They arrived at the edge, a rope leading down the pit resting on the ground directly between Faa's legs.

"Alright," Ne Ime whispered, "say something, loud enough for Lourry to hear, to make sure she's paying attention. Then I'll push you. Ready?"

"Yes."

"Go," said Ne Ime, and she held her breath.

"Jennifer Dash, I love you," Miles said.

Jump, Jump!

Jenn was stunned. Shocked. No one but Antonio d'Anconia had ever said that to her. And while the attempted rapist didn't mean it, she knew in her heart, her soul, that Miles Faa did.

Ne Ime froze. She forgot all about pushing. I love you. He had said it. Miles Faa loved her. This is what love looked like. Jenn thought, *Where do we go from here?* She was too busy processing the surprise words to hear the thundering footsteps. Then it was too late.

BAM! A figure slammed into Miles Faa. Miles was knocked off his feet, but didn't fall over. He managed to land on his back, still on hard ground. His shoulders and head jutted out over the edge, but he hadn't gone over. Not yet.

A figure.

Someone was on top of Miles. Challenging him. Breaking him. Beating him.

But Miles was strong.

The two wrestled on the edge of infinity for eternity.

Under the moonlight.

Marshall Winston. He was trying to throw Miles off. He was the wrestler. The second figure.

Ne Ime remained frozen. In shock. Now, unlike before, traumatized with conflicting thoughts. Jenn wanted both men to win. Not just both men to be safe, no. She wanted Miles

Faa to throw Marshall Winston over the edge, AND she wanted Marshall Winston to hurl Miles into the Wisps.

Where had Miles been when she needed him? He had abandoned her. On more than one occasion. Now he thinks *I love you* makes everything better?

Again ,Jenn's internal processing blocked out hearing what came next.

More footsteps. Then.

Hit.

In the air.

Falling.

Quick, old girl. Grab.

Thud.

Jennifer Dash's body slammed against the rough side of the pit. The shock of the hit chocked her with pain. Her broken ribs sang out in agony, her hands trembling. But. Okay. It was okay. For now. She somehow had grabbed onto the rope, dangling above the glowing Wisps.

She looked up. Lourna Von Schloss. She'd sprinted. Hit Jenn.

Lourry had everything planned out. Marshall Winston was never supposed to be there. Ne Ime would come with her lover, and, before Ne Ime hit the kissing stranger to his doom, Lourry would end Ne Ime. It was a dog-eat-dog world. Lamb's blood had to be shed, and it was not going to be Lourry's. And it was not going to be the man who swept her off her feet that morning, changed her world in an instant, kissed away her past, and with his tongue welcomed her to a future ripe with love. With Ne Ime gone, Lourry and the mystery man could be together.

That was the plan, but then she had heard him say, "Jennifer Dash, I love you." That caused a pause, confusion. She had watched, in horror, as her newfound love was absolutely crushed by that stupid, brooding skeptic. She'd been re-energized to see that her lover had fought back— wasn't down for the count. She had to move. She'd decided to take out Ne Ime while she was distracted.

It seemed to work. Until, that is, she saw Ne Ime still hanging on for dear life, dangling onto the rope. Her first

380

thought was to cut the rope, but with what? How? The two boys still grappled, Marshall sticking his stupid, little fingers into her lover's eye socket. It would be such a bummer if the dirtball gouged out an eyeball. But, Lourry considered, it'd be okay. They'd just have to go with a pirate courtship.

Let go! Jump! Echoed the Wisps from below.

Lourry got on her knees. She gripped the rope Ne Ime clung to and thrust it against the wall of the pit, hoping to dislodge her fellow mulcher.

Marshall Winston caught it first. He was still in the strong man position, having Miles pinned and his limbs incapacitated. He eyed Lourry. What on Earth was she doing? Where was Ne Ime? As Miles screamed Marshall looked past him, towards the deep maroon colors on the side of the pit. There, Ne Ime!

Marshall leaped up and took a step towards Lourry.

"Put the rope down, Lourry," Marshall said in an effort to diffuse the situation.

Fall. Fall. Join us.

Miles saw now.

Bleeding from his left eye, he got up, took notes from Marshall, and mimicked him. "Yes, Lourry, you have to let go of the rope."

Lourry did what her lover commanded and let the rope go.

Jennifer was hanging on, but the release of the rope from Lourry offered little help. She felt she was being pulled down, something tugging on her feet, invisibly pulling, pulling, pulling. She kicked her feet, but nothing, nothing took the pressure away. She could here the wisps now, louder than ever, the vibration of their calls strumming through every muscle of Jenn's aching body.

Come to us. Join us. Fall, the lights spoke.

"I'm just making it so we can be together," Lourry pleaded to Miles.

"That's crazy," Miles said firmly. "You remember what you came here to do. You came here to jump."

Jump. Jump. Jump.

Marshall Winston turned a confused look at Miles, who was still working on coaxing the bald, bleached blonde from San

381

Diego. "You're going to jump. And you're going to do it now."

"We were going to be together, and it was going to be so lovely."

Yes, Jump! Do it. Join and Jump!

"Yes," Miles said. He turned to Marshall, "Help Jenn."

It took a second for Marshall to associate the word Jenn with the girl he knew as Ne Ime. But he when he did, he raced to grab the rope and pull up.

Let go! Join. Jump! Join. Give in!

Let. Go.

Jenn reached up for Marshall's hand. Like nothing at all, he pulled Jennifer Dash up and out of the pit to hell. The Wisps went silent in her head.

Jenn and Marshall Winston scurried away from the edge. They watched, everyone tense and unbelieving, as Miles worked his remorseless magic.

"We're going to be together forever," Miles said sans emotion.

Jump!

"Really?" Lourna Von Schloss cried, hopeful for the first time in minutes. She opened her arms and waited to be embraced by her tongue-ful lover.

Jump!

"No. Not here. Down there."

Jump! Do it!

The wisps pounded louder.

Join us! Join!

"They're waiting for you... and so am I."

Let go!

"Miles, don't!" Jenn pleaded.

He ignored her. Jenn, realizing that Lourry's life hung in the balance of this moment, decided to intervene physically. She wanted to pull Lourry away from the brink, but Marshall held her in place.

Jump!

The men were running the show. Running the world.

"Once you're down there, we'll finally be together."

Yes! YES! Join us!

"You'll come too?" Lourry asked in the voice of a little girl.

382

"I'm already there. Let go. I'll be there. I already am. I'm waiting. Don't keep me waiting, Lourry."

"You know my name?"

Jump.

"Of course."

"What's your real name?"

"You don't know it, silly?" Faa said.

"No." The look on Lourry's face showed not the confident get-it-done personality that Ne Ime knew, but a little orphan girl, hoping to find a parent to love her and make everything okay. Miles somehow was reverting her.

"The answer's down there."

Let us in. Jump!

Lourry peered into the depths. "Down there?"

"Right. Down. There."

Down! Jump! Down.

Lourry smiled.

Jump.

In one moment of decision, her muscles released.

Lourry let herself fall.

She fell.

She was gone.

For the moment, the four-person dance of death was over. The three remaining silhouettes in the night locked at each other, each wondering what happens next.

Miles Faa broke his promise that night. With "Jennifer Dash, I love you," he'd crossed a line. He didn't just say the words, he projected them, projected them into the heart of the object of his affection. He'd gone and done it. He rigged the game. And even so, here he stood, alone, Jennifer Dash firmly in the arms of another. The look on Jenn's face towards Miles was scornful. Anger from Jennifer. Rage from the man that just tried to kill him.

The situation was tender: One wrong move, and the dance could commence once more. Four had gone down to three. Three could easily go to two.

Protecting Jennifer Dash was getting trickier and trickier. It was under this stress that Miles Faa played his next card. "I

383

have to show you something."

~~~

The mental athleticism of Miles Faa has been something that's long been hinted at, but until this evening never on full display.

Now we know.

Miles Faa, with merely a few choice words, sentenced Lourna Von Schloss to a mortal fall down a deep pit. Was it worth it? Will Lourna's death prove necessary? Miles is gambling a lot to be here at the Center, and we're about to find out the full extent of his motivation.

Jenn, Miles, and perhaps Marshall Winston are about to set course for a new adventure, all while Scout Further, with soon to be thousands of children, learns the ropes in the undisclosed OMNO safe haven.

The stakes are piling up.

Chapter 49: Up in the Air

#25 David Foster Wallace

There's no coming back from suicide. This is a logically true statement, but it is unavoidably true in grand narrative form as well. Suicide makes your life a tragedy. You can't avoid it. It can be a beautiful tragedy, but as a whole, your entire life, if you chose to snuff it out, shall be marred by your final volition. David Foster Wallace was the best American writer possibly since Melville. Long ago, I picked up his magnum opus Infinite Jest, *read all 1200 odd pages, end notes and all. As I read the epic tract, I was bored, grossed out, unamused, disenchanted, lost, frustrated, and skeptical that this universally lauded work of genius could ever live up to the hype. Here's a secret to be told in the dark: the book doesn't live up to its hype. Not while you're reading it. But with time, years later, the words, the design of those idea structures, they remain. When all else begins to fade with mediocrity and memory,* Infinite Jest *does not. It haunts me. It laughs at my menial triumphs, and it mocks my routines. Mr. DFW, you made this. Why did you go? Why did you choose to end your story with tragedy? Some say that all stories eventually end in tragedy. This writer doesn't know if that's true. Maybe when I quit sucking air, you'll all turn to me, point, and mock my pitiable death. Maybe. But until that dreadful day, I can play comedy. I can play fun. I can play the fool. I can play anything. I can play. David Foster Wallace can't. Why did he choose not to play anymore? I don't understand. That's the tragedy. Part of it, at least.*

REMEMBER REMEMBER: This world is merciless. It kills us all. But try to play. Everyday. Play with the innocence of a newborn. Play, play, and play until the world steals your breath. Don't force tragedy's hand. I beg you.

"I have to show you something."

There is a list. That list is usually revised once a year, but on occasion, certain names sneak onto the list in the middle of a year. When it happens, it's remarkable.

The word was out on young Miles Faa pretty early on. By his seventh birthday, he was already getting invitations into smartypants cliques like Mensa. He could run calculations like the square root of 9872 in his head in under two seconds just to show off.

By Master Faa's ninth birthday, he was on the list.

Few people know about the list, but if you think about it, it's a very logical thing—a rational idea. An international firm known as the Darwin Amadeus creates this list. They sell it each year for several billion dollars.

The idea is simple: History tells us that once in, say, every 100 million births, a true genius is born. Michelangelo, Einstein, Oppenheimer. 500 years ago, the world population was between 300 and 500 million. That's roughly equivalent to the population in the United States in the early 21st century. During the year 1500, there were, according to Darwin Amadeus, five true geniuses walking the face of the Earth. That number, now that we live in a world populated by seven billion souls, should be around 70 true geniuses. The Darwin Amadeus list enumerates those 70.

Once on the list, nine-year-old Miles Faa and his family became accustomed to visits from mysterious suitors. Most came representing certain industries: Big Pharma, Big Tobacco, private competitors to the CDC, heads of states. Miles could recall for you today a memorable day in which a consulting firm tried to convince him to begin working towards a career in politics. If Miles' parents agreed to give the youngling over to the firm's custody, they'd see to it that the family had access to an overseas account with a $100 million dollar balance. This offer the Faa family declined. They figured rightly, that if Miles was worth a 100 million in the political world, he'd be worth at least double that to the figure heads in more lucrative fields.

Miles was 11 when the family finally sold him out. The payoff was supposed to be worth a billion dollars (between annuities and certain IRAs and property values). Miles was transferred into the custody of an unnamed source. This anonymous bidder would see to Miles' expert education in any field Miles so desired.

Young Miles chose for the longest time not to choose a specific expertise, but more and more, as his teenage years paddled on, he found himself interested in his own mind and what power he could wield with it. This led him to spend the vast bulk of his time understanding the art of propaganda. But geniuses do what geniuses do, and that, perhaps more than anything else, is to meld one sphere of influence with another. Propaganda as a whole had too low a ceiling for a developing child with nearing-infinite possibilities. But, add a dash of applied theoretical physics to Leni Riefenstahl, Ayn Rand, and Kamikazi-ism, and you have a recipe for true power.

Here's the secret. A seventeen-year-old Miles discovered a tonal range that played in conjunction with the spoken word. The tone increased the hearer's probability to accept the words spoken as truth by 94%. The tones are above the spectrum of sounds our ears can hear, but it doesn't matter. In fact, not hearing the tones manifestly adds to its potency. Say to a stranger, "Give me your wallet," and you will be scoffed at. But say that while the right high pitch is played, and the words vibrate deeper into your body. They reverberate through your bones, instinctively informing you that what is being said is internally true—so true that your body echoes the message through your entire physical cage. Over and over.

Now, there are a couple snags in this mind-controlling technique; for one, the tone is based on the proportions of the recipient's passageways. A small child will vibrate to a much different tone than a tall basketball player. Finding each person's tone takes great calculations. Calculations that, say, a mathematical genius can do in his own head while the rest of us would sweat over pen, paper, and calculator.

To this day, Miles hasn't been able to entirely solve the equation. His success rate is somewhere around 91%, three percent lower than it should be. 91% is fantastic, but not unbreakable.

When he first made the discovery, it was by blaring an electronic tone while he spoke. That was okay, but not ideal. His invention, greedily taken from him by the powers-that-be for whom Miles worked, was a little voice modulator that sat in the back of the mouth. The device was far too awkward. Miles knew as much. No one wanted to carry around a mind-controlling instrument in their pocket all day long, just waiting for the right moment to slip it into their mouth. No.

That's why Miles Faa worked with an underground surgeon over the span of two years to have an operation. The surgery was an utter success. Miles had a small incision cut into his vocal cords. It worked something like LASICS for eyes, causing his voice to vibrate on two spectrums at once. Miles Faa, whenever he so desired, could calculate the frame of the person he wished to manipulate and voilà! The thoughts of said person were influenced with secret tones and vibrations.

Having the power of suggestion at the ripe age of 19 made Miles Faa something less than a good man. If a list were made that enumerated his wrongdoings, we would be here a fortnight. He used his powers to get the big three: money, women, and power. It also, however, garnered the attention of someone who didn't give a flying pig who was on the Darwin-Amadeus annual list—someone who would skew the rest of his life—someone who would teach him what the real war is about.

Tonight, Miles had used his 92% effective power of suggestion to make Lourna Von Schloss plummet to her death. It hadn't been the first time he'd manipulated a suicide.

Marshall Winston glared at Miles Faa while he scratched his tattoo. The soothing sensation calmed him, yes, but more importantly, re-centered him, reminded him of his objective. He was thankful for the note he'd gotten from Fater Beck that evening, the note that simple read, "Don't lose her." It'd been months now since he sat down with the master Beck, receiving instructions as to how to deal with this Ne Ime. Most people don't tag around with leprechauns and still maintain an innocent, open demeanor. Jennifer Dash, now re-branded as Ne Ime, showed off these traits with a certain chemical mixture that Fater Beck had rarely seen. He knew: this one's important, connected somehow, but she might not even know how. So, the die was cast: Marshall Winston would be the provocateur to solve the enigma that was the bright-eyed

388

teenage girl from Louisiana.

Had Jenn Dash listened in on that conversation between Fater Beck and Marshall Winston all those months back, she wouldn't have guessed that they were talking about her. Fater Beck used adjectives like young, naive, friendly, innocent, open. Once upon a time Jenn could have associated these words with herself, but not now. Not after killing Tiff, not after having her hand cut off, not after praying away Leviathan (the one thing she desired to see for so long), and especially not now, not after she witnessed her work partner, Lourna Von Schloss, fall into the pit of wisps. In this moment, the words Jenn would use to describe herself would be: senseless, disorderly, confused... but always, a survivalist.

Ne Ime needed to decipher Miles Faa. He may be working for the enemy. He may be trying to extract something from Jenn. Did she have a secret that he might want? Why did he say he loved her? She believed him in her head, in her mind, but as she scratched the small of her back, Ne Ime's heart told her to shut the doors, let no man enter here. Abandon all hope.

"What do you want?" Ne Ime said in a defiant tone to Miles.

"I have to show you something."

"Okay, show us."

Miles looked to Marshall, "Not with him. He stays behind." Marshall scratched his own tattoo and spat on the ground, his spit wad brightly illuminated under the big moon sky.

"Nope. I'm coming with," Marshall stated.

"You're responsible for a young woman's death. You've done enough." That one, that tone, struck. It didn't matter what toxins Marshall's tattoo released, that one had to stick.

"You killed her," Ne Ime said, "Don't play games, just... say what you need to say... before I ask you to jump after Lourry."

This was all challenging to Marshall Winston. He'd heard of mind manipulators before, knew that this Miles Faa character was supposedly the best, but Marshall had never comprehended how hard it is to resist the puppeteer. To defy Miles, Marshall had to defy himself, to act against his own conscience. It felt horrible, and he wouldn't have had the guts to do it, but somehow Ne Ime broke through. She was defying the trespasser's words. If she could find a way... maybe he....

"I'm confused," Marshall said dumbly, and buried his head in his hands. James Bond-esque figures never say, "I'm confused."

"Can we just walk away from this pit? It makes me nervous," Miles said.

Again, to Marshall Winston, the words were like music. Yes! Of course! That's all anyone has ever wanted! To get away from the pit! Who likes the pit? It's creepy! Come to think of it, the pit made Marshall nervous too! Maybe this Miles guy wasn't so bad! At least he's asking reasonable things!

"Yes, let's get away from here," Marshall said.

"No. Not until I know why you're here," Ne Ime again said defiantly to both men.

"I told you, I love you."

Marshall sighed. He'd only known Ne Ime for a few months. Whatever feelings he'd begun to muster for the pretty young thing surely were no match for the cavernous depths of truth and beauty that Miles felt for her.

"That's not a reason."

"I care about you."

"That's not an answer."

"I need to show you what happened to Lillith Babbit."

"What happened?"

"The whole world knows. The whole Earth is seduced."

"Ne Ime," Marshall said, "We need to figure this out. Let's see what the man has to show us."

"No! Marshall, no! I don't even know if I believe in love, so why should I believe you right now, Miles? Give me some evidence. Give me something to hold onto."

With that statement, the situation crystallized for Miles. Suddenly, he understood. His projection of 'I love you' hadn't fallen on deaf ears. Jenn hadn't been one of the 8% that, for whatever reason, weren't susceptible to his powers. No. He'd hit her, straight in the gut, but the problem wasn't his words. It was love. Jenn didn't know what true love was. Miles had believed, after long talks waiting way down in Pishtaco's lair, that Jenn did believe in love. What had changed?

"It's the end of the world, Jennifer. It's the end of the world, and when you realize that, it becomes perfectly clear that the most important thing is to be with the people you love."

Tears welled in Jenn's eyes. "You killed Lourry, didn't you? You killed my friend."

Marshall eyed Miles discretely, trying to gauge his reaction. A wrong answer here could unhinge the third party, and another wrestling match above the endless hole wasn't beyond the pale.

"I didn't know how else to manage the situation."

"I was safe, you didn't have to do anything!" Jenn protested.

"Jenn, this girl knocked you down just moments earlier. She was a wild card. With this guy here trying to take me out... I did what I thought best."

"Punching women in the face, telling them to commit suicide, it's all part of your plan, isn't it?"

"No. I have no plan."

"DON'T LIE TO ME!"

"Ne Ime, it's okay." Marshall Winston offered. "Let's call a truce. You show us what you want to show us, and then you'll let us do whatever we want to do, yes?"

Miles frowned at Marshall's recasting of the situation, "I'm not holding you hostage. I just want to show you something."

"Where is it?" Ne Ime demanded.

"Maybe two hundred paces..." Miles swirled around looking as if he was struggling to get his bearings. "That way."

The odd trio marched towards whatever it was Miles wanted to show them.

Jennifer Dash was nearing panic attack. This sudden incident with Miles brought up gunky thoughts and memories that Jenn hadn't yet fully processed. She wanted answers from Miles. Why had he hit Lex and command his two female counterparts to drown themselves? How had he convinced the Numbered Man to let Jenn and Lex go? Why had he been so angry with the Orion when they decided to hunt for the diseased island? Why had he lost his cool then? And why, why, WHY had he just told her he loved her? Like a rushing river, these thoughts swept over Jenn's mind, fogging up her vision. And yet, she couldn't bring herself to ask Miles anything more. He never gave a real answer in his life.

Nearing an open pasture, Marshall realized where they were and shivered. "Hey look, we're nearing the perimeter of the Center. I'm not sure where the exact mark is... but...."

"But what?" Miles said.

"But if we trip the perimeter, the Center will know we're leaving."

"And then what happens?"

Marshall glared at his competitor, "They'll come after us."

"Who?"

"Hard to say what—"

"Then what're you worried about?"

"It's hard to say what, but I know who it'll be."

"Inform us."

"The spirits of the Druidry."

Ne Ime didn't expect Miles to take that line seriously, but his face turned ashen at his hearing. He nodded solemnly and replied. "Okay, this clearing, do you think we're safely in bounds in the middle of this pasture?"

"Yeah, the edge is somewhere beyond those rocks." Marshall pointed with two fingers at a point maybe 150 meters off. Marshall never pointed with one finger, always two. One was weak. Two was firm.

In the middle of the field, under myriad stars, Miles sat down, took his shoes off. He seemed to be examining the heel of his foot. "Anyone have a knife or sharp point?" he asked.

No answer, just a mumble from Ne Ime, "What are we doing here?"

Miles surveyed the land, hobbled on one foot to a spot a couple meters away, picked up one palm-sized stone, scanned the ground, then picked up another. He sat back down and beat the two rocks together until one of them broke off into several shards. He held one shard up in smug satisfaction. "Sharp point."

Ne Ime and Marshall watched as Miles used his sharp point to surgically remove what looked like a red grain of rice out of his heel. "Uh—got it!" Miles showed off the rice-ling before smashing it on the ground with the unbroken rock. "Now, we wait."

"What was that?" Marshall asked.

"Just calling for a taxi."

"Huh?" Marshall asked in grunt form, a grunt Miles chose to ignore.

"Jenn, I feel like I owe you an explanation."

"Why you said you love me," Jenn blurted out.

"Uh—no, not that. I thought that one was rather self-explanatory. I meant about the island. The last time we were together."

"I'm listening."

"Remember when we split up, searching for a way out?"

"Lex found a classroom, I found that cave painting and all those steps. You found just a... a river and mud."

"Yeah, I didn't quite tell the full story."

When Miles had written in the ground, directing Lex, Jenn, and himself to explore the cave tunnel system individually, he'd found himself in a perilous situation, stuck in mud and water, in some cramped hedgey tunnel, sinking. Death was leaping towards him, reaper in tow.

He was too crammed, couldn't turn around. He tried desperately several times to keep his head above the mud-water horizon, but he kept slipping downwards. His muscles were fatiguing. His up-down orientation in this void of black death was enveloping his mind, reaching beyond his ears and strangling his sense of direction.

So Miles stopped fighting. Like a car sliding on ice, he made the executive Hail Mary call, that rather than fight against the gnawing, grabbing mud, he'd push into it.

Most likely the sinking would seal his fate, and do so in a speedy manner. This choice, though, was the only one with wild cards. He'd tried backpedaling. That didn't work. He couldn't go forward any longer. The mud's pull made up a constant, fruitless stalemate of a struggle. Down was the only mystery.

And in mystery, Miles found life.

He sank and sank and sank, the air in his lungs evaporating, his body spasming for oxygen, for a lifeline.

Then he hit the netting, the same sort of stuff that he, Jenn, and Lex were stuck in for days on end. The netting stopped

Miles from sinking. It held the muddy earth above him in place.

Just beneath the netting—air, sweet air. Miles pushed his face against the net straps... and breathed again.

After sufficient oxygen intake, Miles was able to open his eyes and take in the long stadium hall below him. Miles Faa had managed to find the artificial mud-dripping ceiling of Pishtaco's main lair. There was a throne, covered in mud. Wet earth dripped down onto the throne through the netting, at least thirty feet down.

He was here.

The Numbered Man.

On his throne.

Miles stared down at the huddled mass of flesh— a big, fat thing, bald, as if his skin itself had been dripping off his skull. The top of the Numbered Man's head was pink, purple, and pasty white, and the white top layer looked to have, over time, been melting from the top down, revealing grotesque layers of under-flesh: pinks, reds, purples, and all bloody hell.

He was speaking loudly, apparently to a herd of five hedgeys. The hedgey at the front of the pack looked different from the others, different from any of the ones Miles had seen before. It was taller, maybe four feet high, and it looked more human than the rest. Miles surmised that it was likely a split creation; half human, half hedgehog, with a humanish face and speaking English.

"113 says they split up. Gone exploring."

"Good. Good. I'm glad they'll see my many wonders. And the couple, they too split?"

"Yes, all three went separate ways."

"Hmm... that may be problematic for us. We should convince Lex that the other two are in cahoots. If she feels abandoned, she'll be more likely to accept our generous offer."

"Yes, sir. How should we do that?"

"When they're all back together, once they're asleep, let's cause a little landslide. Separate Miles from the other two. Let's send Merkyl to him. Have Merkyl make up a story—that he has a plan. That he can save Lex if she's the one left behind. Bring Merkyl here. We'll come up with a story. If we can convince Miles that he can win, from all sides, if we get him and one-hand off the island, then everything will fall into place. Miles will bring the rescue team, maybe some military, and we'll have our world platform! Ha! This is working better than I could have dreamed! God is blessing us, 038, oh how he loves us! You understand your orders?"

"Yes, sir, just, which one is Miles?"

"He's the man. Isolate the man."

"Yes, sir, just, which one is the man?"

"The one with a deep voice!"

"Beg your pardon, sir. Is there anyway, sir, that we can see which one she is?"

"He! Which one HE is!"

At that moment, the ever-pushing mud found a crevice in between the netting and Mile's mouth, causing a rather large glob of mud to suck into Mile's nose as he attempted to breath. He instinctively choked on the mud up his nose causing something of a ruckus. A sizable ball of mud down the sanctuary fell, plopping a foot behind the Numbered Man's throne. Miles froze as the Numbered Man turned his face to the ceiling. Miles was spotted. But... no! His face! His eyes, or, the place where his eyes should be! It was all melted.

The Numbered Man was blind.

Miles understood.

There were speakers throughout the cave system, but no microphones. The Numbered Man relied on eyewitness accounts of his mutant henchmen to convey news to him. But, they had a weakness. They apparently couldn't tell the difference between genders. And Merkyl, seemingly, was working with them.

"Ah, it looks like I'll have to finish the story later," Miles said, as he looked up into the sky.

Intuitively, Marshall and Jenn followed Miles' upward glance and saw for themselves what was descending: a large, gray, hot air balloon.

"Our taxi is here."

A woman manning the balloon threw down a rope.

"Shall we make our exit?" Miles smirked.

"This is what you came to show us?" Marshall said,

unamused.

"No." Miles called up to the woman in the balloon, balancing now ten or so feet above the three on land, "Bashreena, would you throw down my tablet?"

The woman grabbed a tablet out of a backpack and tossed it down, which Miles delicately swooped into his hands.

"Let's see if we have a signal way out here, shall we?"

Marshall and Jenn huddled around Miles, peering down at his tablet.

"Well, would you look at that? One strong little bar! We're in business." Miles logged onto Youtube. He clicked a video that boasted 2 billion views titled simply, "Summer Solstice at Stonehenge".

Jennifer was nervous. As it stood, she was right to be. Her demons were back to haunt her. Her decisions were on full display.

A phone video is turned as its narrator and friend who appear to be lying in a field. The main guy and his gal both look nervous, but hyper as well, a common blend of fear and excitement.

"Okay, so, we came to Stonehenge today, only to be cordoned off about a kilometer away. We drove in, pretty much a big circle—"

"More or less," the other person staring at the camera interjects.

"Yeah, more or less, and everywhere we went there were these uniformed guys that said Stonehenge was closed today. We talked to like 10 different people. We gave up, drove to a bar nearby, asked the barkeep what was up. He said Stonehenge had been bought out today. He thought some group had paid off the authorities to use Stonehenge exclusively during the solstice. So we walked here, snuck around some officers, and here, you can see."

The guy turns his phone around. There is Stonehenge, ancient monoliths erected in a circle in the middle of nowhere. It's sunset, and walking from stone to stone, an aging woman, well groomed and dressed, splashes buckets of blood onto each pillar.

"Ah!" the narrator remarks as the woman dunks her head in

the bucket of blood.

The sun is cresting just over the horizon.

The woman meticulously marks herself, pacing back and forth, seemingly counting, from each stone to the center of the circle.

She stands, head black-red with blood, stretches her arms out crucifix style. Raises her head to the heavens.

"What is she doing?" the narrator quivers.

She holds the position for ten seconds, twenty. The edge of the sun drips under the horizon's bow.

Screams.

"Ooh! Oh! OH! OOOH!"

The bloody woman (Jennifer clearly recognized as Lillith Babbit) flies up into the sky. Not flies. She looks to be picked up by an invisible hand. She ascends like a dart into the atmosphere, like a marionette wretched up by the heart.

The phone man runs, still yelping screams of disbelief. The video stops.

"It's a fake, right?" Marshall asked.

"No," Miles said resolutely. "Every expert in the world has given it their thumbs up. This is no joke."

"Lillith," Jenn said.

"Yeah, and I think you know who's blood she used."

No.

Jenn turned, hopped onto the hot air balloon now hovering just a few inches off the ground. She got in, not acknowledging Bashreena, the air taxi operator.

No. She hunkered down, putting her hands on her knees. Jenn was no dummy; she put the pieces together, saw how her decisions along the way played into Lillith's plans. Mrs. Babbit had found the fountain of youth, but no one lives forever on this wicked ground. Lillith Babbit was communing with the gods, and that is not done here on Earth.

Miles, always unpredictable, sprinted. Not to the balloon, not at Marshall Winston, but to the edge of the field, to the rocks that Marshall had pointed at with two fingers.

Marshall was a smart guy, but he couldn't process all this. What did he just watch? Where was Miles going? He stood, watching the world unfurl around him. Miles ran, literally tagged the rocks, and sprinted back. He whizzed past Marshall, flying up and into the balloon. Bashreena, the half-Nigerian, half-Arabian assistant set the air on fire. The balloon took to the skies.

"I'd thought I'd make your decision easier," Miles called to Marshall. "They should be coming for us now, right?"

"Yeah," Marshall replied dumbly from the field.

"If you want to live, you better get in then." Miles didn't know this man, didn't know what he was up to, but he figured it was better to take this talker with them than have him stay behind and blab to the Neo-Druid powers-that-be.

In the distance, barking. They were coming. Hunting.

The words on Fater Beck's note rang through Marshall's mind, "Don't lose her."

Clutching the rope that dangled from the balloon, Marshall pulled himself up the floating carriage. As he ascended, the spirits came.

There are rules, friends, and in this case the rules spared Marshall's life.

The dogs came, barking their faces off at the gently floating albatross above their heads. Realizing they couldn't catch the balloon (the air above the Center not their territory), they did what they do. For Marshall, they turned into a dozen versions of his parents. He huddled down into the base, besides the curled up Jenn.

"Don't look down," he said.

Jenn, seized with human curiosity, hoping for some reprieve from her torturous self-condemnation, looked down. The pookahs looked up at her with the eyes of dead Tiff, dead Flusher O'Malley, dead Redjeb Heller, and there, there she was, dead Lourna Von Schloss.

Beside the imitation of the fallen blonde from San Diego was the image of a little boy, a boy Jenn had helped save from a witch and a Leprechaun, a boy she thought she was saving, a boy who had lost his mother, betrayed by his father, a boy who knew no happiness.

The Lost Boy of Liechtenstein looked up at Ne Ime, now returned to us as Jennifer Dash, from the sacred groves of the Druidry Center at New Grange, Ireland.

Little Robin was the sacrifice, a goat to send the Leprechaun on his way, and the blood of an orphan virgin to send Lillith Babbit into the heavens.

This world seemed infinitely complex, and every turn had rotted from within.

She hunkered back down in the hot air balloon, not caring to take in the beauty of the silent night countryside.

"Jenn, there's more," Miles sighed.

"No, no more. There's no more," Jenn pouted.

"Yeah, there is," Miles flipped the tablet onto Jenn's lap. Another video, this one a news report, began playing.

Jenn and Marshall watched and listened as they took in scene after scene, report after report, of millions dying. They watched videos recounting the innumerable radical laws being passed to stop the death tolls. Slowly, Jenn succumbed to the reality that a virus, the very one that robbed Jenn of her natural hand, was destroying the world.

"We don't have much time," Miles said. "That's why I had to get you... and, well, we have a plan."

They floated on. Marshall and Jenn kept watching videos. It was intoxicating, addicting. Everyone, at some point in life, fantasizes about the end of the world, but to actually see it unfolding in front of you—it's weirdly riveting. You find yourself searching for a reason. Surely, at the end of days, the meaning of life will come into focus. You reach the end of humanity's story, and you're going to find that either everything had an ultimate purpose, or it didn't. What's it all for? Chaos or Reason?

Jenn learned that night also of OMNO: Operation No More Orphans. She caught the American President's address, but it was the honest face of Scout Further that caught her heart. How could that just be coincidence? She made no mention of it to Miles, Marshall, or Bashreena. She kept that card safe.

Then came the last bit. In the wake of Lillith Babbit's magical abduction into the skies, a worldwide cultish obsession with her was developing. Investigations into Lillith Babbit, former heiress of Magical Kingdom, ran rampant, with no end to the conjectures and the often-suicidal attempts to recreate her magic trick. But the one name that followed Lillith

399

everywhere she went was the name Jennifer Calling.

"The world's looking for you," Miles said. "They think you're the link to Lillith."

"Why?"

"Because of the book."

"The *Croatoan*?"

"Bingo."

"I don't have it."

"The world thinks you do. Lillith left a note with her lawyer."

"Mark Janner."

"Yeah, according to him, she gave Janner a message saying that she left the book in your hands. Are you sure you don't have it?"

"What? No. Do I look like I have it?"

"Maybe she left it somewhere where she knew you'd find it?"

"No... I... No."

Marshall stared at Jenn, still unable to get a handle on the string of events that just took place. He had sensed that Ne Ime was special, but this special?

Life was moving fast. Jenn had to reconcile herself to this new reality. Things moved fast now. That was truth. That was the way of things. Jenn had to move fast too. Before they made landfall safely outside of the Center's grasp, Jenn had come up with three new conclusions. These were the new guidelines. Not ten. Three.

1) The world had gone to hell. Remember that.

2) Save Scout Further.

3) Kill the Piper. All this, everything that lies broken—it had to be him, the architect of all the world's suffering. It wasn't Tiff's fault. She was born on the streets. The world was already in motion to the ocean long before she was born. It wasn't the Patriots fault, or the Numbered Man's. As weird and wicked as they were, they were just byproducts of a broken world. It had to be the Piper. If Jenn could succeed in snuffing him out, maybe the world could be fixed. Maybe all things could be put back together again. Pain could be undone. Maybe.

The test of her true success, of her hypothesis, will be whether or not Scout's life and innocence is saved in the end. It's not just Scout's life, but her mind. Keep her innocent. Scout was an emissary of the world. She represented the world not undone. She represented Jenn, before all the world's hardships seeped into her soul. Save Scout and save yourself.

Jenn liked these new guidelines. They were no longer Jenn-specific, not a list of personal do-s and don'ts. Jenn wasn't a character in the story any longer. At the end of all things, who was? Everyone on Earth is just pawns, obstacles, and agents of movement and chaos. That was all. Individuality didn't matter. Except for Scout.

Who cares about a stupid mythical sea serpent anyway?

Land. They were in the backyard of a little cabin in the middle of who-knows-where. Jenn, Miles, Marshall, and the hot-air pilot Bashreena.

Running out the door to meet them, a familiar face: the venerable Sir Isaac.

"Do you have it?" he called out to Jenn, "Do you have the book?"

~~~

Sacrifice has power. Sacrifice an innocent and you are rewarded. "Rewarded with what?" you may ask. We don't yet know.

The Jennifer Dash who began her trek in Louisiana has been spoiled. Ripped apart both physically and emotionally by pain and never-ending hardship.

Despite the weirdness of the Center, it's leaving lasting marks on Jenn's subconscious. She's learned that in order to move forward, you have to forget, and you can't empathize. The haunting of the pookahs is no match for you if you just don't care.

Now we'll follow Jenn to yet another continent. The world's after her, desperate for an answer before it dies out. But as is always true, the real danger doesn't come from without, but from within. Our Jenn's going head-to-head with herself in a battle of meaning and mind, while Marshall and Miles position themselves to reap the rich rewards of her power.

To the Middle East

<u>Main Cast</u>
Jenn
Marshall Winston
Miles Faa
Sir Isaac
Bashreena

Chapter 50: Event Horizon

Right now, Rabbi Levi is reading this passage in his copy of the Tanakh:

Psalm 106:36-38
They served their idols,
which became a snare for them.
They sacrificed their sons
and their daughters to the demons;
they poured out innocent blood,
the blood of their sons and daughters,
whom they sacrificed to the idols of Canaan,
and the land was polluted with blood.

You know about Schrodinger's cat, right? It's dead and alive simultaneously, and only solidifies, in this life, as one of the two options once someone looks at it. Or something like that. There's a dead cat. There's a living cat. It's the same feline. Opening the box to see for yourself the duplicitous nature of the beast casts it fully from potential to automatic static eternality. Or something like that. The point is, until it actually happens, until someone opens the box to look at the cat itself, somehow, the cat is both dead and alive. Or something like that.

In Mecca, the ancient city nestled in present-day Saudi Arabia, Jennifer Dash is currently dead and alive. She is dead. She is alive. Her blood paints the walls of the most sacred site in all of Islam, the walls of the perfect square that is the Ka'aba. Or something like that.

The reason blood drips freely is because Sir Isaac, shrewd mathematician that he is, has had a personal breakthrough in the last weeks since Lillith Babbit ascended into the heavens. All his life he believed in the immutable laws of math and logic. Babbit just broke that framework.

In the wake of the viral video (and of course, the reality of the Lonely Plague that's giving rise to humanity's first truly existential threat since the height of the cold war), Sir Isaac conceived a plan to hedge his bets. There was a way yet to think of magic quite logically.

Reality was clear: Lillith Babbit's ascension broke the laws of physics, and nothing, absolutely nothing in the natural world, predicted such an astonishment. Unless there were other unknown variables involved—namely, unseen agents, distant forces. Or something like that.

While most of nature is predictable enough, to a mathematical mind like Sir Isaac's, human volition remained the most chaotic, severe condition in all of existence. To say it frankly, Isaac didn't understand people. Folks have weird preferences. Some collect figurines. Some drink obscene amounts of coffee, which is (did you know?) just hot water sifted over beans. Folks say they favor one color over another. This is wholly unpredictable. Sir Isaac could know every detail about a person's anatomy, and even their environmental influences, yet he remained clueless when trying to predict a person's favorite color.

Sir Isaac's equations allowed for, under certain conditions, an event horizon such as was caught on video at Stonehenge during the solstice. But there were, on the surface, severe problems. Just standing at Stonehenge during the solstice should not have produced the event. Not now, not ever. There just aren't enough gravitons there. Not enough. I'll say it again in case you were skimming: not enough.

How'd Babbit do it? There were only two options available that Isaac could imagine. Either, for some reason, during this particular solstice, by some bizarre concurrences, there were an unnatural, unfathomable amount of gravitons there to propel Babbit through the event horizon, in which case the blood on the stones was utterly unimportant. Or there were unknown agents involved. Call them gods, call them unseen agents, call them super-humans, call them Mother Nature. It didn't matter. What did matter was that, apparently, they were fickle. They have favorite colors. And they respond to the spilling of virgin blood in the hot zones—the thin places where, due to higher volumes of the sub-atomic particles known as gravitons, the distance between our plane of existence and theirs is, well, thinner.

Five people sitting in a circle in a cabin in the woods: Bashreena, the Saudi/Nigerian hot air balloon pilot, Jenn, Miles, newcomer Marshall Winston, and the resident Professor X of this assembled team of raggedy misfits, Sir Isaac.

"I still don't get why you need me," Jenn asked Sir Isaac. The group was beginning to bond as they went over their plan of attack.

"When I first asked you, back in Peru, I only wanted you because of your youth and dexterity."

"Dexterity?" Jenn said incredulously.

"I needed a specimen more suited to physical maneuvering than myself. But now your name is everywhere. The world is hunting you. Now, you can go the way of Mrs. Babbit. You can escape."

8. When escaping, know beforehand what you're escaping into.

"Wait, wait," Marshall butted in. "Explain it again. One more time." Marshall was a bright enough guy. He'd understood the game plan the first time Sir Isaac had walked them through it, but he was listening for incongruous details. The bizarreness of the situation caused him the first time round to focus on the big picture, to miss some of the component parts.

"The force of gravity is exerted through tiny particles called gravitons. Until recently, they've only been theoretical. No one has found them. When my colleagues and I did find them, we discovered why they're so hard to capture. They fall in and out of our dimensions, our reality. There are places on Earth where these gravitons reappear in greater number. I like to call these 'thin places.'"

"Stonehenge is a thin place," Jenn said, picking up on the narrative.

"Yes, and so is the Ka'aba in Mecca."

"If enough matter is surrounded by these gravitons, when the gravitons 'jump' or 'fall' into one of the other planes of existence, the gravitons carry the matter with it."

"We think that's what happened with Babbit," Miles added.

"So then we go to this Ka'aba, and... then what?"

Miles picked up the mantle and continued, "That's where Bashreena becomes our true Arabian Princess. Since Mohammad, one family line has had the keys to the Ka'aba. Bashreena's negotiated with them. Day after tomorrow, they'll open the doors for us. Right at sunset."

"Because there's a higher probability of there being more gravitons at sunset."

"Yes," said Isaac.

"And, okay, so we get Ne, I mean, Jennifer... we get her in there, and then what?"

"That's where it's nice to have you with me," Miles said. "The doorkeeper of the Ka'aba will open the door and want all of us to go in. We will, and then you and I will convince the key handler, and whatever ensemble he brings with him, to close the doors for a moment with Jenn and Isaac inside."

"Why are you staying inside?" Marshall said, staring at Isaac.

"I need to observe with my own eyes."

"Yeah," Miles continued, "We get the clerics outside, and wait while Jenn says bon voyage... with the device."

At the center of the circle of five rested a small wooden box.

"Why can't we just turn it on now?"

Isaac had previously explained the device, created by his engineer friend, essentially worked like a graviton magnet. It produced a certain seismic vibration using photons or beta rays, or something like that, to propel gravitons to it. Problem was, gravitons pull stuff with them. So, if you have a room with a regular amount of gravitons in it, the device turns on and is immediately shorted and destroyed by the density of non-graviton particles that are hurled at it.

"The device only works in a place with a percentage of gravitons over 0.007% of the atmosphere. Even then, it'll only work for a second or two at the most. But that should be plenty of time."

"Okay, I get it, but, if it works just like it worked for Babbit, then wouldn't Jenn" (Marshall stumbled a bit in calling Ne Ime Jenn) "be thrust through the roof?"

There was a long silence.

"No. The math says that what we saw was just an illusion of

407

the light. Babbit was pulled into the other realm. Instantaneously. The soaring into the sky was just a... a shadow reflection through dimensions." Sir Isaac was lying through his teeth, but he was the only person in the room who had any idea what they were talking about, so the lie stood firm.

"I'll just... poof... into thin air?" Jenn asked.

"Yes."

"I want to go with her." Marshall blurted out. "Why does she have to go alone?"

"Too heavy, only one can go." Isaac replied.

"Can't we rinse and repeat? She'll go, then I'll turn the device back on, and I'll follow."

"We only have one device, and it'll only work once."

Silence fell on the room.

"Do you want to do it?" Miles asked Jenn, "You don't have to. No one's asking you to do anything you don't want to."

"So, I go... then what happens? What will all of you do?"

"Once we know it works, we'll build another device and look for ways to repeat."

The plan dawned on Marshall. He saw the whole of humanity before his eyes. "It's an Ark. You want to use it to save the human race from extinction."

Sir Isaac smiled, "Yes. This is something of a practice run."

"The Lonely Plague hasn't reached the Eastern hemisphere, but it will. We can't stop it. No one can. This... is a way out... a way to escape death." Miles added.

"How many realms are there? Is it possible I end up somewhere different than Lillith?"

No one in the room knew the answer... but I do, and I'll tell you the secret. There are three realms, three planes of existences.

"Can I sleep on it?" Jenn said.

"Of course," Isaac replied, "But in the morning, we go. With or without you."

It just so happened that Bashreena had a pair of handcuffs with her. There were plenty of rooms in the cabin for everyone to get their own bed. Marshall was given an option: he could be escorted out of the cabin, left behind from the upcoming adventure, or he could be handcuffed to his bed, for safety's sake.

He agreed to the handcuffs.

Late in the night, Jenn and Miles sat on a couch in her bedroom side-by-side.

"If I do this, what will you do?"

"I'll work with Isaac to build more devices, get as many people through the void as possible."

"What do you think's on the other side?"

"I think—I think whatever it is, it has to be better than this place."

"Ireland?"

"This world."

"Why?"

"Because there's gotta be a place where the answers to all the questions lie. I assume the place that has the answers... will have comfort."

"Comfort?"

"Yeah. I've never been able to capture it."

"If I stay, would you stay with me?"

"Why do you ask?" Miles said, fishing.

"I need your help."

"With what?"

"I think this world can still be saved."

"Whoa, big words for a teenager."

"Did you mean it, Miles? What you said... before."

"Yeah, I meant it," Miles leaned over and kissed Jenn on the forehead. "I'm with you. I'm for you, through whatever and wherever."

"I have a plan to fix everything, and it doesn't involve jumping through a wormhole."

"Yeah, and what's that?"

"I'm going to kill the Pied Piper."

"I have to go to bed. You need sleep. Even if you're not going through with it, someone will. I promised Isaac I'd help."

Miles walked out of the room, leaving Jenn alone with her thoughts. Her plan had upset him.

The coming hours, mostly spent trying to sleep, worked heavily on Jennifer Dash. A few hours after leaving the New

Grange Druidry, Jenn's body was beginning to revolt. She scratched and scratched and scratched, but the sweeping calmness that usually accompanied the tattoo itch wasn't paying the bills. Jennifer Dash was in withdrawals.

The burning sensation, for some reason, started in her calves, as though someone was exchanging her bones for hot wax. The thrusting burn felt like it was coming from the core of her being, her innermost parts, the marrow of her bones. Jenn got up and walked across the cabin to Marshall's room. In the foyer, in the dark, Bashreena stared at the passing Jenn, eyes wide open, unmoving and un-asleep. Jenn didn't notice.

"Marshall?"

A twisting, seething Marshall Winston responded. "Yeah?"

"Are you feeling what I'm feeling?"

"I'd say so."

"When's it going to stop?"

"I don't know."

Jenn vomited on the carpet in the entrance to Marshall's room. Poor Marshall Winston now had to deal with being handcuffed to the bedpost, his seizure-like withdrawals, his very full bladder, and now the echoing stench of Jenn's vomit.

It was an unpleasant time.

Jenn returned to her bed. Amazingly, Jennifer Dash found a way to slip past the reverberating withdrawals, and fall fast asleep, where, as always, she was greeted by the same delightful fable. To return to the high mountain, the great land of the king—what an experience it is. That was the place Jenn wanted to go. Someday, she would.

In the morning, Miles sat at the foot of Jenn's bed.

"Hey, I have a thought."

"Miles, do you have something to take for... for addiction or something?"

"Here," He handed Jenn a glass of water and four pills. "Marshall woke up a couple hours ago. We were surprised you were able to sleep through the pain. These seem to be helping him."

Jenn unhesitatingly gobbled down the pills and water as the process of waking up was now hurdling with it a fresh fusion of bone-wringing pain.

"Here's what I'm thinking," Miles said. "Either the place you're going is better than here... or it's the same."

"Okay."

"If it's the same, then there's going to be a Pied Piper figure on the other side too. There'll be another Leviathan to slay."

"And if there's not?"

"If there's no Piper, and it's just another messed up world, then your theory's wrong. There's not just one person at the epicenter of all bad things. There's no need to come back."

"What if it is better?"

"If it is a better place, then you can find a way back. You can be an ambassador to us from over there."

"An ambassador," Jenn repeated.

"An ambassador."

You and I both know what happens next. The truth of the matter is that even inexpressibly huge decisions such as, "Should I go through the fabric of space and time?" come down to relatively mundane motivations. For Jenn, after she woke up, took a shower, she came into the kitchen where four faces stared at her, each hoping for her to say yes. That peer pressure led her to one singular word: YES.

They drove to a small airport. Bashreena piloted them in a small plane to the big continent. Somewhere in Belgium, the five set-down, only to walk across another tarmac and strap into another, slightly larger private aircraft that Bashreena used to whisk them away to the Middle East, to Asia, to Saudi Arabia, to Mecca.

The whole trip, with the quick European layover, took just under 12 hours. No one said much during the trip.

At the hotel, all five members were stuck in a large suite. Miles was watching TV when he called Jenn over.

It was a BBC news report, another deep dive analysis of what happened to the now mythical Lillith Babbit. Forensics had decisively concluded that the blood splattered on the monoliths by Babbit belonged to none other than the Lost Boy of Liechtenstein himself, young Robin. They showed a picture of the boy. Jenn teared up staring at the face of the little martyr. A montage of Liechtensteinians placing flowers by his

411

grave flooded the program. The BBC's narration hung over the mute shots of the boy's funeral, and his grieving stepfather, the mayor of Vaduz that Jenn and Ludwig alone knew was abominable. Then, an interview. A woman named Lara came on camera.

"You are Robin's aunt, yes?"

"Yes. And I know who is responsible for his death!"

"Who is that?"

"Your papers keep calling her Jennifer Calling, but her real name is Jennifer Dash."

"Oh, crap." Jenn said.

"If we don't send you to Wonderland tomorrow, you're going to have to adopt a new name." Marshall joked.

"She already has one," Bashreena handed Jenn a passport. It was a fake, but it sure looked good. Jennifer Darzi, citizen of Saudi Arabia, married to Yousef Darzi.

Just then the interview broke. The BBC went to a direct address of the President of the United States.

"That's odd," Marshall said.

Words on the screen flashed: *Emergency, Breaking News!*

"Good Afternoon," The President said. "Minutes ago, over the Atlantic ocean, our Air Force shot down a nuclear missile headed, assuredly, for our continent. There is no mistake. This is an act of war. There is no doubt, there is no question. The missile was a Russian warhead. In the last few weeks our intelligence has provided substantial proof that the virus referred to as the Lonely Plague came to us by way of Russian experimentation off the coast of Peru. Today, it appears, as an act of cowardice, Russian authorities have decided to erase the plague by destroying our homeland. At this time we are unsure if there are more planned attacks, but our Air Force and Navy are prepared for anything. Due to these chilling events, events unprecedented in human history, America has no choice but to defend herself. The flag of freedom must wave on. We shall endure. Until the Russians subject themselves to an international court, I have no choice but to ask Congress to declare war against the Russian Federation. God be with us."

The President walked away from his podium. For several

412

seconds, the camera stayed unmoving on the empty podium.

"Turn it off," Isaac said. "We all need our sleep."

We have four known characters marching towards the event horizon. Bashreena, the fifth crew-member, the silent one, we know nothing about. But Miles, Marshall, Jenn, and Isaac we have something of a handle on.

A cursory breakdown of those four motivations would do us well at this juncture.

Sir Isaac: mathematician by day, designer of humanity's last hope by night. Isaac had been seeking to find a way to Mecca long before the Lonely Plague hit and before WWIII was declared. We know he's brilliant, but we also know he can kill when he needs to. After all, he was the first to slay one of the plagued zombies of the *Known Triangle*. Though he lacks sufficient street skills, he is cunning and shrewd when he needs to be. He was, to be clear, handpicked by Lillith Babbit once upon a time, and Lillith had very specific reasons for choosing the crew she assembled. At the event horizon, Sir Isaac wants a first hand experience. His whole life, from discovering gravitons and observing their qualities and quirks, has been amping up to this moment. He will not be abated.

Miles Faa: If we are to believe his words, Miles loves Jenn. That may be true, but ultimately his allegiance is not with her, nor with Sir Isaac. His constant twisting and maneuvering is an effort to have his cake and eat it too. He wants to remain faithful to all parties, and he believes in himself enough to have convinced himself that he'll be able to pull it off—that he'll be able to save Jennifer Dash from this horrible world before it dies, help Sir Isaac build an Ark before the metaphorical floods completely drown the world, and remain faithful to his master's goals. As long as no one throws a curve ball tomorrow, and the device works, Miles will be exceedingly happy. Maybe even comforted for the first time in who knows how long.

Marshall Winston: The poor skeptic is scrambling to keep up. Never did he expect this avalanche. Parallel worlds, Saudi Arabia, a worldwide pandemic, a nuclear holocaust—it's a lot for a guy to take in. 24 hours ago, all Marshall had to worry

413

about was keeping Ne Ime safe, and maybe learning her secrets. As it is seemingly turning out, Ne Ime is just a feather in a tornado. She knows nothing, but everyone wants their hands on her. He hates to admit it to himself, but he does too. Additionally, Marshall's trying not to let the excruciating withdrawals imbalance his perception of reality. Right now, more than anything, he wants the shouting pain in his bones to vanish. He wants his tattoo scratching to heal him, to make a difference. He wants freedom.

That leaves us with our own Jennifer Dash: rogue agent of all-too many bosses. How quickly she's slid right back into the arms of another boss barking crazy orders at her. She too is trying valiantly to see beyond her very physical pain. But beyond the pain, there's an unavoidable seduction to tomorrow's plan. Escape. Escape not just from the reporters and myriad fans obsessed with Lillith Babbit's final trick, but escape from ever-deepening guilt. Seeing Robin's face on the TV tonight—gah—what do you do with that?

Answer: you escape.

Remember Schrodinger's cat?

In the morning, Bashreena left the hotel first. An hour later, she returned. The five ate some local cuisine and headed out. Jenn and Bashreena encased themselves in niqabs, shrouding themselves, head to foot, in mystery. They took a taxi. Walked to where they met three men. Few words were spoken.

The Ka'aba when seen online or on TV, doesn't itself look like a very impressive structure. But in person it is transcendent. The Perfect Black Square. It's 40 feet tall, and standing near it, you can only imagine what the Tawaf must feel like, circling this structure counter-clockwise with up to 2 million reverent pilgrims. Wow.

Rather unceremoniously, one of the three men opens the only door to the black cube. Everyone enters. Jenn is surprised that although the exterior is a foreboding black, the inside is a magically vibrant green. The inside is marble lined. There are some engraved scriptures, a couple old things hanging on a string above you, but for the most part, after all

414

is said and done, the room is just a simple box.

Bashreena, speaking in Arabic, somehow convinces everyone to leave Jenn and Sir Isaac alone inside the Cube. Just for a moment. The door closes. It's completely black. Isaac anticipates this. He flicks on a flashlight. He pulls out his little wooden box. He places it on the ground in the center of the room. He tells Jenn to sit on her knees in front of the box. She follows his orders. Isaac opens the box, revealing a convincing system of wires and gears. He turns a nob. At first, all Jenn sees are some gears cranking, but then the thing speeds up. Isaac says it's warming up, that it'll get going in a minute or two. Jenn's heart is racing. Is she about to die? Is this what death is like? Crossing the void? Going to heaven? A small light from the middle of the spinning gears starts breaking out. It's expanding.

Isaac has positioned himself just in back of Jennifer. He stands above her, pulls the razor blade out from underneath his tongue, puts it in his hand. Jenn is entranced by this mysterious light. It's about to engulf, to welcome her past the horizon.

Isaac slips his hand past Jenn's neck.

In one fluid motion he cuts her through.

Jenn's blood splatters out on the marbled floor of the Ka'aba and onto the wooden box.

Sir Isaac has hedged his bets. He's added virgin sacrifice to his dowry of mathematical potentials. His offering is accepted. He is enveloped into the next realm.

Jenn lies dead in her blood.

This is what happens.

This is what happens, that is, until it doesn't.

Or something like that.

Jenn is the cat, both dead and alive... until we actually look at the event horizon and find only one finality.

We're only halfway through our story, of course we're not going to find a dead Jenn at the center of half the world's prayers.

No.

But it almost happens like this.
It all starts the same.

In the morning, Bashreena left the hotel first. An hour later, she returned. The five ate some local cuisine and headed out. Jenn and Bashreena encased themselves in niqabs, shrouding themselves, head to foot, in mystery. They took a taxi. Walked to where they met three men. Few words were spoken.

The Ka'aba when seen online or on TV doesn't itself look like a very impressive structure. But in person it is transcendent. The Perfect Black Square. It's 40 feet tall, and standing near it, you can only imagine what the Tawaf must feel like, circling this structure counter-clockwise with up to 2 million reverent pilgrims.

The man opens the door. Inside. As soon as they enter, everyone else distracted by the green marble decor, Marshall whispers into Isaac's ear, "You let me stay and watch, or I'll kill you right now."

His eyes, Marshall's eyes. Isaac stares at them, and decides instantaneously that he is not lying.

They don't waste much time looking around. Bashreena, speaking Arabic, somehow convinces the group to leave Jenn and Isaac alone inside (it may have something to do with the ungodly amount of money Bashreena forwarded into the man's account that morning). Marshall makes for the exit right away, but pulls back into the door's shadow. Amazingly, no one notices until they're outside. By then, it's too late.

The room is pitch black. Jenn's heart beats out of its socket. No one can predict what's about to happen. Where's she going to go? She's like an astronaut headed for an unknown destination, some Atlantean planet no one's ever seen before.

Sir Isaac chooses to not turn on his flashlight. Rather, he feels for the pillars in the cube. He rests the box beside it. He flips the box open, turns the knob. Marshall is silent, staying put by the door.

"Jenn, I've turned it on. It'll take a moment to warm-up. You'll see a light. When you do, please get on your knees just in front of it. It won't take long."

416

Jenn sees a spark of something. She motions towards it. Sits on her knees. Breathe in, breathe out. It'll all be over soon. *This is the last moment,* Jenn thinks to herself.

Using the box's light as a guide, Isaac steps up behind Jenn. He grabs the razor blade from his mouth.

Jenn is entranced by the light and the box. What does this mean? All her life has come to this. A ringing noise coming from the box distracts Jenn from the sound of choking.

Marshall has tiptoed behind Isaac and is choking him.

Isaac lets out a yelp. Jenn turns back.

SCREAMS. She sees the look of hate in Marshall's eyes. He's a demon. He looks like an evil avenger, the grim reaper. *He must be the villain, a spy for the Piper,* Jenn thinks. He chokes Isaac. Slapping his hand back, Isaac jolts the razor blade into Marshall's abdomen.

Frightened by the pain and shock, Marshall releases Isaac.

The light from the box is eclipsing everyone, Jenn can hardly see anything, it's so bright.

Marshall pulls the box cutter out of his stomach. Isaac turns towards Jenn, arms outstretched scrambling to shed her blood somehow.

Marshall slices the back of Isaac's neck. Badly. He turns. Marshall slices again. This time it's the jugular.

Light enveloping.

Virgin blood on the ground. The graviton box warmed up.

Offering Accepted.

....

Jenn's not in the Ka'aba anymore. She's... somewhere else. A big room, but not the one she was just in. The walls are a deep mahogany. There's a wonderful bed, perfectly wooden, besides the mattress and sheets. A rocking chair beside it. In the corner, a door. *It should lead to the closet,* Jenn thinks. She's compelled to open it.

Creakkkkkkkk.

It is a closet. But crammed in there are no clothes. No hangers. Just a wooden bench, a piece of paper, more like papyrus, and sitting at the bench, hunched over the papyrus

417

with a fountain pen in hand, is... Jennifer.

Jennifer stares at Jennifer. There's a difference. This Jennifer has her natural hand. There's no skin color difference, no marked scars. She's an original. She's writing vigorously on her paper, but Jenn can't decipher the words from her angle.

"Hello, Jenn," the writing Jennifer says to the intruder, not looking up.

"Where are we?"

"I'm not you," says the doppelganger.

"I... I know," Jenn says.

"Jenn, what happened to you?"

"Umm... I don't know."

"Think about it. What happened to you?"

"I... I got up in things I didn't understand."

"I think you understood them as much as anyone else."

"Why do you look like me?"

"I wanted this moment to be about you, not anyone else."

"Oh."

"I didn't want the distraction of someone else. This is just you taking some time to reckon with yourself."

"Where are we?"

"We are in a closet."

"What are you writing?"

The other Jenn stopped writing, looked up at our Jenn, smiled, and handed the paper to her.

Jenn began reading aloud what was on the paper.

"Isaac has positioned himself just in back of Jennifer. He stands above her, pulls the razor blade out from underneath his tongue, puts it in his hand. Jenn's entranced by this mysterious light. It's about to engulf, to welcome her past the horizon. Isaac slips his hand past Jenn's neck. In one fluid motion he cuts her neck. Jenn's blood splatters out on the marbled floor of the Ka'aba and onto the wooden box. Sir Isaac has hedged his bets. He's added virgin sacrifice to his dowry of mathematical potentials. His offering is accepted, and he's enveloped into the next realm. Jenn lies dead in her blood. This is what happens."

"What is this?"

"This is the other outcome."

418

"Did I die? Is this what really happened?"

"No. Sir Isaac was going to sacrifice you, the way Lillith Babbit sacrificed Robin, but Marshall Winston stopped him."

"Oh. So... it worked, right?"

Other Jenn sighed. "All that can be settled in time. Right now, in this precious moment, we need to talk about who you've become."

"Why?"

"Because you've changed."

"Everyone changes."

"That's true, but you have to have the heart and mind of a child to enter through heaven's gates."

"Is that what this is, the gate to heaven?"

"No. But see what you're doing? That's what I like about you—your curious nature—your childlike faith has gotten you in trouble multiple times, but that's a big part of what life is all about."

"I don't understand what you want from me."

"You are on a warpath right now. Is that who you want to be? Someone who makes their heart's mission about killing?"

"But if I kill the Piper, then the world will be a better place."

"Maybe so, but it would be ruined for you. You're not a murderer, Jennifer Dash."

"If you knew me, you'd know that I am," Jenn said defiantly.

"Tiff's death was not your fault."

"Doesn't matter. I still did it."

"Even if you did. You can't control the past. And if you let the past define who you choose to be today, then you're life will just be stuck in a guilty gear."

"Do you know how to solve the world?" Jenn asked bravely, sensing this was a moment to be bold.

"No, Jennifer, I don't. But I have hope that you can find the answer. Would you do something for me?"

"What?"

"On the mattress in the bedroom, there's a wooden box. I want you to walk up to it. Imagine all the guilt and shame you have. Imagine putting that guilt and shame into the box. Then, do it."

"Do what?"

419

"Put your guilt and shame in the box."

"I don't know how to do that."

"In this place, Jennifer, whatever you imagine becomes real. I'm asking you to imagine your guilt and shame and put it in the box."

"Then what?"

"With your permission, I'll hold onto the box for you."

"Who are you?"

"We're focusing on you today, Jennifer. Perhaps another time we can focus on me. Now go. Please do this for me."

Jenn walked back into the bedroom. She had looked at the bed before, and didn't notice the wooden box. It looked just like Sir Isaac's box. Same dimensions and everything.

Jenn thought about Tiff. She thought about Flusher O'Malley. She thought about Antonio D'Anconia and how stupid and vulnerable she felt when those men and women in black shaved her hair. She thought about how naive and wrongheaded she was to reach out to touch the griffin in the cave. She thought about how she missed her original hand and grieved its loss. She thought about the Leprechaun and how horrible it was to watch his eyes be burned out with molten coins. She thought also about Robin, how she had only made everything worse for him. She pictured Lourna Von Schloss falling into that pit. If Jenn had never come to the Druidry, Lourry would still be alive. It was Jenn's fault she was dead. But most of all, and much to her own surprise, she thought about Scout Further. She was an orphan now, being shipped away to some undisclosed location. Jennifer felt guilt that this was Scout's lot in life. It was silly to feel guilty for that, but she did. She felt shame that she left Scout. If she'd only stayed with Atticus and Scout, she could have protected her. She could have been a mother to her.

In Jenn's hands, a black, sticky muck seeped through her fingertips, cold and hollow in her hands, a black putrescence. The form of guilt. The form of shame.

Her hands full, Jenn waddled over to the box, and slowly slopped the stuff inside. It was sticky, like silly putty, and it took a considerable amount of time to slop it all off. When she did, Jenn closed the lid on the wooden box. It was full to the brim.

"Thank you," said the other Jenn, now standing behind her.

"What happens now?" Jenn asked.

"Picture in your mind wherever you want to be, hold that place in your mind... and you'll be there."

"Just like that?"

"Just like that."

"What about Marshall? Is he okay?"

"He's in his own room, having his own conversation."

"Is this what happened to Lillith? Did she visit you, here?"

"Enough questions. Do you know where you want to go?"

"Yes."

"Hold that thought."

~~~

Are you ready to meet the Pied Piper?
He's ready to meet you.

End of Part Two.

Don't Quit Now

Who is the Pied Piper? Why did Sir Isaac turn on Jenn? What will Miles Faa do next? And where on Earth (or out of Earth) is Jennifer Dash?

Solve the World: Part Three begins with a world gone mad. There's no more room for a naive Jennifer to go on adventures now. No. Now the stakes are spiraling ever upward. The world's gone mad, and the fiddler and fife player himself, the Pied Piper of Yore, our resident Mad Hatter, will be our tour guide.

Don't leave Jenn now. Continue the journey. Beware the Pied Piper

About Dante Stack

Dante is a desperate believer.

He has education in religion as well as cinema arts from Biola University. He's lived with his wife in Slovenia, Russia, and America. Sometimes he makes outrageous claims like he invented the question mark. No, wait, scratch that. That was Dr. Evil's father who made that outrageous claim. Not Dante. Mr. Stack would never say that. He's much too humble.

Life is best lived with a dog and a wife.

Solve the World: Part Two is Dante's third book.
Discover the rest of his work at: stockadeamusement.com